The Girl in the Glass

By James Hayman

The Girl in the Glass

A McCabe and Savage Thriller

JAMES HAYMAN

WITNESS
IMPULSE

An Imprint of HarperCollinsPublishers

EPub Edition AUGUST 2015 ISBN: 9780062435156
Print Edition ISBN: 9780062435163

10 9 8 7 6 5 4 3

In loving memory of my brother Matthew,
who more than once urged me to take this path in life.

Chapter 1

Whitby Island, Maine
June 1904

AIMÉE WASN'T DEAD. Not unless this was what death felt like. An odd floating in and out of consciousness without light, without pain, without any sense of time or place. All she could remember was the sensation of falling. And then a kind of explosion. She'd always been terrified of heights and often dreamt of falling, but never as vividly as this.

Slowly, by infinitesimal degrees, Aimée Marie Garnier Whitby became aware of a breeze blowing against the left side of her body. The sound of waves pounding against rock. The scraping of pebbles as retreating waves drew them back into the sea. She shivered as a cold spray struck her skin. Bare skin lying on cold, rough stone. Odd. She didn't know why she wouldn't be dressed. But at least she wasn't dead. Not unless her immortal soul had descended into a hell that smelled, sounded and felt like a cold northern sea.

She heard a squawking of birds close by. Forcing reluctant eyelids open, she was blinded by the sudden glare of a sun almost directly overhead. She quickly closed them, waited a few seconds and then tried again, opening her lids more slowly this time. When her eyes had, at last, adjusted to the light, what she saw filled her with dread. A dozen crows, maybe more, circling above. All large, loud and very black. All focused on this wounded thing that lay beneath them. A murder of crows. That's what the English called them. A parliament of owls. An exaltation of larks. A murder of crows. Birds as black as night. Harvesters of death.

LYING ALONE ON this cold, flat rock, Aimée wondered if perhaps she really had died and her soul had descended to hell. A hell filled not with the fires of damnation that the village priest back home in Provence frightened her with as a child, but a hell nevertheless, to which a vengeful God had condemned her. But for what was she being punished? The sin of adultery? The sin of loving another man more than she loved her husband? All the times she and her lover had been together, it had never felt like sin. Moreover, if adultery was a sin worthy of damnation, why wasn't Edward lying here beside her? She had had only one lover, who was indeed someone she loved. Edward, in their ten years of marriage, had had dozens, many hired for a single night in the high-class bordellos of Boston or New York.

Aimée watched the winged black shapes circle above her. Steeling herself to fight back, she shouted at the birds to get away. Managed to swing a fisted arm, striking one who dared fly too close. The bird and its murderous comrades retreated to higher altitudes. Some circling. Others watching from small outcroppings on the wall of rock rising above her.

She lay her head back down against the rock, her eyes moving past the birds, examining the wall itself. Suddenly, she knew exactly where she was. She'd never seen it from this angle but knew without a doubt that she was lying at the bottom of the sixty-foot metamorphic cliff that formed a nearly sheer wall on the seaward side of Whitby Island.

She had no memory of coming to the island. Had she come alone, or had someone been with her? Aimée often sailed out in the summer to paint. Sometimes alone. Sometimes not. If Mark or perhaps Edward had come this time, surely there was a chance, even a likelihood, of rescue. Sooner or later he would miss her and come looking. The island wasn't big. Only thirty-three acres of rock and piney woods rising from the ocean three miles out from the city of Portland.

Aimée shivered. Soon the sun would be going behind the cliff and she would get even colder. Clutching her arms around herself for warmth, she wondered if crawling closer to the cliff would be a good idea. The large rocks at the base might provide some shelter from the wind and sea spray. On the other hand, being tucked in like that would make it impossible for anyone at the top to see her and come to her rescue.

How strange it would be, she thought, for her life to end here. In this cold, foreign place with its rigid Puritan ways. So far from the Bohemian artist's life she'd lived in Paris. So far from the warmth of Provence. So odd she had come here to live. It was all Edward's fault. No, perhaps her own fault. After all, it was she who had fallen so hopelessly in love with this intense American with his dark, dangerous eyes.

Aimée's mind went back to the wet September day in 1894 when Edward Whitby first walked into the drawing studio at the Académie Julien, the art school just south of Montmartre, where her father was an instructor. The moment Edward spotted her, he stopped in his tracks and stared.

Even as he was setting up his bench and arranging his supplies, his eyes kept darting, not to the nude female model standing on the platform in front of him but over to Aimée, who sat, trying hard to concentrate on her own sketches and not quite succeeding. After class, he walked over carrying his sketch pad.

"Pardon, mademoiselle," he said. "Do you speak English?"

"Yes," she smiled, "quite well. My mother is English."

"That is good," he said.

"Et pourquoi?"

"Because my French is appalling."

"Ahhh. May I see?" she asked, pointing at the sheets he carried.

He hesitated, as if debating whether or not to show her the work.

"It's only fair. It was easy to tell you were drawing me and not the model."

He blushed. The first and possibly only time she'd ever seen Edward blush. He handed her the sheets one at a time. She leafed slowly through them. "They're very good. You've captured me quite well even though I was moving. You should show these to my father."

"Your father?"

"Yes. Auguste Garnier. I am Aimée Garnier."

"Auguste Garnier is one of the most respected portraitists in France."

"So I've heard. But he is also my father. And your instructor.

It is only because my name is Garnier that I am allowed to attend the men's classes."

"And why do you want to attend the men's class?"

"Because the instructors are better." She paused. "And the male students so much more interesting."

Edward smiled at what he took to be a compliment. He obviously thought she was talking about him. And perhaps she was. How very forward of her.

"May I invite you for a cup of coffee? Or perhaps a glass of wine?" he asked.

"Why don't you join us instead?"

"Us?"

"Yes. A group of students meets regularly after class at the Café Lézard just up the street. Mostly Americans. The Académie has more American students than mice in the basement. But that's all right. I like Americans. You all take everything so very seriously."

"Oh, do we now?"

"Oh, yes, you do. Art. Politics. L'amour . . ." She paused. "What is your name?"

"Edward. Are there other women in this group?"

"No. They're all men. Except for me." She said the last with a wicked smile.

He smiled back, and she knew he was hooked. What she didn't know was that from that moment on, for Edward Whitby to share Aimée's attention with even one other man was, for him, intolerable. And always would be.

THE SUN DESCENDED behind the cliff. The air grew colder. Aimée fought a fierce desire to sleep. To sleep was to die. How long had she been lying here waiting for rescue? It seemed like hours, but for all she knew, it could have been days.

"Mark, Edward, someone, anyone. Please, won't someone come and take me out of this place?"

Aimée knew that if she lay here much longer, the crows, sensing her growing weakness, would become ever more eager for their meal. No. She couldn't just wait and do nothing. She had to think of a way to save herself.

She looked out toward the sea. Studying the waves crashing angrily against the rocks, she knew instantly that any thought of swimming around the island to the other side was madness. The water was freezing, the waves fierce, the tide coming in. If she didn't die from the cold, she would almost certainly be dashed against the rocks and drown.

Could she possibly climb back up the cliff? If she didn't look down, perhaps she could summon the courage and strength to struggle back up. She was certain she knew the contours of the cliff better than anyone else. She couldn't count the number of calm, sunny days she'd sailed to this side of the island to study and sketch its craggy face, the sketches serving as starting points for many of her paintings. She knew there were hundreds of possible handholds and footholds to use. Properly clothed and uninjured, she felt certain she could make it. Naked and injured was a different story.

The first thing Aimée needed to know was how badly she was hurt. Whether climbing the cliff was even a remote possibility or just a pathetic fantasy. There was no way she could assess her injuries lying on her back. But raising her head high enough to examine herself seemed an enormous undertaking. Placing both arms flat on the rock, she tried to lever her head and shoulders upwards, toward a sitting position. A shock of pain tore through her middle. She clenched her teeth and told herself to deal with it or die.

As she looked, she saw a deep vertical wound in her abdomen two inches above and to the right of her navel. There were some other seemingly random cuts above her breasts, but it was the lower wound that truly hurt. The intensity of pain told her the cut must have been deep. And, in spite of the drying blood surrounding the incision, she could see it was more than an inch long and perfectly straight. A cut like that had to have been made by a knife. Suddenly it all became clear. There *was* someone else on the island. Someone who *wanted* her dead.

Chapter 2

Portland, Maine
June 2012

GRADUATION WEEK IN Portland. All six of the city's high schools, public, private and parochial, had scheduled their commencement ceremonies to take place at some point during this week. Some of the events would be large, with hundreds of graduates. Others much smaller.

Thursday morning was Penfield Academy's turn. It was a bright, sunny day, warm for early summer, with temperatures edging well into the seventies. By 10:50, all eighty-seven graduating seniors of the smallest and, arguably, most prestigious secondary school in the city had gathered in an excited cluster on the far side of the lacrosse field. Forty-five girls and forty-two boys. Marilyn Bell, the headmaster's assistant, scurried among them, clipboard in hand, determined to create order out of chaos. One by one, she called out the graduates' names in a loud whisper. Told each where she wanted them to stand and, when necessary, pushed and prodded an inattentive body into his or her proper position.

Finally all eighty-seven were in place, waiting restlessly in the warm sunshine for Headmaster William S. Cobb to finish telling the assembled audience what a terrific school Penfield was. How smart and talented the students. How capable the faculty and staff. How generous the trustees, parents and alumni.

At the head of the waiting procession stood the class valedictorian and, by general consensus, the class beauty as well. Veronica Aimée Whitby, Aimée to almost everyone who knew her well. Aimée was the kind of girl teenage boys dream about, talk about, follow in the halls at school. Nearly every one of the Upper School boys had, at one time or another, found themselves breathing a little faster and walking a little more slowly when either good fortune or good planning placed them five or six steps behind her in the halls or on the paths of Penfield. When this occurred, most would try to position themselves to catch the most revealing glimpse of flesh, especially when Aimée came to school, as she often did in warm weather, wearing a low-cut tank top, a high-cut miniskirt or both.

For four long years, several hundred hormonally charged Penfield boys had been inhaling Aimée's scent. Dreaming about burying their faces in her silky blonde hair. Imagining her long, muscular legs, tan from the summer sun, wrapped around their bodies. They'd feel themselves growing hard watching or even just thinking about her perfectly rounded ass as it swung in an easy, sensuous rhythm that was all her own. The shyer, less confident boys looked away when she caught them checking her out. The bolder ones kept looking. Hungrily. Pointlessly. Even though the smiles she bestowed were always warm and occasionally flirtatious, virtually all the boys knew they didn't stand a chance. Perhaps with one of the other Penfield girls, perhaps with Aimée's less beautiful sister, Julia. But not with the princess herself.

Still they couldn't help looking. Try as they might, not one among them could resist a stolen glance, and Aimée enjoyed every one. Enjoyed them even more because she knew, and had known since the beginning of senior year, that the Penfield boys weren't the only ones who noticed her. Weren't the only ones who wanted her. There were others. Older, more interesting and, as far as Aimée was concerned, more desirable. At least for the moment.

To AIMÉE'S RIGHT, at the head of the long line of graduates, stood Aman Anbessa, the class salutatorian. A supersmart Eritrean kid, Aman's parents had come to Portland from their native land eight years ago. After four years in Portland's public schools, Aman had won a coveted full scholarship to Penfield and had proved himself worthy of it, finishing second in the class and winning a full scholarship to Tufts University in the fall. Still, his ambitious father wasn't quite satisfied. He drilled it into Aman's head that if only his son had studied ten hours a day instead of just six or seven, perhaps he wouldn't have gotten that one B that ever so slightly lowered an otherwise perfect record and allowed Aimée Whitby to slip past him into the number-one spot.

Inwardly, Aman didn't resent his parents for their relentless *encouragement*. If he harbored any anger, it was directed at Aimée. He was sure she'd achieved her perfect record not just because she was smart and worked hard but also because she came from one of the richest families in Maine. And because of her endless sucking up to the teachers. Especially the male teachers. Double especially Mr. Knowles, the AP English teacher who had given Aman his only B.

Aman told himself he should hate Aimée. Not just for beating him out as valedictorian but for being rich and spoiled instead of a hardworking scholarship kid like himself. For driving a fancy car to school instead of walking two miles from an apartment off Fox Street. But what made Aman Anbessa truly resent Aimée was the fact that she barely noticed him. That she didn't want him like he wanted her. That made him feel diminished. Like less of a man. And that was something he could never forgive her for.

Nell Barnhart, president of the senior class, stood behind Aimée. Next to Nell, and behind Aman, was Emily Welles, who rated a place up front because she was the winner of the headmaster's award for good citizenship. The rest of the seniors were paired off and lined up behind the first four in alphabetical order. At the end of the line, along with the other two Ws in the class, was Aimée's half sister––her half twin, some said, though they looked almost nothing alike––Julia Catherine Whitby.

All the girls were dressed modestly in knee-length white dresses. Some, like Julia, had their hair up. Others, like Aimée, let it fall loosely around their shoulders. Each carried a dozen red roses. The boys wore khaki trousers, blue blazers, white button-down shirts and ties.

There was a pause in the headmaster's remarks and the kids looked up, wondering if, at long last, he'd actually stopped thanking people. "Ladies and Gentlemen," he said, "parents, relatives, alumni, faculty and staff, as well as other honored guests, please rise and welcome our graduates. I proudly present Penfield Academy's graduating class of 2012."

The strains of the school's traditional processional march

emerged from half a dozen speakers strategically placed around the field. The crowd of more than four hundred rose to its feet. Cameras, smartphones and video recorders were plucked from pockets and handbags. The graduates entered and passed slowly down the center aisle through the crowd.

As she walked, Aimée glanced around, acknowledging faces she recognized. Smiling at some. Finger-waving others. She blew a kiss at her father and Deirdre, her stepmother, who were seated among the trustees. Next to Deirdre was Charles Kraft, Whitby Engineering & Development's director of corporate security. She wondered why Kraft was here. A Penfield Academy graduation didn't seem like his kind of show. Or one where Daddy would need security.

Aimée felt Kraft's eyes study her as she walked by closely enough for him to smell the delicate scent she was wearing. Perhaps he had come for her. A frisson of desire passed through her at the thought. Or was it simply fear? Charles was definitely sexy, but also more than a little scary, even to a girl as sure of herself as Aimée. One of the few men she didn't feel certain she could handle. Still, he was exciting. Maybe she'd play the game a little and see what happened.

She wondered if Charles would show up at the party tonight. She wouldn't have expected him to, but then she wouldn't have expected him to come to graduation either. Having passed, she glanced back for just an instant. He caught her look and smiled. She turned away. Felt herself blushing. Aimée hardly ever blushed.

REACHING THE FRONT row of seats, the two lines of graduates split left and right and climbed the steps on either side of the wooden stage constructed for the occasion. Aimée, Aman, Nell and Emily took their designated places, front and center. The other graduates filled the remaining front-row seats, then filed into the second, third and fourth rows. Aimée glanced back and spotted Julia off to the side in the last row. Threw her a smile and a wave. Jules smiled back.

When the graduates were settled, Headmaster Cobb began talking again. He introduced the Penfield trustees one by one, asking each to rise and be acknowledged. He then launched into his favorite subject. Money. For ten minutes he spoke about how generously the families of the graduating seniors had supported the school once again this year. And how he hoped he could convince those few families who hadn't yet given to do so soon. "Any amount helps," he said. "Even just a few dollars will help sustain this school we all love and the programs it offers." Cobb paused for effect . . . and then went on. "While we've received many generous gifts, I feel obligated to make particular mention of one very special graduation gift given by one of Portland and New England's most prominent business leaders in honor of his two daughters, both of whom are graduating today."

Aimée could see the eyes of her classmates and their parents honing in on her father.

Cobb continued. "Two million dollars has been given by Edward Whitby, a sixth-generation Penfield alumnus and the father of both this year's valedictorian, Veronica Aimée Whitby, and her sister, Julia Catherine Whitby. It represents," said Cobb, "the largest single donation this school has ever received and will be used, as Mr. Whitby has directed, in the construction of a new visual and performing arts center that will rival and, I daresay, surpass any offered by any other independent school in New England. An appropriate use of the money I think, given that one of Mr. Whitby's two graduating daughters"—Cobb turned and gestured with one hand toward Aimée, who smiled back— "is not only this year's class valedictorian but also one of our most talented artists. And his other daughter . . ." Cobb turned and stretched a hand in Julia's direction. She raised a hand in response. " . . . Julia has proven herself an exceptional actress, whom many of you applauded for her brilliant performance in the lead role of Blanche DuBois in this year's senior production of *A Streetcar Named Desire*. Naturally, our new facility will be named the Edward V. Whitby Center for the Arts."

The audience rose and applauded. Ed Whitby rose and waved. Cobb waited for silence, then started speaking again. "Now it's my distinct pleasure to introduce the valedictorian of the class of 2012. A young woman who has achieved an unprecedented record in her four years in the Upper School. Thirty-six courses. Thirty-six A pluses. All the while distinguishing herself not just as a student and an artist but also as a member of both the women's soccer and lacrosse teams. Next fall Aimée, as we all call her, will be taking that remarkable record to the Rhode Island School of Design in Providence, where she will follow in the footsteps of her namesake, a celebrated turn-of-the-century artist and her great-great grandmother, Aimée Marie Garnier Whitby. When Aimée enters the American art scene four years from now, I would warn all the current icons of the contemporary art world to pick up their game. Aimée will be gaining on you. Ladies and Gentlemen, it is now my distinct pleasure to present Penfield Academy's newest valedictorian." Cobb again extended his hand.

As Veronica Aimée Whitby stepped to the dais, she was thinking that she had seldom, if ever, felt so good or so excited about the future. This indeed would be the first golden day of the rest of her golden life.

She had no inkling it would also be the last.

Chapter 3

AT ELEVEN FIFTEEN that same morning, Detective Sergeant Michael McCabe hissed the words *selfish bitch* into the old-fashioned telephone receiver before slamming it down. He didn't know if the woman on the other end had heard the words or not, but if she had, she was probably enjoying having goaded him for the hundredth, if not the thousandth, time into a barely controlled rage. The fact that his ex-wife could still manage that trick after all these years added to McCabe's irritation. He resisted a strong urge to pick up the phone and slam it down even harder, no doubt destroying city property in the process.

Instead he ordered himself to calm down. Breathed in deeply a few times. Breathed out. He glanced around at the old wooden desks lined up in neat rows in the squad room on the fourth floor of Portland PD headquarters at 109 Middle Street. Looked to see which, if any, of the half dozen detectives seated behind them had the balls to return their boss's gaze when he was so obviously pissed off.

Tasco, Cleary and Sturgis pretended to focus on their work.

On the other side of the room, Detective Will Meserve was, as usual, oblivious. Either he hadn't heard the hiss and bang, or, if he had, he couldn't care less. Meserve was leaning back in his chair, phone to his ear, guffawing loudly at something somebody on the other end had said. Detective Bill Bacon was on his way back from the men's room. Bacon had probably missed the whole thing.

Only Maggie was looking at him. Detective Margaret Savage. McCabe's number two in the Crimes Against People unit and, when serious cases arose, his partner.

He ignored her look, picked up the file he'd been reviewing and opened it. For more than a minute he tried to focus on the words on the page. They refused to fall into place. Finally he tossed the file on his desk and leaned back, closing his eyes and massaging first his temples and then the hard little knot he could feel forming on the back of his neck. It had been a hell of a spring, and not just because of the call.

Sensing someone approach, McCabe opened his eyes. Maggie was leaning against his desk, studying him.

"What?" he asked.

"Can we go somewhere and talk?"

McCabe frowned. "Talk about what?"

Maggie shrugged. "The Bronstein case?"

"What about the Bronstein case?"

"I'm writing up probable cause for a warrant to search Bronstein's house, and I'd like your thoughts."

McCabe knew Maggie needed his "thoughts" writing up probable cause like a fish needed water wings. Bronstein in theory was an open-and-shut case of domestic violence. Unusual only in the fact that the guy accused of beating up his wife badly enough to land her in the hospital was a respected anesthesiologist and not some punk or drunk. His defense was that he wasn't home at the time, but he didn't have an alibi. He said he was out "driving around," and Rita Bronstein had been attacked by someone else. He claimed she wouldn't admit to that because the someone else was a lover she was trying to protect. For her part, Mrs. Bronstein denied the existence of any such lover and said that Jacob was both full of shit and guilty as sin. Claimed the doctor blew up when she told him she wanted a divorce. Maggie wanted to search the house, because after several long interviews, she suspected the doctor might be telling the truth and that the wife and her lover might be addicted to one or more illegal substances. Maggie figured if she could find both the drugs and evidence of the lover's existence, the case against Bronstein would fall apart and the case against the lover would gather momentum. With Rita still in the hospital, Jacob awaiting bail hearings in the Cumberland County jail and the presumed lover nowhere to be found, Maggie figured this would be an excellent time to take the place apart.

McCabe glanced at the wall clock: 11:25. "Okay. The Bronstein case. How about we get out of here and I buy us some coffee? You can tell me what you need while we sip."

Maggie smiled. "Thanks."

McCabe put on his jacket, retrieved his gun and holster from his bottom drawer and slid the file folders that populated his desk into the space where the gun had been.

Sharing the elevator with Will Meserve, they rode down in silence.

"Where do you want to go?" asked Maggie as the doors slid open and Meserve departed. "Starbucks? Bard?"

"Nah. They'll both be mobbed. Let's walk for a while."

"Okay."

They headed out into bright sunshine and turned right on Middle Street. "Now what's all this baloney about needing help with Bronstein?" McCabe asked.

"Just baloney. The warrant's already signed. I thought you might want to talk about what got you so worked up back there. And maybe why you look like you haven't had a good night's sleep in weeks. Or possibly months. Not to put too fine a point on it, McCabe, but you look like shit."

"That obvious, huh?"

"That obvious. Plus you spend most of the time being cranky, irritable and, frankly, a royal pain in the ass."

"Some people would tell you I'm always a royal pain in the ass."

"Well, they'd be wrong. Now what was going on back there?"

"It was nothing. Just a phone call."

"Nothing? Really? You damn near destroyed the receiver over nothing?"

"Listen, Mag, I know you're trying to help, but if I said it was nothing, just accept that it was nothing. Okay?"

Maggie stopped in the middle of the sidewalk and turned to him. She arched a single dark eyebrow. "I wonder if it's all men," she sighed, "or just the men I care about who have such a hard time talking about their feelings? In that respect, you're so much like my father it makes me want to scream."

McCabe smiled. "How is the old coot? Still cancer-free?"

"Yes. He's doing fine, but let's not change the subject. At the moment, Sergeant, I'm probably the best friend you've got in the world except maybe for Kyra and Dave Hemmings." Kyra was the woman McCabe lived with. Hemmings had been his partner for six years working homicide at the NYPD's Midtown North Precinct. "If you'd rather talk to them instead of me about what's going on, fine. But please don't keep bottling it up inside. It isn't good for you.

McCabe started walking again. Maggie kept up.

Now that summer was almost here, the streets of the Old Port were crowding up with tourists and shoppers. In Tommy's Park, a small urban green space on the other side of Exchange Street, clusters of tattooed teens talked and smoked cigarettes they were technically too young to buy. Toward the back of the park, near the outdoor tables belonging to a popular steakhouse called The Grill Room, a young street entertainer expertly juggled four burning torches. The kid looked like he knew what he was doing, since he hadn't set himself or anybody else on fire. An Abe Lincoln top hat sat on the ground by his side. A passerby tossed in a few dollar bills before moving on.

Closer by, a girl singer in an ankle-length gypsy skirt and bright orange dreads was seated on a bench, playing acoustic guitar and hitting all the right notes on Patsy Cline's *Walkin' After Midnight*. McCabe and Maggie stopped for a minute to listen.

"Okay," McCabe finally said. "Maybe you're right. Let's walk some more and then we'll talk. How about lunch?"

Maggie checked the time. "A little early, but why not? Tallulah's?"

"Yeah. The walk up the hill should help me burn off some steam."

They cut through the park back to Exchange Street and headed up past the old *Press Herald* building. The paper would soon be vacating the space it had occupied since 1923 in favor of a couple of floors in a bigger building near Monument Square. Like papers all over the country, Portland's only daily was facing tough times.

It had already closed its D.C. and Augusta bureaus and laid off as many people as it could. Now it needed to economize even further. Rumor had it the old building was going to be turned into a hotel. Another place for the growing hordes of tourists to bunk. It seemed to McCabe that there were already too many.

They turned right on Congress and headed up Munjoy Hill. Tallulah's sat on the far side of Washington Avenue, about a third of the way up. At this hour, it was mostly empty. Just a couple of regulars hanging at the bar. Lou greeted McCabe with one of her trademark bear hugs and told him his favorite booth in the back was free. She'd once promised to put up a brass plaque over the booth proclaiming *Reserved permanently for M. McCabe*, but she'd never followed through. Passing through the bar, Maggie stopped for a quick hello and a peck on the cheek from a defense lawyer she'd dated a few times. McCabe and the lawyer exchanged nods. When McCabe and Maggie reached the booth, they slid into their accustomed seats, McCabe with his back to the wall, Maggie facing him.

"You still seeing that guy?" McCabe nodded in the direction of the lawyer.

"No. It didn't work out."

"His idea or yours?"

"Mutual but mostly mine. A little too slick for my taste. Plus I couldn't get used to being with a guy who makes his living defending the creeps I knock myself out putting behind bars."

"Sort of like sleeping with the enemy?"

"A: Who said anything about sleeping? And B: who I sleep with or don't sleep with is none of your business. Anyway, we didn't come here to talk about my love life. We're here so you can get whatever's bugging you off your chest."

McCabe heaved a sigh. "You really want to know?"

"If you can force yourself to talk about it, I'm a good listener. If not, we can just have lunch."

A heavyset waitress with short-cropped black hair and thick arms tattooed from wrist to shoulder came up and told them her name was Max.

"Max?"

"Yeah. Short for Maxine."

"You're new," said McCabe.

"Started Monday. You come here a lot?"

"A whole lot. My name's McCabe. This is Maggie."

"Pleased to meet you both. What can I get you?"

They both ordered hamburgers. Medium rare. No cheese. Sweet potato fries on the side. McCabe with a pint of Geary's HSA. Maggie with a Diet Coke.

The drinks arrived. Max disappeared.

McCabe took a long pull of his beer.

"So?" asked Maggie.

McCabe waved her off. "Really. It's not that important."

"Okay."

More silence. The burgers and fries arrived. Maggie slathered hers with ketchup. McCabe, his with A.1. Sauce.

After a couple of minutes of munching, Maggie asked, "So how *is* Sandy these days?" Sandy was McCabe's ex-wife, who had walked out on both their marriage and their only daughter to marry a zillionaire Wall Street banker.

McCabe's eyes narrowed. "What makes you think it was Sandy?"

Maggie shrugged. "She's the only *selfish bitch* I know of who has the ability to get you that pissed off in public. What did she do this time?"

"Maybe, like with your lawyer friend, it's none of your business."

Maggie nodded. "Okay. That's fair. Let's finish our burgers and head back to the office."

McCabe signaled Max, and instead of asking for the check, he ordered another drink. This time a Scotch. Twelve-year-old Macallan single malt. Neat.

"Starting a little early, aren't you?"

"If you wanna know my secrets, this'll help."

Maggie declined another Coke. Instead she pulled herself back against the end of the booth, lifted her long legs up onto the wooden bench and waited for McCabe to start talking.

Tallulah's was starting to fill up, and the level of noise was rising exponentially. McCabe looked around. The lawyer was gone, and he didn't see anyone else he knew. His whiskey arrived.

"I guess what set me off is that the lovely Cassandra just announced she's not coming to Casey's graduation." McCabe's eighteen-year-old daughter, also named Cassandra, was graduating from Portland High on Saturday morning, just two days away.

"And you thought she was?"

McCabe sighed. "Yeah, we both did. Casey and I. Silly us. True to form, Sandy calls me at the office forty-eight hours before the commencement. Tells me 'I'm so sorry but I won't be able to make it. Could you let Casey know?'"

"She couldn't call Casey herself?"

"I don't think she wanted to listen to her only daughter tell her that she doesn't give a shit if Mommy Dearest shows up or not. That, in fact, she'd rather not see her at all."

"So if Casey doesn't care, what's the problem?"

"There really isn't one except Sandy made such a huge deal about coming to the graduation and taking Casey out to a celebratory dinner tomorrow night at Fore Street blah blah blah. Then, at the last minute, she calls it off. It just pissed me off."

Maggie narrowed her eyes. McCabe was being evasive. So far, he hadn't told her anything that would explain his depressed state for the last few weeks. "What supposedly came up?"

"England."

"England?"

"Yeah. She's leaving today. Won't be back for a week."

"And she just called this morning?"

"Yeah. Actually called from JFK. Flight leaves in . . ." McCabe paused to check his watch. " . . . twenty minutes now. First class of course."

"Why's she rushing off to England? Maybe it's something urgent."

"Oh, yeah. Definitely urgent."

Maggie waited for the explanation.

"You're familiar with her rich husband?"

"You've mentioned him. Peter Ingram, right?"

"Yeah, Peter Ingram. Well, Mr. Ingram left for London on business last Sunday night. Sandy was going to be on her own for ten days. Sandy hates being alone. She needs amusement, and she needs an audience. I guess she thought the graduation would provide both. But then she got a better offer. Turns out Ingram's been invited for the weekend to the la-di-da country estate of Lord somebody or other who asked if"—McCabe put on a faux British accent—"'any chance, old man, your wife could join us?' Obviously a bit part in *Downton Abbey* appealed to Sandy more than the title role in *Mother of the Grad*. So off she went."

McCabe finished the Scotch. Caught Max's eye. Ordered another.

"You sure you want that?"

"Yeah, I'm sure. Just carrying on a McCabe family tradition. My old man was a drunk and his old man before him. I'd hate to let the team down."

Max brought the second glass.

"You're not a drunk."

McCabe smiled bitterly. "Kyra might give you an argument on that." He raised the glass and toasted Maggie.

"You're not a drunk," she said softly, reaching out to take his free hand in hers.

"Thank you," he said, squeezing back. "I don't think so either."

"You just," she sighed in frustration, "I don't know . . . drink too much sometimes. Mostly when you're hurting."

"I guess that's one way of putting it." McCabe smiled and let go of her hand. One of the things he liked best about Maggie was her need to defend him. Even against himself. His mother had been that way with his father. On the other hand, maybe it was because Mag had once saved his life, putting a bullet in a bad guy's head nanoseconds before the guy would've cut McCabe's throat from ear to ear. Maybe, like the Chinese, she felt saving his life made her responsible for it forever.

"There's more going on than just Sandy not coming to the graduation, isn't there?"

"Yes and no." McCabe leaned back. The booze was kicking in, and he felt more relaxed. "I guess what's really bugging me is that here's this shallow woman who would rather fly fourteen hours round trip to spend a weekend with people she's never met than go to her only daughter's high school graduation. Yet, in spite of that uncaring attitude, she's nevertheless paying Casey's entire way through Brown University. More than 60K a year. A quarter of a million over four years."

Maggie looked at him questioningly. "And that bugs you because?"

"Because I'm Casey's only real parent. Not Sandy and sure as hell not Ingram, who barely knows her. It's my job to pay my daughter's way through college, but unfortunately I can't afford it. And because of that Sandy's trying to stick it to me like she always has. Prove once again I'm nothing but a lowly cop. In her mind a complete failure who can't even scrape together enough money to pay for his own kid's college education."

Maggie gave him the look she always used before telling him he was being an asshole. But she surprised him. Instead she asked, "What about applying for financial aid? Student loans? Surely, as a lowly cop and a complete failure, you'd qualify."

McCabe sighed. "We tried. Turns out not to be an option. Not when the applicant's mother is married to Peter Ingram, who, apparently, has just donated what he calls three bucks to found Brown's Peter A. Ingram School of Management."

Maggie looked puzzled. "Three bucks?"

"Rich people lingo for three million. The lady at Brown implied giving Casey money would be like giving financial aid to Warren Buffett's kid."

"Well, pardon me for saying so, but I think maybe it's time you swallowed your macho pride, accepted the money and just said 'Thank you.' In spite of everything, Sandy's still Casey's mother."

"I already did that. Months ago. Still, the whole thing sticks in my craw. Casey even picked up on it, though I'd never said a word to her."

"How do you know?"

"She chimed up one day and said she didn't think she wanted to go to Brown. Said she'd prefer U. Maine, Orono. Which, by the way, I'm not sure I could afford either."

"Orono's a good school. I know. I went there."

"I know you did and yes, it is. But Casey's earned her way into Brown. One of the toughest schools in the country to get into. I don't want my hang-ups to be the cause of her missing something I know she wants. So I told her Orono wasn't an option."

Maggie studied McCabe in silence. "What does Kyra think about all this?" she finally asked.

McCabe smiled. A thin bitter smile. "These days she thinks I'm an asshole pretty much all around."

"What do you mean?"

"Kyra left me. Nearly two months ago. She didn't want to hang around with a cop either."

Maggie signaled Max and asked her to bring her a beer. A Geary's HSA. She had a feeling that this was going to be a long afternoon.

Chapter 4

Whitby Island, Maine
June 1904

WHAT AIMÉE HATED most about dying was that she would never see her children grow up. Never see them fall in love. Or marry and have children of their own. Charlotte, the eldest, at eight. So bright and bossy. Always telling the others what to do. Always in charge. Like her father in that regard. Young Teddy, rambunctious and noisy at five. And the baby, Annabelle, not yet three, named for Aimée's English mother.

The children's lovely pink faces floated above her. They seemed so close, so clear. She reached out a hand and stroked Teddy's cheek. Felt its softness against her palm. Teddy. The one she loved most of all though she could never breathe a word of it. Not to Edward or anyone else. But Teddy had always been her favorite. So full of life. So eager. So naughty. So beautiful. There was nothing of Edward in his face. It was all a boyish version of her own. Teddy smiled down at her. "Bonjour, Maman," he said in his sweet soprano. She reached up to pull him closer, but as suddenly as he had appeared, he was gone. She felt tears warming the coldness of her cheek at the thought of never seeing Teddy or the girls again. Never seeing them grow up was too awful to bear. Still, it would be so easy now to simply succumb to the pull of night.

Through the spreading veil of darkness, she heard the crows circling above her again. Quite close now. They must have sensed her time was growing short. "Be patient mes amis," she whispered through drying lips. "Luncheon will be served quite soon."

She saw the children again, walking away from her across a field filled with yellow flowers. A woman Aimée didn't recognize held Teddy and little Annabelle's hands on either side. Who was this woman leading her children away? A maid? No. Not a maid. Edward's next wife? Perhaps. Charlotte, in a gauzy white dress and a brimmed straw hat, skipped ahead of the others. Suddenly Teddy wrenched his hand from the woman's. He turned and began running back toward Aimée.

"Maman, Maman," he shrieked through his tears. "Maman, no! Don't go! Please don't go!"

Aimée opened her arms and waited for Teddy to leap into them. Bury himself against her bosom and fill her face with kisses.

The woman was on him in a flash. Catching him. Lifting him. "You are never to do that again," she scolded. "You will get lost and die."

Teddy reached one arm toward Aimée. "Maman, Maman," he cried, "please come back!"

"Your mother is dead," the woman said in a voice too harsh for such a message. "She's never coming back!"

Aimée wanted desperately to rise and run after them. But her legs wouldn't move, and the harder she tried, the farther away the children seemed to be. Finally, all of them, her three children and the woman who was taking them from her, were nothing but specks on a dark horizon. And then not even specks. The field of yellow flowers faded.

THE SOUND OF men's voices roused Aimée from her reverie. They seemed to be real, not just a dream, and were coming from the ocean.

She opened one eye and saw the dim outline of a fishing boat. Of course. St. Peter the fisherman, who, in the words of the Negro spiritual, must be "Comin' for to carry me home."

Or maybe it was Jesus Himself come to take her in his arms and carry her to heaven. Then there was another voice, younger than the others. A voice only beginning to change to manhood.

"See. Over there!" the boy shouted. The excitement in his cries brought Aimée back to the moment. "By that craggy bit to the left."

"I don't see anything." An older voice. Hoarse and guttural. Both man and boy spoke in that peculiar clipped Maine accent that had become familiar to Aimée.

"It's a woman," the young one shouted. "Holy Jesus! She ain't got no clothes on. Nekked as the day she was born! And there's blood on her body!"

"A naked woman?" a third voice chimed in, laughing, as if he thought that was funny. "Sure she don't have seaweed for hair? And maybe a large scaley tail instead of legs?"

"Don't joke me, Harry. She's real. Look! Right over there!"

"I see her too," said the older man. He sounded grim.

For what seemed a long time, no one spoke. There was only the sound of the sea and the cawing of the crows.

Finally, the old voice said, "All right, one thing's clear. She needs help. That is if she's not already dead."

"Fallen from the cliff, d'ya think, Dad?" asked the one called Harry.

"Look up to the top," said the father. "There's a man at the top. He's leaning over. Looking down."

"Why don't he climb down to help her?" said Harry. "Maybe he meant to kill her."

"You mean he pushed her off the cliff?" asked the younger boy.

"I don't know," said the older man. "The Whitbys don't take kindly to strangers. Never have. But I wouldn't have thought they'd have murdered one."

"We have to go in and help," said the boy.

"Damned if I can get any closer," said the old man. "Not in this sea. Those rocks will knock us to pieces."

"I'll go in the dinghy," said Harry. "Jack's right. We can't let her die."

There was a silence.

"She'll die if we don't," Harry said again.

"She may be dead already."

"No," said Harry, "she's alive. I just saw her move."

"You're lying."

"I just saw her move," Harry insisted

Above, Aimée heard a flapping of wings. A flutter near her face. A pair of sharp talons pushed into her leg. A beak dug in and tore a piece of flesh from the opening. She tried to scream, but no sound would come. Within seconds she felt another peck. And then another. In a moment birds were all over her. Only death would bring relief. She longed for it to take her quickly.

A rifle shot rang out. Its echoes reverberated against the crevices of the cliff wall. The murder of crows retreated. A second shot followed.

"Bastards," said the old man. "I'll not have those damned birds feeding on a Christian woman. Dead or alive."

That seemed funny. Aimée hadn't been a Christian woman for years. Not since she was a child. Perhaps this fisherman really was St. Peter, even if he had a rifle and sounded like a Mainer.

"Then let us go in," said Harry. "We'll get her."

After a minute the old man said, "All right, son. Take the dinghy. Young Jack, you go with him. Tie lines around yourselves so I can haul you back if you run into trouble. When you get there, signal if she's alive. If she is, try to get her into the dinghy. If she's dead, I'll leave you to keep the birds away and head for help. But, for God's sake, be careful. I'd hate to lose both my sons trying to recover the body of one dead woman. Could be a damned Whitby woman at that."

Aimée felt a glimmer of hope as she waited for the two sons, Harry and Jack, to arrive.

Another shot rang out, followed again by the flutter and cries of retreating crows. She wondered how many bullets the fisherman had. Didn't really matter. Crows were smart. The sound of shots wouldn't frighten them for long unless one or more of them was hit. A difficult task with a rifle even if the man had a very good eye. She wished the boys would hurry.

Aimée's eyes opened. The light seemed dimmer. The air colder. Perhaps it was night. She didn't know. She felt her body growing weaker. She closed them again.

After what seemed an eternity, she heard the scraping of a small boat being pulled up onto the beach. Heavy boots crunching the stones, coming closer.

"I think she's dead," said young Jack.

"Sure as hell lying still as death."

Aimée wanted desperately to tell them she was not dead. But no sound would come from her mouth.

"Not just dead, Jack," said the one called Harry. "This woman was murdered."

"Murdered?"

"Damned right. Look at these cuts. This straight one here to the left of her middle. That wasn't made by her falling off any rocks. It's a gut wound made by a knife. And look here. See that? The letter *A* carved into her chest."

Hearing Harry's words, the horror of what had happened today on the island, first at the studio and then at the cliff, came flooding back into Aimée's memory.

"*A*?" asked Jack. "What do you suppose *A* stands for?"

"Beats me. Maybe her name starts with an *A*."

Aimée concentrated as hard as she could on moving something. A finger. A lip. Anything that would convince them she was still alive. At last, with the greatest of effort, an eyelid fluttered.

"She's not dead," said Jack.

"She's dead."

"She's not. I saw her eye move." The boy went down on his knees and put his ear to her chest. "I don't know. Maybe she is dead. No, wait. I can feel her heart beating."

He put his ear to her lips. "She's still breathing. We have to take her back."

Four strong hands lifted and carried Aimée to the dingy. They gently lowered her into a puddle of freezing water. And then pushed off.

"Christ, if she survives this it'll be a damn miracle."

Yes, it would, she thought. *A damn miracle indeed.*

She could feel the waves pushing them back toward the cliff, but somehow the boys managed to get themselves up and over the breakers without damage.

She felt the dinghy banging against the side of the larger craft. Perhaps she would live after all.

"Here, slip her into the net." The older man was speaking again. "And you, Jack, you climb up here and help me haul her in. Hell, she don't look no heavier than a big cod anyway."

Aimée felt herself swinging for a moment in the air. Then she was lifted up and over the gunwale and lowered onto the deck of the rocking craft.

"Here. Wrap her in this."

She felt rough wool encase her body.

"All right, let's get her the hell back to port. With any luck, we'll run into the police boat and pass her on to them."

The rolling of the waves slowed. The boat moved.

She felt the boy's ear press gently against her lips. His cheeks were smooth, like a child's. Like Teddy's.

She mouthed a single word. But it was barely a whisper.

Still, the boy must have heard it. He looked up.

"What did she say?" asked his brother.

"Dunno. Couldn't quite make it out. Sounded like . . ."

AIMÉE NEVER LEARNED if the boy called Jack had correctly heard the name she'd whispered, because before he could tell his brother what it sounded like, darkness fell all around her. And Aimée Marie Garnier Whitby, of Paris, Provence and Portland, Maine, in her twenty-eighth year, slipped into death as quietly and smoothly as she might have slipped into the depths of the ocean.

Chapter 5

PENFIELD ACADEMY'S NEWLY minted valedictorian walked to the lectern. She waited, scanning the audience, smiling warmly, until the applause died down. With the exception of a few toddlers squirming in their parents' arms, every eye was focused on her. Aimée experienced a shiver of excitement.

Her eyes went to the faculty seating area. Sought and found Byron Knowles. Her AP English teacher was a married poet with languid looks and a perpetual two-day growth of beard. Byron, or as she so often teased him, Lord Byron, looked back. His smile communicated nothing more than a teacher taking pride in the achievements of his star pupil. But Aimée knew there was more to it than that. She remembered the two of them sitting naked in bed just days ago, eating ripe peaches and reading erotic poetry to each other. Dripping peach juice both on the sheets and on their bodies. Then grabbing each other and licking it off. Delicious.

A few of her closest friends knew she was involved with someone, but she hadn't offered even a hint as to who it might be. Not even to Julia, with whom Aimée shared most things. Keeping the secret made the affair seem dark, romantic, illicit. Which was, for Aimée at least, part of its charm. But there was also the near certainty Byron would be fired, his career ruined, if their secret came out. That seemed dreadfully unfair to Aimée, since it was she who'd started the whole thing.

The applause continued, and Aimée delighted in it. All these people focusing only on her. Then, with perfect timing, she held up a hand to quiet things down. "Thank you all," she said. "Thank you all so very much."

When there was silence, Aimée began to speak. She didn't need a script or even notes. She'd worked hard, endlessly re-hearsing every word, every gesture, every pause. As she did with everything else in her life, Aimée wanted the speech to be per-fect. "Headmaster Cobb," she began, "trustees, faculty members, family, friends and fellow graduates, today is a day for those of us leaving Penfield to reflect on and be thankful for all we have been given." As her words tumbled out flawlessly, Aimée scanned the audience. For the first time, she spotted her mother, Tracy Carlin, seated way in the back on the aisle. Typical. As the *Press Herald*'s top crime reporter, Tracy's mantra had always been to sit as close to the exit as she could in case of a breaking news story.

Across from Tracy, Aimée spotted Will Moseley. Gorgeous Will. Once a boyfriend but never again. He sat sprawled on a fold-ing chair too small for his six-four frame, long legs stretched out into the aisle, hands folded casually behind his head. A two-day growth on his cheeks and chin. Will wore no suit or blazer, as others did. No necktie. Just black jeans, Frye boots and a checked shirt with tails hanging out loosely.

"The world we, as young people, will be inheriting," Aimée told the attentive audience, "faces challenges on a global scale unlike any faced by previous generations. It is our responsibility as the next in line to shake ourselves loose from the narrow focus on self and look outward to a world that is crying out . . ."

She continued to the end, her speech timed to last precisely twelve minutes, no more, no less. "To paraphrase Benjamin Franklin," she said, wrapping it up, "everyone is born ignorant. Even valedictorians. But for all of us who, for the last four years, have benefited so profoundly from the wisdom, knowledge and guidance of the teachers, coaches and staff here at Penfield, well, it would be impossible for any of us, valedictorians or not, to leave here the same way. For this reason, I'd like to ask all my fellow members of this year's graduating class to stand and join me in thanking you— our teachers, parents and friends of the school— for the love, wisdom, support and, yes, the tuition money you so generously doled out . . ." Aimée waited until the required chuckle died down. " . . . to provide each and every one of us with the very best start in life we could possibly get.'"

She accepted a long, standing ovation, then returned to her seat as Headmaster Cobb replaced her at the dais to present Emily Welles with her citizenship award.

Once seated, Aimée looked again at Moseley and wondered what he was doing here. She hadn't invited him, though he'd hinted more than once that she should. Any interest she'd ever had in Moseley had died two summers ago in a particularly loud and ugly sexual incident out on the island. She thought of it as rape. Hell, it *had been* rape. Yes, they'd had sex before and yes, they'd been making out, but on this day she'd told him she didn't feel like taking things any further. She'd gotten up and tried to leave. He'd gotten pissed off. Called her a cock-teaser. Grabbed her. Thrown her down on the bed, pulled her legs apart and pushed into her. She'd said she was going to tell her father but he knew she wouldn't, since the Moseleys and the Whitbys were best friends and, at the time, she and Will had been having regular sex for over a year. She didn't want Daddy to know about that.

Perhaps Julia had invited him. Jules lusted for Will like a cat lusted for cream. Somehow she didn't get it that making her desire so obvious made her less desirable to him. So much so that Will rarely gave her a second look. Except on those few occasions when he felt particularly horny and Jules allowed herself to be used to satisfy his immediate needs.

Still, it was possible that her father had issued the invitation. He made no secret of the fact that he thought Moseley—two years out of Penfield, two years into Yale and the only son of one of the other richest families in Maine—was exactly the kind of man one of his daughters should marry.

Daddy, no doubt, would think of such a marriage as a kind of business deal. R.W. Moseley and Company, the private bank Will's family owned, had been looking after Whitby money for well over one hundred years and were major underwriters and investors in Whitby Engineering & Development (symbol WED on the New York Stock Exchange). Moseley weds Whitby. In Daddy's mind not so much a marriage as a merger. Or possibly an acquisition. Either way a royal affair. Hell, if Daddy thought he could pull it off, he'd probably try to talk the Brits into renting him Westminster Abbey for the occasion. And maybe even the Queen's golden coach. Failing that, he'd no doubt settle for St. Luke's, the Episcopal cathedral on State Street where Whitbys had been christened, married and mourned since shortly after the Civil War. The wedding of the year, to be followed, no doubt, by the reception of the year in front of the cottage on the island.

Aimée snorted. She had no intention of marrying anyone any-time soon. She had her own life to live, and she sure as hell wasn't going to dedicate it to some hot little frat boy who wanted nothing more than to drink as much booze and screw as many women as he could in the shortest possible time.

When Emily Welles finished her citizenship speech, she was followed by three middle-aged former jocks who were being in-ducted into the Penfield Academy Athletic Hall of Fame. Aimée tuned them out and thought instead about tonight's party. She reviewed the guest list in her mind. All her fellow graduates, plus some of Aimée's and Jules's other friends. Parents of graduates, some of whom were friends of the Whitbys, others who probably just wanted a chance to poke around a cottage that had been fea-tured in three separate issues of *Maine Home and Design*. Check-ing out the lifestyles of the rich and famous.

Most of the faculty would attend with spouses. Except for Lord Byron, who, they'd agreed, would find a way to leave Gina at home. There would also be politicians. Governor Kevin Hardesty and his wife. Maine's First District congressman. And Senator Ann Colman, Vice Chairwoman of the Senate Armed Services Committee, who would be flying up from Washington. Daddy had instructed Charles Kraft to keep an eye on Colman and make sure she was happy. A natural assignment. Kraft liked keeping women happy. Even fifty-something female senators.

A few of Daddy's lobbyists would be present to keep the poli-ticians stoked and stroked. Plus one Pulitzer Prize–winning novelist who lived up in Camden and whose books Aimée liked and an aging Hollywood star who had a house down in Prouts Neck.

Guests who made the cut would be flown to the island on Daddy's helicopter. The less favored would either sail their own boats or sail out with friends. The true commoners, the untouchables, would be relegated to the Casco Bay Lines ferry that had been chartered for the occasion. The only person Aimée could think of who wasn't invited and wouldn't come even if she had been was her own mother, Tracy Carlin, the first Mrs. Edward Whitby.

Chapter 6

McCabe leaned in closer to Maggie. "Why don't we go over to your place," he whispered even though Tallulah's had pretty much emptied out.

She shook her head. "A tempting offer, but no thank you."

It was after three in the afternoon. In the course of telling Maggie about the final breakup between Kyra and himself, McCabe had managed to polish off five Scotches. Actually, in most places, they would have added up to seven or eight, since Lou's bartenders always poured McCabe a good three ounces per drink. As a result, while going over to Maggie's seemed like a really good idea to him, it was a game she definitely wasn't going to play.

"Be more private than my place," he said. "Casey's probably home from school by now."

"I said no. I meant no. But thank you for the offer anyway."

McCabe peered at her with a self-satisfied expression, like this conversation was a test in which he knew all the right answers. "Y'know, you once told me," he said, "that the reason we couldn't get together was because I was taken. Well, guess what?"

"What."

"I'm not taken anymore."

"No, but you are drunk."

"Yeah. But . . ." McCabe grinned broadly. He knew the answer to that one as well. "But I'm not *a* drunk. You told me so yourself just a little while ago." He looked at his watch. "Well, actually quite a while ago."

"Yes, I did, and I meant it. You're not a drunk."

"Good." McCabe turned away, looking for the waitress to order another round.

Maggie reached across the table and took one of McCabe's hands. "Look at me, McCabe, and stop searching for Max. You don't need any more drinks."

McCabe frowned but did as she asked.

"We once made love," said Maggie, "at a time when I was in a bad place and really needed you. I've never been sorry about that. But before we go over to my place or anywhere else for whatever you have in mind, there are a lot of things I have to sort out in my own mind. And probably just as many you should be thinking about as well."

McCabe closed his eyes and took a deep breath, trying to clear the fog in his brain. When he felt about as articulate as he was going to get, he opened them. He looked into Maggie's soft brown eyes, so different from Kyra's blue ones. He spoke slowly, managing not to slur his words. "Mag, we care for each other. We always have. Call it love. Call it friendship. Call it whatever you want. But it's a fact. We have something special. There have been a thousand times over the past six years when I've thought about us being together, and I don't mean just for sex. I mean really being together. And I'm pretty sure you've thought about that too."

"You know I have. But it's not going to happen. Not until I know the answers to a couple of things. For one, Kyra may have left you, but I have a feeling you may not be entirely done with her. Not emotionally anyway. I think if she changed her mind and said she wanted you back, you and I would be right back where we started. And as much as I care for you, I don't want to be anybody's rebound or second choice. Not even yours."

"Maggie, Kyra and I are history."

"I'm sure you believe that's true. And maybe it is. But I'd rather wait till we both know it for sure."

"Okay. I understand. I'm not sure you're right, but I understand."

"There are also a few other problems," said Maggie.

"Like what?"

"Like the fact we work together. That you're my boss. That we work with other detectives, none of whom are stupid."

"Well, there is Will."

"He's no dummy either. If our relationship changed, people would know, and a lot of things about our jobs would have to change as well."

McCabe sighed. She was probably right about that too. "Okay, so what do we do now?"

"Now? Now I'm going to call a cab to take you home. No way you should go staggering back to the office in the shape you're in. And do me a favor? When you get there, don't have another drink. Okay? Just go to bed. You look like you haven't had a decent night's sleep in weeks. We'll talk more tomorrow."

Chapter 7

IT ONLY TOOK a few minutes of flying time for Whitby Engineering & Development's AgustaWestland 139 helicopter to go from the company helipad on the Portland waterfront to Whitby Island. Aimée always loved the ride. Especially on brilliant days like this. She leaned as far forward on her soft white leather seat as the seat belt would allow and pressed her face against the window.

As the island came into view, it seemed to Aimée that the green of the trees bathed in summer sunshine made the place seem like a glittering emerald floating in the middle of a sea of sparkling diamonds. She glanced quickly at her fellow passengers. None was looking. Julia was too absorbed in Gillian Flynn's *Gone Girl* to notice emeralds, diamonds or anything else. Julia was smart. Quite pretty. A very good actress. Amazing how she could transform herself into someone like Blanche DuBois on the stage. Aimée sometimes wished she and Julia could overcome the twin thing. The two had been competing for both accolades and their father's love since they were in the cradle. It was something Aimée wanted to resolve. She wanted them to be friends as well as sisters.

In the middle seat, her stepmother, Deirdre, sat staring straight ahead. Deirdre hated the helicopter. Flying in it frightened her, and she avoided it whenever possible. Up front, next to the pilot, Daddy was talking loudly into his cell. Something about some Pentagon procurement officer fucking up some specs on some job or other. Charles, of course, was snoozing. It always amazed Aimée how Kraft could fall asleep instantly, even if only for a couple of minutes, then wake up alert and ready to go.

As the chopper descended toward the helipad, Aimée watched dozens of white-jacketed caterers stop their frantic scurrying to stare as it gently touched down.

When they had safely landed, the worker bees returned to their activity, setting up dozens of tables, three bars and a large outdoor dance floor. Other workers went back to stringing lights from the trees. The main summer cottage, an eight-thousand-square-foot mansion, was surrounded by patios and manicured gardens. Tonight all would be bathed in lights as soon as the sun went down and darkness fell. Everything would look stunning.

Once on the ground, the misnamed Mr. Jolley rushed out to greet them and grab bags. The dour, skinny, sixty-year-old Scot was a retired cop from up in Houlton and the male half of the couple who took care of the place. He was also someone Aimée generally avoided when she could. Three years back, she'd caught the old fart peeping at her through a corner of the studio window as she was getting dressed after giving Will Moseley what he claimed was one of the best blow jobs in history. Will had reciprocated by providing Aimée with equally good treatment with his own tongue. She didn't know how much Jolley had seen, but most likely the entire performance. He'd scurried away the instant Aimée spotted him. When she'd asked him what was he was doing there, he apologized profusely. Claimed it had been a total accident. Said it was part of his job to check on the cottages and he hadn't seen all that much anyway. Aimée hadn't pushed it. She sure as hell didn't want Mr. Jolley, in his own defense, telling Daddy what she and Moseley had been up to. It wouldn't sit well, since she was only fifteen at the time. Anyway, Jolley had been giving her sly glances and creepy smiles ever since. She told him if he didn't cut it out she would tell Daddy he was a habitual Peeping Tom. So far she hadn't bothered. She preferred the threat to the reality.

Jolley took Aimée's suitcase in one hand and Julia's in the other. He offered to take the dress-bag Aimée was carrying, but she held on to it. The dress was a secret. She'd had it made specially for her dramatic entrance at tonight's party. The dressmaker, the best in Portland, had been instructed to duplicate the design in an old book Aimée had found in the Penfield library. *Hidden Masterpieces of American Art.* She'd actually had to steal the damned book, since it wasn't allowed to circulate.

Once safely in her room, Aimée locked the door, took the dress from the bag and tried it on. She opened the book to the appropriate page. Propped it up and compared her image in the full-length mirror to the one on the page. A perfect match. Identical. She just had to get the hair, makeup and timing right. If she did, there was absolutely no doubt that she'd steal the limelight from everyone else. Daddy, the governor, the famous author, the movie star, and also, alas, poor Jules. Fantasizing about their likely reaction to her performance gave Aimée immense pleasure.

Chapter 8

AT THREE THIRTY in the afternoon a cab deposited McCabe at his front door. He handed the cabbie twenty bucks and told him to keep the change.

Wobbling toward the front door, he started digging around in his pockets for his keys.

The driver, a round-bellied black man in his fifties, leaned out the window of the cab. "What floor's your apartment on?"

McCabe turned and appeared to be giving the question serious consideration. "Three," he finally said.

"Long way up," said the driver.

"Yup," said McCabe, looking up at his windows on the top floor.

The driver exited the car, put one arm around McCabe's shoulder and told McCabe to do the same. He took McCabe's key, opened the door and returned the key, then side by side the two of them struggled up three flights of stairs.

"Anybody else live here?"

"Yup."

"Your wife?"

"Nope. My little girl."

"Your little girl? How old?"

"Eighteen."

"Okay," said the driver and rang the bell.

Casey answered after two rings, looked first at McCabe and then at the man who was holding him up.

"There's my little girl," slurred McCabe.

"This your father?" asked the driver, not wanting to leave a strange drunk with the wrong daughter by mistake.

Casey sighed. "Yup. That's him. Where'd you find him?"

"Picked him up at Tallulah's. Drove him here in my cab. Where's he sleep?"

Casey directed the cabbie to McCabe's bedroom. After her father had been deposited on the bed, she thanked him. "Have you been paid?"

"Yeah. Gave me twice what he should have." He reached in his pocket and pulled out a roll of bills. "Here. Take this," he said, handing her a five. "What's left will be more than enough."

When the cabbie was gone, Casey stood in her father's bedroom door. "All right, what the hell is this all about? It's the middle of the damned afternoon."

"Please don't. You sound exactly like Kyra. It's all right. I just spent the afternoon with Maggie at Lou's pouring my heart out."

"You told her about Kyra?"

"About that and everything else. I did a lot of talking."

"And a lot of drinking?"

What McCabe detected in her voice was more like concern than disapproval. "Yup. Seeking solace in the demon rum."

"You know, I'm the kid in this family. You're the one who's supposed to be giving me lectures about stuff like that."

McCabe held up a hand. "Please. No lectures."

"Well, I'm glad you were able to open up to somebody even if you had to get drunk to do it. You've been wound up so tight lately I thought you were going to explode."

She walked over to the bed, turned his face toward hers and gave him a kiss. "You gonna be okay?"

"Yeah. I'll be fine. And you're right. I did need to let it out. And now I need to sleep. So buzz off, bambina."

"I probably won't be here when you wake up. I'm going out tonight. To a party. Remember?"

McCabe closed his eyes. "I remember everything. You know that. Try and be home by one."

"I will."

"You need the car?"

"No. Somebody's picking me up."

"Who?"

"Just this kid."

"Boy kid or girl kid?"

"Just a kid."

"Okay. No drinking."

Casey decided not to dignify that with an answer. She just leaned down and gave him a kiss. And then, thinking it wasn't such a great idea to fall asleep with a loaded Glock 17 riding on his hip, she reached over and undid the buckle to his holster. After she locked the gun in the small safe McCabe kept for the purpose, she came back and kissed him again. "I'll be back by one," she said.

"Make sure that you are," he said and turned over. In less than a minute he was sound asleep.

Chapter 9

THE GUESTS BEGAN arriving before six. A flotilla of private boats, some motor, more sail, moored in the broad cove on the leeward side. The largest was a ten-million-dollar, eighty-nine-foot, Bill Tripp–designed, world-class sailing yacht called the *Sea Witch*, owned by the movie star. There were half a dozen other good-sized yachts and scores of smaller boats. From the moorings, a dozen twenty-something "parking valets," identically dressed in white sneakers, khaki shorts and blue polo shirts bearing the Whitby E&D logo, ferried guests from their boats to the smaller of the two docks and directed them up the pathway that led to the "cottage," which stood two hundred feet back and fifty feet above the cove.

Most of the arrivals were dressed informally, as the invitations had instructed. Of course, *informally* had been interpreted in a variety of ways, from blazers and ties for the men and elegant slacks and silk blouses for the women down to jeans or shorts and T-shirts for the graduates.

FRESH FROM HER shower with a towel wrapped around her, Aimée gazed through the window as clusters of guests arrived on the stone terrace below. One group after another shook hands and air-kissed Daddy and Deirdre. She was a little pissed her mother hadn't been invited, even as a gesture. But both she and Daddy knew Tracy wouldn't have come anyway. Still, the invitation should have been offered.

Daddy, a warm smile plastered to his face, was listening to a pair of chatty Penfield parents. Periodically he glanced over their shoulders to see if there was anyone more important or more interesting in the area he ought to be talking to. Spotting the approaching figures of Margaux Amory and her husband, John Roach, he excused himself from the Penfield pair. Still exquisite in her mid-sixties, Amory was once considered one of Hollywood's best and most versatile stars. In fact, only a couple of weeks ago, Aimée and Tracy had enjoyed a "girls' night in" watching Amory's Oscar-winning performance in a twenty-five-year-old movie called *Wet Work,* in which she played a high-class call girl who doubled as a paid assassin. Amory's character had been hired to murder her hot-looking client, who also happened to be a leading candidate for president. The storyline was bullshit, but Amory's performance as a whore was amazing. It was a role for which, Aimée thought with a smile, Margaux was a natural.

Aimée turned from the window and walked back to her dressing table. Using the image in *Hidden Masterpieces* for reference, she started preparing for her entrance. It took over an hour to get everything exactly right. The hair. The makeup. Finally, the dress and a single strand of antique pearls around her neck.

Aimée examined herself in the mirror one last time. Practiced the smile in the painting until she was sure she had it right. Turned her head this way and that. Adjusted a blonde curl that seemed out of place and looked again. The final touch was the earrings. An exquisite pair of deep blue teardrop sapphires, each surrounded by two rows of diamonds set in gold dangles. They were the only things Aimée would wear tonight that weren't in the painting. Her great-great-grandfather had purchased them in New York at the old Tiffany's on Union Square West because, according to family legend, the stones almost matched the deep, nearly violet blue of the first Aimée's eyes. He had planned to take the earrings to the island and surprise her with the gift. But it never happened. She was murdered first.

Finally, when everything was truly perfect, Aimée took a cut-crystal highball glass from the tray she'd instructed Anna Jolley to leave for her. She dropped in a handful of ice cubes, retrieved the bottle of Ketel One she kept in her bottom drawer and poured herself a good four ounces. Raising the glass, she toasted the image in the book. "To my inspiration, the first Aimée," she said. Then, turning her attention to her own image in the mirror, she added, "And to me, Aimée again."

Taking the drink with her, she rose and went to the door. Opened it silently. Looked both ways. Seeing no one on the landing, she moved into the shadows at the top of the stairs, where she could watch her father speaking in front of the big stone fireplace without being seen herself. She waited, certain the wait wouldn't be long. Edward Whitby enjoyed being the center of attention as much as either of his daughters did. He also enjoyed being prompt. He invariably stuck to schedule.

A scant two minutes later, she watched Daddy nab a delicate flute of Perrier-Jouët from a passing waiter and position himself at the center of the fireplace. He took a few sips, waiting until he felt the timing was right.

"Ladies and Gentlemen," he finally called out. "I'd like as many of you as possible to please join me here in the living room. Please, everyone, this way. I have a special treat for you all."

Prodded by the waitstaff, guests began to move. More than a hundred managed to squeeze into the large living room. Another hundred and some clustered outside on the stone patio, where they could watch Whitby's image and listen to his words on two large CCTV screens set up for the occasion.

Aimée looked past her father to the painting that hung, covered with black baize cloth, above the mantel. She'd only seen reproductions before and hadn't realized how big the original was. At least five feet high. Three or a little more across. She was sure the size of the painting would heighten the effect. For people looking up at it from the floor, her great-great grandmother would appear to be very nearly the same size as her living namesake.

"Ladies and Gentlemen, graduates and parents, friends," Edward Whitby began. "Let me start by welcoming you all here to our humble . . . well, perhaps not so humble . . . summer cottage on Whitby Island. For those of you who've been here before, welcome back. For those who haven't, please know that, for tonight at least, *mi casa es su casa.*"

The guests applauded. Aimée sipped her vodka on the landing and waited. With his back to the large stone fireplace, Daddy raised his champagne flute. "We're here tonight to honor not just my two beautiful daughters." He turned a palm toward Julia, who had positioned herself up front. "Julia." Jules nodded her thanks. Daddy looked around the room for a few seconds more and not seeing Aimée, he continued, "One of whom seems not to be here at the moment. Rare for Aimée to miss a moment like this. Ah, well. We're also here to honor all the other wonderful kids who graduated from Penfield today. May you all succeed, prosper and find fulfillment in whatever career and on whatever road you choose to travel in life."

Shouts of "Hear! Hear!" boomed from the crowd. Other guests applauded. Still others stood quietly and sipped expensive champagne or martinis.

"However," said Whitby, "I also have another purpose. As I said, a special treat. I'd like you all to be present for the first public showing of an important work by one of America's greatest and most respected artists, Mark Garrison. The piece under the cloth is Garrison's last great work, one which was never quite finished before his death. A large portrait of my great-grandmother, and Julia and Aimée's great-great grandmother, Aimée Marie Garnier Whitby."

He scanned the room, looking for Aimée. He still couldn't find her.

"This portrait of the first Aimée," Edward Whitby continued, "was commissioned by her husband, my great-grandfather, Edward Whitby Jr. He had wanted John Singer Sargent to paint his wife, but Aimée, a fine artist in her own right, insisted that she preferred the work of Garrison. Since Garrison was considered by many at the time to be very nearly Sargent's equal and, as Sargent was in England, Edward agreed.

"The story that follows the awarding of that commission is well known. It is surrounded by tales of infidelity, scandal, murder and suicide that no member of my family has ever been willing to publically discuss. I don't plan on breaking with that tradition tonight to regale you with any of the lurid details.

Those who are interested can find accounts in the newspaper reports of the time.

"Rather, I'd like you to focus your attention on a great painting whose creation ended in tragedy and turned out to be Garrison's last masterpiece. *Portrait of Aimée* was painted here in this room, with this stone fireplace as background. It was originally meant to hang over the fireplace, where it hangs now, but it never has. Some may wonder why I want to own or hang a canvas created by a man who murdered a member of my own family. The simple answer is that I have always regarded this work as belonging more to Aimée than to Garrison, and I believe she would have wanted it here, gazing down on her descendants. I know I've wanted to return it to this house all my adult life. And now I have.

"Garrison painted the portrait in the spring of 1904. In late May of that year, he took the almost completed canvas back to his studio in Boston for a few finishing touches. After Garrison's and Aimée's deaths, it remained in the studio for a time. Almost but not quite finished. My great-grandfather, who commissioned the work, couldn't bear the thought of having it in the house. He also refused to pay what was still owed on the commission. So, after a year, Garrison's widow, in desperate need of money, sold it, along with a number of his other paintings, to a wealthy family from New York. It remained quietly in their hands for over a century. For me the subject of the painting and the quality of the work, which is superb, have always been more important than the tale of murder surrounding it. Over the years, I've tried to purchase it many times, but always without success. Then, last winter, I learned the descendants of the original owners were putting Garrison's *Portrait of Aimée* up for auction at Christie's in New York. Naturally, I attended. I think everybody in the room knew

I wouldn't let the painting go to anyone else at any price. Perhaps that's why the bidding was so stiff. I suppose the owners of the auction house will get mad at me for saying this, but I wouldn't be a bit surprised if they placed a few ringers in the crowd to push the price even higher. No matter. I felt strongly that it was well past time this great work of art, this treasure, be restored to the place where it was meant to hang regardless of price and regardless of the circumstances of Aimée's death. I believed then as I believe now it is one of Garrison's finest works and that Aimée's place is here in the house she loved. Ladies and Gentlemen, after one hundred and eight years, my great-grandmother, Aimée Marie Garnier Whitby, has come home."

Whitby pulled a cord, releasing the baize covering to reveal a nearly perfect likeness of the first Aimée. Upstairs, her great-great-granddaughter waited a few beats to allow the crowd time to study and admire the portrait. Then she put her empty vodka glass on the floor and moved from the shadows. She smiled the practiced smile and started down the curved staircase. On the sixth step down, she called out, "*Bonsoir, mes amis, et bienvenue.*"

There was a collective hush. Every face in the room turned, almost in unison, to watch Aimée slowly descend the stairs. The gown she wore, low cut and black, and the pearls around her neck were both identical to the ones in the painting. She had also styled an identical arrangement of her blonde hair. Even the smile, some might say a Mona Lisa smile, matched Aimée's in the portrait. It was nearly impossible to distinguish the face or figure of the young woman descending the stairs from the face and figure in the painting. Except for the brilliant blue sapphire-and-diamond earrings young Aimée wore, the resemblance was exact, the effect stunning.

On the next-to-bottom step she paused to introduce herself. *"Je suis Aimée."*

Edward Whitby came over, put his arm around her and walked her back to the fireplace and positioned her beneath the portrait.

"It has never ceased to amaze me," he said to the crowd, "how my beautiful eldest daughter has such an uncanny ability to upstage her father at the most dramatic moments of his life." He raised the glass of champagne. "To my dearest, favorite girl, who is, as you can see, a true incarnation of the first Aimée."

Aimée kissed her father, then turned to the guests. "Once I saw the painting," she said, "and saw how much I looked like her, well, as you can imagine, it was just too tempting not to give it a whirl."

Most of the guests spontaneously applauded.

Aimée bowed her head, thanked everyone and then plunged into the crowd.

Chapter 10

"ABSOLUTELY PERFECT ENTRANCE," Margaux Amory whispered in Aimée's ear. "You were born to be a star."

Aimée resisted a strong temptation to simply say *I know* and leave it at that. Instead she told the Oscar-winning actress, "Thank you. Coming from you, Ms. Amory, that really means a lot."

"Please. Call me Margaux and not Ms. Amory. And please call me next week. Your father has the number. There are some people I think you really ought to meet. Or, perhaps more accurately, who ought to meet you."

Aimée promised she would and headed toward the bar. She briefly noticed her sister watching her intently. Jules wasn't smiling.

Charles Kraft fell in beside her. Took her by the elbow. She could feel the bulge of his SIG Sauer 9 mm automatic pressing into her arm from under his jacket. "Y'know, you really are something else," he said.

She smiled at Charles. "Thank you, Charles. I'll take that as a compliment."

"Oh, definitely a compliment."

She asked Mr. Jolley, who was tending bar, to pour her a vodka on the rocks. Ketel One. He hesitated. She was, after all, only eighteen.

"Don't worry, Mr. Jolley. I won't tell a soul," she said, adding after a pause, "not about anything."

Jolley frowned. Then tossed some ice cubes in a glass and filled it with vodka.

Kraft watched the exchange, then asked Jolley for the same.

When he had it, he took Aimée's elbow again and began steering her toward the terrace. "Y'know," he said, "now that you've become a real grown-up . . . ordering vodka, threatening the staff . . ."

"What do you mean, 'threatening'?"

"You know exactly what I mean. You and I are too much alike not to recognize the threats we each make. Even the more subtle ones."

"I see. And how else are we alike?"

Kraft held her arm a little tighter. "We both like things a little dangerous."

"Yes, perhaps we do. But not tonight, Charles. I have other plans. Now, if you'll please let go of my arm. You're hurting me."

"Yes, Charles," Julia's voice came from behind them. "I think you should let go of Daddy's 'dearest, favorite girl.' He won't like it."

Kraft glanced at Julia. Apparently deciding a tactical retreat was in order, he released Aimée's arm. "If you'll excuse me," he said and walked away.

"That was some performance you gave," said Julia. "How long have you been planning this?"

"I first saw the painting in a book last year. Noticed the resemblance. Then when Daddy told us he was buying it and that it would be presented at the graduation party, I figured what the hell."

"And you didn't bother to tell me."

"I didn't tell anyone, Jules. For one thing, I wasn't sure I could pull it off. For another, I wanted it to be a surprise. To everyone."

"And I thought I was the actress in the family," she said with a snort. "But look at you. Hair. Makeup. The dress. All of it perfect. Everything except for the earrings. I don't remember Daddy giving them to you."

"Now Jules, don't have a hissy. I haven't absconded with the family jewels. Let's just say I borrowed them for the occasion. Now, if you'll excuse me, I don't think either of us should be ignoring our guests."

Aimée left Julia standing there and walked out through the French doors. She noticed Aman Anbessa standing alone at the far end of the patio. He was wearing the same blazer, khakis and tie he'd worn for graduation and was drinking a Coke out of the can. She walked over and congratulated him on getting a full scholarship to Tufts. "Your parents must be very proud. Are they here?"

"They didn't want to come. Said they would have felt out of place. But I wouldn't have missed it for the world."

"Good. I'm glad. Are you coming to the kids' after-party? After the grown-ups go home."

"Oh yes? Where will it be?"

"At the top of the cliff."

He shook his head. "I haven't been invited."

"Of course you're invited. It'll start around eleven. Hot dogs. Beer. Vodka if you want it."

"I don't drink alcohol. Or eat pork."

"No pork? Heavens, you're not Jewish, are you?"

Aman visibly stiffened.

"I'm sorry. I was only teasing. There'll be a lot of other things to eat. You can have whatever you want. Stay. It should be fun. You'll see where to go by the big bonfire. You'll also see a bunch of the other kids headed that way."

"If I don't catch the ferry, how will I get home?"

"Oh, don't worry about that. There'll be boats going back and forth all night. But some of the kids brought sleeping bags so they could sleep out by the cliff. If you wanted to do that, we could lend you one."

"No. I think I need to get home."

"Well, it'll be easy to get you a ride. If you get stuck, I can give you a ride myself."

"You know, Aimée, I've always been put off by you, not just for beating me out for valedictorian but . . ." He paused, then waved his arms in all directions. " . . . for having all this. For looking like you do. Are you telling me I was wrong?"

"I don't know. Were you?"

Aman looked into her eyes and said without smiling, "Time will tell."

"Yes, I suppose it will. Anyway, welcome to Whitby Island." She leaned in and gave him a kiss on the cheek. To her surprise, he kissed her back, his lips lightly brushing hers.

"See you later by the cliff?"

"Perhaps."

She left and headed back toward the bar for a refill.

Before she got halfway, she felt a hand descend on her ass.

Moseley. Of course. She hadn't noticed him approaching.

"What's up with you, Aimée?"

Not eight o'clock yet and Will was already slurring his words. He took a sip from the whiskey he was holding, and then glanced over at Aman.

"Getting it on with our friends from Africa now?" he said. "Eager to see how a little dark meat tastes?"

Aimée's slap across Moseley's cheek had enough power behind it to snap his head back. He balled his hand into a fist and drew it back. Aman moved toward them.

A number of guests on the patio turned and stared.

"Stay out of this, monkey boy," Moseley snapped. Still, he relaxed his fist.

"Jesus Christ, Moseley. You are such an asshole." Aimée spat out the words. "I can't believe the garbage that comes out of your mouth. Now why don't you apologize to our guest and then get your racist ass off my island and leave me alone?"

Moseley didn't move.

"All right. If you won't apologize, I will. I'm sorry, Aman, for what this jerk said."

"Don't worry. I've heard worse."

Aman turned and started walking into the darkness, away from the house.

Aimée watched him go, then started toward the French doors. Moseley followed. He was stopped short by Charles Kraft, who stepped between them.

"Give me the drink."

"Who the fuck do you think you're talking to, Kraft?" said Moseley in a voice loud enough for everyone on the terrace to hear him. "What are you, the bouncer or something?"

"Or something," Kraft said quietly. "Now give me the drink. You've had too much."

Moseley insolently took another sip.

Aimée stared at the two of them, wondering if Moseley was drunk enough to take Charles on, kind of hoping in a way he would. He was two inches taller, maybe twenty pounds heavier, played football for Yale. Still, she was sure he'd get his ass kicked.

"Give him the drink, Will." Daddy had come out the door. He didn't look happy. "Right now. Before you embarrass yourself any further."

"Yes, sir." Moseley handed the glass to Kraft, who took it and went inside.

"And you're not to have any more tonight."

"No, sir."

"Do I make myself clear?"

"Yes, sir."

"Ladies and Gentlemen," Daddy said to the half dozen or so guests who'd gathered around to watch, "I apologize for the interruption. Just a young man getting carried away with the joys of alcohol. Please go back to enjoying yourselves."

The gawkers wandered away. Daddy followed.

"You liked that little show, didn't you?" Moseley said to Aimée.

"Actually," she said with a small smile, "I was hoping for a little more action at the end."

Moseley glared at her for a minute. *If looks could kill,* Aimée thought to herself. *If looks could only kill.* Will stormed off in the direction of the dock where the Moseley yacht was moored. She knew for a fact there was plenty of booze on board.

Chapter 11

BY MIDNIGHT MOST of the guests had left. Julia found herself growing more and more irritated by the minute. Her mother was in the hall, locked in conversation with a hard-looking man Julia didn't know. From her expression, Jules could tell she didn't want to be disturbed, and she couldn't think of anyone else she could commiserate with. Everyone, aside from Julia and her mother, thought the painting and Aimée's little star-turn were so very wonderful. She walked over to the bar near the patio door. Mr. Jolley was gone, so Jules poured herself another glass of champagne from one of the bottles he'd left for the remaining guests.

Julia knew she'd already had too much, but she was in no mood to stop. She took a sip and studied the century-old image of her half twin hanging on the other side of the room, a self-satisfied smile on her face, as if this room, this house, this entire fucking world had been made for her and her only. It made Jules crazy knowing that every time she came into this room, probably for the rest of her life, her bloody bitch of a sister would be staring down at her with that fucking smirk.

Of course, Jules had gushed appropriately when Daddy unveiled the painting. But even then she knew she'd never be able to enjoy this room again the way she had in the past. It was as if Aimée was laying claim to it. Just as she'd laid claim to the old studio because she, and not Julia, was a painter like the first Aimée. And laid claim to Will Moseley, who wanted Aimée so much more than he'd ever wanted Jules.

According to the *New York Times* Arts Section, Daddy had paid $2.4 million for the painting. And he probably would have gone higher. All for his beloved Aimée. His two beloved Aimées. Would he have paid so much if the painting had looked like Julia instead of Aimée? If the genetics had gone the other way and she'd inherited the Whitby genes, or, perhaps more accurately, the Garnier genes and Aimée hadn't? But there was no way to answer that, because then she'd be her sister and her sister would look like a blonde reporter for the *Press Herald*. Julia told herself to stop thinking that way. It would make her crazy.

She walked across the living room, where her father was still talking to the few remaining guests, and into the empty study, closing the door behind her. She went to a glass case that stood against the far wall. She looked down at the Tanto, the antique Samurai dagger, with its elaborately carved bone handle and sheath. Dating back to the fourteenth century, it was purchased by the first Edward Whitby on one of his voyages to the Far East. It was still sitting where it was supposed to have been, but wasn't, the day Garrison used it to murder his mistress. What if she followed Garrison's example? She imagined herself climbing a ladder late at night, slipping the Tanto from its sheath, raising it high and shredding the fucking painting into a million worthless pieces. Daddy would get his money back. She was sure he'd insured it for at least what he'd paid for it. Maybe more. But of course he'd never forgive her. She'd be disowned and disinherited, assigned forever to Whitby purgatory, if not to hell. On the other hand, was there any reason he had to know it was she who'd wielded the blade? Julia reached for the sides of the glass case and began to lift it. She just wanted to feel the heft of the knife in her hand.

"A real bitch, isn't she?"

She started at the sound of Will Moseley's voice coming from behind the back of the leather couch. She hadn't noticed him lying there. Had he seen her opening the case where the knife was kept? She couldn't be sure.

"A real honest to God bitch," he repeated. "Aimée, I mean."

Moseley got to his feet and took a long swig from what looked like a glass of whiskey. He must have brought it from his father's boat, or perhaps filched it from the kitchen. The bartenders had all been instructed not to give him anything more to drink. Still, that had been four hours ago, and he seemed more sober now.

"Aimée?" Julia responded. "A bitch? Don't be silly, Will. Everybody knows how wonderful Aimée is. No, I take it back. *Wonderful*'s not nearly a good enough word. Not for Aimée. *Perfect* is better. Yes, perfection in every way. The perfect daughter. The perfect student. The perfect girlfriend. And, oh yes, I guess when it comes down to it you really are right, the perfect bitch."

Julia flopped down in a big leather chair opposite the sofa. "And there she'll be, the bitch over the fireplace, staring down at us forever."

Will said nothing.

"I wonder if you have any idea, my darling Will, what it's been like having to play second fiddle every day of my life to such an amazing, beautiful, perfectly wonderful sister."

Will smiled. "Don't worry, Jules. You'll get your chance to shine."

Julia smiled a bitter smile. "Will I? Who knows? But I can promise you one thing. I have no intention of living in Aimée's shadow forever."

Moseley rose, went to the chair where Julia was sitting and pulled her to her feet. He put both his drink and her champagne on a side table and put his arms around her waist. He pulled her close.

She pulled away. "Don't play games with me, Will. Not tonight. I know it's Aimée you really want. Just like every other male in the place. At least the ones who don't need Viagra. And, frankly, I'm in no mood tonight to play the role of *that other Whitby girl. You know, the not quite so pretty one? The one who didn't quite make valedictorian. Oh darn, what's her name? I can't seem to remember.* No. No more of that. Not tonight, Will. Not with you. Not with anyone. Not ever. I've been cast in that role for far too long. It's time for me to put a stop to it."

Moseley, still hopeful he could somehow work his magic, moved in and nuzzled her neck. "Oh, come on, Jules. You know how much I've always liked you. Because you're you and not 'that other Whitby girl.'"

"Maybe some other time, Moseley, but not tonight."

Will sighed. "Fine." He moved his hands from around Julia's waist. "So who's the perfect bitch hanging out with tonight? That black guy? Or maybe that asshole Kraft? Or has she found some other poor sucker?"

"You really want to know?" asked Julia, lowering her voice to a whisper, as if she was about to reveal a deep, dark secret.

Moseley nodded. "Yeah. I really want to know."

"Who'd you have for senior English?"

"At Penfield?"

"Yes, at Penfield."

"You have *got* to be kidding. That poetry-spouting twink? He's got to be at least twice her age. And, frankly, I always thought he was a fag."

Julia smiled. Exactly what her mother had said when Julia told her about Aimée's affair a couple of weeks ago. She was certain her mother would put a stop to it. But she hadn't. At least not yet.

"Ssssh." Julia put a finger over Moseley's lips. "Not so loud. They'll hear you. But you're at least half right. He's thirty-six."

"Jesus. Did Aimée tell you this?"

"Of course not. It's her secret. And his. If it ever went public, Penfield would kick his tail out of there so fast it'd make his head spin. And God knows what Daddy would do. Of course, Will, I know I can count on you not to breathe a word of it." She smiled at him conspiratorially. "I mean I can, can't I?"

"If it's such a big secret, how come you know about it?"

Jules smiled her cat-who-swallowed-the-canary smile. "Oh, I have my ways."

"Such as?"

"Such as figuring out people's passwords. But I *can* count on you not to say a word about this, can't I?"

"Who would I tell?"

"Oh, I don't know. Your old Penfield buddies. Your father maybe."

"Not a word." Moseley smiled and took another slug of his whiskey. "Not a word."

Chapter 12

McCabe woke with a start when he heard the front door open and then softly close.

A male voice came from the living room. "You got any beer?"

He instinctively reached for his weapon. It wasn't there. He didn't remember locking it up. He sat up, ready to get out of bed and find it, when he heard Casey's urgent whisper. "Sssh. Be quiet. My father's here. He's sleeping."

He looked at the bedside clock to see if she'd made curfew. Just after midnight. Nearly an hour early. Which he would have felt good about if his head wasn't hurting and his mouth didn't feel like sandpaper.

The male voice came again, this time speaking in not quite a whisper.

"Sorry. You got any beer?"

"Yes. But you can't have any."

"Why not?"

"Because he's a cop, you jerk, and you're underage. If he woke up, he'd probably throw both of us in the clink."

"C'mon. You're kidding, right?"

"Yeah, I'm kidding. He'd only throw *you* in the clink." There was a brief silence. "All right. He wouldn't throw you in the clink either, but he wouldn't be happy."

McCabe knew he shouldn't have been eavesdropping on his daughter and somebody who might be her boyfriend, but it was too much fun not to. He was tempted to wander out and say hi and give the kid the once-over, but he knew Casey would give him absolute hell if he did. Not knowing what else to do, he piled up four pillows—his two and Kyra's two—and lay back on his bed without turning on the lights. Parenting was hell.

Okay, he told himself. It was just after midnight. He'd been dead to the world for nearly nine hours. Unlikely he'd get any more sleep. He wondered if the world had changed in any meaningful way since he'd gotten himself so stupidly, staggeringly drunk. He checked his phone. No calls from Kyra. It was only a little after nine in San Francisco. She was probably out at dinner with some guy who wasn't a cop.

Nearly dawn in England. He supposed Sandy was still snoozing in London, dreaming about shooting grouse or riding to the hounds or whatever the hell it was Lord MuckyMuck had planned for the weekend. On the other hand, maybe her plane had crashed and she was dead. That'd suit him just fine, except a lot of other people would have died with her. So maybe her plane had just developed engine trouble and had been diverted to someplace like Gander, Newfoundland. Man, would Sandy ever be pissed off finding herself in Gander. Who the hell can you show off to in Gander?

Tired of lying down, McCabe got up again and listened to Casey and the boy speaking softly. Nothing of consequence. Then the talking stopped. He supposed they were making out. Hoped the kid, whoever he was, deserved whatever affection he was getting. He was pretty sure things wouldn't go very far. Not with Daddy, the cop, supposedly asleep in the next room. He heard soft laughter. A whispered good-night.

I love you.

Yeah, I love you too. See you Saturday.

The door to the apartment opened and closed. The door to Casey's bedroom opened and closed. McCabe walked to the window and peered through the blinds. He watched a tall skinny kid with carrot-top hair leave the building. Kind of geeky looking. Geeky is good, McCabe told himself. Geeky wouldn't push things too far too fast. The kid stopped. Took out a cell phone. Began texting. With his fingers still pecking away at the phone, he got into his car, an old Saturn, started the engine and drove away.

I love you. I love you too. See you Saturday.

Probably wouldn't come to anything. She'd be in Providence come September. Ready for new adventures with college boys. The idea of being without her, of being alone with both Casey and Kyra gone, was painful.

Okay. No way was he going to sleep any more. He supposed he could go to the office, but he didn't have much to do there either. Maybe go for a run? Nah. Running while hungover wasn't appealing. He looked around the room. The bed, the rocking chair, the empty closet where Kyra's clothes used to hang. It all felt like it was closing in. He needed air. And space. He went to the kitchen. Put on a pot of coffee. Came back. Took off the clothes he'd been sleeping in. Blue button-down shirt, crappy tie and gray pants. Clearance rack stuff from Men's Wearhouse. The raspy voice from the commercials growled through his mind. *You're gonna like the way you look.* But he didn't like the way he looked. Point of fact he thought he looked like shit. Still, you had to save money somewhere.

He took a one-minute shower. Dried himself and found a pair of jeans and a blue sweatshirt with USM written across the front. He pulled them on. Sorted through the shoes in the closet and found some black Nikes. He unlocked the gun safe, pulled out his holster and service weapon, checked the load and strapped it on. Pulled the sweatshirt down over it. Not that he thought he'd need the gun, but he never left it unattended in the apartment.

He poured a large travel mug of black coffee. Crept into Casey's room. Watched her sleep for a few seconds, her face softly lit by moonlight streaming through the window. A face so like Sandy's. A personality so different. He kissed her softly on the forehead. *Sleep well, my love.*

"G'night, Dad," she murmured.

He double-locked the apartment door and headed down and out into the pleasantly cool night air. He walked over to the only good thing—not counting Casey—that had come out of his eight-year marriage. A cherry-red '57 T-Bird convertible he and Sandy bought the first year they were together and had spent innumerable weekends restoring. Even more weekends driving out to the Hamptons with the top down.

He turned the key and listened with pleasure as the big Ford V8 came to life with a throaty roar. He took a minute to connect his smartphone to the newly installed Bluetooth player and tapped *Bird: The Complete Charlie Parker on Verve.* Hadn't listened to much else since he'd downloaded the life's work of the musician he considered the greatest and most innovative jazz man of all time. As the sounds of Bird's sax tumbled out of the speakers, McCabe pulled his own Bird out onto the Eastern Prom and roared off to the left, heading for the interstate. He lowered both windows and sucked in cool, fresh air. He didn't know where he was going, but there were plenty of empty places in Maine, and he just wanted to lose himself.

As he drove, McCabe's mind went back to the final scene with Kyra. She'd threatened to leave him before. Had actually done it a couple of times when he'd been so absorbed in a case he barely said hello. He knew that pissed her off. He'd be pissed if she did the same to him. He couldn't count the times he told her he was sorry. Mostly she forgave him. Said it was just the way he was made. An obsessive personality obsessing about catching and punishing one slime ball or another who thought he could get away with rape, murder, assault, whatever.

He'd asked her to marry him half a dozen times, and the response was always the same. "The day you stop being a cop."

"Kyra, people marry cops. My mother married a cop."

"Not a cop like you."

"What do you mean?"

"The problem with marrying you, McCabe, is that you're already married to your job. When you're in the middle of a case, you barely know I'm alive. Sometimes I wonder if that's what happened with Sandy."

When she said that two months ago, she hit a hot button. He lost his temper and slammed out. When he came back four hours later, she was gone. He didn't think much of it. She'd left in the past and had never gone far. Just down the hill, back to the small artist's loft on Chestnut Street that doubled as her studio and bolt-hole. When she'd come back days later, she'd tell him she loved him. And ask him once again to quit the department. Say she couldn't take much more of either the loneliness or the angst of never knowing if he'd come home dead or alive or maybe not come home at all.

He'd tell her he loved her too. Enough to want to live with her forever. But he didn't know what he would do with himself if he stopped being a cop. It was part of his genetic code, his DNA, and he didn't know if there was anything he could do about that.

Her response rang in his ear. "Enough of this, McCabe. Either get another job or get yourself another girlfriend. You can't have both."

He never thought she meant it. But then came that day eight weeks ago when the phone rang and he discovered she hadn't just gone down the hill to Chestnut Street.

"Where are you?"

"San Francisco."

He frowned. She hadn't said anything about going to San Francisco. "What are you doing there?"

"Starting a new job."

He didn't respond. Just tried to figure out what she was talking about.

"A tenure track job at the San Francisco Art Institute," she said. "Too good to turn down."

"You didn't tell me you were applying for that."

"You weren't around."

"What's wrong with teaching at MECA?" MECA, the Maine College of Art, was right down the hill on Congress. Five minutes from the apartment even if you didn't make every light.

"What's wrong with MECA," she said, "is the same thing that's wrong with my loft on Chestnut Street. It's way too close. Whenever I go there, all you have to do is leave me alone and, in no time at all, I'll come home, wagging my tail behind me. And we're right back where we started. McCabe, I can't take it anymore."

"If I stopped being a cop, would you take me back?"

"In a heartbeat."

"What would I do with myself in San Francisco?"

"I've told you before. You could teach."

"Teach what? Where?"

"I'm sure they've got courses in criminal justice out here. As far as I know, it's the only thing you're a certified expert in. Or maybe you could do corporate security. That guy you went to NYU with once offered you a job doing that. Six-figure salary, as I recall. Probably some tech companies out here that would love to have you."

McCabe shook his head. "Kyra, I don't teach. I don't do tech. I chase bad guys. That's who I am."

There were ten seconds of silence before she said, "I know." The two words pregnant with regret for what might have been. For what would never be. "That's why I'm in San Francisco. Too far away to pop over when missing you really starts to hurt. Which I know it will."

"Or when I start missing you?"

"Which I know you will. And guess what? You'll always be welcome."

"Even if you fall in love with another guy? One of those Bay Area painters. Like that Richard Diebenkorn guy you're always talking about."

"Unfortunately, Diebenkorn's dead. Almost twenty years now."

"All right then. Somebody who's alive."

"I'll let you know if that happens."

That pretty much finished the conversation.

He asked her what he should do with her paintings that hung in the apartment.

"Just keep them as a reminder of what might have been."

He hadn't taken them down yet. But he knew he would.

Chapter 13

"Do you know what today is?" Aimée asked.

"Graduation day?"

"For me, my lovely Lord Byron, today is Independence Day." Her warm breath blew softly in his ear as her hand explored her AP English teacher's slender white body, still moist from love-making.

"What do you mean?"

"As of today, according to the official rules of the game, I can fuck you anytime, anywhere and in any weird way I want. And nobody can do a damned thing about it. Isn't that delicious?"

Knowles smiled. "Not for the next ten minutes you can't. I don't care how delicious you are."

She slipped her tongue in his ear. "Wanna bet?" she murmured, sliding her hand between his legs. He began growing hard.

"C'mon, Byron," she breathed playfully, "rise to the occasion." Her voice little more than a whisper, she pulled him toward her, sliding her legs around his.

Aimée suddenly tensed. She could have sworn she'd heard

someone laughing outside the window. Could Mr. Jolley be up to his old tricks? Or was Moseley spying on her? She slid out of bed, walked to the window and peered out. Saw nothing but moonlight broken by the blackness of trees. Heard nothing but the sound of a gentle wind blowing through the leaves. Perhaps that was all the sound had been. A gust of wind.

"What's the matter?" asked Byron.

"Nothing. Just thought I heard something. Or maybe someone."

She made sure the curtains were as tightly closed as they could be, checked the lock on the door and returned to bed.

Byron slipped his arms around her body, stroked her back and pulled her down on top of him. They began to move together, slowly, rhythmically. Not the eager, breathless coupling of twenty minutes earlier, but a gentler, more measured lovemaking. Knowles murmured poetry in her ear as they moved.

> She walks in beauty, like the night
> Of cloudless climes and starry skies;
> And all that's best of dark and bright
> Meet in her aspect and her eyes;
> Thus mellowed to that tender light
> Which heaven to gaudy day denies.

He knew Aimée loved it when he recited Lord Byron during sex.

When they'd finished, the two of them lay silently, side by side, on the pull-out sofa bed in the same small studio on the far end of the island where the first Aimée had painted her paintings and pleasured her lover. The same studio where, a little more than one hundred years ago, Mark Garrison was said to have stabbed and then chased her as she'd fled toward the cliff two hundred yards away.

Some of Garrison's studies of her, paintings and drawings both clothed and nude, hung on the wall, having been methodically hunted down and purchased over the years by the first Aimée's son, Edward Whitby III. The one they called Teddy. Daddy's grandfather. Most of the drawings predated the large portrait in the main house. The story, the way it was told, was that their affair had been going on long before Garrison painted the portrait. Mostly they met in Boston, but occasionally, when Edward was away, here on the island. It was said that the affair was the main reason the first Aimée had wanted Garrison, rather than Sargent, to paint her portrait though Sargent was generally considered superior.

Byron Knowles slid off the bed and walked over for a closer look at the drawings. This was his first time in the studio. His first time on the island.

Aimée followed and stood behind Byron as he examined them. She wrapped her arms around his body. Rested her head on his shoulder.

"You know, it's amazing," he said. "Even in these gestural drawings you look exactly like her. Face. Body. Physical attitude. Everything. It's quite remarkable." He turned, slipped his arms around her and hugged her tightly. "And now, my darling girl," he said softly, "it's time for me to leave. I promised Gina I'd be home by midnight. And it looks like I'm going to be more than two hours late. There'll be an almighty row when I get there. I know she suspects what's going on."

Aimée pulled him even closer. "Byron, please. Isn't it time you told your wife you're leaving her? That you're coming to Providence with me? You don't love her. You love me. You've told me so at least a dozen times."

"We've talked about this before. You know it can't happen. At least not right now."

"Why can't it happen? You know you'd be happier."

"Yes, I probably would be. At least for a while. Until you grew bored with me."

"That wouldn't happen."

"If you were being honest, you'd know it would. Besides, what could I do in Providence? Having walked out on my pregnant wife and child and run off with a former student, no school would ever hire me. In Providence or anywhere else. I'd be lucky if I didn't get sent to jail."

Knowles smiled sadly and kissed her softly on the lips. Walked over to the window and looked out into the night. "There's a law against teachers falling in love with their students. At least those under eighteen."

Aimée retreated to the bed and covered herself with the sheet. "I'm no longer your student. And I'm no longer under eighteen."

"No, but this affair didn't start twelve hours ago, and people would surely figure that out. If that somebody happened to be your father, I hate to think what he'd do. Probably pay somebody like that Kraft guy or my wife's macho-man father to come down to Providence, cut me into little pieces and throw me in the river."

"Daddy's not like that."

"I wouldn't be so sure. He strikes me as a man who doesn't take kindly to people who mess around with what he considers his."

"He's not a thug, and I'm not his property."

"No. But he loves you and he'll want to protect you."

"Byron, this isn't fair. I don't want to lose you." Aimée felt tears coming. She'd always been capable of crying on demand, but these were genuine. "If you came to Providence, you could concentrate on your writing. Your poetry or maybe the screenplay we talked about. You said your friend Meyers thinks it's a great idea. And at night, when I come back from my classes, we'd drink wine, eat dinner and make love all night. Wouldn't you like that?"

"Sounds delightful. It really does. But poetry doesn't pay enough to keep a mouse alive. And while Meyers thinks the movie idea has potential, potential is not a contract. Besides, I'm not even halfway done with it."

"Why does any of that matter? I'm rich, remember? My grandfather's trust fund became all mine last April. Which makes me . . . what would Lord Byron have called it? A woman of independent means?"

"That wasn't Lord Byron," he said. "If I'm not mistaken, it was Sally Fields. At least in the movie version. Anyway, even if I didn't get arrested and go to jail, there's still no way I could allow myself to live off your money."

"You let me pay rent on the apartment."

"Yes. And I feel guilty as hell about that."

"You also told me you planned on divorcing your wife."

"Aimée, we've talked about this before. Yes, I want a divorce. I've told Gina I wanted one. Not once but three or four times. But she's a good Catholic girl and she won't hear of it."

"You're not her slave. You could just leave."

"Yes, I could. But she's eight months pregnant and I'm sleeping with a teenager and former student. Gina's vindictive. She'd let everyone from Cobb to your father know what happened. She'd try to humiliate us publically. And if she ever did agree to a divorce, even a semicompetent lawyer would make sure she got every nickel I ever made. Now and forever more. She's a self-righteous bitch who'd hang us both out to dry."

Aimée folded her arms across her chest. Her mouth went into classic pout mode. "What good is being rich if I can't have the things I want?"

Knowles shook his head. "I don't know what to tell you. Life isn't easy? Even if we suffered the slings and arrows of public humiliation and I allowed you to support me, what would happen when you lost interest? When you got bored playing house with an aging poet and wannabe screenwriter and decided you wanted somebody new? Somebody younger. More exciting. More interesting."

"I won't get bored. I promise."

"Yes you will, and I think you know that as well as I do. What do I do then?"

Aimée stared at him angrily. He was being an asshole. "I don't know," she shrugged. "Get a job. Write a book. Make your fucking movie. Jesus Christ, Knowles, get a life instead of letting your nasty little wife treat you like a fucking floor mat."

"I'm afraid, Aimée, I already have a life," he said as he pulled on his clothes. "Which at the moment includes not just my wife but a little girl, just four years old, who I love. Not to mention another child due in a month. No, I don't think so. As amazing as you are and as sad as it makes me to say this, I think this will have to be our last time."

Her body jerked, as if shocked by an electric current. "As *amazing* as I am? Don't you really mean as amazing as the *sex* has been? Isn't that what you *really* meant to say? Probably all you ever wanted from me was sex. All that 'I love you' stuff and 'I want to divorce my wife' stuff? That was all bullshit, wasn't it?"

He reached out for her. She slapped his hand away.

"I'm sorry, Aimée. I do love you. You're one of the most beautiful, talented, irresistible women I've ever met. But you're also my student. Which makes my behavior over the past few months not only illegal but also unforgivable." He smiled ruefully. "It was stupid and self-indulgent. I've never been strong enough to say no to you, but now I have to be."

Aimée's face contorted in anger. "You stupid, stupid man. Don't you know what you're throwing away?"

"Not throwing away. I'm giving you your life back."

"You bastard," she hissed between clenched teeth. "You've taught me well. I can quote your namesake as well as you: *'Remember thee! Remember thee! Till Lethe quench life's burning stream. Remorse and shame shall cling to thee, And haunt thee like a feverish dream!'*" She spat out the words. "Remember thee, my dear Byron, remorse shall haunt thee like a feverish dream!"

Byron Knowles barely heard the last few words before he closed the door and headed for the Whitby family's private dock, where his boat was tied up.

Chapter 14

HAD BYRON BEEN less distracted by the angry parting with Aimée and less preoccupied with the coming confrontation with Gina, he might have realized he was being followed. But Byron neither looked back nor paid attention to the occasional sound behind him of dry leaves rustling or the odd twig snapping.

He was too involved with his own thoughts as he walked the wooded path toward his boat, the *Patti Ann*. Byron's father had originally named the old boat for Byron's mother. But Byron had told his four-year-old daughter, whose name was also Patti Ann, that Grandpa had named it for her as well. Yes, a lie, but only a little lie—in most families a harmless thing which pleased both his mother and his daughter.

It was only Gina who disapproved. Gina with her rigid moral stances. If lying was wrong, she said, lying was wrong. Little lies as wrong as big ones. White lies as wrong as black. Which really cut to the core of the problem. If Gina found out what he'd been up to and who he'd been having an affair with, she'd demand a confrontation. Not just with him but also with Aimée. Edward

Whitby would find out. Headmaster Cobb would find out. The trustees of Penfield Academy would find out. The whole damned world would find out. It was all too distressing to even think about. The best thing he could do was deny, deny, deny. Keep the lies consistent and behave as if the whole thing had never happened.

No question Gina suspected the affair. All the signs were there. The frequent suspiciousness in her voice. The close questioning about where he'd been and who he'd been with. And, most damning of all, the time he woke in the middle of the night to find her going through his wallet and briefcase. He remembered the conversation verbatim.

"What are you doing?" he asked.

"The Chart House," she said.

"What?"

"The Chart House. The restaurant in Cape Neddick." She waved a slip of white paper at him. "You had dinner there on April twenty-third." She paused and looked again at the slip of paper. "Paid the bill at 9:53."

Byron's mind was racing. How in God's name was he going to get away with this one? April twenty-third. Aimée's eighteenth birthday. She'd wanted to go out to dinner to celebrate. He'd tried to talk her out of it. Told her it wasn't a good idea.

"What's the matter? Afraid we'll get caught?" she'd teased.

"Damned right I am."

She'd pouted. He'd relented, since Gina would be out at her church group. They'd driven all the way down to Cape Neddick to avoid running into anyone they knew. It had been the only time they'd ever gone out together in public, and, schmuck that he was, he'd left the fucking receipt in his wallet.

"Two hundred and eight dollars and twenty-six cents," said Gina.

Aimée had insisted on paying the bill. He wouldn't let her.

"No way," he'd said. "It's your birthday. My treat."

"I had dinner," he told Gina, "with Barry Meyers." Meyers was his old roommate from Bowdoin and still his best friend. "He flew in from L.A. for some meetings in Boston and he called me and suggested we get together."

"And you paid for it? Meyers is a damned Hollywood screenwriter. Makes zillions, and I can't even afford to buy new underwear."

"We split. I insisted. Barry gave me his half in cash. And you know damned well you can afford underwear." Jesus, she drove him crazy with that "I can't afford underwear" bullshit.

Byron knew she didn't believe him about Meyers. As soon as he was sure she had gone back to sleep, he slipped out of the bedroom and called Meyers on the coast. It was only midnight L.A. time. He asked his old friend to cover for him.

Lacking a flashlight, Byron proceeded cautiously, particularly in places where overhead branches blocked the ambient light of the moon. Every once in a while he would stop altogether and probe a dark patch in front of him with his foot for unseen roots or stones that might trip him up. It would be just too damned stupid to compound his infidelities by arriving home with a broken ankle or worse. Whenever Byron stopped, his follower stopped and waited silently for Byron to start moving again.

As soon as Byron stepped onto the dock, he felt something hard press into his back.

Byron turned.

He saw a slender figure dressed in black trousers and one of the white jackets the catering staff wore at the party. A black balaclava with small holes cut for the eyes and mouth covered the face and head. Whoever was under that mask didn't want to be recognized. He . . . or she . . . was pointing a handgun directly at Byron's face. Byron couldn't tell one gun from another, but this one looked like the kind the cops in Portland carried on their hips.

The color drained from his face. "W-w-what do you want?"

"What do I want? What I want is to punish you for having sex with one of your students."

Byron failed to react. Just stood motionless, eyes wide open, like the proverbial deer in the headlights.

"Oh yes, I know what you were doing. You really should have checked things out when your girlfriend told you she heard a noise outside. If you had, it would have made things a lot tougher for me. But no. You were so eager to get back into action you couldn't be bothered. Well, for your sake, I hope it was a good fuck, Byron, because if you don't do exactly as I tell you, it just might be your last."

Byron looked back at the *Patti Ann*. Forty feet away. He wondered if he could make it. He'd run track in college and was pretty fast. But no. There was no way he could outrun a bullet. He imagined one crashing through the back of his skull before he even got halfway.

"What . . . what are you going to do?" Byron stammered.

"Interesting question. What I'm going to do is punish you for the sin of fucking one of your students when you have a wife waiting faithfully at home. I may kill you. I may not."

"You, you, you're not going to kill me?"

"Maybe not. Not if you do exactly what I tell you. I mean, why else would I have this mask on? To keep you from identifying me if I do decide to let you live."

Byron felt a small glimmer of hope. Maybe this person wasn't going to shoot him after all. Of course, mask or no mask, he was certain he would never forget his assailant's voice. But maybe this wasn't a good time to bring that up. "I promise I won't say a word to anybody."

"No, I'm certain you won't. Now, what I want you to do now is turn around and walk slowly to the end of the dock."

Byron did as he was told.

"Okay, now take out your cell phone and put it down gently. Not too close to the water. We don't want to get it wet now, do we?"

Byron followed instructions.

"Now lie down flat on your belly, head toward the water, hands flat on the dock in front of you."

Byron did what he was told.

"Let me have the pass code for your phone."

Byron tried to speak, but the only sound that came out was a small mewing sound, like a kitten.

He suddenly felt the barrel of the gun press against the back of his neck. "Your pass code. Now."

Byron Knowles started shivering and weeping. "Please," he blubbered, "please don't kill me."

The gun was pressed harder into the back of his neck. "Give . . . me . . . your . . . fucking . . . pass code or you die now. One number at a time."

"Gina," Byron squeaked.

"What about Gina?"

"Gina. Her name's the pass code. G-I-N-A."

"Pass codes are numbers."

"Numerically, it's four-four-six-two."

Now that he'd given up the information, Byron closed his eyes tightly, waiting for the bullet that would end his life. It didn't come. Instead he peeked around and, out of the corner of his eye, watched the person who might or might not decide to kill him punch in the numbers and, satisfied that they worked, pocket the phone.

"Good. Now I want you to get up and climb down into your boat."

Byron climbed down.

"Now pick up that black bag there by the cockpit."

Byron looked and saw a large black vinyl bag he'd never seen before. He picked it up.

"All right, now, nice and slowly, I want you to climb into the bag. Feet first. Arms by your side. Make one sound and, trust me, you'll be dead."

Byron was sure this thing must be a body bag, though he'd never seen one before. As instructed, he put his feet into the bottom.

"Now grab the zipper and pull it up as high up around you as you can. Then put your hands inside. If you make a single solitary sound, I'll be forced to shoot and get my brand-new bag all dirty with the gooey bits of your brain."

Byron managed to pull the zipper up almost as high as his neck. Then he squeezed his hands back inside.

"Now lie down on the deck and close your eyes."

Again he followed instructions. He felt a gloved hand take hold of the zipper and pull it up the rest of the way. Byron opened his eyes. He could see nothing but black. He was totally encased in dark, heavy vinyl with no way to get out. Byron, always afraid of the dark, was now sure he was going to die. He imagined himself buried alive in this bag, dying slowly and horribly under the earth. He began whimpering and shaking uncontrollably.

"Goddamit, stop blubbering. Lie still, or I'll kill you now."

Byron lay still and tried to keep the sound of his weeping as quiet as he possibly could.

FOR THE FIRST fifteen minutes after her lover left, Aimée lay on the rumpled sheets of the sofa bed, mourning the end of the affair. She really had loved Byron. At least she thought she had. Finally, tired of feeling sorry for herself, she got up, found her clothes in the corner where she'd thrown them and pulled them on. Denim cutoffs over a pink thong. A white tank top. An old Yale sweatshirt of Moseley's. A pair of pink sneakers. She opened the door and looked out toward the cliff. The kids' after-party was still going on. She could hear the sound of distant voices and somebody playing a guitar. She could see the glow of a bonfire light up the night sky. She wondered who might still be there. Jules for sure. Some of her friends. She wondered if Aman Anbessa had stayed. Probably not. The after-party wouldn't be his scene. Especially when he realized the silent promise of her kiss was never meant to be kept. Moseley? Yeah, he'd be there for sure, still looking to get laid. Unless, of course, he'd already found a willing victim. Maybe Jules. Maybe not.

Truth be told, Will or no Will, the idea of sitting around a bonfire with a bunch of high school kids had zero appeal. Partly because none of them was all that interesting. But more importantly because the guy she thought she'd loved turned out, in the end, to be nothing more than a pussy-whipped English teacher too afraid of his ugly, boring wife to take a chance on living life to the fullest.

Still, she had thought she loved him.

She'd planned their affair so carefully. Rented the apartment on Hampshire Street so they'd have someplace to go and not worry about Tracy or her father bursting in on them. Or Mr. Jolley peeping through the window.

And next year was supposed to have been even better. Aimée had checked out some really cool apartments near RISD, on the hill overlooking Providence. Places that would have been perfect for their evenings together. How many times had she imagined the scene? Byron working on his screenplay or maybe posing nude while Aimée sketched his beautiful, slender body. It all would have been so much fun, and now he had gone and screwed everything up. It really wasn't fair. Not fair at all.

She got up, straightened the sheets and closed the sofa bed. Found the vodka, poured herself a drink and sat quietly sipping. She thought about all the boys and men who wanted her. Why was it, she wondered, she was always attracted to the older ones? The impossible ones. She wondered if what she was really looking for wasn't some poetic wuss like Byron but somebody more like Charles or, even better, Daddy. Her father was almost perfect. Smart. Warm. Handsome. Funny. And, most important, unafraid of living life to the fullest. She wanted someone like that. Someone who could be gentle and tender with her yet tough as nails with anyone who had the balls to confront him head-on. And that sure as hell wasn't Byron. Byron with all his poetry didn't come close. She supposed she'd always known the affair wouldn't last. But she didn't think it would end this soon. And the way it ended hurt. She wanted to make Byron suffer for that.

The vibration from the phone in her pocket made her jump. A

text from Byron. *How could I have been such a jerk?* he wrote. *I'm so sorry. We need to talk. Please meet me by my boat. I love you.*

Aimée smiled to herself. Less than half an hour after his big speech, and the gutless wonder was already crawling back. She texted back, *OMW.*

Chapter 15

WITHOUT REALIZING HOW far he'd driven, McCabe found himself passing through the town of Rumford, heading toward the Mahoosuc Land Trust on a small two-laner. That's when his phone rang. Caller ID told him it was Kelly Haddon from Portland Police Dispatch.

"What's up, Kelly?"

Kelly's voice emerged from the Bluetooth speakers. "Looks like you're up, Sergeant," she said. "Body of a woman was just found off the Loring Trail. Bob Hurley was first at the scene. Says the vic looks pretty young. Maybe a teenager. Shift commander said I should call you direct."

"Murdered? Or just dead?"

"Murdered, I think. Possibly raped is what Hurley said."

It was weird. Just hearing the words *murdered, possibly raped* emerge from the speaker triggered a familiar rush in McCabe. His breathing and heart rate shot up. His muscles tensed. His senses went on heightened alert. It was a high he'd always been addicted to. A high for which there were no rehab centers or twenty-eight-day cures. McCabe knew it. Kyra knew it. A murder junkie, she'd once called him. And she was right. When the bell went off, it turned him on. More than booze, more than pot, even more than sex. A high that stayed with him until the bad guy was caught. Or, better yet, dead.

"What do you want me to do?" Kelly's voice asked from the speakers.

As with all addictions, McCabe's came with a price: the inevitable guilt of knowing that the excitement he drew from the act of murder was both ethically and morally wrong. Reprehensible. The problem was, he couldn't help himself.

"McCabe?"

Fueled by adrenaline, McCabe hit the brakes, downshifted to second, spun the wheel hard to the left and slammed the Bird into a tight one-eighty. He floored the accelerator and shifted to third.

"McCabe, are you still there?"

"I'm here," he responded.

"What do you want me to do?"

"Call Maggie. Tell her I'm up near Rumford. Tell her to get on down to the scene. I'll be there quick as I can."

He ended the call.

The night was clear. The road before him empty. McCabe turned on his flashers and pushed the Bird up to 110 . . . everything the old V8 was able to give.

His mind went to his daughter sleeping peacefully in her bed. The red-haired kid leaving the building. He imagined Casey getting up. Sneaking out for a secret late-night rendezvous. *I love you. I love you too.* He saw them kissing. Groping. And then . . . what? Rape? Murder? He told himself to stop it. Stop getting weirded out by stupid thoughts. Stop being an asshole. Still, he couldn't push the image from his mind.

KELLY HADDON'S CALL woke Maggie from a restless sleep in her apartment on Vesper Street on Portland's Munjoy Hill.

"Yeah. What is it?" she mumbled into her cell.

"Some kid's gotten herself killed," said Haddon. "McCabe says he wants you to get to the scene. Seems he's up near Rumford. He's on his way back."

Rumford? Rumford was the back of beyond. What in hell was McCabe doing in Rumford at three in the morning? She wondered if he was still drunk. Or maybe just hungover.

She flipped the phone to speaker, took it with her into the bathroom. "Okay. Tell me what you know."

She listened to Haddon while she washed her face and brushed her teeth.

"Young woman, maybe a teenager, was found stabbed and naked on the Loring Trail just off the end of the Eastern Prom. Patrol guys are there now. Jacoby's people are on their way." Bill Jacoby ran the PPD's Crime Scene unit. "I don't have a lot of specifics."

"Okay. Thanks. Be there in five."

Maggie hit End. She threw on some clothes, attached her gold shield to her belt, strapped on her weapon and headed downstairs.

Less than three minutes later, she pulled her red Chevy Trail-Blazer in behind a cluster of PPD cruisers and a MEDCU ambulance that practically filled the small circular parking area around the Loring Memorial. Located at the far end of the Eastern Prom, the place was a vest pocket park dedicated to the memory of a dead war hero.

"Hiya, Mag, how you doing?" The greeting, called out in a throaty growl, came from one of the PPD's veterans, Sergeant Pete Kenney. Kenney'd been one of Maggie's trainers when she first joined the department fourteen years ago, and she still had a soft spot for him. He'd put in his thirty and was now only weeks from retirement. She'd just RSVP'd yes to the invite for his farewell party, a family affair at Bruno's Tavern, an Italian place located in front of the Portland Boxing Club on Allen Avenue.

"Hiya, Pete. Any reporters pick up the scent?"

"Not yet. But it won't be long. It never is."

Kenney had given himself the job of keeping anyone, but especially the press, from heading down the steps toward the scene.

The Loring Trail was a narrow dirt path descending at a sharp angle from the memorial down to the water. It was both the shortest and steepest way to cut down the backside of Munjoy Hill to the running and biking trails that ran along the edge of Casco Bay and Back Cove for miles in each direction.

"Who's watching from below?"

"Walt Ghent and John Freeman."

Maggie started for the trail. Kenney stopped her. "Take this," he said, handing her a MagLite. "Dark as doom down there and plenty to trip over."

She nodded her thanks, slipped under the yellow crime scene tape that'd already been stretched across the opening to the trail and started her descent.

Chapter 16

From the journal of Edward Whitby Jr.
Entry dated June 20, 1924

I begin this journal by noting that while my heart died twenty years ago this month, the rest of my body will only be joining it now. To be precise, not exactly now, but surely within a few short months. I write seated at a simple wooden table and chair in Aimée's studio on Whitby Island. I have decided to spend my last months here alone with my memories of the woman I loved more than any other, in the place we both loved more than any other, tended only by a private nurse and my manservant, Alfred Kinney.

My doctors have done all they can to prolong my life. I've undergone several surgeries, as well as radiation treatments by Dr. Gioacchino Failla at Memorial Hospital in New York. I hope these procedures have given me the few months I need to tell the story of that love as only I know it before I join Aimée and Garrison in death.

I am in constant pain, but I refuse the morphine my doctors offer, for I know it will cloud my mind and make it impossible for me to finish the task I have set myself.

I write for no other eyes but my own and those of my children and grandchildren, and then only when they are old enough to understand the tragic events that transpired in that wretched summer of 1904. It seems right to me that those whom Aimée and I brought into the world should be allowed to know the truth of how she left it. And the guilt I have suffered ever since for the role I played in her death. But no one else. Our family has already suffered too much from the lies and from the public shaming of the remarkable woman who was my wife. Showing these pages beyond our direct line would only revive the chatter we were forced to live through and would serve no purpose whatsoever. The dead would remain dead.

Sitting here on the island, as darkness falls, I ponder how to tell the tale. I suppose I should begin at the beginning. Not with my birth, like Copperfield, but with my year in Paris. The year my father gave me to "sow my wild oats." The year I met Aimée and fell in love with the most remarkable woman I have ever known.

In June 1894 I graduated from the Massachusetts Institute of Technology, near the top of my class, with a degree in Naval Architecture. Though I'd pursued my studies assiduously, my true passion at the time was art. From my earliest years I'd seldom been without a sketchpad or paints and canvas. While completing my degree at MIT, I simultaneously completed a course of study at the School of the Boston Museum of Fine Arts in the basement in Copley Square. I was a good painter, and my work earned high praise from my instructors. While I knew I was talented, I was not yet as good as I wanted to be.

The Sunday after graduation, the Whitby family went en masse, as was our wont, to services at St. Luke's Cathedral on State Street in Portland. After returning to the house, I planned to tell my father that before I joined the firm, I intended to go to Paris to study art.

The coach let us off under the porte cochere. Before going in, I stopped my father and told him there was something important we needed to discuss. He looked at me with his dark eyes and invited me into his private study overlooking the back gardens. I always hated that room, for it was there, throughout my childhood, that punishment had been meted out. I still bore the scars, mental as well as physical, of the beatings I suffered in that room from the buckle on my dear papa's favorite leather belt.

We entered the study. He sat at his desk. I sat in the same straight-backed chair he'd once used for the beatings. He waited for me to speak. It was like being called into the headmaster's office. But my father, in his silence, was far more frightening than any mere headmaster.

"What is so important we need to talk about it today?" he finally asked.

"Art," I said. Actually, I think it came out more as a squeak than the actual word.

"Art. What about art?" He said the word *art* in a sneering way, as though it was something unworthy of serious discussion by a man of his stature. I sensed this was going to be one of the most difficult conversations we'd ever had.

"I graduated MIT just as you wanted me to. Magna cum laude, just as you hoped."

"Actually, I hoped for summa. Which I think you might have made had you not snuck out to Copley Square three evenings a week."

I wasn't sure how he knew about that. I'd paid the art school fees myself out of an inheritance I'd received from my maternal grandfather. I'd felt it wiser not to ask. "Honors nevertheless. I learned the skills I needed, and, as I have often said, I am prepared to spend my life in service to Whitby & Sons."

"But? I assume there is a but."

He was staring at me with such icy malevolence that I thought that in spite of the fact that I was now both bigger and stronger than my father, he might just order me to bend over the chair, drop my trousers and take a dozen of the best. I remember squeezing my hands into fists, thinking that instead of bowing to his will, this time I would defend myself even if it meant disinheritance.

"But?" he said once more.

I forced myself to relax. "Yes, there is a but. I will join the company, but before I do, I intend going to Paris to study with the masters at the Académie Julien. Bougereau, Lefebvre and Garnier. I need to find out how good an artist I am. If I am as good as I hope, I will come back, join the company as promised and do my best to help it succeed."

"And your art?"

"I will paint evenings and weekends and try to exhibit

my work with Homer, Stevens and others in shows at the Society of Art."

"I see. And if I say no? If I say that I need you, the son I've always seen as my successor, at Whitby & Sons now. What will you do then?"

"I'll go anyway. I still have enough of Grandfather's inheritance to pay my own way and live for a year or so."

"And not join the company?"

"If that is the retribution you wish. Thanks to you I have the credentials to find a position with another company."

"A competitor?"

"If need be."

He didn't speak. Didn't move. I could see rage rising in his face. A rage I had always feared. Perhaps he *would* try to beat me with his belt. "You'll always have Charles to succeed you if I don't," I said. My brother was three years younger than me, but, instead of going to college, he had been working at the company since leaving Penfield a year earlier.

My father turned to look out the window at the formal gardens he'd always loved.

"Edward," he finally said. "You've just completed an honors degree at one of the finest schools of naval architecture in the country, if not the world. I commend you for that. I'm even more impressed you managed a magna while simultaneously pursuing your passion for art. I commend you for that as well. However, now is the time for you to put away childish things and come to work for the firm."

"No."

"No?"

"No. I am going to go to Paris to study figure painting at the Académie Julien. When I return from Paris, I will take up my duties at the company. But I intend to enjoy Paris first."

"I see. Will a year be enough?"

"I'd prefer two."

"One."

"Two."

"Only one."

Before I could answer, he continued, "However, I will pay for your trip and for your studies there. In addition, I will provide an allowance generous enough for you to enjoy the pleasures Paris has to offer. Knowing you, Edward, I suspect you'll be doing considerably more with the female form than simply painting it, and doing more with your nights than simply eating well and sipping fine wine. However, I will give you a year to study art, sow your oats and hopefully get certain appetites out of your system before you return home to your true vocation. But first you must sign a contract that at the end of the year, you'll return to Portland and take your place both at Whitby & Sons and in Portland society."

He had given in more easily than I had imagined. I gave him my word and agreed to his conditions. The following day, I signed the contract. After all, a year was the most I'd expected and, of course, my father was right in his assumption that my eagerness for Paris was rooted at least as much in the carnal as it was in the artistic.

Chapter 17

THE LORING TRAIL was bordered on either side by dense woods and interrupted every ten yards or so with short, sharp flights of granite steps installed to make the climb up or down a little easier.

About thirty feet down, Maggie saw two more cops, Bob Hurley and Diane Rizzo, blocking the way to an even narrower dirt path, no more than twenty-four inches wide, that veered off to the right from the main trail. Through the darkness she could see a pair of evidence techs setting up their equipment.

A young man, maybe thirty, stood shivering near Hurley and Rizzo. He was bare-chested, wearing nothing but nylon jogging shorts and sneakers and looking more than a little the worse for wear. His face and body were covered with scratches and dirt and what looked like blood. His arms were folded across his chest, presumably for warmth. He had one hand connected to a leash. A reddish-brown vizsla stood wagging her tail at the other end. With Maggie's arrival, the dog nudged her leg and started licking her hand.

"Who's this?" she asked.

"The guy who found the body," said Bob Hurley.

"My name is Dean Scott, and actually, my dog found her first. She was still alive when Ruthie found her."

"Well, she sure as hell isn't alive now," said an EMT who was passing by, heading up the hill. "Nothing more we can do here," he said to Maggie. "Dr. Scott here tried his best. You want us to hang by the van?"

"Yeah. Unless you get another call. We may need you to take her to the morgue."

Maggie turned back to Scott. "You're a medical doctor?"

"I am. First-year resident in the ER at Cumberland Med. Like I said, the girl was still alive when I found her. Barely. But I did what I could to save her."

"What happened to your shirt?"

"She'd been whacked hard on the back of her head. I used the shirt as a compress to try to slow the bleeding. I think it helped a little."

Maggie turned to Diane Rizzo. "Any idea when the ME's getting here?"

"Be a while yet. Shift supervisor said Dr. Mirabito was gonna handle it herself. She's driving down from Augusta."

"All right. Do me a favor, Diane. See if you can find Dr. Scott something to cover up with? I need to talk to him, and it's got to be a little chilly standing around half naked."

Rizzo headed back up the hill toward her cruiser.

"Thank you," said Scott. "I take it you're the boss here?"

"For the time being. I'm Detective Savage. Margaret Savage." She pushed her jacket aside to reveal the gold shield attached to her belt. "I need to ask you some questions about what happened."

"You don't suppose I could go home first, clean up and get dressed?"

"I need to ask the questions first if you don't mind. It's important that we get started quickly if we're going to find out who did this."

Scott sighed, shrugged and finally nodded. "Okay. I get it."

Down on the narrow dirt path where the girl's body lay, a generator roared to life. As it did, a pair of floods fastened to tall aluminum tripods lit the area as brightly as center field at a Sox game. The victim came into view, along with Bill Jacoby and two of his evidence techs, all three dressed in Tyvek coveralls. The girl lay on her back on the side of the path, head pointing uphill toward Maggie, feet pointing down. She was naked except for a pair of bright pink sneakers and shorty socks with pink pom-poms poking out from the backs. What looked like a blood-soaked rag was tied to the back of her head. Maggie could see some blood on her chest.

She called Jacoby over to where she was standing. "Find any ID yet?"

"We're still looking, but so far, nothing. No wallet. No clothes. No nothing. Any missing person reports filed?"

Maggie shook her head. "I asked Kelly Haddon to call if any came in. Meantime, you go do your thing. I'm gonna talk to the guy who found her. Yell if you find anything."

Diane Rizzo handed Scott a blue nylon jacket with the word *Police* stenciled on the back. Probably her own. He slipped it on. A little small, but only a little. Diane was a big woman.

Maggie walked fifty feet down the trail, both for privacy and to get away from the noise of the generator. She sat on an old wooden bench that was decaying on one side of the trail and called McCabe.

"Where are you now?" she asked.

"Forty miles out. I've got my flasher on and I'm doing over a hundred, so I shouldn't be long."

"You sober?"

"I'm sober. Think I'd be driving a hundred drunk? Want me to meet you at 109?"

"No. We're not even close to done here. Plus you need to see the scene. Not just the pictures. Park up at Loring and walk down the trail. You'll see the floods."

"Got it."

"Meantime stay on the phone. I'll be talking to the guy who found the body. You ought to listen in."

Maggie waved Scott over to the bench. He sat on one end. She sat on the other. She put her phone between them, flipped it to speaker for McCabe's benefit, turned on a small digital recorder and put it next to the phone. "I'm recording our conversation, and my partner, Detective Sergeant McCabe, is listening in by phone."

Dean Scott shrugged. "Fine by me."

"Good. This is Detective Margaret Savage of the Portland, Maine Police Department," she said for the benefit of the recorder. "The time is 3:11 a.m. on Friday, June 24, 2012. The following is an interview with Dr. Dean Scott recorded on the Loring Trail in Portland. Dr. Scott, what is your address, please?"

"52 Quebec Street here in Portland. It's a small three-unit between Lafayette and North Street. I'm on the top floor. Apartment three."

52 Quebec sat in the middle of a gentrified section of Munjoy Hill. There were some single-family houses on the street; others had been divided into two- and three-unit apartments. Many had undergone fairly recent face-lifts.

"And you work as a resident in emergency medicine at Cumberland Medical Center in Portland?"

"That's right. First year. Graduated med school at UVM last year."

"Okay. Good. Now would you please tell me in your own words what you know about what happened here tonight?"

"Well, one thing I can tell you for sure is your crime scene's majorly fucked up."

Scott's answer rubbed Maggie the wrong way. It seemed arrogant, and she didn't like the way he casually used the word *fuck* in an official police interview.

"And I suppose you know a lot about crime scenes?"

"Just what I see on *CSI*. But trust me, this one's fucked up."

"Okay, how?"

"First off, the victim was discovered by my dog, and Ruthie's a licker. She was alone with the girl, who was still alive at the time, for maybe two, three minutes. Probably licked her from head to toe. Then I arrived. Pulled Ruthie off and did what I could to save her life. In terms of your scene, I'm afraid I made things a lot worse."

Maggie took a deep breath. Scott was right. The crime scene *was* fucked up. Badly compromised.

"Okay, here's what I want you to do," she said. "Start at the beginning and tell me, step by step, what you were doing before you found the victim, how you found her and what you did between then and now."

Scott shrugged. "Okay. When I got home from the hospital, I changed into running clothes and took Ruthie for a run."

"Just you and the dog?"

"That's right."

"At three in the morning?"

"Twenty of. I was supposed to finish my shift at midnight, but there'd been a bad accident out on Route 22 in Westbrook. Ambulance pulled into the ER about 11:30. Three teenagers. Two boys and a girl. One of the boys was DOA. The other two critical. I joined the trauma team working on the second boy. He was sent up to surgery around two. I cleaned up and left around 2:10 or so."

"Anybody see you leave?"

Scott thought about that. "Obviously, the trauma team. Woman at the admissions desk. Probably some people waiting in the ER. There'll be a record of their names at the hospital. Anyway, I got home a little before 2:30. Washed up. Threw on my running clothes, clipped on Ruthie's leash and off we went."

"You live with anybody?"

"Just the dog."

"No girlfriends?"

"No one serious at the moment. At least nobody who's moved in."

"You ever see the victim before?"

"Before tonight?"

"Yeah."

Suddenly it seemed to Maggie that Scott was looking more thoughtful. Like he was trying to figure something out. "Before I answer any more questions, I need to ask you one. Are you thinking maybe I had something to do with this? With killing her, I mean?"

"I don't know. Did you?"

"Jesus. No, I did not. I tried to save her life."

"Then you have nothing to worry about. All I asked you, Dean, was if you'd ever seen her before."

Scott hesitated. Then apparently decided to answer the question. "Yes. I have seen her," he finally said. "I've never talked to her, but I've definitely seen her."

"Where?"

"Around."

"Around where?"

"The neighborhood. I think she must have lived around here."

"Where specifically?"

"You know the Hill?"

"I know it."

"I saw her a couple of times over at Hilltop Coffee. Doing homework, I think."

"What makes you think she was doing homework?"

Scott shrugged. "She had a couple of textbooks on the table and was banging away on a laptop, so that's what it seemed like."

"Was she alone?"

"Yes."

"Did you talk to her?"

Scott smiled sadly. "I tried to. Once. Asked if I could share her table. She just nodded. I sat down and tried to start up a conversation. She gave me a couple of one-word answers."

"Answers to what?"

"Standard conversation starters. I think I asked her what she was working on. If it was anything interesting."

"What did she say?"

"Biology term paper. Just the three words. That was it."

"When was this?"

"I don't know. A while ago. April, maybe. "

Okay, so the victim was in school. No surprise there. And she probably lived on the Hill. "She say anything else?"

"I asked her where she went to school." Scott smiled sheepishly. "I was hoping it was USM or something. I'm a little old for high school kids."

"Did she tell you?"

"No. Just looked annoyed and said something like 'This paper's due tomorrow so would you mind not talking?'"

"What'd you do?"

"I stopped talking. Just sipped my coffee, opened my own computer and spent twenty minutes surfing the net."

Maggie made a mental note to check with the owners of Hilltop Coffee. If the vic was a regular there, they might know her name. Where she lived.

"Ever see her anywhere else?"

"Passed her a few times running. I'd nod and smile. Sometimes she'd notice me. Nod back. Sometimes not." Scott smiled ruefully. "Ruthie's usually a chick magnet, but not with this girl."

"She was running alone?"

"Yeah."

"Think hard about what she was wearing when you saw her running. Any caps or shirts with a school or team logo that might help us identify her?"

Scott thought about it. "One time she was wearing a Red Sox cap. But I don't think that's gonna help you much."

Scott was right. It wouldn't. "Okay. Let's go back to tonight. Which way did you run?"

"My usual route. Took Lafayette over to Congress. Turned left on Congress and ran down to the park. Then down the hill to the running trail."

"See anybody along the way?"

Scott thought about that for a second. "Not there, no. Just a couple of cars. One heading west on Congress. One heading down the hill on the Prom. That's all."

"Both heading away from the direction you were headed in?"

"Yeah. That matter?"

"So either one of them could have been coming from Loring when they passed you?"

"Yeah, I guess so. I didn't think of that."

"What kind of cars?"

"Jesus, I don't know. Just cars. The one going down the Prom was an SUV. Explorer, TrailBlazer, something like that. Mostly I saw their lights."

"New? Old?"

"Newish, I think. At least not old bangers."

"Keep going."

"Like I said, I ran down the hill to the running trail. I let Ruthie off the leash. She's well trained and pretty much always comes when I call. We took the path along the water toward Back Cove. I usually go that way and then circle the cove and then double back toward Congress. Six miles in all. This time we only got about halfway to the sewage treatment plant when Ruthie must have caught a scent."

"Not the one coming from the plant?"

Scott smiled at that. "No. She smelled something on top of that and took off like a bat out of hell. I called her to come back, but she kept going. I called again. She still didn't come back. I figured she must be chasing a squirrel or some other small animal, so I ran after her, calling her name. Telling her to come. But she paid no attention, and I lost sight of her.

"I stopped for a second near the sewage plant, trying to figure out which way she went. That's when I did see somebody. An old woman scurrying by. A bag lady pushing a cart full of stuff. I tried stopping her and asking if she'd seen my dog, but she just kept going as fast as she could. I suppose she might have seen something."

"What did she look like?"

Scott shrugged. "I don't know. Like a bag lady. Gray, stringy hair. Kind of dirty. Mismatched clothes. Maybe sixty something, but you never know with homeless people. Sometimes when they're brought into the ER they turn out to be twenty years younger than you would have guessed. Anyway, she was maybe five foot two or three. Kind of fat. Pasty face. Her legs were all swollen up with edema. Whoever she is, she's had a hard life."

"She was coming from the direction where you found the body?"

"Yeah."

Looked like they might have a possible witness. That is if they could ever find the woman. "Okay, what then?"

"I ran to the Loring and turned up the trail."

"Had to be pitch black on the trail. How could you see anything?"

"I was wearing a headlamp. Which, by the way, is still lying in the dirt near the body. It belongs to me, not the killer, so I'd like it back."

"Sorry. It'll have to go into the evidence locker for the duration."

"Yeah? Well, in that case, maybe you guys could buy me a new one. It's something I use a lot, and first-year residents aren't exactly rich doctors."

"Fine. Remind me later. Right now it seems to me that between Ruthie's barking and the light from your headlamp, the killer must have seen and heard you coming from quite a distance away."

"I'm sure of it. But at that point I didn't know anything about a murder or anyone being attacked. I was just trying to find my dog and stop her from catching what I thought must be a small animal and eating it. Anyway, right up there"—Scott pointed—"where the trail meets that little path to the left, I saw some splotches of what I was pretty sure was blood. More blood was visible further along the path. I didn't hear Ruthie barking anymore, but I could hear her making licking sounds. So I figured she must have caught whatever it was she was chasing and carted it into the woods to finish it off."

"You didn't see the girl lying on the path?"

"No."

"Why not?"

"Because she wasn't there then."

Maggie frowned. "Where was she?"

"Let me finish. The woods right there are pretty thick on both sides of the path. Small trees. A lot of bramble bushes. Other prickly stuff. With my light I could just see Ruthie on the right side, head to the ground, poking at something. I figured she was probably eating whatever she caught. Since the last thing I need is my dog puking squirrel guts all night, I got down on my haunches and crawled in after her. About ten feet in, I saw the girl. Ruthie was standing over her licking whatever she could off her body."

"Blood?"

"Blood for sure. Probably other stuff as well. Sweat. Tears if there were any. Salt. Saliva. Whatever. And along with it, I would guess any trace of whoever attacked her. I put Ruthie on the leash. Tied it around a small tree trunk and crawled back. I found a pulse. Weak but definitely there. She wasn't dead yet.

"She had a deep stab wound about two centimeters above and on the right side of her navel."

"Her right side or yours?"

"Hers. Looked like the knife punctured the small intestine. Maybe the colon. No way to tell how bad, but there wasn't a whole lot I could do about it either way. What I could do something about was the bleeding from the back of her head. I took off my shirt and used it as a compress to at least try to stanch the bleeding enough for her to survive till an ambulance could get here. I tied the shirt in place with the laces from my running shoes. One around her forehead and the other around her chin. Then held it on tight with one hand. While I was doing that, I called 911 with the other."

"Anything else?"

"Yeah. Something weird. She had a letter carved into her chest. Just starting to scab over."

"A letter?"

"Yeah. A capital letter *A*. All I could think of was Hester Prynne. Y'know? The one accused of adultery in Hawthorne's *Scarlet Letter*? Except in the book, the *A* was pinned to her dress."

Maggie frowned. A letter *A* carved into the victim's chest. What in hell was that all about? "All right. What happened then?"

"Then she died. She was just a kid. No more than twenty. I'll tell you, between the DOA at the hospital and this one, it's been a bitch of a night."

"What did you do?"

"When I couldn't find a pulse, I picked her up and carried her back to the path."

"Carried her how?"

"Upright. Like this." Scott formed a circle with his arms. "Arms around her waist. Her body against mine. It was the fastest way to get there. Her feet dragged along the ground most of the way. We both got scratched."

"Why move her at all?"

"I needed a clear space to start CPR. Both chest compression and mouth to mouth. No way I could do it in the brambles."

Maggie narrowed her eyes. "Why do CPR if she'd most likely bled to death or maybe died from organ failure? How would CPR help?"

Scott gave Maggie a dismissive look. "Any full arrest deserves a full resuscitation. That's one of the first things they teach you in med school. It may not help, but when the alternative is certain death, you do what you can to get the heart started again. Specially when there's an ambulance only a couple of minutes away. That's it. The whole story. I did CPR until the EMTs got here. We both knew it was over."

Maggie sighed. "So what we've got now is a body covered not just with dog lick but also with your blood and sweat from you carrying her and your saliva in her mouth. Plus your crawling around most likely wiped out any footprints or other signs of the killer."

"'Fraid so. Sorry. Like I said. A fucked-up crime scene. But I tried to do what was best for the girl."

Maggie studied the young doctor, wondering if maybe he had killed the girl himself and all the rest was bullshit.

"Can I go home now?" he asked.

Maggie didn't hear him. She was thinking maybe he was pleased because his strategy seemed to be working. The fact that his blood, saliva, fingerprints and footprints were all over the place, on the body and at the scene, couldn't be used to convince a jury, or even a prosecutor, of his guilt. Neither could the fact that her blood was on him. All it would convince them of was his heroic efforts to save her life. An almost perfect cover-up for murder.

"Detective, I asked you if I could go home now."

"No. Not yet," she said distractedly. Her mind was racing. Okay. Scott said people saw him leave the hospital at 2:15 a.m. That could be easily checked, easily substantiated. But what if instead of just taking the dog for a run, he also had a date to meet the girl here? A date in which he planned to kill her. Did it have to be planned? Could it have been spontaneous? No. It had to be planned. Why else carry a knife with him? On the other hand, if he planned to rape and kill somebody, why bring the dog? Ruthie the licker. Answer: To screw up the evidence. Okay. So he went home. Changed into running clothes. Got the dog. Got the knife. And jogged on down for their rendezvous. It sort of fit. Including the fact that he was admittedly present at time of death. Except if he was the killer, maybe he delayed the 911 call till he was sure she was dead. But that was no big deal. Okay, so what about the letter *A*? Maybe it had nothing to do with Hester Prynne. Maybe he was signing his work. Maybe his name started with an *A*. No, she reminded herself, his initials were DS. Okay, maybe the *A* meant that this kid was destined to be the first of many. They'd find his next victim with a *B* on her chest. On the surface, Scott didn't seem to fit the profile of a serial killer. He'd chosen a career in which his job was saving lives. On the other hand, who the hell knew? Serial killers did weird stuff. Dennis Rader sent notes to the media and the cops telling them he wanted to be called BTK. That was his signature. Bind. Torture. Kill. Then there was that alphabet guy in New York State whose victims' first and last names and towns in which the bodies were found always started with the same letter. Carmen Colon in Churchville. Wanda Walkowicz in Webster. Michelle Maenza in Macedon.

"I'm sorry, I think I have to go home now. I've got to be back at the hospital by noon."

"One last question. Do you remember anything else that might have some meaning? Anything else, anything at all that you saw or heard on your way to the scene? Think hard. Put yourself back in that place and think hard if there was anything else."

Scott took a deep breath. Leaned his head back. Maggie waited.

"There was one thing, now that I think about it, that seemed a little strange."

"What?"

"A boat engine. Judging by the sound, a midsized outboard. It started up just about the time I stopped the bag lady. Then the sound diminished, like the boat was pulling away from shore. I didn't pay much attention to it at the time—I was too focused on finding Ruthie. It probably should have occurred to me that it was strange that someone should be running a boat at that hour of the morning. I don't know." Scott's face brightened. "Maybe it was your killer making his getaway."

"Yeah. Maybe." A boat engine. Okay. Might mean something. But maybe nothing more than a lobsterman getting an early start. On the other hand, Scott could be right about the guy getting away by boat. Maggie looked up and saw McCabe standing a few feet away, studying her. She wasn't sure how long he'd been there.

"Can I go home now?" asked Scott.

"Yes. You can go. Get some sleep. Get cleaned up. But don't go far. We may need to talk to you again." She asked for his cell number. Wrote it down. Handed him her card. "If something occurs to you that you didn't think of while we were talking, anything, no matter how small, please call me. Even if you think it's totally irrelevant."

Scott smiled what Maggie figured was his charm-the-girls smile. "How about I give you a call anyway?" he said. "Even if I don't think of anything, maybe we could get together for a drink or something?"

She suppressed a strong desire to say *Hey, asshole, we're in the middle of a murder investigation and I'm a cop and I don't date witnesses.* Instead she left it at a pleasant, "Sorry, Dean, I don't think so."

She waited till Scott and Ruthie were out of sight before asking McCabe, "What do you think?"

"Sort of a jerk, specially that 'let's get together for a drink' business, but I don't think I buy him as the killer."

"I dunno. You're probably right. Let's go look at the body."

Chapter 18

From the journal of Edward Whitby Jr.
Entry dated June 24, 1924

I sailed from Boston on the liner *Bretagne* on the 20th of July 1894 and arrived in Paris eight days later. With the help of Peter Comstock, a friend and fellow artist from the Museum School who had been in Paris for over a year, I found appropriate rooms one flight above his, in a building on the Rue des Trois Frères in the Montmartre section of the city, just north of the Académie Julien. My rooms were comfortably, if not lavishly, furnished and afforded me a pleasant view of the rooftops of the city. The building itself was almost entirely populated by Americans more or less my own age who had come to Paris to eat good food, drink fine wine and get to know as many ladies of the demimonde as we possibly could. Of course, with whatever time we had left over, we also studied art, music, medicine or French literature.

If allowing me to get "certain appetites" out of my system was the reason my father agreed to finance my year in Paris, I am the first to admit that at least for the first month or so, I did not disappoint. I spent Whitby money lavishly. Ate with Peter and other friends at the city's finest restaurants and drank heavily. I experimented with absinthe, cocaine and morphine, and spent more than a few nights a week cavorting with *les filles de joie* within the rooms of Paris's most exclusive *maisons de tolerance,* most particularly Madame Kelly's Le Chabanais, where the other patrons included the famed artist Henri de Toulouse-Lautrec and Queen Victoria's corpulent son "Bertie," the Prince of Wales, a pleasant, if self-indulgent, fellow who would later become King Edward VII.

On a warm, rainy day at the beginning of September, I began classes at the Académie. It was a little after two in the afternoon and I was hurrying, because I was nearly twenty minutes late for my first studio session and I arrived soaked both by perspiration and rain. Every face in the room turned as I bolted in. Twenty-one men and one woman. Two if you count the model.

Le professeur, Monsieur Garnier, approached.

"Monsieur Whitby?"

"Yes, sir. I mean oui, Monsieur."

"You are late," he said in excellent English.

"Oui, Monsieur."

"I will excuse your tardiness, as this is your first session. However, in the future, kindly make sure you arrive on time.

Now find yourself a bench and please stop staring at my daughter."

I tried. I truly did. But as I started my sketches, I found it nearly impossible not to look at her. And soon I was sketching Aimée and not the far-rougher-looking woman who was modeling. Indeed, at eighteen, Aimée was the most beautiful woman I'd ever laid eyes on. Her silky blonde hair was tied back with a black ribbon. Her soft red lips pursed in concentration as she worked. She had deep blue, nearly indigo eyes that, as I recall, occasionally glanced back at me in playful curiosity. It wasn't just Aimée's features and figure that attracted me. Even if these had been more ordinary, she exuded a radiance of spirit I'd never before encountered in a woman. Indeed, by the end of our two-hour session, I was hopelessly in love without a word having passed between us. I gathered up both my sketches and my courage and walked over to introduce myself, hoping my less-than-satisfactory Penfield Academy French would suffice. Happily she spoke perfect English. I was half-expecting to be sent packing for my forwardness in so obviously sketching her, but instead she asked to see the sketches. I hesitated. She was, after all, the daughter of one of the most famous artists in the world. To my amazement, she complimented my work. Told me I had talent. And, to my delight, invited me to join her and a group of other students after class at the nearby Café Lézard.

I readily accepted the invitation and followed as she led us through the rain-soaked streets to the café. It turned out that Aimée was the only woman, as well as the only *Francaise,* in the group. Whether she was included for her

beauty, for her family connection to one of the most important *professeurs* at the Académie, or because they liked
her strong opinions and prodigious talent was a matter of
debate. Still, it pleased Aimée to be there. She made no
secret of the fact that she preferred the company of men,
flirted shamelessly with all of us and basked in the attention
we paid her.

I remember those afternoons so well. There we were,
seven young peacocks, seated around a large table, all
puffed up, strutting and shaking our tails in our eagerness
to impress the one extraordinary female in our midst. Every
time she favored me rather than one of the others with a
look, or asked my opinion on something, my heart would
leap. But whenever she turned her attention to someone
else, it wounded me like a knife to the heart.

Ten months later, to my own amazement, as well as the
amazement of everyone who knew us both, Aimée agreed
to become my wife. Never in my wildest dreams had I ever
imagined anyone as beautiful and talented, anyone with so
much life, could ever find someone as intense and moody
as myself even remotely attractive. But apparently she did.

Not wanting to give my prize a chance to change her
mind, I promptly presented her with a large diamond purchased at the most expensive *bijouterie* in Paris, and two
weeks later, despite the protests of both Aimée's and my
own parents, we were married in the village church near
the farm in Provence where Aimée was born. After the
wedding, we traveled by train to Le Havre and boarded *La
Bretagne* for the trip back to Boston.

Chapter 19

At 4:20 A.M., the air on the Loring Trail was dry, crisp and surprisingly cool for early June. A steady breeze was blowing in from the water. The stars that had filled the night skies just a little earlier faded as the first streaks of dawn appeared in the east.

Maggie and McCabe waited at the top of the path where the girl's body lay in the glare of the floodlights. A pair of evidence techs were still taking measurements. Drawing diagrams. Shooting photographs and videos both of the body and the scene.

Finally, Bill Jacoby came up and handed them gloves and Tyvek booties. "My people will be done in a minute. You can go have a look."

As the techs moved away from the body and disappeared into the woods to search for evidence, McCabe and Maggie walked down the narrow path, single file, to where the body lay.

They squatted side by side next to the girl. She looked to be twenty at most. Even in death it was easy to tell she'd once been pretty. More than pretty. Beautiful in that same rare way few women are. "She looks like a young Catherine Deneuve," said McCabe. "Features. Shape of the head. Everything."

"Catherine who?" asked Jacoby.

"A famous French film star."

"Lucky film star," said Jacoby.

"Deneuve must be in her seventies now. Still a beauty though. Too bad this girl didn't make it that far."

"Find any ID yet?" Maggie asked Jacoby.

"Nope. Nothing. Unless her name starts with an *A*. She's still Jane Doe as far as we're concerned. But check out the earrings she's wearing. They look like the real thing and damned expensive."

The earrings did indeed look expensive and not like anything a kid her age would be wearing with pink sneakers. Deep blue sapphires surrounded by diamonds set in gold dangles.

"Well, the motive doesn't seem to have included robbery," McCabe said. "I'm pretty sure they're real. You check them for prints?"

"We'll do that back at the shop," said Jacoby. "Then we'll have them appraised."

It was a little over an hour since presumed TOD. Rigor hadn't fully set in. McCabe looked into Jane Doe's eyes. Deep blue that nearly matched the blue of the sapphires except that they had started clouding over. Both were open and staring up with a look of puzzlement. As if she couldn't believe anything this bad could possibly happen to her. She had none of the wasted look of kids who were druggies or runaways. This girl had been healthy and fit. Well fed and well cared for. Her face was lightly but carefully made up. A little eye shadow. A little lipstick. Like she might have been getting ready for a date or a party. Or had been to one. Maybe that's why the earrings. McCabe imagined her long honey-blonde hair floating in a summer breeze, like a model in a commercial for what Casey called *product*. But now her life was over, and her beautiful hair was matted with drying blood and held in place by a T-shirt and shoelaces tied around both her forehead and chin.

McCabe's eyes moved down the body. He estimated the girl's height at five-eight or five-nine. Flat stomach. Well-muscled arms and legs. Probably an athlete. Or at least someone who exercised a lot. More capable, he imagined, than most women of defending herself from a rapist. She had a small, irregularly shaped, light brown birthmark on her thigh, the kind sometimes called a café au lait mark. It was shaped like a fist with one finger pointing out. He noted the stab wound on the right side of her navel. The three cuts on her upper chest forming the crudely carved letter *A*.

The cuts looked deep enough that scar tissue would have formed if the girl had survived the attack. The letter *A* would have been permanently etched on her body.

Was that the killer's intention? If so, why didn't he let her live? McCabe pointed to it and threw a questioning glance at Maggie. She shook her head and shrugged.

"I guess it's a clue," she said, "but I'm not sure of what. *The Scarlet Letter*? First in a series of serial killings? First letter of the victim's name? Maybe the first letter of the killer's name? Maybe he was just giving himself a grade, like in school. Like he'd done a grade A job of killing her. I imagine it's got to mean something, but who knows what."

A short, round-faced woman with dark curly hair walked down the path toward them, carrying an old-fashioned black doctor's bag. Maine's newly appointed chief medical examiner, Dr. Terri Mirabito. Maggie filled Terri in on what they knew, which wasn't much. Terri listened without comment, moved in and squatted down next to McCabe, and looked closely at the body. Shook her head. "What a waste," she sighed. "Why do they have to kill them so young?"

Without saying any more, Terri pulled on a pair of surgical gloves, took a small high-intensity light from her bag, knelt by the body and began examining the wounds. As she looked, she murmured, "They say great beauty can be more a curse than a blessing. I guess this kid proves the point."

While Terri was checking the wounds, one of Jacoby's evidence techs crawled out of the underbrush clutching a bunch of plastic bags. "Clothes," she said. "Presumably the vic's. Found 'em bunched up together under a prickly bush."

"No knife?"

"Not yet. But we did find this." The tech held up a bag containing an iPhone in a pink protective case. "It was lying on the ground, not far from where the clothes were. Almost certainly hers."

"Weird," said Maggie.

"What do you mean?"

"Knowing how much information a smartphone can contain, why on earth would the bad guy toss it into the woods with the clothes? Is he just stupid? Or did he want us to find it?"

McCabe thought about that. "More likely when he heard Ruthie and Scott coming, he panicked, dropped everything and got the hell out of there as fast as he could."

However it had happened, the phone was a gift. McCabe asked Diane Rizzo to get it back to 109 to be checked out ASAP. He next took the plastic bags containing the clothes. "You find any ID with this stuff? For the girl or anyone else?"

"Nope. Nothing at all in her pockets. Just the stuff she was wearing."

The first bag contained a white tank top. In the second was a dark blue sweatshirt caked with dirt but with no blood and no indication of knife cuts. Which meant her clothes were already off when the knife was plunged in. There was a big white Y in the middle of the sweatshirt. Y *for what?* McCabe wondered. Yale was the obvious choice, but maybe something else starting with Y? There was always Yeshiva. But for this Waspy-looking blonde in Portland, Maine, Yeshiva didn't seem likely. Yarmouth High School was possible. Yarmouth was an affluent suburb just up the coast from Portland. But unless Yarmouth's school color was the same shade of blue framing the same shaped Y, McCabe was ready to bet on Yale.

"Scott tell you where he went to school?"

"Med school at UVM."

"How about undergrad?"

"No idea."

"Let's find out."

Maggie nodded. McCabe opened another bag. He held up a pair of blue denim short shorts with raggedy hems. The kind Casey and what seemed like half the teenage girls in Portland were wearing these days. At least the half with good legs. The shorts were supposed to look like ratty cutoffs, except they cost forty bucks a pop and were cut about as high up the crotch as possible for the wearer to avoid arrest. There was dirt smeared on both sides of the back. It was likely she'd still been wearing them when she'd gone down. Next came pink thong underpants, which he supposed went with the pink sneakers and pom-poms. There was no bra.

McCabe shook his head. The way this girl was dressed sure as hell would get guys to notice her, lust for her, and maybe, if they wanted to go too far, too fast, to kill her to avoid charges of rape.

"Stop thinking what you're thinking, McCabe. I don't care what this kid was wearing. This wasn't her fault."

"How do you know what I'm thinking?"

"I just know."

"How come you're always right?"

Maggie smiled but said nothing.

McCabe turned to Jacoby. "How about a condom? Your folks find any condoms?"

"On this hillside?" Jacoby snorted, "only about a thousand of them." The area was popular for trysts. Especially gay trysts. "If we pick 'em all up, we'll be testing DNA from now till hell freezes over."

"Just go for the fresh ones."

"I don't think he used a condom," Terri called out.

They walked back to the body. Terri was kneeling, shining her light between the girl's legs.

"He didn't?"

"Doesn't look like it."

"Semen?" asked Maggie.

"I think so. I suppose it could be dog lick. Or maybe both. Be able to tell better at the morgue. Also there's no sign of vaginal bruising. If he raped her, he didn't try to hurt her while doing it."

"Blow to the head the cause of death?" asked Maggie.

"I doubt it. Head wounds like this can bleed like stink, but probably not enough to kill her. More likely the knife wound in the abdomen caused enough internal bleeding to do the job. Either way, cause of death was hemorrhagic shock due to blood loss. You can quote me on that. Now, unless you guys have something more, I'll have the EMTs wrap her up and take her over to Cumberland. I'll be able to tell a lot more there. I'll do the autopsy tomorrow afternoon."

TERRI CONTINUED TALKING, but McCabe had stopped listening to what she was saying. He just kept looking at the girl's face, certain there was something about it and that sooner or later something would click. After a minute it did. An image from 2004, the year he moved to Portland, of a little girl, ten years old, blonde and beautiful, handing him a cup of coffee. Thanks to an eidetic memory, McCabe remembered in exquisite detail nearly everything he'd ever seen, heard or read that had even slightly interested him. He could reconstruct in his mind, down to the last dust mote floating in the summer sunshine, a morning eight years ago that he'd spent in an apartment in South Portland.

At 9:21 on that particular morning, McCabe had just walked out of his date's bedroom. As he closed the door, he noticed the little girl sitting cross-legged in front of the TV set. She turned. Saw him. Muted the Sunday morning cartoon she was watching. There was no sign of shock or surprise at having a strange man emerge from her mother's bedroom. Apparently, she'd seen that before, how many times McCabe didn't know.

The girl rose from the floor. She was wearing a pair of pajamas covered with little red hearts and a pair of furry slippers with bunny ears. She walked over to McCabe, held out her hand and introduced herself. "How do you do?" she said formally. "I'm Veronica. Most people call me Aimée."

McCabe took her hand and shook it. "Why do they call you that?"

"It's my middle name, and I think it's prettier than Veronica.

It means 'beloved' in French. My mother insists on calling me Ronnie, though."

McCabe remembered thinking how incredibly self-possessed this child was. Ten years old, going on thirty. "How do you do, Aimée," he said. "My name is Michael. Most people call me McCabe."

"Why do they call you that?"

"It's my last name and I think it's prettier than Michael."

"You do not." She smiled a smile so beautiful it almost took his breath away.

"No. I'm just teasing about the pretty part. But most people do call me McCabe."

"Okay, McCabe. Would you care for a cup of coffee?"

"Yes, thank you, Aimée, I'd love a cup of coffee."

"How do you take it?"

"Black, please."

"I'll pour two. My mom likes coffee in bed if you want to take it to her."

"Of course."

McCabe closed his eyes and concentrated on the details of ten-year-old Aimée's face. How it might have changed as she'd matured and grown. And the more he thought about it, the surer he was that the girl who lay dead beneath his gaze was Tracy Carlin's daughter, Veronica Aimée Whitby. He wondered if she still called herself Aimée because she thought it a prettier name than Veronica. He knew he was the one who'd have to tell Tracy—who, though no longer a girlfriend, was still a friend—that her daughter was dead. But before he did, he had to be sure beyond any shadow of a doubt. Beyond one percent. Beyond even one-tenth of one percent.

He took out his iPhone. Connected to the Internet. Typed in *Veronica Aimée Whitby* and hit Images. The last scraps of doubt disappeared. McCabe signaled Maggie to follow him up the hill. "I know who she is," he said, showing her the pictures. "And where she lives. By an interesting coincidence, Dr. Scott happens to be a rather near neighbor."

Maggie took the iPhone and looked. "She's Edward Whitby's daughter? Jesus."

"As far as anyone else is concerned," said McCabe, "she's still Jane Doe."

Chapter 20

From the journal of Edward Whitby Jr.
Entry dated June 26, 1924

Even in the beginning, when I was begging her to marry me, I should have known Aimée was ill suited for the role I had cast her in, wife of a wealthy Portland businessman. I suppose I assumed once she became mistress of the house on the Western Prom, she would somehow be magically transformed and begin to behave like the women I'd grown up with, the women who'd married my friends. Of course, if that had happened, she'd no longer have been the woman I fell in love with.

That Aimée was a free spirit, a Bohemian, a supremely talented artist and a woman of strong emotions and stronger opinions who had allowed herself to be trapped in a marriage to someone who had once been a fellow artist but was no longer. Alas, as my father had foreseen, the artist in me withered and died as, over the years, I became more and more enmeshed in the business of Whitby & Sons. While Aimée escaped the tedium of Portland society by creating beautiful portraits and seascapes and socializing with other artists, I was busy designing and building warships for the Navy Department.

"For what purpose?" she frequently asked.

"To keep our country strong," I would reply, sounding more pompous than I intended. I suspect she knew, probably before I did, that the reason I worked so hard was a desperate need to outdo my now dead father. To make Whitby & Sons far more profitable than he'd ever dreamt it could be. To earn more money than he ever had. I deluded myself into thinking that outdoing him in the things he prided most in himself would, in some way, constitute revenge for all the humiliation I suffered at his hands. In the end, of course, all it did was turn me into the son he'd always wanted. Like almighty God, he had created me in his own image. His ultimate triumph.

"Come back to Paris with me," Aimée pleaded time and again.

"We visit often enough," I'd say, pretending not to understand what she meant.

"Oh, Lord," she would sigh. "Where has the beautiful boy I married disappeared to?"

"I'm the same man I always was."

"No, you're not. But if we move back to Paris to live, perhaps you'll rediscover yourself, Edward. We're still young. We have more than enough money to last three lifetimes. What's the point of making more? Together, we've created

three beautiful children. I want them to grow up appreciat-
ing the beauty of life. Not the beauty of warships."

Of course she was right. I look now at the images she
created of the sea and the island. Canvases that captured
both the extraordinary light and power of the Maine coast. I
see them now and realize how good they were and wonder
if I myself could ever have reached such heights.

As talented as she was, I didn't want Aimée selling her
work. I felt accepting money from strangers was beneath
the dignity of the wife of Edward Whitby. That, if friends
wanted them, she should make them a gift.

This, of course, made her angry, and rightfully so. "I'm
an artist, Edward," she said. "Art is my business. I make
paintings and I sell them. It's an honest and honorable pro-
fession, and it's what I do. I was an artist when we met in
Paris. And so were you. But unlike you, I'm still an artist.
And I will be till I die."

We argued about that dozens of times, and each time
Aimée adamantly refused to give in. Her paintings sold for
good prices and were hanging in the homes of the wealthy,
not just in Portland but also in Boston and New York. Two
had even been purchased by the famed Boston collector
Isabella Stewart Gardner and were included in the collec-
tion of the new museum Mrs. Gardner had established just
eighteen months before Aimée's death in a grand building
on the Fenway. The idea that Aimée's paintings would soon
be hanging in the same building, perhaps even in the same
room, with works by Titian, Rembrandt and Sargent thrilled
us both. But since her death, I've never gone to see them. I
was always afraid the sight of them would break my heart.

Chapter 21

MAGGIE AND MCCABE watched as two EMTs slid Veronica Aimée Whitby's remains into a black vinyl-coated bag and zipped it up. They placed the bag on a stretcher, lifted it easily, their burden weighing no more than one hundred and thirty pounds, and began carrying it up the hill. The two detectives followed.

"I should be the one to tell Tracy about this," said McCabe.

Maggie nodded. "Yes, you should. You want me to do Whitby?"

"Sure. But let's get our people started first. Why don't you call Fortier and bring him up to speed? Especially on that cell phone. It could be the key to the whole case." Lieutenant Bill Fortier was the head of Portland's CID and McCabe's direct report. "Bill should also drag in as many warm bodies as he can for a full court press on the neighborhood. Find out if anyone else saw the homeless woman Scott said was coming from the Loring."

Maggie and McCabe reached the top of the hill just as the MEDCU ambulance pulled away, heading for the morgue at Cumberland Med. The newshounds were already out in force. TV. Print. A couple of local stringers for the Boston and New York papers. Spotting the two detectives, they moved in and started calling out questions. Portland was a small city, and McCabe knew just about all of the reporters by name. Tracy Carlin was the one he knew best. He saw her in the middle of the pack. She smiled as she caught his eye.

McCabe held up a hand calling for silence. "Okay, quiet down," he shouted. The questions kept coming for maybe another ten seconds. "You all know me well enough to know I'll play it till you all pipe down." D and D meant deaf and dumb.

Finally there was a semblance of silence. "Okay. First I'll make a brief statement. But after that no one here will be answering any questions of any kind from anybody." McCabe ignored the collective groan. "What I will tell you is that the body of a young woman was found at roughly three o'clock this morning on the Loring Trail by a jogger, a young doctor at Cumberland Medical Center. She was the apparent victim of a homicide. She was stabbed and may also have been raped. We have no information at this time as to her identity, and when we do, we won't be making the information public until next of kin have been notified. That's not going to be for a while yet, so if I were you, I'd go home and get some sleep. Now if you'll excuse us, Detective Savage and I have work to do."

"Come on, McCabe," Tracy Carlin called out. "You've got to give us more than that."

"As soon as we know any more, Tracy, we'll let you know. That's it for now except to say our crime scene specialists are still combing the area for possible evidence. So please don't try to sneak in."

Chapter 22

MAGGIE HEADED FOR her Blazer, McCabe for the Bird. He started the engine and pulled out. It only took a couple of minutes to drive to Tracy's new home, a small, single-family on the corner of Howard Street and Quebec, two short blocks from Dean Scott's apartment. He looked at the place in the early morning light. A hundred-year-old frame house with pale yellow clapboards and black shutters. She'd bought it five years ago and spent two years and a lot of money renovating it from top to bottom. McCabe and Kyra had gone to the housewarming when the renovations were finished. He hadn't thought about it at the time, but Aimée hadn't been there. At least he hadn't seen her. Strange, considering it was her new home as well.

He considered calling Tracy to meet him here but decided that if she was with people, texting might be more discreet. *Where R U?*

On my way to office to file story, she texted back.

Meet me your house ASAP. Need to talk. Privately.

She instantly responded. K.

Then he called Shockley's landline. A sleepy voice answered on the fourth ring.

"All right, McCabe, what do you want? And trust me, my friend, it better be good."

"Are you alone, sir?" Shockley's supposedly secret live-in girl-friend was an on-air reporter for News Center 6 named Josie Tenant. McCabe hadn't seen her at Loring, so she might well be lying in the chief's bed. The last thing he needed was for Tenant to get wind of the murder before Whitby was informed. "I've got some highly sensitive information. I don't think you'll want your friend listening when you hear it."

He half expected Shockley to bust his chops for mentioning his friend, but Shockley didn't. Just said, "Wait sixty seconds and call back on my cell."

McCabe waited, then called.

"All right, what is it?"

"Edward Whitby's daughter, Veronica Aimée Whitby, was murdered at roughly three o'clock this morning just off the Loring Trail on the East End. Possibly raped before she was killed. Body was nude. No ID, but we did find a cell phone we're sure is hers."

"Jesus Fucking Christ. You've got to be kidding."

"Definitely not kidding."

"Are you sure of this?" Before McCabe could answer, Shockley said, "Hold on for a sec." His voice fell to a muffled whisper. "Josie, I'm in the middle of a confidential conversation. Would you mind going back to bed? And please shut the door." Shockley's voice returned to normal. "Jesus, McCabe. You have any idea how much money Whitby has?"

"Not a clue."

"Well, suffice it to say he regularly appears on the Forbes Richest People in America list."

McCabe wondered if Peter Ingram made the cut. Doubted it. Sandy would have been sure to let him know. "Just 'cause the guy's rich doesn't mean his daughter is any less dead."

A long sigh on the other end. "McCabe. Are you sure of this?"

"I'm sure."

"Who else knows?"

"Just Maggie. She's letting Fortier know. I gave a statement at the scene identifying the vic as Jane Doe."

"You said there was no ID?"

"We found what we think is her cell phone. Won't know for sure till it's checked out."

"So how do you know it's her?"

"I've met her before." McCabe didn't bother telling Shockley Aimée was only a child at the time. "I also found pictures of her on the Web. They match. Maggie's talking to Fortier now, organizing the investigation. I'm about to inform the victim's mother, who happens to be an old friend of mine."

"What about Whitby?"

"Maggie's gonna do that. I'll join her when I can."

"Maybe I should go with her when she tells him. Whitby will want to know I'm personally involved in the investigation."

"With all due respect, Chief, I think it's better if Maggie does this. She's about as good as they get at this kind of thing. We'll let Mr. Whitby know you're running the show."

Shockley didn't object. In fact, he sounded a little relieved.

"The girl's mother? Whitby's ex-wife?"

"What about her?"

"She still covers crime for the *Press Herald,* doesn't she?"

"I don't think she's gonna want to write about this. But I will ask her not to tip off any of her colleagues before we go public."

"Hmmm. I guess that's okay. But we better damned well close this case fast, or fucking Whitby will hang us all out to dry."

TRACY'S THREE-YEAR-OLD HONDA Accord turned into one of the two spaces in the small driveway. Next to the Honda, McCabe could see a gleaming new Mercedes SL 560. No way Tracy could afford a car like that unless she won the Powerball. Had to be either a boyfriend's or the kid's, and McCabe was willing to bet on the kid. He wondered what kind of asshole would spoil a teenager with wheels like that. Probably the same kind of asshole who'd make finding his daughter's killer a whole lot harder.

Tracy exited her car and rapped on the driver's side window of the Bird. McCabe rolled it down.

"What's going on, McCabe?" She leaned in with a conspiratorial smile. "You thinking of giving me a little scoop on this job? You owe me a couple, you know."

"Let's go inside and we'll talk, okay?"

McCabe exited the car and followed Tracy up the concrete steps that led to the landing. He hated next-of-kin notifications. All cops do. But with this one—with the victim being someone he'd met as a little girl and her mother a former girlfriend and now just a friend—there was no question it was going to be brutal.

Chapter 23

AT FIVE O'CLOCK in the morning, the fourth floor of 109 was deserted. Maggie sat down, flipped on her desk lamp and called Kelly Haddon in Dispatch.

"What do you need, Mag?"

"See if you can find me an address and phone number for Edward Whitby."

"Whitby? What's he got to do with this?"

"No questions, Kelly. Just see what you can find, okay?"

Maggie broke the connection. Her next call woke up Bill Fortier. He answered on the second ring.

"Problems?"

Maggie filled him in on what had happened during the night on the Loring Trail. Bill listened in his quiet, thoughtful way. Said uh-huh a couple of times. Asked a few questions.

"All right," he finally said, "I've got it. You go do your NOK. I'll be there in fifteen and pull in every warm body I can find to start a canvas. I'll also get Cleary working on getting the lowdown on the phone. Don't worry. I've got it covered."

"Do me a favor, Lieutenant."

"What's that?"

"Assign somebody to do a backgrounder on Dean Scott. I want as much on the guy as we can find. Hometown. Family. Friends. Education. I also want to check ViCAP and CODIS." These were FBI databases that kept a record of anybody who'd ever been implicated in any violent or sexual crimes anywhere in the US. "If your folks find anything remotely suspicious, ask Cleary to bring him in and put his ass through a wringer."

Detective Brian Cleary was a tough little fireplug and a certified expert at playing bad cop. An ex-prizefighter who looked the part, he was capable of scaring the shit out of most suspects. She was certain he'd have that effect on Scott.

"You think Scott's our perp?" asked Fortier. "I mean the guy's a doctor, for chrissake."

"I don't know. Maybe not. But doctors aren't saints, and Scott's young, definitely horny and he was the last person to see the girl alive. Far as I'm concerned that automatically makes him a suspect."

As soon as Maggie hung up, Kelly Haddon got back to her with an address and the unlisted phone number for what she described as the Whitby mansion on the Western Prom. Maggie was pretty sure she knew which house it was. She tried the number twice. Got voice mail twice. Finally, she said the hell with it and decided just to go and bang on the door till someone answered.

Chapter 24

TRACY UNLOCKED THE door and led McCabe inside. The place looked much as he remembered it from the night of the party. To the left, a graceful oak staircase led up to the second floor. To the right, an open living room extended some twenty-five feet to the back deck. The furniture was modern. Black leather, glass and chrome. Some good art hung on the walls, including one of Kyra's. Without the fifty party guests who'd filled the room the last time he'd been here, it looked bigger. And messier. Books and newspapers scattered both on the glass coffee table and under it. A heavy glass ashtray filled with dead butts. A pair of wineglasses colored by the dregs of last night's red wine sat on a side table, an empty bottle of good California Cabernet next to them.

"Okay, so what's the deal, McCabe? What do you want to talk about?" Her eyes narrowed suspiciously. "Is there something you want me to plant in my story?"

"Nothing like that, Trace. We just need to talk."

She pointed him to the couch in the middle of the room and slipped into the matching armchair next to it.

"All right, so talk."

"You alone?"

Tracy noticed him looking at the empty bottle and the glasses. "Yes, I'm alone. I had dinner with a friend last night. A friend who went home. Aimée's out at her father's place on Whitby Island." She pulled a box of Marlboros from her shoulder bag. Slid one between her lips. Lit it with a cheap plastic lighter.

She sucked in the smoke. Blew it out. He realized he had no idea how to start. "It's about Aimée."

Tracy frowned. "What about Aimée? Like I told you, she's on the island."

McCabe struggled to find the words to begin.

Tracy filled the silence. "Her father threw a big graduation party out there last night supposedly in honor of Aimée and his other daughter, Aimée's half twin, Julia. She spent the night there."

"By any chance," asked McCabe, "does Aimée have a small café au lait birthmark on her right hip?"

Tracy's expression changed from curious to alarmed. She nodded silently.

"She's not on the island, Trace."

For as long as McCabe had known her, Tracy always liked to assume a kind of tough, no bullshit, newspaper woman persona. Sort of like Rosalind Russell as Hildy Johnson in *His Girl Friday*. But McCabe knew, as he always had, that Tracy's toughness was a thin veneer masking a sensitive and now suddenly frightened woman.

She retreated into her chair as if she might find safety there. "She said she was staying there," she repeated, as if saying it might make it so.

"She's not on the island." McCabe took a deep breath. Blew it out slowly. There was no gentle way to say it. "It was Aimée we found this morning."

"Oh, Jesus." Tracy put both hands up, palms out, as if to push what he was saying away from her. "No. No. No way. You said you didn't know who the dead girl was. You called her Jane Doe. Aimée's on the island."

"I'm sorry, Tracy. It's her. She was here. In Portland."

"How do you know it was her? You haven't seen her in what? Seven or eight years? Lots of people have birthmarks."

"I wouldn't be telling you this if I wasn't sure."

Tracy found her cell phone, poked at it a couple of times, then pushed it at him. "Here. A dozen pictures I took yesterday. Look at them. And then I want you to tell me it was somebody else you found and you're sorry for scaring the shit out of me."

McCabe sighed. Took the phone. Fingered through a series of photos of a young woman in a white graduation dress. In a couple, she was smiling at her mother's camera. Others showed her at a dais making a speech. There was one of Aimée walking down the center aisle carrying a bouquet of red roses, her head turned toward her mother's camera, smiling, fingers waving.

Had McCabe harbored even the slightest doubt, it would now be gone. He shook his head, handing back the phone. "I'm sorry, but it is her."

Tracy speed-dialed a number. A voice message came on immediately. "Hi. You've reached Aimée. Leave your number, and I'll call you back."

"Her phone's in the crime lab at 109. We found it by the body. Tech knows enough not to answer."

Tracy hit the Off button, suppressed a choking sound and just managed to get out the words, "Is there any possibility . . ." She closed her eyes. Swallowed hard. Opened them again. " . . . that you're wrong?"

McCabe pictured himself sitting across from a cop hearing the news that his daughter, Casey, had been murdered. He couldn't begin to imagine the pain she must be feeling.

Chapter 25

As MAGGIE DROVE across town in the early morning light, the streets were empty save for a few poor souls sleeping "al fresco," as McCabe often described it. Maggie headed west on Middle Street past where it turned into Spring, followed Spring till it ended on Vaughn, then circled down around the bottom of the West End Cemetery, hooking a sharp right up the hill onto the Western Prom.

Edward Whitby lived in a large, white-columned mansion she'd driven by a thousand times. The place always reminded her of Tara in *Gone With the Wind,* except this particular Tara was improbably sandwiched between a pair of large, plain, New Englandy shingled jobs.

Maggie parked her unmarked Police Interceptor under a white portico supported by six large white columns. Doric, she thought. Or maybe Ionic. Or Dork and Ironic, as she and her best friend, Emily Kaplan, called them in high school. Either way, Maggie could never remember which was which.

She spent a good five minutes ringing the doorbell and banging a brass knocker on a large pair of twin mahogany doors. No one answered. Certain that a house this big had to come with at least one or two live-in staff, she decided to try telephoning again. Before the call went through, a light went on and the door opened about six inches.

"Who are you and what do you want?"

A woman in her late sixties or early seventies glared out at Maggie through the narrow opening. She had steel-gray hair cut short in a mannish style and was dressed in a nightgown and robe. She'd clearly been woken up by the ruckus Maggie had been making outside.

"Mrs. Whitby?" Maggie asked, pretty sure it wasn't.

"No. Mrs. Whitby isn't here."

"I see. Can you tell me where I can find either Mr. or Mrs. Whitby? Or preferably both. I'm Detective Margaret Savage of the Portland Police Department, and I'm here on a rather urgent matter." She took out her wallet. Flipped it open and showed the woman her ID.

After waiting vainly for the woman to introduce herself, Maggie said, "May I ask what your name is?"

"Mrs. Boatwright," the woman said. "Brenda Boatwright. I'm the housekeeper here. And what may I ask is so important that you have to come banging on our doors at the crack of dawn?"

"I need to talk to Mr. and Mrs. Whitby as soon as possible. This is a police matter, and, trust me, it is important. Now, can you tell me where I can find them?"

"No. Not unless you tell me what it's all about."

"I'm afraid I can't do that."

"Then I can't tell you where the Whitbys are. I'm sorry, but I'm under standing orders not to give anyone, detective or not, their private phone number."

Boatwright began to push the door closed. Maggie stuck out an arm and stopped her. "I respect your loyalty to your employers, Ms. Boatwright. But trust me when I tell you I'm here on very urgent police business and that if the Whitbys don't get to hear what I have to tell them because you decided to stonewall me, well, I suspect they'll kick your loyal ass out of this house before you can say boo. And even if they don't, I just might take it into my own head to charge you with impeding a criminal investigation."

"Are you threatening me?"

"Yes, ma'am, I sure as hell am. Now where are Mr. and Mrs. Whitby?"

Chapter 26

Tracy's face crumpled in on itself. She covered it with both hands and, bending almost double, let out a long, loud, low-pitched wail so filled with pain that McCabe thought her heart must be literally breaking in two.

He reached out and put a hand on her shoulder. She shook him off. "Just give me a minute alone to absorb this."

McCabe rose and went out onto a back deck overlooking a garden he knew his friend lovingly tended. He closed the screen but left the sliding door open so he could hear her, then sat in one of a pair of deck chairs that were still damp with morning dew. He looked down at the clumps of blooming azaleas and rhododendrons running along the back fence, alive in a blaze of pink and white. The white peonies about to pop. Red roses climbing a trellis attached to the side of a garden shed. There was a profusion of other flowers McCabe couldn't begin to name. A small granite fountain sat off to one side, burbling water. Tracy had often said her garden was her refuge, the one place where she could truly relax and shake off the evils of the world she wrote about day after day.

After about five minutes, he heard her get up and head for the deck. He rose as she walked out.

"Tell me what happened," she said, her voice flat and empty. "I want to know all of it. Everything you know."

He nodded, thinking how little they really knew and wondering how much he could allow himself to say. She was, after all, a reporter.

They sat side by side on the deck chairs. She lit another cigarette, then tossed the box on the small glass table in front of them. She took a deep drag, blew out the smoke and stared down, as he had, at the profusion of color below.

McCabe reached over and took one of the cigarettes. Lit it and sucked in the smoke. He hadn't smoked in at least a couple of years. Amazingly, it still tasted good.

"Talk to me, McCabe."

He told her most of what they knew, holding back little.

Chapter 27

BRENDA BOATWRIGHT STARED at Maggie for maybe five seconds. Blinked about twenty times. Then opened the door wider and said, "Follow me."

She led Maggie across a large marble-floored entrance hall to an antique table with a telephone. She picked up the receiver and dialed a number. Maggie waited, drumming her fingers against the side of her leg, listening as the phone rang about ten times before it was finally answered.

"Mr. Jolley?" Boatwright said. "It's Brenda at the house. I'm afraid I have to ask you to wake Mr. Whitby. There's a police officer here, a detective, who says she must talk to him immediately.... No, I don't know what it's about, but she says it's urgent.... That's right, urgent.... Yes, she showed me identification.... Okay, fine."

Mrs. Boatwright pressed the receiver against her chest. "Mr. Whitby's out on the island. Mr. Jolley says he'll wake him and ask him to call back immediately."

"What about Mrs. Whitby?"

"Mr. Whitby will call back."

"I see."

Maggie supposed the island Boatwright was talking about was Whitby Island. The family's private playground. She'd read about it often enough in the society pages but had never laid eyes on the place. She didn't know anyone else who had either. Not even Shockley.

Not wanting to talk to Whitby with Brenda Boatwright hanging over her, she handed her a card. "Ask him to call my cell phone," she said. "The number's right there." Boatwright relayed the number to Mr. Jolley, whoever he was.

"I'll be waiting in my car."

Chapter 28

"YOU SAW THE birthmark," said Tracy. "That means she had to be naked. At least from the waist down."

"She was."

Tracy's eyes narrowed. "You said she was found by a doctor. You think he did it?"

McCabe shrugged and shook his head. "At this point the old cliché applies, everyone's a suspect. Specially the last one to see her alive. Specially when it's a guy who lives in the neighborhood."

She frowned. "Where?"

"On Quebec. Near North Street."

"You called him young."

"Yeah. First-year resident. Probably twenty-six or so."

"Will you let me interview him?"

"Absolutely not."

"I'm really good at it."

"Sorry. No way."

"Can I at least come up to 109 and watch you talk to him?"

"Negative."

"Can you tell me his name?"

McCabe shook his head. He'd already said too much. Old affection overwhelming procedural rules. "I'm sorry, no. Tracy, you can't write about any of this. Or tell anyone any of what I've told you. At least not yet."

He sensed the wheels turning in her head, her investigative reporter instincts kicking in, constructing a story line. McCabe knew Tracy well enough to know she might just find Dean Scott and talk to him on her own. There was really no way he could stop her. At least not legally.

"I'm sorry. I can't answer any more of your questions. But I do need to ask you some of my own if you can handle it."

She sat for a minute looking out at the garden. Finally she sighed, "There's a bottle of bourbon in the kitchen cabinet to the left of the fridge. I'd like you to pour me a large glass with three ice cubes. When you come back out, I'll try to answer your questions."

McCabe went to the kitchen, found a glass and a half-empty bottle of Wild Turkey. Before pouring the drink, he texted Maggie. *Tracy notified.*

He returned with the drink and handed it to her. She took a sip. "Let's say this doctor has seen her before." She spoke softly and slowly, taking deep breaths, as if trying to hold back tears. "Maybe running on the Prom. She did that a lot. Or maybe here in the neighborhood. Walking or driving by. Maybe she's got the top down on the car. He smiles at her. She smiles back. They talk. Maybe he asks her out. She says no and nothing happens. Then last night she decides, for whatever reason, to come back from the island after the party. Probably a little drunk. Maybe a lot drunk. Ties up at the marina off Fore Street, y'know, near Portland Yacht Services. She starts walking home along the jogging trail. The doctor sees her when she gets to East End Beach. Says hi. Tries to get friendly. Maybe she's drunk enough to get friendly back. They fool around a little. He pushes things. She tells him to back off. He gets pissed and wham, the bastard goes for her."

She ties up at the marina? McCabe held up a finger to signal a break.

"Is that how Aimée would have come if she decided to come back from the island? On her own boat? She wouldn't have taken a ferry or some such?"

"I don't think so. The boat's how she usually goes back and forth. It's not technically hers. It's one of Edward's. He's got half a dozen out there. All sizes. But there's one she uses most of the time."

"Would she have taken someone with her? Someone from the party?"

Tracy shrugged. "I guess so. Why not?"

"What kind of boat is it?"

"I don't know. Just a small white cruising boat. Nothing fancy. Outboard motor. Maybe twenty feet. No cabin. Just a cockpit. You're thinking she might have brought somebody back to Portland who might have attacked her once they got here?"

"It's possible. Does she always use the same boat?"

"Pretty much. She likes it because it's named after her. The *Aimée*. That makes it her own. I'm told there's an identical one with her sister's name on it. The *Julia Catherine*."

"And she would have tied up at the Yacht Services marina?"

"Most likely. It's close by, and Edward owns a couple of slips there."

McCabe got up. "Excuse me a minute, Tracy. I have to make a call."

He went back inside and speed-dialed Fortier.

"What do you need, Mike?"

"I need you to send some people down to the marina at Portland Yacht Services. You know? The place off Fore Street? See if they can find a smallish white boat, maybe tied up in a slip, maybe moored. Named the *Aimée*."

"Named after her?"

"Yeah."

"Sail or motor?"

"Outboard. Twenty feet give or take."

"And we're looking for this boat because?"

"The victim may have used it to come back from a party on Whitby Island. Could've brought somebody with her."

"The bad guy?"

"If we're lucky. If we don't find it at Yacht Services, have people check every other dock and marina in town. Anywhere a small boat can tie up."

"This one of Whitby's boats?"

"Yeah."

"Okay, then we better also check the private dock at Whitby E&D."

"If you do find it, have Jacoby's people go the whole nine yards. Prints. Hair. Fibers. The works. Including blood. Either the victim's or someone else's."

"Someone else being the perp?"

"Like I said, if we're lucky. And if we're really, really lucky, maybe we'll even find the knife he stabbed her with."

McCabe went back to the porch. Tears were rolling down Tracy's cheeks.

"I'm sorry I have to put you through this."

"It's all right. I want to catch this guy even more than you do. Ask your questions."

"You called Julia and Aimée half twins," he said.

"That's what they are. Born three days apart, same father, different mothers. Me and a woman named Deirdre McClure. I was Edward's first wife. We'd been married about two years. Deirdre worked for him. Did PR work, which in those days consisted mostly of press releases. He hired her out of a security firm in D.C."

"How old?" asked McCabe.

"About my age." Tracy sucked at her cigarette. "Though I didn't know it at the time, Edward was screwing both of us. Deirdre just physically. Me in every way you can imagine. He got us both pregnant at pretty much the same time.

"I knew nothing about his goings-on till Deirdre showed up at the house one winter day in our mutual seventh month. The bell rings. I answer it, and there we are at the door, both out to here. Face-to-face and belly to belly.

"I'd met her once at the office, so I smiled and congratulated her on her pregnancy. Told her Edward wasn't home. She said she'd come to talk to me, so I invited her in. We went to the living room. I offered her coffee. She asked for tea. I called Brenda Boatwright, who was our housekeeper, and asked her to make a pot.

"Deirdre sits down and starts talking. She skips the prelims and goes right to the main event. Announces loudly enough so even Brenda could hear that she and Edward have been having an affair pretty much since she started at the company two years earlier and that the baby she was carrying was his. I wasn't surprised by the sex. Only that he'd let it result in a baby. I knew Edward had been fooling around almost from the day I married him. Business trips. Late nights at the office. For all I know, early mornings at the office as well. Remember the old song? 'When I'm not near the girl I love, I love the girl I'm near.' Of course you do. You remember every song ever written. Anyway, that was Edward to a T. Always ready, willing and able to *schtup* any female who was even modestly attractive and could actually walk, talk and spread her legs.

"So there we are. Deirdre sipping her tea ever so demurely on one of the Whitby family's eighteenth-century silk damask chairs. She tells me she loves Edward and wants to marry him.

"'Really?' I said, frankly a little surprised. 'And how does Edward feel about marrying you?'

"'The same. He loves me too.'

"'You're sure of that?' I ask.

"'I'm sure.'

"'Well, don't expect any money out of the deal. The Whitby attorneys will write a prenup that's tighter than . . . well, I don't want to get vulgar.'

"'I don't care about the prenup,' she said. 'It's Edward I love, and not his money.'

"'The attorneys will be relieved to hear that,' I said.

"'Edward wants us to get married just as soon as he can arrange a divorce. I would like the wedding to take place before our baby is born.'

"'And why is that?' I asked. 'So you can walk down the aisle in maternity white?'

"'No,' she said, placing the Royal Doulton teacup back on the silver tray. 'So our baby can be born in wedlock.'

"'Ah,' I replied, 'you'd rather my child be the illegitimate bastard and not yours?'

"'Edward won't renounce either of his children.'

" 'That's a comfort,' I told her. 'And just what, may I ask, is the purpose of this visit, Deirdre? I'm sure it's about more than just giving me fair notice of my impending dismissal as Mrs. Edward V. Whitby?'

" 'Yes, actually . . .' and the bitch actually had the gall to say this, 'I just wanted to get a look around the house. Give me enough time to order the fabrics and furnishings for the nursery so it's ready by the time my baby comes.'

"That's when I kicked her ass out the front door. Anyway, Aimée was born first, on April twenty-third. Julia three days later. Edward and I agreed on joint custody, with Edward paying a fair amount for childcare and all of Aimée's education. He's actually way too generous with her. Gives her anything she asks for. And a lot of things she doesn't. Edward loves all women, but I always get the feeling the one he loves most, in the true sense of the word *love,* is his beautiful eldest daughter."

"Tell me about Julia. What's she like?"

"She's pretty enough. Also a good student, I'm told. And a talented actress. I saw her in the senior play this year in the role of Blanche DuBois in *Streetcar,* and she was really very good. *I have always depended on the kindness of strangers.* But it's Aimée who's the gorgeous one. She inherited the Whitby looks. Much more like her father than me. Julia, on the other hand, looks like her mother."

"Was Aimée involved with any boyfriends at the moment?" McCabe asked.

"Give me a minute, would you?"

McCabe nodded and watched his old friend take a series of deep breaths while staring at her garden for what was more like two or three minutes.

"Okay, sorry," she finally said. "What was your question?"

"Did Aimée have any current boyfriends?"

Another deep breath. Another sigh. "Probably. But she didn't bring guys home. Or give me any names."

That was too bad. Knowing who her current boyfriend or boyfriends were could prove important. He studied her. A top-notch investigative reporter who'd just lost her only child. "Tracy, you've got to promise me one thing. I'll keep you as informed as I can, but please, please don't start trying to find the killer on your own. If something important occurs to you, just let me or Maggie know. Leave the investigating to us."

"McCabe, I won't get in your way. That's a promise. But here's another promise. If you don't find the creep who did this and put him away; if, after all your efforts, this remains an open investigation, all bets are off. I'm pretty damned good at this game. And I won't rest until I find him. And when I do, I may kill him myself."

Before McCabe could respond, his phone rang. Bill Fortier. McCabe went back in the house.

"I just got a call from Tommy Holmes," Fortier told him.

"Who?"

"Tommy Holmes. He's a detective on the South Portland PD. They just got a missing persons report. I suggest you follow up immediately."

"Who's missing?"

"Guy named Byron Knowles. Teacher at Penfield Academy. Teaches junior and senior English, so Aimée could've been one of his students. Knowles's wife called it in to SoPo about forty-five minutes ago. She said her husband went to Whitby's party last night. Took his own boat out there. Wife didn't go cause she's eight months pregnant, and just the thought of being on a boat makes her seasick. Anyway, he was supposed to be home by midnight . . ."

"And he never showed?"

"No. He texted her instead. At 2:21 in the morning."

"Saying what?"

"Quote: 'I can never forgive myself for the terrible things I have done. Please know that I have always loved you.' "

"Jesus. What's that supposed to be? A suicide note?"

"Either that or a farewell. Suicide would be a little weird, though. Guy goes to a party and then kills himself? Most suicides don't include merrymaking."

"You don't know your Bible," said McCabe.

"What?"

"Isaiah 22:13. 'And behold, joy and gladness, killing oxen and slaughtering sheep, eating flesh and drinking wine. Let us eat and drink, for tomorrow we die.' "

Chapter 29

MAGGIE WENT TO her car to wait for the call. It took seven minutes before she heard the first four notes of Beethoven's Fifth. *Da-da-da-dum.* Caller ID said Private Caller. "This is Detective Margaret Savage," she said. "Is this Mr. Whitby?"

"Yes. It is." Another irritated voice. "Now, Detective, please tell me what's so urgent that you're waking me at the crack of dawn."

"It's about your daughter, sir. Aimée."

"What about Aimée? Is she in some kind of trouble?"

"I'd rather speak to you about this in person."

"I'm sure you would. But that's not possible, since I'm on an island three miles out in the bay. If this is so urgent, why don't we just forget about the niceties and you tell me what's going on with Aimée? And please, try to make it quick."

Taken aback by his abrasiveness, Maggie paused for a moment, then thought to herself, *All right, Mr. Whitby, you want to forget about the niceties, we'll forget about the niceties.* "Your daughter is dead," she said.

"What?"

"She was murdered early this morning just off the Loring Trail in Portland. Possibly raped before she was stabbed to death."

"Dear God in heaven . . ."

There was a moment of silence before Whitby spoke. "Could you hold on a minute? I need to check on something."

"What?"

"Please, just hang on for a minute."

Maggie stayed on the line for what turned out to be more like three minutes.

Whitby returned. "And she's not at her mother's?" he asked.

"No, sir," said Maggie, certain McCabe would have let her know if a live Aimée had somehow turned up on Howard Street.

"I see. How sure are you that the person you found is Aimée?"

"One hundred percent," said Maggie. "When was the last time you saw your daughter?"

"Give me a minute to absorb all this, will you? I feel like I've just been sucker-punched."

So much for the man's aggressiveness. Perhaps he'd now appreciate *the niceties* a little more. "Of course," she said. "But the sooner we get the investigation underway, the better."

There was a brief silence on the other end.

"Mr. Whitby?"

She heard Whitby let out a long, slow breath on the other end. "I'm sorry," he said. "I was just thinking how beautiful Aimée looked at the party last night."

"What party?"

"We threw a large party on the island last night. To celebrate my two daughters' graduation from Penfield Academy. Aimée and her sister, Julia. Both just starting out in life." He paused, his voice choking up. "Now one of them's gone."

"And Aimée seemed okay last night?"

"Better than okay. She was positively glowing. I've never seen her looking so alive. Or so beautiful."

"About what time did you last see your daughter, Mr. Whitby?" Maggie asked.

"Let me think. It was probably around ten thirty. Most of our guests had already left. I was chatting to some old friends. Aimée had changed out of the gown she was wearing and into some cut-offs and a sweatshirt . . ." Whitby's voice quavered. He was finding it difficult to talk. He cleared his throat. Cleared it again. Finally continued. "She gave me a kiss and thanked me for being . . ." Another cough. "Shit. This is hard . . . the best daddy in the whole world."

Maggie was sure Whitby was weeping but was trying hard not to be heard.

"Said she was going off with some of the Penfield kids."

"Off where?"

"A bonfire near the cliff on the other side. An after-party for the graduates."

"How many people were on the island last night?"

"A lot. Between two and three hundred, including help."

"How many were left when you last saw Aimée?"

"God, I don't know. Maybe forty or fifty. Plus the caterers and other help."

"When did they leave?"

"Nearly everyone was gone by midnight except for a few of the kids and some other hangers-on. I don't know for sure, but I'd say that by 2:00 a.m., the island was empty except for my family and the couple that looks after the place for us."

"Mr. Jolley?"

"Yes. And his wife. Oh, and my director of security also spent the night."

"Name?"

"Charles Kraft."

"It would be helpful, Mr. Whitby, if you could put together a list of everybody who was on the island last night. Not just your guests but bartenders, caterers, musicians, whatever. Also if you could indicate those whom you know were still there when you saw Aimée for the last time. We'll also need contact numbers. Everyone who attended or worked at the party will have to be interviewed."

"Some pretty important people are on that list."

"We'll need to talk to everyone."

"Even Senator Colman? Or Governor Hardesty? Or Margaux Amory? Obviously none of them had anything to do with Aimée's death."

"I'm sure not. But it's impossible to know who, if anyone, may have seen something or someone that might turn out to be important to the case."

Whitby sighed. "Fine. My assistant can make up a list with contact numbers. I'll call her at home and have her get started. I'll try to figure out if there is anyone else still here and ask them to stay."

"Who catered?"

"A company called Great Expectations. They handle all our parties and events. Both corporate and personal. I guess I better come back to town so we can talk face-to-face."

"I'd rather you stayed on the island for the time being. My partner, Sergeant McCabe, and I will need to come out to the island to have a good look around. We'll also want to talk to you and your family and whoever else still there who might have seen Aimée last night. Oh, by the way, do you get cell service on the island?"

"Intermittent. On the side facing Portland, where the house is, it's quite good. On the backside by the cliff, practically nothing." Whitby paused and then asked, "Where is Aimée now? Her body, I mean?"

"In the morgue at Cumberland Medical Center. The medical examiner will be performing an autopsy this afternoon."

"Is that really necessary? It just hurts. The idea of someone cutting up my child."

"I'm afraid it is. In all cases of homicide, an autopsy is required by law. It can also be very helpful in identifying the perpetrator."

Maggie heard another deep sigh on the other end of the phone. "Have you told Aimée's mother yet?"

"Sergeant McCabe is with her now."

"Poor Tracy. This has got to be absolutely devastating for her."

"And for you as well."

"Yes. And for me. Let me know when you're coming."

"I will. Let me have the best number to reach you."

He gave it to her. Then added, "Call me before you come. I can have my helicopter waiting for you."

"No need. The Portland fireboat can bring us out."

"The chopper's faster. By the way, I suppose Tom Shockley knows about Aimée?"

"Yes, sir. He's assigned Sergeant McCabe and me to head up the investigation." That was only a small lie. "We're the department's senior homicide investigators. We'll be running things. And, of course, Chief Shockley will be fully involved in the investigation."

"Frankly, if I were you, I'd keep him as far away from this as you can. I suspect you know as well as I do, Shockley's an ass."

Maggie didn't say anything. And, of course, Whitby couldn't see her smiling.

When they'd broken the connection, she texted McCabe. *Whitby notified.*

Chapter 30

McCabe left Tracy's house and called Maggie from the car.

"Can you talk?"

"Yes. You've finished with Tracy?"

"All done. But something else has come up." He told her about Byron Knowles's disappearance. "We need to talk to the wife next. Be a good idea if we did it together. I want to drop the Bird off at my place. Maybe you could pick me up there."

As McCabe headed home, his mind focused on the text Byron Knowles sent his wife. *I can never forgive myself for the terrible things I have done.* Okay, so what was it Knowles had done? Given the timing, maybe Knowles got drunk enough at the party to lose control and rape one of his own students. When it was over, maybe she threatened to turn him in and he killed her to avoid punishment. Consumed with guilt, he then killed himself. That seemed possible.

On the other hand, maybe the sex had been consensual and ongoing. An affair between student and teacher, forbidden both by law and moral custom. Maybe Aimée wanted to break it off. Knowles didn't. They argued and Aimée threatened to go public. Not being able to face the scandal, Knowles killed her and then himself. All of it possible, but why in hell carve an A in Aimée's chest? As an English teacher, he certainly would have been familiar with Hawthorne's *Scarlet Letter*. Maybe even assigned it in one of his classes. In which case, the blood red A carved into Aimée's chest stood for Knowles's adultery and not her own.

Of course, he could be overthinking it. Possibly his first guess was the right one. That Knowles just got drunk at the party, made a pass at a beautiful girl, lost control and raped her. She threatened to turn him in. Tell her father. Knowles panicked and killed her. He had a boat. People keep knives on boats they use for fishing. Maybe he was giving her a ride back to Portland when it happened. But if so, why not just dump her body at sea? Why drag it to the East End and up the Loring Trail? Especially if she was still alive. Which Scott said she was. And again, why in God's name carve the letter A on her chest? It had to be meant as a message or a confession.

Of course there was one other possibility. That Knowles's disappearance had nothing to do with Aimée's death other than the coincidence of timing. Maybe he was just an unhappy husband who wanted to run away from a bad marriage. Or throw himself into the ocean and end it all.

He called Fortier back. "Bill," said McCabe, "can you get us Knowles's cell phone records as well as Aimée's? Every number called. Every text. Every voice mail. Every e-mail. We need to know if their relationship was more than just normal student and teacher."

"Cleary's already on it. Let you know when we get them."

He next texted Casey, who, at this hour, would still be asleep. *Out working. Brand-new homicide. Talk later.* He briefly considered changing his plan to use Sandy's uncanceled reservation at Fore Street for the celebratory dinner she was supposed to have had with her daughter. On the other hand he didn't want to disappoint Casey the way he'd so often disappointed Kyra.

Chapter 31

From the journal of Edward Whitby Jr.
Entry dated June 28, 1924

I have, for many years now, suffered a recurring dream, the images of which have lately tormented me night after night. In this dream, I see Aimée gazing out from within the glass of an old mirror. I can see no reflection of myself in this mirror. Or of the room in which I sit. It is as if I am looking through a window darkening with age. There is only Aimée on the other side. Behind her, the clutter of her island studio as it was in that fateful final year.

She stands before her easel, working on a canvas. It is turned toward her, so I cannot see the image she is working on. However, from time to time, she looks into the glass at herself, unaware both of my presence and the longing I feel for her, just feet away. Unaware, as well, of the tortured wreckage I have become. As she looks, she turns her head, first this way and then that, studying, I assume, the structure and color of her own face. Then she turns back to the canvas and works the colors into it. I think this must be a self-portrait she is working on. She painted many of these in the years we were together. I have kept them, and they are precious to me.

She looks pleased with her work. As she examines it, she smiles the same smile I remember so clearly from our first day at the Académie in Paris. The face and smile I fell so hopelessly in love with. I yearn to again hold her. To take her into my arms. To press my lips against hers. To make love as ardently as we did back then, when we were both too young and eager and, in the way of youth, too selfish to understand where love might lead.

I reach out, wanting to touch her face, but my hand is stopped by hard glass. I press harder. Still I cannot penetrate this brittle barrier. I knock, as if knocking on a doorway to the dead will convince Aimée to open it and allow me to join her on the other side. She appears not to hear my knocks, so I knock louder. Still the door will not open. She will not let me in.

An uncontrollable rage builds within me. I get up and lift the chair I am sitting on. I swing it with all my might. The glass explodes. Knifelike shards fly toward her. They strike her face and body. She erupts in blood from a thousand cuts. She stares at me with a horror which, in my life, I have never seen on another human face.

I fly through the open space where the glass once was. I reach out, wanting to comfort her. To heal her wounds. She turns and flees. Runs toward the cliff. I follow, desperately calling her name, trying to stop her before she gets to the edge.

I am too late. I peer over the edge and see her naked body falling. Arms flailing, face looking up into mine. She falls for what seems an eternity, reaching up for me to save her as she goes. I try, but cannot. I tell myself to follow her over the cliff. But I don't. I simply watch as she falls faster and faster and finally lands on the rocks below, breaking into a thousand pieces like a glass figurine, its delicate and now broken parts strewn across the bottom of the cliff. As I look down, I scream in anguish at the sight of her lying there, and it is my screams that, night after night, wake me from this ghastly nightmare.

Chapter 32

MAGGIE HANDED MCCABE a large Styrofoam cup of coffee and a paper bag. "Here. Stopped for these up on the way over. Figured you hadn't had a good nutritious breakfast yet."

She pulled the unmarked Interceptor out onto the Eastern Prom and turned right toward the Old Port.

He peered inside. Two chocolate-covered donuts. "Both for me?"

"Both for you. I gobbled mine on the way over."

He bit into one, licked chocolate off his finger and washed it down with a generous slug of the coffee.

"Do you suppose," he asked, "that we became cops because we like donuts? Or that we like donuts because we became cops?"

They crossed Franklin and continued west on Fore Street, still quiet at six thirty on a Friday morning.

McCabe finished his first donut and pulled the second from the bag.

"I think," said Maggie, bearing left onto York Street and heading for the Casco Bay Bridge, "that we like donuts because, as responsible, health-conscious adults, we are both aware that a good, nutritious breakfast is the most important meal of the day."

"Exactly what my mother used to say when she poured me my Sugar Pops."

"A wise woman. How's she doing?" Maggie stayed in the middle lane as she crossed the bridge that spanned the Fore River and separated Portland from South Portland, or SoPo, as it was called. She turned right onto Cottage Road, then left onto Ellesmere.

"Not so great. According to my brother Bobby, she's getting more and more forgetful all the time. He thinks it's Alzheimer's."

"Sorry to hear that," said Maggie. She navigated a series of lefts and rights that led to Willard Haven Place, where Byron Knowles and his wife, Gina, lived. "Changing the subject, how convinced are you that Knowles killed Aimée?"

" 'I can never forgive myself for the terrible things I have done'? I suppose that could refer to a lot of things, but given the coincidence of timing, it sure seems likely that what he can't forgive himself for is killing her."

"Jesus, her English teacher. If you can't trust your English teacher, who can you trust?"

"Yeah. It makes me happier than you can imagine that Casey's English teacher is a fifty-five-year-old overweight female."

They pulled up in front of a small, light green Cape Cod on Willard Haven Place in the Willard Beach section of the city. Another unmarked police car was parked on the opposite side of the street. A big man with a dark black mustache exited the vehicle. Maggie and McCabe crossed over to meet him.

"Detective Holmes?" asked McCabe.

"Yup, Tommy Holmes."

"Anybody ever call you Sherlock?"

"Only folks who don't mind getting their asses kicked." Since Holmes stood a good six foot three and probably weighed 220, most of it muscle, there was no question he could have kicked most asses without breaking a sweat. Including McCabe's.

"I'll keep that in mind," said McCabe with a smile. "Anyway, I'm Detective Sergeant Mike McCabe. This is my partner, Detective Maggie Savage."

They all shook hands. "You talked to the wife yet?" asked Maggie.

"Yeah. One of our patrol guys answered the missing persons call. When she showed him the text, he alerted me."

"You checked the source of the text?"

"Yeah. It definitely came from Knowles's cell phone. He sent it at 2:21 a.m. Phone's been offline ever since. Pops right to message. I asked her where Knowles was last night. Apparently he teaches English at Penfield and went to a school graduation party out on Whitby Island. Went in his own boat."

"What kind of boat?"

"An old nineteen-foot Midland he fixed up himself. Mostly uses it for fishing. He was supposed to be back by midnight. Never showed. He keeps the boat at the Sunset Marina off Front Street. We checked, and it wasn't there. But his car was still in the lot. A maroon '02 Camry."

"Anything of interest in the car?"

"Nah. Just some empty coffee cups and a kid's toy."

"Did you look in the trunk?"

"Yeah. Just in case he'd been murdered and stuffed in there. But there was nothing there. It's possible he had some kind of problem with the boat on the way home. Engine conking out or whatever. But given the contents of the message, I've got a feeling he took a dive. Coast Guard Search and Rescue are looking for both the boat and for Knowles if he's in the water. When I heard you guys had a brand-new homicide, a female teenager, and since Knowles taught teenagers, seemed like there might be a connection. I don't know. Like maybe he killed your vic and then himself. Or maybe he's using the boat to make a getaway."

"Definitely a connection. Our victim was in Knowles's class and was at the same party with him."

"Well, there you go then. Anyway, the Coasties are patrolling the area looking for him and/or the boat."

"What's the boat's registration number?" asked McCabe.

Holmes took out his notepad. "Want me to write it out for you?"

"Not necessary. Just read it out loud. I'll remember it."

"You got a photographic memory or something?"

"Or something."

Holmes shrugged and read off the six-digit registration number.

"I've also got somebody watching the car in case Knowles turns up. Also to make sure nobody else touches it till it can be checked for possible evidence."

"Mag, would you see if Jacoby's got anybody left who can go over the car?"

"If it helps, I could have our people do it," said Holmes. "We'll send over whatever we find."

"That'd be a big help. Thanks. We're stretched thin at the moment."

Holmes nodded and made the call. After he'd arranged for South Portland evidence techs to check out the Camry he hung up and asked McCabe, "Can you tell me the name of the victim yet?"

Since it'd be all over the media in just a couple of hours, there was no point in holding back. "She was Edward Whitby's daughter. Veronica Aimée Whitby."

"Whitby?" Holmes made a whistling sound. "That ought to make things interesting."

"Yep. She took senior English from the missing Mr. Knowles. You get anything more from Mrs. Knowles?"

"Not really. I didn't want to get into her relationship with her husband. Figured I'd leave that to you. By the way, you do know she's gonna have a baby any minute?"

"We heard. Thanks for your help."

"No problem. Let me know if you need anything else."

Just as Holmes was getting in his car, McCabe called out, "Give my regards to Dr. Watson." Holmes smiled and extended the third finger of his left hand.

Chapter 33

AS THEY WENT up the walk, McCabe suggested that Maggie do most of the talking. She was good at it, and he preferred watching for visual reaction. McCabe knocked. A very pregnant but otherwise slender-looking blonde in her midthirties opened the door. A little girl about four peered curiously out from behind her mother's trousers.

"Mrs. Knowles?" asked Maggie.

"Yes. Gina."

"I'm Detective Margaret Savage. Portland PD. This is Detective Sergeant Michael McCabe. May we come in?"

She eyed them suspiciously through large black-framed glasses. "Why Portland? I already talked to two people from the South Portland Police."

"Detective Holmes called us because we're investigating another case that might shed some light on your husband's whereabouts. May we come in?"

The door opened wider, and they walked into a small, neatly

furnished living room. Maggie looked down and smiled at the little girl. "What's your name?"

In response, the child shoved two fingers into her mouth and buried her face in her mother's leg.

"Her name is Patti."

"Hi, Patti."

Patti peeked out and smiled shyly.

"Would you two like some coffee or anything while we talk? I'm drinking some."

"No, thank you. Where's the best place to sit?"

"Over there." She pointed Maggie and McCabe to a table on the other side of a Formica counter that separated a dining area from the open-plan kitchen. "But let me get her set up first. "Hey pumpkin, c'mon, let's watch *Curious George,* okay?"

Ms. Knowles pushed a DVD into a player and sat her daughter down in front of the TV with a pair of earphones that had cartoon tigers covering each ear. When the program started, she joined them in the dining area. Maggie sat at the head of the table. Gina Knowles took the side chair, which gave her the best view of her daughter. McCabe distanced himself at the other end.

"She won't be able to hear anything but the TV with those earmuffs on."

A Toshiba laptop sat open in front of her, a smartphone next to it. Maggie placed her digital recorder next to the phone and told Gina she was going to record the conversation.

"Okay."

"Gina, you sound like you're originally from Boston?"

"Born and raised. Been in Maine for eleven years now, but the accent sticks with you."

"Are you a full-time mom?"

"Don't I wish? But no way can we afford to live on one salary. Especially when one of them's a teaching salary from a private school. I work as a lab technician for Intex." The company, one of the largest in the area, made veterinary pharmaceuticals. "My mom takes care of Patti while I'm at work. She'll also help with the new baby when it comes."

"She live nearby?"

"A few blocks away. She and my dad came up from Boston after he retired. Wanted to be closer to their granddaughter. Anyway, I'll be taking four weeks maternity leave when the baby comes, but after that it'll be back to the grindstone."

"Please tell us about your husband's disappearance."

"Yes. That's why you're here, isn't it? All I know is that I'm worried sick. What I told the people who were here before is that his name is Byron Knowles. He teaches at Penfield Academy in Portland. Here . . ." She slid some copy paper across the table. " . . . I printed out a bunch of pictures. Maybe these will help you find him."

Maggie picked them up. Studied the slender, handsome face for a few seconds, then slid them down to McCabe. "Good-looking guy," she said.

"Yeah," said Gina. "Sometimes I think too good looking."

"Why do you say that? Do women make a play for him?"

At least thirty seconds passed before Gina Knowles spoke. "Some do."

"You were telling us about what your husband does," said McCabe.

"Byron teaches eleventh- and twelfth-grade English. Been at Penfield eleven years. The job offer from Penfield was why we moved to Portland. Graduation was yesterday morning. Byron went. I didn't."

"Why not?"

"Faculty spouses aren't invited. Seating's limited. Besides, I had to work."

"Did you see your husband at all after the graduation?" asked Maggie.

"Yes, he got back around one o'clock and was still here when I got home from work at four fifteen. We're converting his home office into a nursery for the new baby, and he spent part of the afternoon painting it. He took a shower and got dressed for a graduation party out on Whitby Island. Left about five. Took our boat out to the island. Two of the Whitby girls, twins I think, were both students of Byron's, and all the Upper School faculty was invited."

She delivered this information in a flat voice, as empty of emotion as if she'd been reading out a shopping list. McCabe wondered if she was working hard at keeping her emotions bottled up. Or maybe she just didn't give a damn where her husband might be.

"When Byron left for the party, what was he wearing?"

"What he always wears for school events. Blue blazer. Striped or checked button-down shirt. I don't remember which. Red tie. Loafers."

"Wouldn't he have gotten kinda wet in a small boat dressed like that?"

"He keeps waterproofs in the boat. Bright yellow coveralls. They fit right over his clothes."

The yellow ought to make it easier for the Coasties to spot Knowles if he was still floating around somewhere. Or trying to escape by sea.

"Generally wear a life jacket?"

"Always."

Unless, thought McCabe, he was planning to kill himself.

"Spouses not invited to the party either?" asked Maggie.

"I was invited. But I wasn't about to go cruising out to Whitby Island in this condition." She placed a hand on her pregnant tummy. "I probably would have thrown up before we got out of the harbor. Didn't really want to go anyway. I can't stand all that preppy party chatter. The Penfield crowd thinks they're all so high and mighty. Particularly the Whitbys. The invitation from them made me feel like one of the serfs being summoned to the manor house. Yes, m'lord. No, m'lord. And since I can't even drink in this condition, I declined."

"But Byron went?"

"Yes. Said it was part of his job to be there. Headmaster expected it. Students expected it. I asked him if he could just put in an appearance and maybe be home by nine or ten, but he didn't want to do that. We compromised on midnight."

"But you weren't happy about that."

"No, I wasn't happy."

"Did you wait up for him?"

"No. I went to bed around eleven. I couldn't wait up any longer."

"When did you notice he hadn't come home?"

"Three fifteen. I woke up to go to the bathroom. There's a digital clock right next to the bed."

"You didn't call the police till after five. Why didn't you call at three fifteen?"

Gina Knowles took a deep breath. "Sometimes Byron doesn't come home when he's supposed to."

"I see. What about the text message?" Maggie picked up the phone on the table. "That came in at 2:21."

"I keep the phone on silent when I sleep. And I didn't look at it when I woke up."

"Why not?"

"I just didn't."

"Your husband was over three hours late coming home from a party across open water in a small boat in the dark. Didn't that worry you enough to at least check if he'd sent any kind of message?"

"No."

Maggie waited for some kind of explanation. There was none. "Why not?"

"I already told you. Sometimes Byron doesn't come home when he's supposed to. Or he calls and says he's working and he'll be home late. Eight. Nine. Sometimes even midnight."

Maggie frowned. "Working? Does he have a second job?"

"The romantic poets are his specialty. He's supposedly writing a biography of Lord Byron. He used to work at home but he says there are too many distractions here, so now he works at the university library at USM. During the week it's open till 11:00 p.m."

"Does he do that frequently?"

"Frequently enough. At least for the past year or so. Before that hardly ever."

"Why do you think that is?"

"Well, if you really want to know the truth, I don't think he's doing anything at the USM library. And I don't think he's been working on his book. If he is, he certainly doesn't seem to have made much progress on it."

"Do you think he's having an affair?"

Gina Knowles glanced over at her daughter, who was still immersed in *Curious George*. "That's right, Detective. I think my husband is having an affair. In fact, I don't think it. I know it."

"How do you know it?"

"I just know it. A wife knows things like that. So when I woke up at three fifteen and saw he wasn't here, I didn't get worried. I got angry. So angry I couldn't go back to sleep. I just lay in the bed picturing him out on Whitby Island, or maybe back here with whoever the hell he's having sex with these days."

"Did you ever discuss divorce?"

"He brought it up a couple of times. I told him I wasn't interested. We were married in the Catholic Church, and I firmly believe when you make vows before God, you keep them. No matter what. Till death do you part."

"Is Byron Catholic?"

"He used to be."

"But not anymore?"

"No, he hardly ever goes to church except at Christmas, and then only because he likes the music."

"But you go regularly?"

"Yes. Every Sunday. To Holy Cross over on Cottage Road."

"What did he say when you told him you wouldn't agree to a divorce?"

"He got angry. Yelled at me. Told me our marriage was a sham."

"When was that?" asked McCabe.

"When I first realized I was pregnant. Back in early November. I thought he'd be overjoyed. Like I was. Like he'd been when we had Patti. But all he said was 'Oh,' as if he was disappointed. Then, 'Are you sure?' like another child was the last thing he wanted even though we'd talked about it a million times. It was like he was wondering if I might be willing to end the pregnancy."

"Did he ask you to have an abortion?"

"No. But I could tell that's what he was thinking."

"Did that make you angry?"

"Of course it made me angry. He knows how I feel about abortion. A new life is a gift from God. You don't destroy it."

"Did you fight about it? Lose your temper?"

"Yes. Well, at least I did. But it's hard to fight with Byron. Whenever I get angry or shout at him, he just retreats into a shell and doesn't say anything. Doesn't even try to defend himself. When he doesn't want to talk about something, he can be so damn passive, it makes me crazy."

"Any idea who the other woman, or women, might be?"

Gina looked first at Maggie and then at McCabe. He got the sense that she was debating her answer to the question.

"I don't know," she said after a minute. "I do think it's just one woman. Byron was never like this before this year. This not showing up when he was supposed to and then offering some flimsy excuse. I think it's probably one of the young female teachers at Penfield. There are a lot of single women on the faculty, some quite attractive, and I can't think where else he'd have an opportunity to meet someone. He doesn't hang out at bars. And I don't think he'd have the nerve to start prowling around online. He's just not aggressive enough for that. Byron's a hopeless romantic, but at the same time, like I told you, he can be passive. When we met, I was the one who had to ask him out first. I expect it's the same thing with whoever he's been seeing lately. She came on to him and he didn't have the strength or integrity to say no. Like you said, Byron's a good-looking guy."

"Did you ever ask him or accuse him directly of having an affair?"

"Sort of. Once. I went through his wallet and found a credit card receipt for dinner at an expensive restaurant. The Chart House in Cape Neddick. $208.26. April twenty-third."

McCabe's mind clicked back to his conversation with Tracy. April twenty-third. Aimée's birthday. The evidence was beginning to squeeze a little tighter around Mr. Knowles's neck.

"I asked him who he was having dinner with. He said it was with his old roommate from Bowdoin. Guy named Barry Meyers."

"How do you know he wasn't?"

"I just know it. Byron's fallen for some woman. Probably some little cutie in the English Department."

"Do you have a contact number for this guy Meyers?" asked McCabe.

"No. He's Byron's friend, not mine. But you shouldn't have any trouble finding him. He's a very successful screenwriter. Nominated for a Golden Globe last year. Lives in L.A."

"So what time was it you first saw the text?"

"About five fifteen. Since I couldn't sleep, I finally decided the heck with it and got up to do some work. I made some coffee. Brought my laptop and phone down here, and the first thing I did was check for messages. And there it was. 'I can never forgive myself for the terrible things I have done. Please know that I have always loved you.' My first thought was maybe his girlfriend dumped him and he was trying to make it up with me. Or maybe, with the baby coming, he was starting to feel guilty about the whole thing and managed to work up the courage to dump her. My second thought, since he still wasn't home, was that it sounded like a suicide note. Detective Holmes agreed. He notified the Coast Guard. They sent a helicopter to look for Byron's boat."

"There's a third possibility," said Maggie.

"What?"

"If Byron decided to run away, disappear, to hide out for a while, where do you think he'd go?"

"Why do you think Byron might have run away?"

Maggie didn't answer Gina's question. "Where do you think he'd go?"

"Lord, I don't know. He doesn't have any money. Just our bank debit card. There's less than a thousand dollars in the account, and one other Visa card that's pretty near maxed out. His parents are both dead. He has a brother, Paul, who lives just outside of Asheville, North Carolina."

The western mountains of North Carolina were not easily accessible by boat. Neither was Los Angeles. At least not from Maine. McCabe figured that if Knowles was running, he'd probably ditched the boat down the coast somewhere and gotten himself some wheels. Maybe Barry Meyers had wired him some money.

"What about his buddy Meyers?" asked Maggie, as if she had read McCabe's mind. "Would Byron have gone to him for financial help?"

"Barry's got plenty of money, but he's way the hell out in L.A."

"Can you give us contact numbers for brother Paul? Also numbers for the credit cards?"

Gina provided the numbers and Maggie wrote them down.

Maggie studied Gina Knowles for a few seconds before pointing at the computer on the table. "Is that your laptop or his?"

"This one's mine. Byron's got his own. A new MacBook Pro, which we frankly couldn't afford. Byron said Penfield was going to pay for it, but I'm not sure that's true. They've never done anything like that before."

"Is his computer here in the house?"

"No. I don't know where it is. Probably in his car. Or in his office at school."

Tommy Holmes had told them they hadn't found anything of interest in the car.

"Is it password protected?"

"Yes."

"Do you know the password?"

"Not for sure. But Byron uses the same password for everything. GGB1788. Stands for George Gordon Byron, AKA Lord Byron. 1788's the year Byron was born. You didn't answer me when I asked you why you think Byron might have run away."

Maggie figured it was time to shake Gina up. "We don't know if he has, but one of the Whitby girls, Veronica Aimée Whitby, was murdered early this morning in Portland."

Gina stared at Maggie with a look of disbelief. She seemed literally speechless.

"Given the timing, I'm afraid we have to consider the possibility that your husband was involved."

"Are you saying you think Byron murdered one of his students and then ran away? Or maybe killed himself?"

"We're saying it's possible," said Maggie. "More importantly, I'd like to know what you think."

Gina Knowles shook her head. Tears formed in her eyes. "I don't know what to think." She shook her head again. "He could be crazily impulsive. But murder? Maybe I just didn't know the man as well as I thought I did."

McCabe's cell vibrated. Bill Fortier. He got up and went outside before answering. "What's up, Bill?"

"You still with Knowles's wife?"

"Yeah. We're here."

"Well, I'm afraid I've got another next of kin for you. Knowles's body just washed up in Dyer Cove. Right near Two Lights in Cape

Elizabeth. Looks like he went for a swim still dressed in his party clothes."

"Suicide?"

"Sure looks like it. I suppose he might've lost his balance and fallen from the boat, but based on the contents of the text message, I'd say he jumped."

"He wasn't wearing yellow waterproofs?"

"No."

"How about a life jacket?"

"Nope. Just a wool blazer and pants and shoes. Like I said, his party clothes."

"Where's the body now?"

"On its way to Cumberland Med. Looks like Terri will be doing a twofer."

"Would you ask her to put a rush on Knowles's DNA analysis? We'll need to match it up with any semen she finds in Aimée Whitby."

"Already asked."

"What about the boat?"

"No sign of it. Probably left the engine running when he jumped. Coast Guard's still looking. Probably just going around in circles, but who knows? Maybe it'll end up in Spain."

Chapter 34

AT 6:30 THAT morning Lucy McCorkle found herself at the back end of Washington Avenue. She'd been pushing the heavy shopping cart up and down the streets of the Munjoy Hill neighborhood for more than three hours now. Though more tired than she could ever remember feeling in her life, she was afraid to stop moving. Afraid that if she allowed herself to rest for even a couple of minutes, the man would find her. And kill her. Just like he killed the girl. Once or twice Lucy found herself wondering about that white jacket he wore. Wondering if maybe the guy was a waiter. Or a pharmacist. Or a dentist. She wondered how many dentists went around killing people. It seemed crazy. It made her think that maybe none of what she'd seen had actually happened and that she was getting as nutty as some of those guys who hung out at the dump. She knew booze could do that to you, and she sure as hell drank a lot of booze.

No, she told herself, it wasn't the booze. It really *had* happened, and the proof of it was right in her pocket. One hundred and seventy-one dollars in cold hard cash. All she had to do was stick her hand in, feel the money and know everything she'd seen was real. Just as real as the handle of the cart she was pushing. Just as real as the constant pain in her legs.

Every once in a while Lucy couldn't resist putting her hand in her pocket again just because she liked the feel of it. One hundred and seventy-one dollars minus the four bucks and change she'd spent on the pint of vodka. It was more money than she'd had at any one time in the three years since she got fired from her job as a greeter at the Walmart store in Falmouth. She was fired for telling the asshole shift supervisor that he was an asshole. Hell, everybody who worked in the store knew he was an asshole, but she was the only one who had the guts to tell him so to his face, so she was the only one who got kicked out. When he said those words, "You're outta here," she took off her little blue vest and threw the stupid thing right in his face. One of the best moments of her life. Made her chuckle even now. Even though she hadn't been able to find a job since then. She earned what money she could wandering the streets the night before trash pickup and taking as many cans and bottles out of the recycling bins as she could, then cashing them in for the deposit money. That was pretty much her only source of income these days, and the competition to get to the bins first was getting fierce. That's what made the one hundred and seventy-one dollars in her pocket so special.

Lucy leaned forward into the cart as she pushed. Damned thing was always heavy, seeing as how it contained every single piece of crap Lucy owned. But right now the crap felt heavier than ever. Her whole body was aching from pushing, and she knew she had to rest or she'd just fall down in the street and the cops would come and haul her away and she didn't want anything to do with the cops. Especially with all that money and the girl's wallet still in her pocket. Hell, they'd just take it and maybe even accuse her of being the killer. Which was stupid, because if she ever did kill someone like the dentist killed that girl, she wouldn't bother pulling off her clothes and fucking her victim before she did it. Lucy just couldn't get the image out of her head of the guy pulling down his pants, pulling a rubber onto his big hard boner, kneeling down and sticking it into her. After he fucked her, he pulled his pants back up, then stabbed her and started dragging her body into the woods.

That's when he noticed Lucy peering out from the nest of old clothes and blankets she slept in most nights. He pulled the girl's body under some brambles and looked straight at Lucy, still holding the knife he'd killed the girl with. Lucy was sure he was going to kill her too. Though if he was gonna kill her, she was pretty sure he wouldn't try to fuck her first. At least she didn't think he would. Course you never knew with some guys. While he stood there looking at her, Lucy tried to figure out which way she could run. But there wasn't anywhere. Not up the hill. Not down. Not anywhere. No way she could run on her fucked-up legs anyway. The guy started walking toward her. Real easy like. Like this was something he'd done plenty of times before. Lucy would sure as hell be dead now if that dog hadn't come racing toward them barking its fool head off. And that guy down on the trail shouting at the top of his lungs, "Ruthie, come. Ruthie come. Goddamn it, Ruthie, you eat that squirrel and you're dead meat."

All the commotion made the dentist stop dead in his tracks. He saw the dog rushing up the hill and the guy with the light on his head coming this way and he just heaved the girl's clothes into the woods and turned and ran like stink past the dog and down the hill toward the water. Lucy wouldn't have bothered checking any of the girl's stuff except for the fact that her shorts had landed plop on Lucy's head, which momentarily cut off whatever view she had. When she took the shorts off her head, the dentist was gone and the dog was sniffing and licking the girl's body. Lucy was about to toss the shorts into the pile with the other clothes when she felt something hard in one of the pockets. She stuck her hand in and, bingo, there it was. One cell phone. One thin leather wallet and one hundred and seventy-one dollars in cash. Plus about a dollar twenty-five in loose change. Sometimes God smiles, Lucy thought to herself. Sometimes he surely does. She tossed the cell phone, stuck the wallet and money in her pocket, and got the hell out of there, pushing her cart as fast as she could down the trail toward East End Beach. When she passed the guy with the light on his head, she just kept going.

Lucy stopped pushing for a minute, looked up and saw she was just across the street from The Sahara Club. Sahara as in the desert. As in dry. The place had pictures of sand dunes and a big camel painted on the front wall and was a social club for local alkies who'd stopped drinking to get together and talk about not drinking. This time of the morning it was empty. Seemed as good a place as any for an alkie who had no intention of stopping drinking till she was dead and gone to plop down on her ass and take a rest. And maybe, just for the hell of it, she'd take a swig of her vodka and raise a toast to those that saved her life, one big barking dog and one guy with a light on his head.

She pushed the cart across the club's parking lot and around toward the back, where she wouldn't be so easily spotted. She dug around in one of her black garbage bags and pulled out the pint of Five O'Clock Vodka she'd bought at the mini-mart store with four bucks of the girl's money. It was cheap shit that tasted like rubbing alcohol. With all that money in her pocket she'd been tempted to go for something better, like Smirnoff or Absolut, but she didn't want Roger behind the counter to start wondering where Crazy Lucy, which she knew is what he called her, had gotten that kind of money.

Pressing her back against the side of the building, Lucy let herself slide slowly down until she was sitting. She stretched out her aching legs, rubbed them for a little while. Then she unscrewed the bottle, tipped it back in her mouth and took a long slug. Took a couple of deep breaths and then another long slug. Lucy closed her eyes and waited for the rotgut to kick in and ease her tension a little. She wished Kaz was here so he could rub the knots out of her neck and shoulders like he used to do when he wasn't pissed off. But Kaz was dead, so there'd be no more back rubs. On the plus side, there'd be no more getting the shit kicked out of her either when Kaz was pissed off about something or other, which he usually was.

Lucy knew she ought to tell somebody about the dentist fucking and then stabbing the girl, but who the fuck was she gonna tell? She took another swallow and let the problem percolate around her mind for a couple of minutes. Maybe she could tell that female cop who lived over on Vesper Street. She seemed pretty nice. Even helped her out every now and then with a couple of bucks. But the more she thought about it, the more she figured, nice or not, the cops weren't an option. First off, they wouldn't believe somebody like her. Just a dirty old ex-hippie drunk living rough in the woods on the side of the hill. Second off, she didn't get all that good a look at the guy's face. Good enough so she thought maybe she'd remember him if she ever saw him again or maybe even pick him out of a police lineup, but maybe not good enough to give the cops an accurate description. Third off, there was the problem of the money. She probably shouldn't have taken it, but how often do you have one hundred and seventy-one dollars literally land on your head?

She took another swig of the booze. She wished again Kaz was here. He would've known what to do. She couldn't remember exactly how long Kaz had been dead, her memory wasn't so good anymore, but it seemed like a long time now. Two years. Maybe three. It was a couple of months after she lost her job that Kaz died and then she was kicked out of the shithole apartment they shared and she'd ended up homeless. She'd probably be joining old Kaz soon if next winter turned out to be as bad as the last one. The cold would kill her if the booze didn't do the job first. And, truth be told, she'd just as soon die as let the do-gooders push her back into the fucking women's shelter, where they were always on her case about getting her life back together. She didn't *want* to get her fucking life back together. She just wanted to be able to afford decent booze till she passed.

Lucy found herself wondering if God let the souls of homeless drunks into heaven. Ought to. She'd already had her share of hell right here on earth. If He was gonna be fair about it, wasn't it time for her to have a little taste of heaven? Anyway, if He did let her in, it'd be good to see ol' Kaz again, assuming he was there too. Been lonely without him. Hadn't had his body lying next to her to help keep her warm since he died. She tried to figure out what he'd say if he was sitting next to her right now. She was pretty damned sure it'd be *Hold on to the goddamned money, Luce, and don't tell the cops or anyone else a goddamned thing about what you saw. You don't need the trouble.*

Still, it didn't seem right. The dentist guy was a murderer. A real nasty-looking murderer. First time she saw him, he was coming up the hill from the water, pushing the girl in front of him. Then the girl broke away and tried to make a run for it. Didn't get far though. The dentist grabbed her and pulled her down. She musta hit her head on a rock or something, cause she started bleeding like crazy. He dragged her along the trail, blood dripping from her head, and set her down on the path. Then he pulled her clothes off, pulled on the rubber and fucked her. Then he stabbed her. Lucy watched the whole thing from where she lay all wrapped up in her nest of ratty old clothes and blankets. Afterwards she could hear him dragging the girl into the woods. That's when he heard Lucy scuttling around.

Lucy pulled the girl's wallet out of her pocket. She hadn't taken a real good look at it yet. She opened it. Stared at the photo on a driver's license. Veronica Aimée Whitby. She also found an American Express Platinum Card and a TD Bank debit card with the same name.

Lucy took another slug of the vodka. She was feeling much better now, but she still didn't feel like moving. She could hear Kaz's raspy old voice saying, *That money was manna from heaven, Lucy. Manna from heaven. Reason it landed on your head was cause God wanted you to have it. If you tell the cops, they'll just take the damned money and spend it on themselves. Toss you in jail for killing the girl.*

"But Kaz," she said, as if he was sitting right next to her like he used to, "it doesn't feel right taking money from a murdered girl."

"Shit, lady," said Kaz. "Use your damned head. A, she's dead and that ain't gonna change, and B, that kind of money'll buy you more hooch'n you had in years. Decent meal or two as well."

Kaz was right of course. Without thinking, Lucy passed the

bottle over to where she supposed Kaz's ghost must be sitting. But he didn't take it. Never knew Kaz to turn down a drink before. Maybe it was because they didn't let you drink when you were dead. You were nothing but . . . what'd they call it? Ectoplasm? Booze flowed right through your non-body and just went to waste. Since she herself wasn't dead yet, she raised the bottle and drank to Kaz's health, such as it was.

"What about the credit cards?" she asked him, but this time he didn't answer.

Lucy supposed she should just toss the wallet in the next Dumpster she saw and be done with it. But those credit cards kept nagging at her. She was trying to think if there was any way she could use them. She pictured herself handing some bozo behind a counter an American Express Platinum Card and saying in her most refined voice, *You do take American Express, don't you?* The idea actually made her cough out a throaty laugh or two. First time she'd laughed all morning. No, trying to use the credit card was way beyond stupid. If Kaz was around, he'd beat the shit out of her just for thinking anything that stupid. God knows he beat her up often enough when he was alive for stuff that was a whole lot less stupid.

On the other hand, Lucy thought to herself, there was that debit card. Now, that was another story. If she could figure out the password, maybe she could get even more money. She opened the wallet and looked again at the girl's license. Veronica Aimée Whitby. Born 4/23/94. Poor kid was only eighteen years old. Lucy wondered if she was any relation to *those* Whitbys. If she was, it'd sure as hell be worth a try. Kaz said lots of people use their birthdays backwards as passwords. In Veronica's case that'd be 4932 or maybe 9324. She looked through the rest of the stuff in the wallet but couldn't find anything that looked like it might be a clue to the password. Lucy decided that if one of those two worked, great. If not, fuck it. She'd toss the thing. Nothing ventured, nothing gained. She got up, tucked the now mostly empty bottle back into the black bag and started trudging down Washington toward the mini-mart store where she'd bought the vodka. They had an ATM there. Way in the back where nobody would see what she was doing.

Chapter 35

MAGGIE AND MCCABE were sitting in Bill Fortier's office debriefing him on their next-of-kin notifications and their interview with Gina Knowles when Detective Brian Cleary stuck his head in. "Phone records just came in."

"And?" asked McCabe.

"No question something hot and heavy was going on between them. Something illegal as well. Tom's got the records for both phones laid out in the conference room."

They went down the hall and joined Cleary's partner, Tom Tasco. Once there, they all leaned over the long table and pored over the documents.

"Finding her phone was a gift," said Tasco. "Seems she deleted practically nothing. The phone tells us as much about what was going on between them as we need to know."

"There were hundreds of calls, texts and voice mails between the two. Sometimes as many as twenty round-trip texts in one day," Cleary added.

"Starting when?" asked Maggie.

"The first ones date from November just before the Thanksgiving holidays. Initially nothing more than flirty. Stuff like her asking, 'Did you like the poem I sent you? Wrote it specially for you.' And him responding, 'Stop by my office and we can talk about it.' Course we don't know what went on in the office. Bill Bacon checked with the Penfield headmaster. As department head, Knowles rated a private office with a door."

"Lockable?" asked McCabe.

"Yes," said Tasco. "But teachers aren't supposed to even close their doors, let alone lock them, when they have a student in the office. Closed doors leave the teacher vulnerable to charges of sexual harassment."

"Man," said McCabe, "times sure have changed since my days at St. Barnabas."

"The texting back and forth picked up steam in December. She apparently bought him a Christmas present. First edition of something called *Childe Harold's Pilgrimage* by a poet named Lord Byron. Must have been expensive, cause he wrote her a big thank-you note. Asked . . ." Tasco checked his notes. " . . . 'Where on earth did you find this? It must have cost you a fortune.' By the middle of January they were texting back and forth pretty much every day, and it was obvious they were doing more than just texting. Voice mail content, specially the ones from her to him, was getting pretty steamy. Not quite *Fifty Shades of Grey* but some pretty damned close. She also sent him a couple of nude selfies. I don't know about Knowles, but if a hot-looking kid like Aimée Whitby sent me some of the stuff she sent him, I think I'd turn fifty shades of scarlet."

Maggie smiled. Tom was no prude, so Aimée's messages must have been pretty hot. Not to mention the photos. "How about his replies? Equally explicit?"

"No. His were more discreet. Even so, he was saying stuff like 'I've never loved another human being as much as I love you.' Love notwithstanding, he made it pretty clear he was as eager for sex as she was."

"Where'd they do their dirty dancing?" asked Maggie.

"In the beginning at Tracy Carlin's house. I'm assuming Tracy wasn't home while they went at it. Then in February he rented a studio apartment in a building on Hampshire Street a couple of doors up from Angelo's."

Angelo's was a down-at-the-heels tavern popular with a lot of the local drinkers and brawlers. Cops were constantly being called to the place to break up fights. Just two months ago a melee in the parking lot ended with somebody getting stabbed to death and the stabber being sentenced to a long stay at the state prison in Warren. The city council was thinking about lifting the tavern's liquor license.

"Reading between the lines," Tasco said, "it seems Knowles told the landlord he planned to use the apartment as an office for writing his book. Don't know if he ever told his wife anything about it."

"I doubt it," said Maggie. "Knowles's wife implied they were pretty much broke. Said he worked at the USM library."

"Anyway, the apartment wasn't his idea, it was Aimée's. When she suggested it, he told her he couldn't afford it. She texted back, 'My treat.' He signed the lease, since she was only seventeen, and I guess probably because the name Whitby would have made more than a few waves. But she paid the rent. Six fifty a month."

"A kept man," said McCabe. "Usually it's the other way around. Especially when the woman's young and beautiful. Mag, when you get a chance, take a look at the place, talk to the landlord. Find out what you can about who went in and out."

"Aside from the two of them?" asked Maggie.

"Yeah, I'm just wondering if anybody else ever dropped by."

"Like who?"

"Like maybe the murderer. We're all assuming Knowles killed her and then himself. I'd rather not be that hasty in our assumptions. Anyway, take a look yourself and then have the techs go over it and see what they can find. Also ask the landlord to give you a copy of the lease. I'll write up a subpoena for her bank records and get copies of her canceled checks. I'm curious how much money of her own this kid had."

Maggie turned to Cleary. "After February, did they always use the apartment for their get-togethers?"

"Yeah. They e-mailed a few times about going out to Whitby Island. Some place called the studio. But Aimée said they couldn't because somebody named Mr. Jolley might be nosing around."

"Jolley and his wife are the caretakers," said Maggie.

"Any communications between them in the last twenty-four hours?" asked McCabe.

"Quite a lot there too," said Brian Cleary. "The most interesting are the last ones. At 10:52, when we know they were probably both on the island, she texts him, 'Meet you in 15 u know where.' He texts back, 'Gotcha.' Then nothing until 1:41, when he texted, 'How could I have been such a jerk? I'm so sorry. We need to talk. Please meet me by my boat. I love you.' She texted back, 'OMW.'"

"OMW?" Fortier looked puzzled.

"Kids texting abbreviation," Maggie explained. "Means 'On my way.'"

"I wonder what he was apologizing for? Kind of sounds like they had a fight and he wants to make up. Anything else?"

"After that, just the final text he sent to his wife," said Cleary.

"The so-called suicide note. At least one scenario of what happened here seems pretty obvious to me."

"Really?" said McCabe. "Well, maybe you can enlighten the rest of us."

"Since they were on the island, I'd say they went to the studio to do their thing. In her texts, she was always saying how it was her favorite place and she wished that they could be together there. So they go, but when they get there, they have a fight. About what? Who knows. What do lovers fight about? Something he said. Something he didn't say. His sex technique? Hers? Maybe she's pissed because she didn't have an orgasm. Maybe she wants to do it again and he doesn't. Maybe she wants him to leave his wife and he says no. Since they're both dead, we'll never know. Point is, they have a fight. During which he says something that hurts her and storms out."

"Lot of suppositions there," said McCabe.

"Just hear me out. Knowles storms out, but as he heads to his boat, he's horrified by the nasty things he's said. He needs to apologize. 'I'm so sorry,' he sends in a text from his boat. 'How could I have been such a jerk?' Followed by a plea to make up. 'I love you.' To which Aimée responded, not by telling him she's sorry too but rather, 'On my way.' Maybe she's still pissed and hasn't finished telling him off. So when she gets there, she starts the fight up all over again. Maybe she threatens to tell her father about the affair. Or the police. He knows if she does that it'll cost him. Not just his marriage but also his job and possibly even jail time. He panics and knocks her down. She hits her head against a rock or maybe the back of the boat and starts bleeding. She tries to hit back. He panics. Sees his future going down the drain. Grabs a knife."

"Aha," said McCabe, "the handy knife."

"C'mon, McCabe, this is a fishing boat. It's next to certain there's at least a gutting knife on board. He grabs it as she comes for him. In the melee he stabs her. Or maybe she just runs into the knife and it really is an accident. He pulls out the knife. She falls down, not dead but dying from the wound. Knowles realizes that if anyone finds out what he's done, he won't just do a year in the county jail for screwing a student, he'll most likely spend the rest of his life in prison for killing one. Or at least a lot of years for stabbing and wounding one.

"That means he can't leave her where she is. He's got to get the hell out of there before anyone sees them. He starts up the boat and heads back to Portland. He thinks about throwing her body overboard but she isn't dead yet, so he can't bring himself to do it.

"He convinces himself that if he hides the body up by the Loring, he can tell the police she asked for a ride to her mother's place and he dropped her off as near as he could. He'll tell them the last he saw of her, she was climbing up the Loring Trail to head for home.

"He thinks maybe it'll all be blamed on some random rapist who just happened to be on the prowl. If they find his DNA on her body, he can admit to consensual sex. He leaves her there, gets back in the boat and starts for home. On the way, he has a real *Oh my God* moment. Twenty-four hours ago he was an upstanding father and a respected teacher. Now he's nothing but a murderer. He's overcome by guilt and self-loathing. Decides he can't live with himself. He texts the suicide note and dives overboard. He drowns and his body washes up at Two Lights. There you have it. Means. Motive. Opportunity. Q.E.D."

"Q.E.D.? What the hell's that?" asked Fortier. "More of that texting stuff?"

"No," said McCabe, "it's Latin for *Quod Erat Demonstrandum,* which means 'thus it is demonstrated.'"

"Jesus, Brian, where the hell did you learn Latin? Your old man make you go to church?"

"Nah. I picked it up on an episode of one of those new Sherlock Holmes shows. Holmes says 'Q.E.D.' to Watson after proving a point. Only the Watson on this show is a cute girl. I thought it was kind of cool." Cleary looked pleased with himself. "Now if you all will just admit I'm right about all this, we can wrap it up and I won't have to miss tonight's Sox-Yankees game. I planned to meet up with a couple of buddies at Rivalries to watch it." Rivalries was a popular sports bar on Cotton Street in Portland.

McCabe sighed. "Sorry, Brian, you better let your pals know you won't be making it."

"Why? What do you mean?"

"I mean I think there may be a few holes in your theory."

"Such as?"

"Well, for starters, you've got too many what-ifs and not enough facts. *What if* they had a fight. *What if* she texted OMW because she wanted to yell at him some more. What if she falls and bashes her head. C'mon, I know it's a big game, but you know as well as I do that any defense attorney would tell any judge this is all just random speculation on your part. Any or all of it might be exactly how it happened, but it's just as likely that it's not. There's no way you can prove it. Which means if Knowles were alive, there'd be no way you could convict him of anything other than having sex with a student, which at least we have some hard evidence for but frankly isn't the main issue here."

Cleary looked crestfallen. "Anything else?"

"Yeah. What some might consider gaping holes in your solution."

"Such as?"

"Such as why in hell would a panicked or maybe guilt-ridden Byron Knowles take x minutes to carve an *A* in her chest? You've suggested no reason, and I can't imagine any unless it's some weird reference to a Nathaniel Hawthorne novel. Then there's the question of her cell phone. Why on earth would Knowles leave her cell phone with all its sexy text messages lying ten feet from her body? If he wants to hide the sexual relationship, especially if he wants to hide what you called the *Fifty Shades of Grey* stuff, no way he'd leave it there. All it does is implicate him. Especially when his last message to his wife was 'Please know that I have always loved you.' I mean if you were him, wouldn't you want to hide the dirty things you were doing and not have them become part of the official record?"

"There's one possible reason he might have left it," said Maggie.

"Okay, what's that?"

"If he had to leave in a hurry. If he heard Scott's dog charging up the trail with Scott not so far behind, he might have just dropped it and run like hell."

"Okay, that's a definite maybe," said McCabe. "But what about this? We know Aimée was still alive when Scott found her. She was breathing. She had a pulse. If Knowles didn't want her to die, why would he drag her body a hundred feet up a rough incline and then hide her in some brambles where she was so hard to find it took a dog to actually sniff her out? Not to mention the fact that he didn't bother calling 911 for an ambulance to come and help her?"

Cleary shrugged. "Because he's no doctor. He thought she was dead and, like I said, he thinks a rapist/murderer would try to hide the body, so that's what he does. As for the phone, maybe Maggie's right. He panicked when he heard Ruthie and Scott approaching and just forgot to take it."

"Yeah, maybe. But it's equally possible that Knowles didn't kill anyone. Not Aimée. Not himself. They may have both been the victims of a third man. An unsub who wants all us cops to believe the scenario you just laid out. I don't think we can do that till we know a whole lot more."

"Me either," said Maggie. "Especially not after spending an hour with his wife. Gina Knowles is an angry and bitter woman, which she has every right to be. But she still couldn't imagine Knowles being capable of murder."

"If there is a third man," said McCabe, "he probably used Knowles's cell phone to send the text that lured Aimée to Knowles's boat. Which means A, the bad guy was on the island at the time, and B, based on the content of the text, he somehow knew that Knowles and Aimée had just had a fight or a disagreement or something else that Knowles felt he had to apologize about. It's like the bad guy had the damned studio bugged."

"Or that Knowles really is the killer," said Cleary.

"Or that," said McCabe.

"So where does all that leave us, folks?" asked Bill Fortier.

"Looking for an alternative killer," said Maggie. "At this point we don't have a clue as to who that might be. Though I guess we can be pretty sure it wasn't Dean Scott."

Fortier shook his head and sighed. "Why couldn't one of these, just for once, be easy?"

"Hey, come on, Bill, cheer up," said McCabe. "We only found the body seven hours ago. We're just getting started."

Fortier's phone rang. He picked it up and listened. Then hung up without a word. "Shockley's going public in exactly three minutes," he told the detectives. "Downstairs in the big briefing room. You guys wanna go down and watch the show live?"

Maggie watched a pair of frown lines appear between McCabe's eyes.

"No, thanks," he said. "You go if you want. I think I'll just watch it from up here." He didn't want to answer any questions thrown at him as the lead detective, but he wanted to see how much information Shockley was going to give out. Shockley was better at the PR stuff than he was anyway.

Fortier nodded. "Okay. Why don't we all watch it from here?" He flipped on the TV in the corner and clicked to the local NBC affiliate. The face of Shockley's girlfriend, on-air reporter Josie Tenant, filled one half the screen. An empty rostrum filled the other.

"And here he is now," said Tenant. "Portland Police Chief Thomas Shockley." The cameras turned to Shockley, in full dress uniform, striding across the stage. He took his place at the rostrum, a serious no-bullshit expression on his face. The chief took a few seconds for the chatter to die down and then began to speak.

"Ladies and Gentlemen, early this morning, at approximately 3:20 a.m., the severely wounded body of a young woman was discovered just off the Loring Trail in Portland by Dr. Dean Scott of Portland. Dr. Scott, who had been jogging nearby, is a resident in emergency medicine at Cumberland Medical Center. In spite of his best efforts to save her life, the young woman died of her wounds just a few minutes later. She has since been identified as Veronica Aimée Whitby. Aimée, as she was known to practically everyone, is the daughter of one of Maine's most prominent business leaders, Edward Whitby, president and board chairman of Whitby Engineering & Development. Her mother, Tracy Carlin, is a journalist with the Portland *Press Herald* and a colleague of many of you in attendance here today. I know you all share, as I do, the profound grief that Mr. Whitby and Ms. Carlin must be feeling over the tragic slaying of their daughter. The motive behind the killing is, at this time, unclear, but there is a definite possibility that Aimée Whitby was raped before she was killed.

"Several hours after the discovery of the victim's body, another body, that of Penfield Academy English teacher Byron Knowles, of South Portland, washed up near Two Lights in Cape Elizabeth. Mr. Knowles was the father of a four-year-old girl, and his wife is expecting another child in the very near future. Our hearts also go out to both Knowles's wife and child. Since Ms. Whitby was a student of Mr. Knowles at Penfield, and since both of them attended the same graduation party on Whitby Island last night, it's likely that the two deaths are connected. However at this time we cannot be certain exactly what the connection is."

"Got to give the old fart credit," said McCabe. "He does this crap well."

Shockley spent the next several minutes describing Aimée's wounds in some detail, including the *A* carved into her chest. "At this point we have no idea what significance this letter might have, but we have to assume that the *A* stands for something."

"I hope going public with that is the right thing to do," said Maggie.

McCabe sighed. "Too late now. What's done is done."

"I will now take questions," Shockley told the assembled reporters.

"Do you think Knowles killed the Whitby girl and then killed himself?" Eric Steinberg from the *Bangor Daily News* shouted out.

"That's one of the possibilities we're investigating, Eric," said Shockley, "but it's still too early to definitively declare this a murder/suicide scenario."

"Chief Shockley, do we know if Knowles was having a sexual affair with Aimée Whitby?" The questioner was none other than Shockley's girlfriend, Josie Tenant. He looked irritated at her question.

"I'm sorry, Josie, I can't comment on that at this time."

"Have there been any reports of his having had sexual relations with any other female students?"

"None that I know of."

Reporters were shouting out a battery of questions, but Shockley had apparently decided not to answer any more.

"In conclusion," he said, "I'd like to assure Aimée's parents and friends and Byron Knowles's family that this department will spare no effort or expense getting to the bottom of these tragic deaths. In the meantime, I urge anyone who has any information about this case to please step forward now and let us know. We've set up a special hotline at 1-800-555-1872. The identity of all those offering information will be kept absolutely confidential."

"That ought to lure all the whackos out of the woodwork," said Tom Tasco. "Hope we've got plenty of people working the phones."

McCabe's phone rang. Caller ID said US Coast Guard.

He muted the TV and flipped the phone to speaker so the others could listen. "This is McCabe."

"Sergeant McCabe? This is Chief Petty Officer Karl Nelson, US Coast Guard Search and Rescue. We found your boat, sir."

"You sure you've got the right one?"

"Yessir. A recently restored Midland 19. Originally built 1984. Registered to Byron Knowles of South Portland. Name's the *Patti Ann*. She was spotted out of gas and drifting. About two kilometers south-southeast of Inner Green Island. No one aboard."

"Okay. Good work. Where is the boat now?"

"She's being towed into our South Portland station. Should be here in twenty minutes or so."

"Do me a favor, Chief. If the boat gets there before my partner and I do, under no circumstances let anybody touch a thing inside. Not till our forensics people have had a chance to go over it."

"Aye-aye, sir. Not a problem. I understand. I'll alert our people at the gate that you're on your way."

Chapter 36

FIFTEEN MINUTES LATER, McCabe and Maggie stood at the end of the Coast Guard dock staring down into the interior of the *Patti Ann*. Nothing to see. Just an empty sport fishing boat. No weapons. No obvious bloodstains. Nothing but a little water sloshing around inside and pair of yellow waterproofs pushed in one corner near the bow.

"You know what I don't get?" Maggie said. "If Knowles wasn't the killer, why would a third man bring Aimée all the way back to Portland, then drag her up the Loring Trail and use a knife? Even if he wanted to rape her, there's plenty of room and total privacy right down there in the back of the boat. When he was finished he could've dumped her overboard, like he supposedly did with Knowles. No leaving of DNA or anything else behind. Cleaner. Easier. Simpler."

"I guess he wanted her body to be found."

"Why?"

"Presumably to set up the murder/suicide scenario, which, if we buy it, puts an end to the investigation. Without a body, Aimée's a missing person and we keep looking. And from what I've heard about Edward Whitby, so would he. Much safer for the bad guy to let us find her and blame Knowles."

"Okay. But why not kill her on the island, carve the *A* and leave her there? If he wants to implicate Knowles, he leaves her cell phone there with all the texts and voice mails. Once he's done with Aimée, he tosses Knowles in the boat, takes him out into the open ocean, sends the suicide note to Gina, and then dumps him overboard never to be found."

McCabe raised both hands, palms out. "I don't know. Maybe he just felt like doing it the way he did."

Maggie shook her head in frustration. McCabe's phone rang. Tom Tasco was on the other end.

"Yeah, Tom."

"Whitby's assistant, a woman named Martha Davis, just sent over the guest list for last night's party. Two hundred and thirty-six attendees, including a lot of well-known names. Plus another fifty-two worker bees hired by the caterer. She included contact info for all of them. Phone and e-mail."

"Efficient woman."

"I agree, but we may need the National Guard if we're gonna interview nearly three hundred people."

"So call in some help. We need to find out if anybody saw anything in any way suspicious on the island last night. Also we need to identify anyone who might have had some motive for wanting to see Knowles and Aimée dead. Or maybe just Aimée. Knowles may have been collateral damage. You know the drill."

"Okay. I'll see if I can recruit some additional manpower from the Staties and start working the list."

McCabe returned to Maggie, who seemed lost in thought.

"What are you thinking about?" he asked.

"The letter A."

Maggie took out her phone and made a call. "Headmaster Cobb, please." Pause. "I see. This is Detective Margaret Savage of the Portland Police Department. I'm investigating the murder of Aimée Whitby." Pause. "Yes, it was a terrible thing." Pause. "Is there anyone there who can tell me if the book *The Scarlet Letter* was assigned in Aimée's English classes? Thanks. I'll hold."

Maggie waited. A minute later she introduced herself to someone else and asked the same question. She waited again. Nodded and thanked whoever she was talking to. "Okay," she finally said to McCabe. "I still don't know what it means, but Byron Knowles has assigned *The Scarlet Letter* to all his senior students for the last eight years."

"So anybody who'd taken his class would know that *A* stands for adultery."

"I guess. But there is one problem with that," said Maggie.

"What?"

"Well, we know adultery was committed. But Knowles was the adulterer, not Aimée. She wasn't married."

"I don't know," said McCabe. "Isn't sleeping with a married man considered adultery?" He looked up the word on his iPhone. "Okay. Here it is. 'Voluntary sexual intercourse between a married person and a person who is not his or her spouse.' So I guess technically they're both adulterers. Anyway, why else carve the *A*?"

Maggie shrugged. "We've been over that. Because it's the first initial of her name? Or she's the first in a series of killings and he wants to sign his work. Or maybe like that guy in New York, he wants to become known as The Alphabet Killer."

Before McCabe could answer, Maggie's phone rang.

"Yes, Mr. Whitby?" she said, flipping to speaker so McCabe could hear.

"I just watched a tape of Shockley's press conference."

"Yes, sir?"

"You didn't tell me about the letter *A* when we spoke earlier."

"No, I'm sorry. The specifics seemed less important than telling you about your daughter's death."

"Well, the specifics are important. I suggest you and McCabe get your tails out here pronto. There's something you need to know. And to see. I'll have the chopper waiting on the company helipad."

"Okay. We'll be there as soon as we can."

Maggie looked over at McCabe, who nodded.

They headed back to the car.

"You drive," said Maggie. "I want to ask Terri something."

"Hi, Mag, what's up?" said Terri Mirabito.

"One more question. What if Whitby had sex with two different guys and there's semen from both?"

"What about it?"

"Can Joe Pines differentiate between two different specimens? Can we get DNA reads for both?"

"Yes. The tests would give us indicators for both."

"Good. Thank you. When are you cutting?"

"I plan on doing both autopsies today. I'll start at three. The Whitby girl first. Then Knowles. Will you and McCabe be joining me?"

"No. Just me." She glanced over at McCabe. "McCabe is taking his daughter to Fore Street for dinner to celebrate her graduation."

"Hey, that's great. Congratulate them both for me."

"I will." Maggie broke the connection and smiled at McCabe.

"We're in the middle of a double murder and you decide, all on your own, that I'm going out for dinner instead of doing my job?"

"Yup."

"A little arbitrary on your part, don't you think? Especially since I just told Brian he couldn't meet his buddies for the Sox game."

"Sox games don't count. They play a hundred and sixty a season. You, on the other hand, have only one daughter. The two of you should be celebrating tonight, and you should be going to Casey's graduation tomorrow. She needs to know you care more about her than you do your job. Which is probably what Kyra needed too. And maybe still does."

"Yes, ma'am," McCabe said, glancing into Maggie's brown eyes. "Thank you. I suspect you're right."

"And don't worry about the autopsies. I'm happy to cover."

Chapter 37

From the journal of Edward Whitby Jr.
Entry dated July 3, 1924

The unraveling of our lives began, as I suppose such things often do, in a most prosaic manner, with a letter that arrived unexpectedly just after breakfast on a beautiful Saturday morning in June. It had come from the Museum School in Boston and was addressed to Aimée. She tore it open as we sat together sipping our coffee on the terrace behind the house.

"Oh my goodness! Oh my goodness! I can't believe it." She was holding the pages of the letter in both hands and was staring down at them. Her excitement was palpable.

I looked up from my morning paper and smiled. She looked particularly lovely that morning, her face so alive, so filled with energy as she read whatever news was contained in the letter that I longed to take her in my arms and thank her again for being my wife and the mother of our children. It had been a long time since I'd felt so close to her. Perhaps that is why I reacted so fiercely to what she said.

"What is it?" I asked. "What is it that is giving you such pleasure? Please share your news."

"I'm not sure I should, Edward. I'm afraid it may be something you won't like. But before I tell you, I want you to know that I am thrilled."

My pleasure turned to suspicion about what she was going to say. "What is it?" I asked again.

"I have been invited by Mr. Mark Garrison to teach a class in painting seascapes at the Museum School in Boston. He says I am the first woman ever asked to be an instructor there."

I'm sure I must have frowned, because she said, "Edward, don't look so downcast. This is something that makes me happy. Don't you want me to be happy?"

"How did Garrison happen to think of you?"

"We've met a few times at gallery openings in Boston, and when he said they would be adding an instructor for this September, I applied for the position, more on a lark than anything else. I never imagined it would actually happen. But listen to what Garrison says. 'I greatly admire your work, Mrs. Whitby, particularly the oils in what you call your island series. They are strong. They are vibrant. They bring the ocean and the rocky coast of your island to life with all the strength and power I'm sure they possess in life. If you are half as good an instructor as you are a painter,

I am confident that you will be a credit to this institution. I must add that, at this time, we can only offer you a part-time position. Your classes will meet only one day a week, one in the morning and one in the afternoon on Thursdays, and the stipend is small. If you are still interested, please telephone me at your earliest convenience so that we can arrange a time to meet in person and discuss the details further.'"

"Well," I said. "I suppose I should congratulate you on the offer. It's quite an honor to be the first woman invited to join the faculty of such a prestigious institution. But I'm afraid you must let Garrison know you weren't serious when you sent in your application 'on a lark,' as you say. You will telephone Mr. Garrison Monday morning and thank him for the offer but tell him that it no longer works with your schedule."

"No. I'm going to call him Monday and accept."

Though her words triggered a barely containable rage inside of me, I said nothing.

"Please be happy for me, Edward," said Aimée, sensing my anger. "Accepting this job is something that could save my life."

The irony in those words didn't strike me until nearly a year later.

Chapter 38

THE HEADQUARTERS OF Whitby Engineering & Development took up three acres on the far end of the Portland waterfront. McCabe flashed his badge at a bored-looking guard, who said yes, Mr. Whitby had called, and yes, he could direct them to the helipad. He provided brief instructions and said that the pilot was waiting for them.

The pad itself was a circular concrete apron extending out over the Fore River with something that looked like a target painted in the middle. A gleaming white AgustaWestland AW139 chopper was perched in the bull's-eye. A tall, skinny kid walked over to meet them. He was dressed in navy blue trousers, spit-shined black shoes and a white shirt with the Whitby E&D logo sewn over the pocket.

"Sergeant McCabe? Detective Savage?" he asked.

"Yup," Maggie said. "He's McCabe, I'm Savage."

"Hi, I'm Jack Summers. I'll be your pilot."

Maggie looked him over carefully. He looked like he hadn't started shaving yet. "You been doing this long?" she asked. "Flying helicopters, I mean."

"Nope. This will be my first time."

Maggie frowned.

"Well, actually, I've had my learner's permit for, heck, let me see, two weeks now, but my instructor says I'm really doing well. But this will be my first time flying solo. And I am *really* excited."

He paused, maybe waiting to see if she thought that was funny. Her look told him she didn't.

"Sorry. Yes, I know I look young, but I've been flying choppers for over eight years."

Maggie raised one eyebrow. "Really?"

"Really. Six years in Army Aviation, including two combat tours in Iraq, mostly flying Kiawas. I got out two years ago, and I've been flying for Whitby ever since. Right over there is my baby. An AgustaWestland 139. One of the best machines money can buy."

"A lot of money, I assume?" asked Maggie.

"Oh yeah. A hell of a lot."

He opened a sliding door. Inside was a luxurious passenger cabin complete with six soft white leather seats facing each other, three and three. Between them, an expensive-looking walnut coffee table. "I can put you both back here in first class, or one of you can ride up front with me. Your call."

"Up front works for me," said Maggie. She wanted to see if she could get any useful information out of Summers.

"You go for it," said McCabe, climbing in. "I'll enjoy pampering myself in the back."

"You'll only get about five minutes to enjoy it," said Summers.

He opened a separate cockpit door and climbed in first. Maggie followed. She watched him check a whole bunch of dials and gauges and then start the engine. "She's got to warm up for a few minutes before we take off."

"You ferry people to and from the party last night?"

"Yup. Ran a regular shuttle service. From about five to ten thirty or so."

"That's when the last guests left?"

"The last ones who were flying with me."

"Anyone interesting?"

"Nope."

"Really? I heard there was at least one movie star and one senator. Any other big cheeses?"

"Sorry, Detective. I don't get paid to give out passengers' names. If Mr. Whitby wants you to know who I flew to and from the island last night, he'll tell you himself."

The chopper rose, hovered in the air for a moment, then set off flying due east over the water.

"I'd offer you snacks and beverages," said Summers, "but you'll be on the island in five minutes."

"How about Aimée? Did you give her rides out here very often?"

"Fairly often. But work for the company always takes precedence."

"Pretty girl, don't you think?"

"Aimée? Oh yeah. Absolutely gorgeous. To die for."

Summers looked relaxed and smiling as he said that. Maybe he hadn't heard about the murders yet. Maybe he didn't watch much television.

Maggie turned her attention to the glittering waters of Casco Bay passing below. It was a breezy morning with considerable chop, evidenced by a number of whitecaps. They flew out between Cushing and Harts Islands, then turned slightly north, passing just to the south of Cliff and Jewell. Eagle Island, where famed Arctic explorer Admiral Robert Peary had a home, could be seen to the north as they began their descent onto Whitby.

Two men and a young woman stood waiting as the chopper came down. It all made Maggie feel like the president coming in on Marine One. It was easy to tell which of the men was Whitby. He looked like a taller, well-tanned, male version of Aimée, as handsome in his way as she was beautiful in hers. She obviously carried the Whitby genes. Whitby was dressed in preppy weekend gear. Khaki shorts, a striped polo shirt and a pair of beat-up topsiders with no socks on his feet. On any other morning here on his island, he probably would have looked relaxed and at ease with the world, but on this morning, even from the window of the chopper, he appeared stiff with tension, his face simultaneously sad and angry. He hadn't bothered shaving.

Following Summers's instructions, Maggie pushed the cockpit door open and climbed down, acutely aware of the rotor blades spinning what seemed just inches above her head. This being her first time on a helicopter, she bent her six-foot frame as low as she could as she walked out from under. While possible death in the line of duty was something all cops accepted, decapitation by helicopter blades wouldn't have been Maggie's first choice of how to go.

Summers climbed down and slid open the passenger door for McCabe and he followed them out.

"Sergeant McCabe? Detective Savage? I'm Edward Whitby."

They all shook hands. Whitby had a strong, confident grip.

"This is my daughter Julia, Aimée's half twin." A young woman with a mane of curly red hair and a face full of freckles offered her hand. Maggie shook it. Julia wasn't beautiful, like her half sister, but she wasn't unattractive. Quite pretty, actually. At the moment, however, her looks were diminished by a pair of tired, reddened eyes, which might have been caused by crying. Or maybe she was still hungover from last night's festivities.

"Julia probably knew Aimée as well or better than anyone else, so she should be able to offer you some helpful insights. And this is Charles Kraft, our director of corporate security. You can count on Charles to help your investigation in any way he can."

Kraft was about the same age as Whitby. He had a hard face with steel-gray eyes and a linebacker's build. He sure as hell looked like a pro. "Are you a former police officer, Mr. Kraft?"

Kraft's smile suggested he found the question amusing. "No," he said, "I've never been a cop."

"FBI then?"

"Not that either."

Whitby filled the silence that followed.

"Charles spent twenty years with Army Special Forces. Served in both Iraq and Afghanistan. After he got out, he spent a couple of years working for an old pal of mine as a private contractor, providing security for US diplomats and corporate clients in Iraq, Afghanistan and other hot spots."

"Blackwater?"

"No," said Kraft. "The Orion Group. We were smaller and, I think, better. Not so many loose cannons."

McCabe had heard of the company. Remembered their logo, a particularly artful adaptation of the constellation Orion, the hunter, wielding a sword with stars and lightning.

"Kill anybody over there?"

"My share."

"Any civilians?"

"My share."

Based on background, the guy was bound to be an efficient and expert killer. Someone like Byron Knowles wouldn't have stood a chance against him. Nor would Aimée. But what possible motive would Kraft have for killing his boss's daughter? The only one McCabe could think of was sexual. Kraft wanted her, maybe was in love with her, and she spurned his attentions. Or maybe he already had something going when she dropped him for Knowles. The lover spurned.

"Are you going to be around for a while, Mr. Kraft?" asked McCabe.

Whitby answered for him. "At the moment both Charles and Julia are taking the chopper back to the mainland. I'll give you their cell numbers. You'll be able to reach them there."

"I wonder if you'd mind coming downtown to police head-quarters for a chat? Maybe sometime this afternoon?"

Kraft studied McCabe for a moment, perhaps assessing him as a possible adversary. "Sure. Why not? What time?"

"We'll let you know."

"Anybody else on the island at the moment?" asked Maggie.

"My wife, Deirdre. She's Julia's mother and Aimée's step-mother. She's in her room. I'm afraid she's too upset by the news to talk to anyone at the moment."

"Really? I spoke at length with Aimée's mother. But her step-mother is too upset to talk to us?"

"Let's just say she's emotionally fragile and leave it at that."

Interesting. "Emotionally fragile" didn't sound at all like the woman Tracy described to McCabe earlier that morning. Brash and aggressive was more like it. Maybe eighteen years of marriage to Edward Whitby had worn her down. Or maybe there were things the second Mrs. Whitby didn't want to discuss. "I'm afraid it's important that we get any information she may have on this."

"She'll be back to town tomorrow. You'll be able to reach her there."

"Anyone else still here?"

"Yes. Mr. and Mrs. Jolley, who live on the island. They have their own cottage."

"Must be a lonely existence living here full-time. Specially in winter."

"The Jolleys seem to like it."

"Did they attend the party?"

"Not as guests. Mr. Jolley tended one of the bars. Mrs. Jolley helped organize the caterers."

"All right. We'll need to talk to them as well."

"That's fine," said Whitby, "but there is something I think you ought to see before you go any further in the investigation."

"What's that?"

"Come with me."

Chapter 39

MAGGIE AND MCCABE followed Edward Whitby across a blue-stone patio toward a large shingled house that was almost but not quite as big as the one on the Western Prom. He led the way through a pair of mullioned French doors into a spacious, tastefully furnished living room. Nothing grandiose, just expensive. Once inside, he closed and locked both patio doors. Then he locked the two doors that led into the room from the interior hallway.

McCabe and Savage barely noticed the locking of the doors. Both were too distracted by the large oil painting hanging over the fireplace. A portrait of Aimée certainly. Not as they'd last seen her, dead on the Loring Trail, but amazingly alive. She was looking down at them as if she was just itching to leap off the wall and join the conversation. She was dressed in an elegant, low-cut black evening gown, her blonde hair swept up high on her head, a string of pearls around her neck and a wry, mischievous smile on her face.

What struck McCabe as odd about the painting was that the canvas itself looked far too old to be a portrait of Whitby's daughter. It showed some of the same signs of aging that Kyra once pointed out as she was giving him a quick lesson in art authentication. There were also some barely noticeable repairs on the gold frame.

Whitby joined them. "I asked you to come to the island because I wanted you to see this painting."

"This couldn't be a portrait of your daughter," said Maggie.

"It's not, but it might as well be. It's a painting of my great-grandmother, also named Aimée, commissioned by my great-grandfather. It's by an artist named Mark Garrison. She was twenty-eight when he painted it. Ten years older than my Aimée."

"The resemblance is extraordinary."

"Yes, the two are practically identical. You can see it not just here but also in some old family photographs. Put them side by side with photos of my daughter and, except for the hairdos and clothing, it's next to impossible to see any difference."

"Interesting," said McCabe, "but why was it so important that you had to show us this immediately?"

"To be honest with you, I don't know if the painting itself has any direct bearing on what happened to my daughter last night, but because of the timing, I think it might. That's when I unveiled it to the more than two hundred people who attended the party. Plus, I suppose, the waiters and other help who were in the room. The fact that Aimée was killed only a few hours later may just be a weird coincidence, but I've been around long enough not to believe in coincidences."

"Had anyone seen it before last night?"

"It's been in private hands for more than a hundred years. I purchased it at auction less than two months ago. Only my wife and daughters and a few close friends saw it when I first had it delivered. But no one else except a restorer who did a little work on it and made some repairs to the frame."

"What possible connection could unveiling a painting have with the murder?" asked Maggie.

"I don't know for sure that it does. But there are circumstances surrounding the creation of this painting that are certainly connected."

"Okay. Where would you like to start?" asked McCabe.

"Why don't we all sit down?" Whitby pointed them to a pair of chairs that faced the fireplace and the painting above it. McCabe supposed he wanted them to look at it as they spoke. Whitby then took the seat facing them. The face in the painting smiled down at the detectives from over Whitby's right shoulder. From this vantage point McCabe had an eerie sense that the first Aimée Whitby was hovering over her great-grandson and, like him, wanted Maggie and McCabe to know something.

Whitby spoke first. "I told Detective Savage that I watched Tom Shockley's press conference this morning. I learned that Aimée's body was found nude, that she was stabbed in the abdomen and that the letter *A* was carved into her upper chest deeply enough to have formed permanent scars had she survived. Accurate so far?"

"Accurate," said Maggie.

"Shockley also said the body of Aimée's English teacher, Byron Knowles, washed ashore in Cape Elizabeth. An apparent suicide."

"Yes."

"Do you think he killed her before killing himself?"

"We think that's one possibility," said Maggie, "but only one. We're not certain that he's the killer."

"Why not?"

A frown line formed between Maggie's eyes. "Just what are you getting at, Mr. Whitby?"

"Answer my question first, then I'll answer yours. Why don't you think Knowles killed my daughter?"

"I didn't say that," said Maggie. "I said we weren't certain."

"Do the two of you agree with Shockley that Knowles's death was a suicide?"

"He sent his wife a text message that makes it look that way."

"You didn't answer my question."

"Again we think it's possible."

"But not certain?"

"That's right. Not certain. Both Aimée and Knowles may have been victims of a killer we have yet to identify."

"Shockley said Knowles was married."

"Yes," said McCabe. "With one child and another on the way."

Edward Whitby paused and took a deep breath before asking, "Do you have any evidence that indicates Knowles was having an affair with my daughter?"

Maggie and McCabe exchanged glances. "We know he was," said Maggie, closely watching Whitby's face as she spoke. "We have clear evidence that Byron Knowles and your daughter have had an active sexual relationship since at least last November."

McCabe didn't know what reaction he was expecting from Whitby, but there was practically none. His expression remained more sad than angry. His eyes drifted to the view of the ocean beyond the stone patio. "How old was Knowles?"

"Thirty-six," said Maggie. "Twice your daughter's age."

"Was he planning to leave his wife?"

"We don't know. All we know is that the marriage wasn't in good shape and that Knowles's wife suspected he was having an affair. She told us she didn't know with who."

"Any evidence that Aimée told Knowles she wanted to break things off?"

"Not that we've seen."

"And you're not certain whether or not Knowles killed my daughter?"

"Either he killed her," said McCabe, "or somebody is trying very hard to make it look that way. Now perhaps you can tell us what connection this painting may have with your daughter's death."

"My daughter is not the first murder victim in this family. The woman you see in that painting, my great-grandmother, the first Aimée, was also murdered. The story goes that she was murdered by Mark Garrison, the artist who painted the portrait. Garrison was also her lover. He killed her here on Whitby Island by stabbing her in the abdomen. He also carved a letter *A* into her chest, just like the one Tom Shockley described this morning. After killing Aimée, Garrison committed suicide in the small studio we have here on the island.

"It seems perfectly obvious to me that my daughter's killer, whether it was Knowles or someone else, knew about and copied the details of a murder that happened here on this island one hundred and eight years ago. Not only were the two victims physically identical, so was the method of killing them and so was the fate of the suspected killer. That's what I thought you should know before proceeding with your investigation. I thought it might change the way you approach it."

Maggie and McCabe exchanged glances. A copycat murder with identical victims. Whitby was right. Knowing that changed everything. Including the possible meaning of the letter *A*.

"What was Garrison's motive?" asked McCabe. "Why did he kill her?"

Looking up once again at the portrait, McCabe had the strangest feeling that the woman looking down from over the fireplace was listening with great interest to every word they were saying. Perhaps only she knew the answer to his question.

"Like I told you earlier, Mark Garrison was Aimée's lover. The police at the time came to the conclusion that after what they called an illicit assignation in the studio, Aimée told Garrison that her husband, my great-grandfather, had learned of their relationship and because of this she could never see him again."

"Did your great-grandfather confirm that he knew about the affair?"

"Yes. He told Deputy Inspector Elijah Handy of the Portland Police Department, who was the chief investigator on the case, that he had discovered what was going on and that he had confronted Aimée with an accusation. He said that after many denials she finally admitted the truth. After which she asked for a divorce. He said no. Divorce wasn't an option for someone in his position. She threatened to leave him. He told her that if she did, he would never allow her to see her children again. He said that with her being an admitted adulteress, he was sure any judge would grant him custody. Since my great-grandfather had most of the judges in the state firmly in his pocket, and since most of them were puritanical and suspected all foreigners, but particularly French foreigners like Aimée, of immoral behavior, I'm sure he was right.

"Anyway, my great-grandfather said at the inquest that he wouldn't divorce Aimée because, in spite of the affair, he still loved her. He also feared that the scandal of divorce would damage the reputation of both the Whitby family and the Whitby business.

"He told the jury that he demanded that she break off the affair immediately, send Garrison packing and say nothing of it to anyone. Apparently she gave in and agreed to tell Garrison that they could never see each other again."

"Okay, then what happened?"

"It's a little murky. As best we can reconstruct it, Aimée must have arranged for Garrison to meet her secretly on the island, where she planned to tell him their affair was over. She may also have allowed him to make love to her one final time, I suppose as kind of a farewell present before breaking it off. After which she gave him the bad news, and Garrison, in a rage at being rejected, grabbed a knife, stabbed Aimée and carved the *A* in her chest."

"What makes you think they made love before she told him she was breaking it off?" asked Maggie. "Was her body ever examined by a doctor for signs of sexual intercourse?"

"Not to my knowledge. Apparently the police concluded they'd made love because she was naked when she was discovered at the bottom of the cliff at the far end of the island by three fishermen. Anyway, it seemed likely to the police at the time that they had made love. I truly don't know the answer to that."

"Okay. So she tells him she's breaking things off, he loses his temper, grabs a knife, stabs her and carves the *A* on her chest," said McCabe.

"Yes. That's what the inquest concluded."

"But there's no proof it actually happened that way?"

Whitby sighed. "Not really. I suspect my great-grandfather applied pressure on the mayor, the attorney general and the coroner to make the whole thing go away as quickly and quietly as possible. Unfortunately, the newspapers didn't cooperate with his efforts. It was exactly the kind of sordid tale they loved, and they played it to the hilt."

"Did anybody have any idea what significance the *A* might have had?" asked Maggie.

"No one knew. Journalists had a field day comparing it to Hawthorne's *Scarlet Letter*. You know the book? Hester Prynne forced to wear a scarlet *A* for being an adulteress? Which Aimée was. But Garrison was also a married man and just as guilty of adultery, so the idea that he wanted to mark her with the label has always bothered me. Of course the *A* could have stood for something else, including her name. So who knows? In any event, the knife wound didn't kill her. She fled the studio and apparently ran, for reasons known only to her, toward the high cliff on the seaward side of this island. Garrison supposedly gave chase, and Aimée either fell or was pushed by Garrison over the edge."

"How does anyone know this?" asked Maggie. "Weren't the two of them alone on the island?"

"No one really does. It was pure conjecture on the part of Inspector Handy, based on the fact that one of the fishermen—just a boy of twelve— who came ashore in a dinghy to try to rescue her later testified at the inquest that, as they were loading her body onto their boat, he spotted a man's face peering at them from over the edge of the cliff. The boy waved at him, but he didn't respond. He simply disappeared."

"Did he know who the man was?" asked McCabe.

"No."

"Did the police show the boy any pictures to help identify him?"

"No, they did not."

"It would have been standard police procedure to do so. Even back then."

"I think there was considerable pressure from the Whitby family to just make the whole thing go away. Blaming Garrison for both Aimée's and his own deaths. Whether she fell or was pushed by Garrison, she was somehow still alive when the fishermen found her. She died on the way back to Portland, where they handed her body over to the police."

"And Garrison? What happened to him?"

"The story is that, overcome with guilt and horror at what he had done, he took his own life. Hung himself in the studio."

"How did he do it?"

"With his belt. He looped it around his neck. Attached the buckle to a large hook that was attached high up on the wall and kicked away the stool he was standing on."

"Did the fall break his neck?"

"No. According to the doctor who examined the corpse, he died of asphyxiation."

"Did he leave any kind of suicide note?" asked Maggie.

"Yes, a note that said 'I am consumed by guilt. I loved her far too much to go on without her.'"

Maggie looked over to McCabe. "'I can never forgive myself for the terrible things I have done,'" she said.

"I'm sorry. What?" asked Whitby.

"Nothing," said McCabe. "I assume the note was handwritten?"

Whitby looked at him oddly. "Why do you ask?"

"I'm just wondering if anyone ever analyzed the handwriting to see if it was actually written by Garrison."

"I have no idea. Are you saying somebody else might have written it?"

"I don't know. But checking it should have been done even in 1904. How about the press? With a famous painter killing the wife of a prominent businessman, I would think the newspapers would be all over it," said McCabe.

"As I said, they were. It was hailed by William Randolph Hearst and others in the yellow press as 'the murder of the century,' even though the century was, at that point, only four years old. Happily, at least as far as the Whitby family was concerned, another murder took the title just two years later."

"The Harry Thaw case."

"Yes, Thaw shot and killed the architect Stanford White in 1906 on the roof of the old Madison Square Garden in New York. Hearst quickly made that one the new 'murder of the century.' You obviously know of that case."

"At least in the Thaw case there was no doubt about who the murderer was. Hundreds of people saw Thaw do it."

"Do you think there should be doubts about this one? That Garrison might not have been her killer?"

McCabe shrugged. "Based on what you've told us, there was almost no real evidence to prove that he was. All they had were two dead bodies, a suicide note, which could have been written by anybody, and an unidentified face peering over the edge of the cliff. Pretty much everything else seems to be based on nothing more than guesswork. And what the victim's husband told the police. Which, I take, no one ever questioned?"

"No one dared. My great-grandfather was the most powerful man in Portland."

"Some might say the same about you."

"They might."

"How about the police records on the case? Are they available?"

"No. In 1904, the police department was located in the old city hall building. Four years later, in 1908, the building burned to the ground, and any records that existed were destroyed."

"Including Garrison's note?"

"Including Garrison's note. What I know comes from the press coverage and from the transcripts of an inquest that concluded that Garrison was the killer, that he took his own life and that no one else was on the island."

"Was there any evidence that might have suggested Garrison wasn't the killer?"

"Just one thing. One of the local reporters, a man named Charlie Hough, wrote in the *Press Herald* that he interviewed the boy, Jack."

"And?"

"Hough wrote that just before she died, Aimée whispered a name into Jack's ear. He said the name Jack heard was Edward and definitely not Mark. Hough asked the boy if he was sure he heard Edward. Jack said yes."

"Doesn't mean Edward killed her," said McCabe. "Maybe she was just asking for him."

"That's what the police concluded."

"Did Edward have an alibi?"

"Not really. He said he was working alone in his office at home. The housekeeper said she saw him there."

"Did Hough write anything more about the case?"

"Not for the *Press Herald*. Shortly after that first article appeared, Hough was fired by the paper and never heard from again. At least not in Portland."

"How many people today know the details of the 1904 murder?" asked McCabe.

"Pretty much anyone who has an interest in the case can learn all about it. All they have to do is go to the Portland Public Library and look it up in the *Press Herald* archives. It's all there on microfiche. Including Hough's piece. Transcripts of the coroner's inquest following the murder are available in the files of the Cumberland County Court."

"Okay. Easy to research," said Maggie, "but to mimic the cutting of the *A,* your daughter's killer, whether it was Knowles or someone else, would had to have been at least aware of what happened with your great-grandmother."

"Yes."

McCabe looked up at the face of the first Aimée. "One thing puzzles me. You said this painting was commissioned by your great-grandfather. Yet you also said you recently bought it at auction. Why hasn't it been here the whole time?"

"After painting it, Garrison took the canvas back to his studio in Boston for a few finishing touches. He was dead before he got around to doing them. Because Edward refused to pay Garrison's widow the remainder of the commission, she refused to let him have the painting. Because she needed the money, she eventually sold it, along with most of the rest of his work. As I said, I purchased it at an auction this past April in New York. Cost me several million dollars, but I'd wanted it for years, and it had only just become available. Garrison's work, and especially this piece, is much sought after because of his talent but also partly because of the scandal that surrounded the end of his life. I unveiled it for the first time at the party last night. I can't help thinking that my daughter's death must somehow be connected to my purchase of this painting."

Whitby spent the next five minutes recounting how Aimée had stolen the show with her breathtaking entrance, dressed as the original Aimée. "My daughter was an incredible young woman," he said. "Much more than just a great beauty. Like her great-great-grandmother, she was also an accomplished artist. Valedictorian of her class. A very good athlete. I could go on and on. But I'm afraid I can't."

He took a deep breath and stopped talking. And wiped both eyes with a white handkerchief.

"Can you think of any reason someone other than Knowles might have had for killing her?"

"No. I have to believe it was Knowles. Perhaps Aimée tried to end the affair and he lost his temper and stabbed her. Just like Garrison. Then in remorse he took his own life. Again like Garrison."

"We're looking into the possibility. Can you think of anyone else?"

"I don't know. Knowles's wife? She certainly had a motive."

"Knowles's wife is eight and a half months pregnant. I don't think she would have been physically capable of murdering either her husband or your daughter."

Whitby shrugged. "Could the motive have been sexual? Simple rape? Might not a random rapist have killed her to keep her from reporting him to the police? Or to me?"

"Detective Savage and I have discussed that possibility," said McCabe, "but what you've told us means that any random rapist would have to have been familiar with the exact details of the first Aimée's death. That seems unlikely, don't you think?"

"More than unlikely."

Chapter 40

AT A LITTLE after 1:00 p.m., Maggie turned her Portland PD Ford Interceptor onto Hampshire Street, a small one-way cut-through a couple of blocks from 109 that connected Congress and Middle Streets. Number 47 was on the right. It was a small two-story covered with gray asbestos shingles and four unpainted wooden steps leading up to the front door.

A heavyset man about fifty, with thinning hair and a face covered with old acne scars, stood waiting out front.

Maggie got out of her car. "Dan Mullaney?"

"That's me."

"I'm Detective Margaret Savage." She showed him her ID and gave him a business card. He looked it over and gave her one of his own.

"You're the landlord here?" she asked.

"Yep."

"Do you live in the building?"

"No. I live out in Westbrook. I own this place and three other rental properties here in town. That's one of the others right there." He pointed to a nearly identical building on the opposite side of the street. Same architecture. Same era.

"How many apartments in this one?" she asked.

"Four. Two up. Two down. All studios."

"I assume you heard what happened to your tenants?"

"Yes. I saw it on the morning news. Real shame. I had no idea she was only a kid. Even less that her name was Whitby."

"Were they good tenants?"

He gave her a squirrely look. "Far as I know. I didn't see all that much of them. I showed them the place. He signed the lease. She paid the rent. All cash. Six months in advance."

"And you didn't know she was Edward Whitby's daughter?"

"Not till this morning."

"You weren't curious when she paid you in cash?"

"I try to mind my own business. He said he wanted to use the place as an office for writing a book. Seemed okay to me."

"But she paid the rent? A little unusual, don't you think?"

"Unusual don't mean illegal. She said something about being a patron of the arts. Don't know if she meant that as a joke or not, but I didn't ask."

"Still a little unusual?"

"Like I said, I mind my own business."

Clearly, Mullaney wasn't going to be very helpful.

"Tenants get off-street parking?"

"Nope. But there's plenty of parking spaces on the street."

"So tenants . . . or maybe visitors . . . can usually find a spot to park in front of the building?"

"Or close to it. C'mon, I'll show you the apartment."

Mullaney sorted through a metal ring with a bunch of keys on it. He found the right one, climbed to the landing and opened the front door.

They went up to the second floor, where there were two apartments. Maggie followed the landlord to the one with yellow crime scene tape stretched across it.

Mullaney unlocked it and pushed the door open. "How long you gonna be?"

"I'm not sure. Maybe an hour. Maybe more."

"I'll leave you to it." He handed her the key. "When you're done, would you mind locking up and returning this to the office. Mullaney Realty. It's in the blue building just at the end of the block on Congress."

The landlord left, and Maggie pulled on a pair of booties and latex gloves. She pushed open the door, ducked under the tape and went inside.

She found herself standing in a decent-sized room, which she guesstimated at fifteen by twenty. Not exactly luxurious, but it looked to be in reasonable condition.

Beneath her booties was a fairly new, or maybe refinished, hardwood floor. Half a dozen of what Maggie guessed were Aimée's paintings and drawings hung on the plaster walls. A couple of self-portraits and one nicely rendered figure drawing of Byron. The kid had talent, no question about that. She'd obviously inherited more than her looks from the first Aimée.

On the far side of the room, two windows were covered with newish up-down shades. Maggie lowered the one to the right and peered down onto Hampshire Street. It would be easy for anyone driving by, especially at night, when the lovers were likely in residence, to look up and see if any lights were on in the apartment. Lights that would be visible even if the shades were drawn. And it would be just as easy to see if a maroon 2002 Camry or maybe a black Mercedes 560 or maybe both were parked nearby. If they were, and if you were patient, you could park your own car just across the street and wait to see if Aimée and Knowles were going in or coming out. Either alone or together. Maybe holding hands. Or kissing good-bye. Or maybe being discreet and each going their own way.

Maggie remembered Gina Knowles, the wronged wife, telling her how she'd looked through her husband's wallet and found a receipt from a restaurant in Cape Neddick. She'd confronted Byron with it. He wouldn't have kept a lease in his wallet. But maybe in his briefcase? Or in his office at school? Had Gina ever looked for and found a signed lease for an apartment on Hampshire Street? She said she knew he was having an affair. "I think it's probably with one of the young female teachers at Penfield. There are a lot of single women on the faculty, some quite attractive."

Maggie wondered if Gina Knowles could possibly have been the killer. McCabe's third man or, in this case, third woman. Motive was easy. As the saying goes, "Hell hath no fury like a woman scorned." Could her fury have been powerful enough to motivate a double murder? As for the letter *A,* Byron taught *The Scarlet Letter.* Had Gina read it? Or maybe, like Maggie, had she just seen the Hollywood version with Demi Moore playing Hester Prynne?

Okay, so Gina had an obvious motive for murder and for labeling Aimée an adulteress by carving the *A.* But what about her denial that she'd been on the island last night? Had anyone seen her? A woman eight months pregnant would have been noticed. Maggie texted McCabe, who was at 109 writing up probable cause to get both Byron and Aimée's bank and credit card records. *Ask the guys interviewing party guests if anyone noticed a large pregnant tummy on the island last night.*

Will do.

The biggest problem with Gina being the killer was obviously physical. Expecting a baby in just a few weeks, there was no way she'd be a physical match for either her husband or Aimée. On the other hand, she didn't have to be. She had the knife. Maybe a gun as well. Would Byron have jumped overboard if she'd threatened to shoot him? Doubtful. On the other hand, what if she'd threatened to shoot Aimée? Would Byron have done the gallant thing and taken a dive to save Aimée's life? That seemed slightly more likely. Still, the whole scenario seemed far-fetched.

Of course there was another possibility. That, instead of going to the island, Gina had hired someone else to kill her husband and his lover. Hired killers can be difficult to find. They don't advertise in the yellow pages or on Facebook. They don't have websites. Plus they tend to be expensive, and Gina said she and Byron were broke. Easy enough to confirm by checking their bank and credit card accounts. No, Maggie decided, Gina wasn't the killer. She was barking up the wrong tree.

She turned from the window and went back to checking out the apartment. One closet with nothing but a few metal coat hangers, a window fan and a beat-up vacuum cleaner. A man's hunter-green cardigan sweater, size large, hung from a hook on the back of the door. Byron's? Probably.

The small kitchen was nearly as empty as the closet. A few glasses and coffee mugs occupied one of the glass-fronted cupboards, along with a pile of coffee filters, paper plates and a half-empty box of plastic utensils. An under-counter fridge held an open bag of coffee, a quart of milk and a 1.75 liter bottle of Ketel One vodka with maybe three inches of booze left inside. The stove and oven appeared to never have been used. Nothing in the drawers. No pots, pans or silverware. A Black & Decker coffeemaker with what looked like week-old coffee grounds in it sat on the Formica counter next to the stainless steel sink. A bottle of Dawn and a sponge on the sink. One coffee mug and two oversized martini glasses sat upside down in a plastic drying rack.

Maggie turned back to the main room. The place looked clean, the furniture new and not inexpensive. The kind of stuff that looked like it'd been ordered straight out of Crate and Barrel's or Pottery Barn's online catalogues. Had Aimée paid to furnish the place as well as paying the rent? Probably. One of the perks of being a girl blessed with unlimited funds. In the immortal words of Lerner and Loewe, *Wouldn't it be loverly?*

An oversized love seat with white slipcovers was pushed up against one wall, with a matching armchair next to it and a wooden coffee table in front. A bright red Navajo area rug covered the floor. A couple of copies of a magazine called *Art in America* were arranged a little self-consciously on top of the table.

Against the opposite wall was an unmade queen-sized bed and two matching nightstands with lamps. Rumpled red sheets and a reddish-brown paisley duvet that had slipped mostly off to one side and four matching pillows. A treasure trove of DNA, which would be worth next to nothing unless it belonged to someone other than the two lovers. Still, she'd have Jacoby haul it all into the lab and go over it looking for hairs, skin and whatever else he could find.

Maggie paused on her way to the desk to look at herself in a full-length mirror that hung to the right of the bed. She was wearing no makeup, and her short, dark hair was sticking out in a few places it shouldn't. Still, she thought to herself, not so bad for someone inching up on thirty-seven. Especially considering she'd been up all night and had thrown on the same clothes she'd worn the day before. Black jeans, black T-shirt, lightweight black jacket and red high-top sneakers. Just for a second she found herself wondering if, with Kyra out of the picture, she and McCabe really might get something going. She pushed the thought out of her head as quickly as it came and got back to work.

Maggie walked over to Byron's desk. A rectangle of solid birch supported by a pair of matching wood file cabinets. A desk lamp and a laptop computer were the only things on top. Before checking the computer, she opened the drawers. Top left was empty except for a roll of packing tape, a stapler and a small bag of rubber bands. Bottom left was totally empty. So was the top right. It was in the one on the bottom right that Maggie hit pay dirt. The drawer was filled with a large pile of papers, probably two to three hundred sheets in all. The top page was a photocopy of a front-page story in the *Portland Press Herald* from one hundred and eight years ago. She lifted several sheets carefully by the sides of the pages and saw other photocopies of subsequent stories about the murder.

Maggie sat in the black Aeron desk chair and read the first story. A reduced-size copy of the front page of the *Press Herald* dated June 18, 1904. A banner headline screamed out the big story of the day: *"Murder and Suicide on Whitby Island!"* A subhead only a little smaller added, *"Portland business tycoon's artist wife and her lover found dead in island love nest. Passion and jealousy apparent motive!"*

Maggie lifted the page up by its edges and began to read the reduced-size type.

"In what can only be described as an enormous loss to the entire Portland community, Mrs. Aimée Garnier Whitby, wife of prominent Portland business and civic leader Edward Whitby Jr., was found near death early yesterday by the water's edge on the Whitbys' privately owned island. Mrs. Whitby had been stabbed in the abdomen and was subsequently either pushed or fell over the island's sixty-foot cliff, known to local mariners as The Eagle's Slide. The fall from the cliff severed her spine, and, had she lived, she would have been permanently crippled. However, Mrs. Whitby died of her wounds as she was being transported back to Portland for medical treatment by Portland fisherman John O'Reilly and his two sons, Jack, 12, and Harry, 16. The O'Reillys discovered Mrs. Whitby's stricken body lying on the rocks beneath the cliff early yesterday afternoon as they were preparing to lay nets on the seaward side of the island.

"At great risk to their own lives, Mr. O'Reilly's two sons braved the fearsome waves that predominate on that side of the island and transported Mrs. Whitby safely back to their vessel, the Jackknife.

"According to Portland mayor Herbert Callaway, who announced that he will be personally heading up the investigation into Mrs. Whitby's death, Mrs. Whitby had been mortally stabbed by the renowned Boston artist Mark Garrison. Garrison's blade, an antique Japanese dagger called a Tanto, inflicted a deep wound to her abdomen. He then carved a crudely formed letter A in her upper chest.

Cumberland County coroner Harley Creamer told this reporter that Mrs. Whitby's death was the result of the abdominal wound. Her assailant later took his own life, hanging himself with a leather belt inside Mrs. Whitby's island art studio."

The piece went on to describe in fairly lurid detail the story of the love affair, then engaged in what seemed nothing more than pure speculation that *"Garrison had slain his paramour when she told him that she was breaking off their relationship. Horrified by what he had done, he then took his own life."*

Maggie carefully lifted the top page. The story continued for two more pages and essentially recounted the tale that Edward Whitby had told her and McCabe back on the island. Below the article were copies of similar stories, including follow-ups from other papers in Maine, as well as all the New York and Boston dailies. The death of Aimée Whitby remained front-page news for nearly a month. Of course, in those days there was no television, no Internet and no twenty-four-hour news cycles with endlessly pontificating talking heads.

Leaving the papers intact, Maggie pushed the drawer closed to await transport to 109 by a team of evidence techs.

She then turned her attention to the laptop computer on top of the desk. A MacBook Pro. Presumably the new computer Gina Knowles told them about that morning. The one on which Byron was supposedly writing his biography of Lord Byron. Byron told Gina the school had paid the two thousand dollars plus that the machine cost. That could be checked. If they hadn't, Aimée might have picked up the tab for this as well. Maggie wondered how a man her own age felt about a rich teenager spending all this money on him. Grateful? Embarrassed? Angry? Afraid of how he would be judged if the affair became public knowledge? Maybe McCabe was wrong and there was no third man. Maybe this was simply a case of an angry man killing his girlfriend and then taking his own life to avoid public disgrace.

Maggie lifted the lid on the computer. At the moment, the screen was dark, either turned off or in sleep mode. She punched the space bar a few times. The machine lit up, and she typed GGB1788 in the login box. The screen opened to page thirty-three of an eighty-five-page Microsoft Word Document titled *A Mourning of Death*1.3.docx. She read:

DISS. TO EXTERIOR SHOT. A GRAY DREARY MORN-ING. THROUGH SWIRLS OF FOG WE CAN SEE THE ISLAND STUDIO.

CAMERA MOVES IN FOR A MCU AS DOOR OPENS. DANIELLE BURSTS OUT. SHE IS NUDE, *HER BODY SPATTERED WITH BLOOD.*

CUT TO CU HILTON'S FACE STANDING IN THE DOOR OF THE STUDIO.

HILTON (OC): Danielle come back! Please come back!

HILTON FOLLOWS HER TOWARD THE CLIFF.

Obviously Byron Knowles was working on more than a biography of his namesake. This was a screenplay based on the events of 1904, a dramatization of the murder on Whitby Island. Byron had changed the name of the place to Barnett Island and also changed the names of the characters. Maggie wondered if Aimée had provided Knowles with any information Edward Whitby had not mentioned. Information possibly not included in the news accounts and court records of the day. Maggie would ask Jacoby to print out the screenplay, and she'd read it tonight after the autopsies. She pressed Save and closed *A Mourning of Death*. Then she shut down the computer, called Jacoby and told him to send a team over to the apartment to do a thorough search for both fingerprints and DNA. They could pick up a key at Mullaney Realty.

Chapter 41

From the journal of Edward Whitby Jr.
Entry dated July 11, 1924

On a cold night in January in the winter of 1904, the seeds of jealousy that had lain dormant in the recesses of my brain for so many months began to germinate. The immediate catalyst was a suggestion I made to Aimée. That night the two of us enjoyed a quiet dinner at home with our children, Charlotte, Teddy and Annabelle. After dessert, we all went into the sitting room, where Charlotte read stories to the two younger ones. When the stories were done, we kissed all three good night and asked Nanny to take them upstairs to get ready for bed. Charlotte objected.

"I'm nearly eight years old, Mommy," she said. "I shouldn't be made to go to bed when the others do."

"You needn't turn your light out for another hour," said

Aimée, "but I'd like you to go upstairs and get ready for bed. There's school tomorrow."

Charlotte harrumphed, then looked at me, preparing, I knew, to appeal her case to higher authority. I cut her off.

"No arguments, young lady. Do as your mother says."

She harrumphed again before trudging up the stairs behind the others.

Aimée and I remained in the sitting room. A heavy snow was falling outside the windows. It had started at about four that afternoon, and by eight o'clock there was a good six inches on the ground, which a strong northeast wind was blowing into drifts.

Even from a distance of twenty years, I can still see myself sitting in the big leather chair in front of the fireplace, smoking a cigar and sipping a snifter of Armagnac as I listened to Aimée at the piano playing one of Chopin's nocturnes. Opus 62 in E Major. I'd rarely seen her look so beautiful.

"I've been thinking of commissioning a formal portrait of you," I said when she finished the piece.

She turned to face me. "Another portrait? We already have the two my father painted."

"You were a child when he painted those. Only twelve when he did the first one."

"Sixteen for the second," she said. "Not such a child."

"No. Not such a child. Still, I'd like another of you as you are now. My wife. The mother of our children. And even more beautiful at twenty-eight than you were when I met you. I'd like to hang it over the stone fireplace on the island."

She looked at me curiously. "Why the island?"

"Because I know how much you love the island. How you think of it as your home far more than you do this house. Besides, the portraits your father painted are already hanging here."

"Very well. As you wish."

Aimée walked over and kissed me on the cheek. I received the kiss gratefully, though I would rather it had been on the lips. It had been a long time, at least six weeks, since we had been physically close. I stood, put my arms around her and tried to kiss her properly.

She pulled away and sat once again on the piano bench.

"Have you considered an artist for this portrait?" she asked.

"I've already written Sargent to see if he'd be interested in taking the commission. He wrote back saying he would but that it would have to wait at least until summer. He's going to be in Europe until then."

"Why Sargent?"

"Because he's the best."

"I'm not so sure."

"Aimée, please. I and just about everyone else in our circle who knows anything about art considers John Singer Sargent the finest portraitist of the age."

I had a feeling that she would object, and she did.

"I'd rather Garrison paint it."

"Mark Garrison? I grant you he's a talented painter, but compared to Sargent?" I made a dismissive gesture with my hands.

"I don't want to hang as one more of Sargent's *grandes dames*. I really don't think you know Mark's work. I think he's every inch the equal of Sargent. And because he and I know each other, I think he's more likely to create a painting that truly captures the spirit of who I am."

I felt the first flutters of jealousy hearing these words. I knew she'd been taking the train down to Boston more frequently of late and not just the once a week required by her duties as an instructor. When I'd asked her why, she'd offered little, other than to say that she enjoyed visiting the city for shopping, visiting the galleries and museums and sometimes sharing lunch with an old school friend of hers from France named Delphine Martineau, who, like Aimée, had married an American. Delphine had recently been widowed, and since the death of her husband she'd been living in a small town house on Beacon Hill.

Initially, I accepted Aimée's explanation. I knew that Delphine had telephoned on several occasions, presumably to make plans for their excursions. Now I was wondering if these visits with Delphine might not just be a cover for excursions of another kind.

"I see," I said, "and exactly how well has Mr. Garrison gotten to know you?"

Aimée knew from our days in Paris how jealous I could be of other men, how easily my suspicions were aroused.

"We're colleagues at the Museum School. Nothing more."

"And there's nothing else going on here that you're not telling me?"

"Edward, if you're implying what I think you are, the answer is of course not. What on earth could you be thinking?"

Against my better judgment, I relented and agreed that we would offer Garrison the commission. Within days the deal was done. He would paint his portrait of Aimée on the island as soon as the weather turned warm enough to open the house for the season and trips across the bay became more comfortable.

Over the next few months, however, I became so obsessed with the idea that Aimée was having an affair with Garrison that I could think of little else. Finally, unable to carry on without knowing the truth, I engaged the services of a private investigator named Albert Whelan, who had impressed me with his discretion while performing some sensitive inquiries in behalf of Whitby & Sons.

The next time Aimée went to Boston, Whelan followed her. She was met at the North Station by a man who fit the description of Garrison. They hired a taxi, and Whelan managed to hear Aimée instruct the driver to take Garrison and herself to number 22 Walnut Street on Beacon Hill. I knew this was the address of the house belonging to Delphine Martineau. Whelan found another cab and followed them. Aimée must have had a key, Whelan said, because when they got to the house, they let themselves in.

Chapter 42

LEAVING THE AUTOPSY room at Cumberland Med a little after seven thirty, Maggie left her car in the visitors lot and walked the quarter mile or so to the big white house on the Western Prom. She rang the bell, and this time Brenda Boatwright opened the door promptly. She peered out at Maggie with scarcely disguised dislike.

"What do you want now?"

"Is Mrs. Whitby here at the house?"

"No."

"How about Julia?"

"Why do you want to know?"

Maggie sighed. "I'm not your enemy, Ms. Boatwright. I'm working hard to solve what you surely know by now are a pair of tragic murders. I'd appreciate it, as I'm sure the Whitbys would, if you would stop putting petty roadblocks in my way. Now, if Julia's at home, would you please let her know that I need to speak with her."

Boatwright harrumphed. "Wait here," she said and turned.

Maggie shook her head. At least the housekeeper hadn't told her to go around and wait by the tradesmen's entrance. A couple of minutes later Julia appeared. She was wearing a maroon Penfield T-shirt and a pair of tight jeans. Her feet were bare.

"Come in," she said. Without another word she led the way into a large, elegantly furnished study overlooking a formally planted garden. She pointed Maggie to a large leather sofa and plopped herself down in a matching easy chair.

"Do you want a drink or anything?"

"No, thank you. Your mother's not here?"

"No. She went out. She said she had some business to attend to."

"And your father?"

"He's here. He told me to come down and help you in any way I can."

"Your father said you knew your sister better than anyone."

"I guess."

"Would you say you and Aimée were friends?"

"Well, sure."

"Best friends?"

"I loved my sister. That's more than just being best friends."

"And she loved you back?"

Julia didn't answer for what must have been ten or fifteen seconds. "Of course," she finally said. "I loved her and she loved me."

Maggie didn't subscribe to the theory that people blink a lot when telling a lie. She'd interrogated too many practiced liars who barely blinked at all. Still, Julia was blinking frequently. Maybe she wasn't practiced enough.

"Did you and Aimée share most things?"

"You mean like clothes?"

"No, I mean like secrets."

More hesitation. More blinking. "We talked about a lot of stuff."

"Like boyfriends and things like that?"

"Well, yeah."

"Did you know Aimée and Byron Knowles were having an affair?"

"An affair?" Julia's tone was suddenly angry. "Is that what you call it? A teacher fucking one of his students. I'm not sure I'd call that an affair."

"All right, did you know Knowles was *fucking* your sister—"

"Half sister," Julia interrupted.

"Half sister, then. Did you know about it before last night?"

"No." Julia paused, perhaps thinking over her answer. "Well, yes. Sort of."

"Did Aimée tell you about it?"

"Not in so many words."

"Well, then how did you know?"

Julia shrugged. "It was more like, I don't know, intuition. I mean we've been together since we were born. A lot of times I know what she's thinking or doing, and she knew the same about me. It's like a kind of telepathy."

"Did Aimée ever drop a hint about what she and Knowles were up to?"

"Not really. It was more in the way she looked at him. Talked about him. Like it made me think something was going on there."

"Did you ever ask her about it?"

"Yeah, once."

"And what did she say?"

"'Oh, don't be silly, Jules. You can't go messing around with your teachers.' Something like that."

"But you thought she was lying?"

"I *knew* she was lying."

"Did that make you angry?"

"I just thought it was stupid. Aimée could have any guy she wanted any time she wanted, and she goes and picks a married, middle-aged English teacher? Jesus Christ, how stupid is that? Still, she always had a thing for older guys."

"Oh, yeah? Like who?"

"Like Knowles."

"Like who else?"

"Like Charles Kraft. I think she's had the hots for Charles for a while. And he kind of has the hots for her. Come to think of it, maybe that's why Knowles killed her. Maybe Aimée dumped him so she could go after Charles, and Knowles got pissed off and did the deed."

"Do you think there's any chance Kraft might have killed your sister? Let's say out of jealousy?"

Julia shrugged. "I don't know. Killing is something he's probably pretty good at."

"I've been trying to reach Mr. Kraft all day. Do you have any idea where he might be?"

"Do you know a place called Nasty's?"

Chapter 43

"Is this seat free?" Maggie asked as she slipped onto the barstool next to Charles Kraft in Nasty's. The place was one of the more popular dive bars on the west end, and at eight thirty on a Friday night, things were just beginning to roar.

"Well, the truth of it is," Kraft said with a smile, "I was saving it for my girlfriend."

Maggie looked around. "Oh, really? Now which girlfriend would that be?"

Maggie felt Charles Kraft's eyes assessing her, dressed as she usually was in her trademark black. Black sweater, black trousers, and a black cotton jacket that barely concealed the black Glock 17 nestled in its black holster. Kraft seemed to like what he saw.

"Haven't decided yet," he said, scanning the crowd pushing in toward the bar. "Maybe you could help me. What do you think of that one?" Kraft nodded toward a small, pretty brunette, no more than five-one or five-two, wearing a T-shirt and pair of tight leggings that revealed every ripple in her very nice ass. She was standing at the end of the bar, laughing loudly with a couple of less attractive girlfriends. They were all drinking Miller Lite out of bottles Maggie figured they were just old enough to buy.

"Cute. Nice body. But a little giggly, don't you think?"

"Umm. Maybe you're right. How about that blonde over there in the booth?"

Maggie nodded. "Not bad as long as you don't mind muscling out the dude she's with." The dude looked to be six-three, with a lean body and heavily muscled arms covered with elaborate tattoos from wrist to shoulder. "Course, for a former Special Ops guy like you, that shouldn't be hard."

Kraft smiled. "Might even be fun. On the other hand," he said, giving Maggie another once-over, "maybe the best is already here. What'll you have?"

"Diet Coke works for me."

"You working or something?"

"Or something."

Kraft signaled the bartender, a bottle blonde with large breasts that were pushing their way out of a low-cut T-shirt two sizes too small. "Damn," the blonde said. "If it isn't Maggie Savage. Haven't seen you in a coon's age? Still chasing bad guys?"

"What else?" said Maggie. "Charles, this is Gloria. Gloria, Charles. Glo's been working the bar at Nasty's for, jeez, what is it? Twenty years now?"

"Twenty-two come next month." She turned to Charles. "You one of the bad guys she spends her time chasing?"

Kraft smiled at Maggie. "I don't know, Detective. Am I bad? And are you chasing me?"

Maggie smiled back. Under other circumstances she might well consider "chasing" him. "Well, you never know, now, do you, Charles? Depends how bad you are."

"Pretty damned bad."

"Is that so? Would that be why you haven't returned my phone calls? I tried you three times. I was beginning to think you were trying to avoid me."

Kraft pulled out his phone and looked at it. "Yup. Three times. Says so right here. So how'd you find me?"

"Julia told me you like to hang out here."

Gloria came back and handed Maggie her coke, then filled Charles's glass with a couple of fresh ice cubes and a double measure of Ketel One.

"Tell me, Charles, what exactly did you have against Aimée Whitby?"

"Oooh, nice interrogation technique, Detective," said Kraft. "Make the witness feel defensive. *Exactly what do you have against the Americans, Ahmad, that convinced you to join the jihad?* Did they teach you that in cop school?"

Maggie didn't answer. Just sipped her Coke and waited for Kraft to answer her question.

"I had absolutely nothing against Aimée. In fact, I've always been rather fond of her. She could be a little arrogant at times. But then she had a lot to be arrogant about."

"Did you find her attractive?"

"Poor choice of words."

"How so?"

"Calling Aimée Whitby attractive is like calling Shakespeare a pretty good writer or LeBron an okay basketball player. Aimée was movie star gorgeous. One of the most beautiful women I've ever seen."

"Did you ever think about making *her* your girlfriend?"

"Think about it? Sure. Probably every guy she met thought

about it. But Aimée was my boss's daughter, and I happen to like my job. And frankly, she was a little young for me."

"Yes. Only eighteen. More child than woman. Too young to die, don't you think?"

"Of course she was. On the other hand, I can't count the number of eighteen-year-old kids I saw getting killed in Iraq and Afghanistan. And that was just on our side. If you count the dead on their side, the bodies started piling up just outside the womb. In some cases even before they got out of the womb."

"How do you feel about what you did in the war?"

"Let's just say I thought it was necessary. At least I did at the time. Either way, I was good at it."

"Good at what? Killing people?"

"Among other things."

"How did you feel about it? Killing people, I mean?" Maggie's own brother Harlan had been a Marine sniper in Iraq, and she knew for a fact that he'd killed twenty-three Iraqis before leaving the war with a serious head wound. To this day the memory of those twenty-three dead haunted him. Not to mention the civilian dead Kraft was alluding to.

"I was doing my duty. Defending my country against people who wanted to do us harm. That's what soldiers do."

"Did you ever get off on it?"

"You mean sexually?"

"You tell me."

"No. But there were guys who did. War does weird shit to your brain."

"Do you think that the person who killed Aimée may have been one of them?"

Maggie studied Kraft's face as he swirled his vodka in his glass.

"Maybe. Probably. I can't think of any other reason to have done what he did. Have you ever killed anyone?" he asked.

"Only once. A psychopathic murderer who was about to cut my partner's throat."

"McCabe?"

"Yes."

"Did you like it? The act of inflicting death?"

"No. I hated it. Even though the guy was a sicko who killed people for fun. He deserved to die."

"So you gave him what he deserved?"

"I suppose so."

"A lot of people in a war zone who see their buddies getting waxed begin to feel the same way. The jihadis deserve to die. So you kill them."

"And you were good at it?"

"Yup."

"How come you quit the army and joined Orion?"

"The pay was better. Base pay for a captain with six years service is roughly sixty-five K a year. Orion paid me four times that for what was essentially the same job. Plus bonuses."

"Because you were good at it?"

"Yeah. Because I was good at it. Look, Detective, if this is going where I think it's going, you've got the wrong guy. I didn't kill Aimée. I didn't kill her boyfriend either. Though I might have if I'd known her teacher was screwing her on a regular basis."

"What makes you think they were having sex?" Maggie asked. Shockley hadn't announced that. Nor had the papers printed it, though they had insinuated the possibility. Perhaps Kraft, in spite of his self-confidence, had just slipped up.

"Julia talks to both of us."

"When did she tell you?"

"On the helicopter flying back to the mainland this morning."

"What exactly did she say?"

"Just that Aimée and Knowles had been getting it on for most of senior year."

"Anything else?"

Kraft shrugged. "She also started spouting a lot of nonsense about Aimée being the reincarnation of their great-great-grandmother and that she was fated to be killed in the same way. To be murdered by her lover who then committed suicide."

"Is that the term she used? 'Fated'?"

"Yeah. But Jules has always been a little weird when it comes to the woo-woo stuff."

"How did Julia know about the affair? Did Aimée tell her?"

"I'm not sure, but I would guess she didn't."

"Why?"

"Because when I asked Jules how she knew, she became evasive. All she would say was that she just had a special way of knowing about things like that."

"Interesting."

"My guess is *her special way* was nothing more than hacking Aimée's e-mails and texts. Probably been doing it for quite a while."

"Why?"

"You want my theory?"

"Sure."

"I know for a fact that Julia was seriously jealous of Aimée. Always has been. Not hard to understand why. Aimée's the prettier sister. The smarter sister. The better athlete. Plus they're exactly the same age. Worst of all, Aimée's the one Daddy loves most. At least in Julia's mind he does."

"Is she right about that?"

"I think so. A situation like that can be brutal for a kid growing up. I think jealousy led Julia to obsess about Aimée. What she was doing. Who she was doing it with. What secrets she wasn't revealing. Turned out one of those secrets was Byron Knowles. You want another Coke?"

Maggie shook her head no. Kraft held up his glass. Maggie watched Gloria fill it to the top, watched Kraft start sipping it. How was it, she wondered, that every guy she found both interesting and attractive seemed to drink too much? Maybe the problem wasn't theirs but hers. Maybe she was just genetically attracted to alcoholics. Hell, even her father found it tough to say no to a bottle of good bourbon.

"Last night at the party," said Kraft, "when Aimée made her grand entrance, dressed exactly like the woman in the painting, Jules couldn't hold her anger in. I was watching her, and I thought for a minute she was really going to lose it and go for Aimée. Rip the damned dress right off her body." Kraft chuckled. "Catfight like that would have been one hell of a show. Of course, there's no way Julia would have come out on top. Aimée would have kicked the crap out of her."

"Did anyone else notice Julia's anger?"

Kraft shrugged. "No idea."

"Why were you watching her so closely?"

"When I saw Aimée make her grand entrance, I had a feeling Jules might react that way. I'm paid to keep things from getting out of hand. Specially stuff like that."

Maggie thought about it. Jealousy again. Just like Gina Knowles. Seems Julia was consumed by it. The oldest motive for murder in the world. Gina was eight months pregnant and physically incapable of pulling it off. But Julia was young and fit. Could she be the one who killed Aimée and Knowles? Could she have murdered her own sister? Maggie thought about words she'd read in Sunday school as a kid. *When Cain realized that God was not pleased with his sacrifice but accepted Abel's, his heart became wicked. He became angry and jealous of his brother and killed him out of envy.* Had Julia Whitby grown angry and jealous of her sibling and killed her out of envy? Certainly seemed possible. Though to pull it off she would have had to have gotten the drop on them somehow. Or have found someone to help her.

"How many people have you killed?" asked Maggie.

Kraft's eyes narrowed. "Quite a few. Either directly or by ordering someone else to do it."

"Don't you remember how many?"

"I didn't keep a running count. In a place like Iraq, death is delivered in so many different ways sometimes you don't even know how many may have died. So no, I don't remember how many."

"But you're capable of killing."

"I already told you I didn't kill her. Or him."

"I know, but what I'm wondering is do you think Julia is capable of murder?"

"Given the right circumstances, I think almost anybody is. But Jules? I'm not sure she'd be very good at it."

"Good at it. Like you, you mean."

"Yeah. Like me."

"Tell me something. How long did you work at Orion?"

"Five years, give or take."

"How many other people like you worked there?"

"Maggie, haven't you figured it out yet?" Kraft grinned. "There are no other people like me."

"I'm not joking, Charles. How many others?"

"At the moment?"

"Either current or former. People you knew?"

"A couple of hundred."

"All good at killing?"

"Maggie, not only did I not kill Aimée but I also didn't pass on any names of Orion people who might have. I swear that's the truth. I liked Aimée. I work for and like her father. I wouldn't do something like that to either of them."

"Are you sure?"

"Yes, I'm sure. Yes, I could have given Julia the names of plenty of people who could do the job. But I didn't. And even if I did, I'm not sure Julia would have had enough money to pay the bill. Mercenary killers don't come cheap."

"So who do you think did it?"

"Me?" Kraft shrugged. "I'm a believer in Occam's razor. In the absence of contradictory evidence, I believe the simplest solution is usually the correct one."

"And what's the simplest solution here?"

"That Knowles killed her. Then killed himself."

"Why did he carve the letter *A*?"

"Who knows?" Kraft shrugged. "Julia said he specialized in the romantic poets. Maybe he knew about the murder of the first Aimée and thought it might be romantic to duplicate it as closely as possible."

"Darkly romantic."

"Very darkly." Kraft slipped off his stool and made his way to the men's room. Maggie sat there and considered the possibilities. Something she hadn't thought about before popped into her head.

Charles returned. "How about we blow this place and go somewhere a little quieter?" he asked.

"Some other time, maybe, and I mean that. But not while I'm working. However, I do have one more question."

"Shoot."

"You worked for Orion for five years, right?"

"Right."

"Why did you leave?"

"I got a better offer from Whitby."

"Were you looking for another job?"

"No."

"So how did you find out about the job at Whitby?"

"They found me. I told my boss, the guy who founded Orion, that I'd had enough of the contract work and was planning on looking for something else. He said he knew Whitby was looking for a security guy."

"How'd he know that?"

Kraft's smile disappeared "At the moment, I'm not sure I'm free to tell you that."

Maggie decided not to press him. Instead she took out her phone and looked up the Wikipedia page for The Orion Group. It was right there in the first paragraph. *The company was founded in 1987 by former Navy Seal Dennis McClure.*

"Is Dennis McClure any relation to Deirdre?"

"Her brother."

Chapter 44

LUCY MCCORKLE SAW the killer before he saw her.

Wanting the cover of darkness, Lucy waited till ten o'clock Friday night before pushing her shopping cart across the parking area of the mini-mart. She left the cart just outside, opened the door, walked into the store and there he was, standing at the counter buying a pack of cigarettes. He was no longer wearing the white jacket. Just a pair of black pants and a blue denim shirt with fancy-looking shoes on his feet. She couldn't quite see all of his face; still, she had no doubt it was him.

She told herself to turn around and get the hell out of there. To disappear. Get lost. Or at least head down to the back of the store, where it was darker and he might not notice her. But she didn't. She just stood there, as if rooted to the spot, right in the doorway, staring at him.

She wondered if, when he turned, he would know she was the one who'd seen him kill the girl.

Of course he would. She recognized him, so why wouldn't he recognize her?

Maybe because while she'd seen not just his face but his whole body, even his ass and his pecker when he was banging away at the girl, he'd only seen her eyes and maybe a little of her face, and even that for only a few seconds in the dark.

When the killer handed the clerk, a kid named Roger, a twenty-dollar bill to pay for the cigarettes, Lucy told herself again to turn around and leave the store. Or disappear into the back. But hard as she tried to make that happen, she couldn't get her feet to work. It was like they were glued to the floor. So she just stood there and stared as Roger put the twenty to the side of the cash register. Counted out the change and handed it over. The killer tucked the cigarettes, a green pack of Newports, into the breast pocket of his shirt, checked his change and stuffed it into his pocket.

That's when he saw her. He studied her for a few seconds, brows furrowed, an uncertain expression on his face.

Lucy stared back. Then she changed the stare to a smile. "Hey, mister, can you spare an old lady a couple of bucks so maybe I can buy myself a little something for dinner? And maybe a pack of them butts?"

His expression changed from uncertainty to an easy smile.

Run, a voice in her head was screaming. *Run out of here, you stupid old bag.*

But she didn't run. She didn't move.

The man reached into his pocket and pulled out a five and handed it to her. "Here. This won't get you the butts, but maybe it'll get you something to eat."

Lucy took the money and looked at it. "Thank you, sir," she said. "Thank you. God will bless you for this. He will reward you in heaven."

The man must've thought that was funny, cause he laughed. "I wouldn't count on it," he said. Lucy moved out of his way.

"See you around," he said, winking at Lucy. Then he pulled the door open and left.

She watched him cross the parking lot and wondered if maybe she was wrong and this wasn't the guy who killed the girl. Sure looked like him though. Maybe he just hadn't recognized her. She visibly relaxed as he climbed into a car. Rear lights blinked as he started the engine and pulled out onto Washington Avenue.

Lucy watched the car go. For a minute she wondered if maybe she really had just imagined the whole thing. But all she had to do was put her hand in her pocket and feel the money and the wallet to know it was real. She was surer than ever she'd just taken five bucks from a murderer then watched him drive away.

"Go get what you want, Lucy," said Roger, "then get out. The boss doesn't like you hanging around here too long."

Lucy limped on her sore legs toward the back of the store, past the rack where they kept the liquor and wine. Made sure Roger couldn't see her. She opened the wallet belonging to Veronica Aimée Whitby, pulled out the green debit card and slid it into the slot. The machine said *Remove card quickly.* Lucy did. *Please enter your personal identification number.* Lucy entered 4932. To her amazement, a group of choices appeared on the screen. Lucy pressed the one that said *Get Cash.* She peered around the corner of the wine shelf to see if Roger might be watching her, wondering what she was doing back there. But he wasn't. He was ringing up a purchase for another customer and didn't seem to know she was still in the store. Nobody else was down this end, so Lucy turned her attention back to the ATM. The message on the machine asked her if she wanted the money from checking or savings. Lucy hit Checking. Then it asked her to select the amount of money she wanted. Gave her a bunch of choices. *$20. $40. $80. $100. Other.* Shit. A lousy hundred dollars. Was that all she could get? She pressed Other. *Please enter the amount of cash you would like to withdraw.* Lucy thought about that for a minute, not being sure how much money the machine was allowed to give her. She tapped in *$1,000* and hit Enter. Another message came up. *Sorry. That amount exceeds the daily limit of cash that may be withdrawn from this ATM. Please enter an amount between $20 and $400.* Lucy entered *$400.* Then the damned machine asked another question. *Your bank charges a $3.00 fee for this transaction. Do you accept this fee? Please hit yes or no.* Lucy peered around the shelf again. Now Roger was sitting behind the counter, reading a copy of the *Forecaster* and drinking some coffee. Lucy hit the Yes button. She held her breath for what seemed like a long time. Then the machine started spitting out twenty-dollar bills like there was no tomorrow. Lucy watched in amazement as one twenty after another came sliding out of the machine, making a sound like *kachung, kachung, kachung* every time another twenty joined the pile. When it seemed to be finished, she removed the wad and folded the bills over and stuffed them into her pocket. *Do you want another transaction?* the machine asked. Lucy pressed No and waited for the receipt. She pulled out the little slip of white paper and looked down at it.

"Jesus, Mary and Joseph," she murmured, her heart beating just as fast as it had when she saw the killer ram the knife into the girl's gut. She closed her eyes for a minute and breathed slowly in and out, hoping the breathing would slow down the pounding in her chest. Then she opened her eyes and looked one more time at the white slip of paper. Not the whole thing. Just the last line where it said, Remaining Balance: $21,476.89.

Staring at the number, Lucy wondered again if she shouldn't tell the lady cop on Vesper Street, the one who called herself Maggie, about seeing the killer. Tell her what he looked like. What color car he drove. Even what kind of butts he smoked. Get the bastard off the street before he killed her or anyone else. No reason she had to say anything about the debit card or about the twenty-one grand. If she could just hold on to that, Lucy could get herself cleaned up, rent a small apartment and fill the place with enough bottles of good vodka to last her just about forever.

Chapter 45

From the journal of Edward Whitby Jr.
July 16, 1924

Over the course of that spring, Aimée and Garrison made a number of subsequent trips to the house at 22 Walnut Street. On each occasion Aimée used the key to let them in. They usually stayed about two hours before leaving and going their separate ways. When parting, they shook hands formally on the street. Whelan reported seeing no kisses, no hugs, no overt signs whatsoever of physical affection or sexual attraction.

Nevertheless, reading Whelan's confidential reports were an agony to me. I pictured Aimée and Garrison together in that house, imagining them engaged in acts not only of intimacy but of the utmost depravity. In my mind I could hear them laughing at how thoroughly they had pulled the wool over the eyes of the unsuspecting cuckold. I was seized with the urge to follow Aimée myself on her next trip. To smash down the doors of Delphine's house and to catch them *in flagrante delicto.* To take out my revolver and kill both of them then and there. Of course, to follow them would have been impossible. Aimée would have noticed me instantly.

Moreover, before confronting Aimée, I told myself I needed absolute proof of her infidelity. I needed Whelan to catch her in the act. All the detective had provided me with thus far was information that Garrison and Aimée had been seen entering a house belonging to Aimée's friend Delphine Martineau. Perhaps all they had done while there was to have tea in the garden with or without Delphine in attendance.

Whelan suggested that he call on Delphine and ask her about the visits. Discover whether she knew of them. Ask why Aimée had a key to Delphine's house. I forbade him from doing so. All that would accomplish would be to alert the lovers of my suspicions. Instead, I asked him if he was capable of picking a lock. He said that he was, but that entering a house belonging to someone else without permission violated the law. If seen in the act, he was liable to prosecution. It took only a little monetary persuasion to convince Whelan to change his mind.

The following Wednesday I received a telephone call from Whelan asking me to meet with him in his small office on Exchange Street. I went around, expecting the worst.

"Take a seat, Mr. Whitby."

With great difficulty I sat.

"Yesterday I followed your wife to Boston, as I have been doing. By the way, she has begun noticing me on the train. Hopefully she thinks of me as someone who commutes regularly for business purposes."

"As you are."

"Yes, I suppose. Anyway, before arriving at the house, I put on a false beard and spectacles and changed my jacket to prevent her from recognizing me. I then allowed them a good forty-five minutes alone in the house before I began working the lock. It only took a minute to trip the tumblers and let myself in. Happily, no one saw me on the street, and there was no one on the ground floor inside. It was a very elegant house, I must say. Many fine paintings and objects of art."

I was growing impatient. "Get to it, man. Did you see them?"

"Yes. In the main bedroom upstairs."

My stomach tightened, waiting for Whelan to describe the scene.

"Your wife was naked."

"And Garrison?"

"Fully clothed."

I frowned. "What were they doing?"

"She was standing by a window. The morning light was shining on her body. A very beautiful woman, if I may say so."

"No, sir. You may most definitely not say so. Where was Garrison?"

"He was standing at an easel near the door, drawing a picture of her. There were many other pictures of her around the room. Some strewn about the floor. Others, as it turned out, in a portfolio case. When I burst into the room holding a revolver, your wife screamed and grabbed a robe and put it on. Garrison came at me with clenched fists but stopped short when I pointed the gun not at him but at your wife. I had a feeling he might have risked his own life to attack me but he wouldn't risk hers. Naturally, they took me for a burglar, which is what I had intended. Garrison offered me money.

"Did you take it?"

"Of course. What kind of burglar would I be if I hadn't? I'll deduct the amount from your invoice. I also scooped up a number of the drawings of your wife, both clothed and naked, and stuffed them into the portfolio case. I then warned them not to follow me or call the police, or I would shoot them. I took the portfolio case and went back down to the ground floor, where I took some silver candlesticks and a few other baubles to support the idea of a burglary. I left the house as quickly as possible and caught the next train back to Portland. And that's it. The whole story. I can write it up for you in a formal report, but I'm not sure you want this all on paper."

"There was a bed in the room?" I asked.

"Yes, but it was neatly made. I have no idea if they had been or were about to be engaged in any sexual acts other than a nude model posing for an artist. When I got back to Portland, I called an old friend on the Boston police force to see if there had been any reports of a burglary on Beacon Hill that afternoon. He said there hadn't."

Chapter 46

By ELEVEN O'CLOCK, Maggie was exhausted. She hadn't slept in over twenty hours, and it had been a rough twenty. She figured maybe it was time to head for home, open a bottle of wine, put her feet up and get back to the investigation in the morning. On the other hand, she thought, since 109 was more or less midway between Nasty's and her apartment, she might as well stop by and catch up on what, if anything, had been learned from the interviews with the guests and catering staff.

McCabe walked into the small lobby right behind her.

"What are you doing here?" she asked.

"I work here, remember?"

"How was dinner?"

"We had a good time. Fore Street was jammed as usual, but we got a reasonably quiet table in the back room."

"Food good?"

"Terrific. But even better than the food, I convinced Casey that I was totally cool with Sandy paying for Brown. Told her it was the least her mother could do after all the years of neglect."

"Good for you," Maggie said. "I really mean that."

"Thanks. I know you do. But strictly between you and me, I'm still mightily pissed off about it. Probably always will be. But no way do I want my anger with Sandy to make Casey feel guilty about going to Brown. It's my problem, not hers. Anyway, enough of that. How was your evening?"

"Watching dead bodies getting sliced up? One of my favorite Friday night activities. On the other hand, we may have a brand-new suspect."

McCabe arched a questioning brow and Maggie told him about her conversation with Kraft.

"The wife, huh? Guess we better have a little chat with her."

"If we can. So far she's stonewalling us."

"Hmmm. Maybe she does have something to hide. How'd the autopsies go?"

Exiting the elevator, they stood for a minute in the darkened hallway.

"No big surprises," said Maggie. "Knowles drowned pure and simple. No sign of bruising or knife cuts anywhere on his body. Like Terri told us, hemorrhagic shock from internal bleeding is the official cause of death for Aimée."

"Any semen?"

"Yep. Like we expected, Terri found some inside."

"Anything unexpected?"

"Yes. A couple of short gray hairs on Aimée's chest. Definitely not hers. Definitely not Knowles's or Dean Scott's, and definitely not Ruthie's."

"Our third man?"

"I think so. The gray suggests he's no kid, so I figure maybe he's somebody who worked at Orion twenty years back when Deirdre was still there. Anyway, Terri sent it all up to Joe Pines in Augusta. Asked him to fast-track the DNA testing. Tox reports, as usual, are gonna take a while. I called Whitby afterward to let him know we could turn Aimée's body over to whatever funeral home he wanted. Called Gina Knowles and told her the same thing."

They walked to the brightly lit conference room, where they found a dozen cops seated around the big table, poring over notes from at least a hundred interviews reports. If the count was right, it meant there were another hundred and fifty that still hadn't come in.

A pair of large black thermoses and some Styrofoam cups sat on a side table at the far end of the room. Maggie walked over and poured coffee into two, then handed one to McCabe. She grabbed a glazed donut from a box next to the thermos and began munching. Donuts and coffee for breakfast. Donuts and coffee for dinner. So much for healthy living.

"I owe anybody?" she called out.

"Department's treating," said Fortier, not lifting his eyes from the sheet of paper he was reading.

"Thanks, Department," said McCabe.

Maggie found a chair and squeezed it into a small space between a rookie detective named Connie Davenport, who'd just been promoted to the Crimes Against Property unit on the other side of the floor and had been pressed into service by Fortier. McCabe leaned against the back wall.

Maggie filled everyone in on the results of the autopsies.

"How're you folks doing so far?" asked McCabe. "Anything interesting?"

"Not a lot that seems pertinent," said Tom Tasco, who seemed to be in charge of collating the interviews. "Everybody says how gorgeous Aimée looked walking down the stairs in her slinky black gown. Half a dozen say, quote, 'she took my breath away,' unquote. Also what an absolute double she was for the woman in the painting.

"The good news is a lot of people took pictures. A couple made smartphone videos. We've got 'em all here."

Tasco passed McCabe an iPhone. McCabe hit the Start arrow.

The first video started with Aimée Whitby arriving at the bottom of the stairs, smiling and announcing, *"Je suis Aimée."* Then Edward Whitby entered the scene, put his arm around her and said, "It has never ceased to amaze me how my beautiful eldest daughter has such an uncanny ability to upstage her father at the most dramatic moments of his life." He lifted his glass. "To my dearest, favorite girl, who is, as you can see, a true incarnation of the first Aimée."

"You said there were others?" asked McCabe.

"Yeah. I sent the whole package downstairs to see if Starbucks could isolate any faces in the crowd who weren't on the guest or catering lists," said Tasco. "Anyone who looked like he didn't belong. Or anybody with an expression that doesn't look quite right. Angry. Crazy. Agitated. Nervous. Whatever. He's working with them now."

Starbucks was a young Somali named Aden Yusuf Hassan, who'd been the department's resident computer geek ever since he started working part-time while still in high school. Aside from a four-year timeout to earn a degree in computer science at U. Maine Orono, he'd been with the PPD ever since. The nickname Starbucks came more from his addiction to strong coffee than for any resemblance to the Melville character. He drank endless cups of the stuff from morning till night. Not surprisingly, he never seemed to need sleep.

"I've got something interesting here," Detective Carl Sturgis called from the other side of the table. He too was holding a handful of interview reports. Everyone stopped talking and looked across at Sturgis. "I've found at least four different people who report seeing Aimée get into a nasty little tussle with a kid named Will Moseley."

"What kind of tussle?"

Sturgis sorted the pertinent sheets and started reading aloud first from one, then from another. "'Moseley was drunk.' 'Slurring his words.' 'Staggering.' According to one witness, 'He patted Aimée's ass.' Somebody else said it wasn't patting. 'He grabbed her ass then made a clumsy pass.'" Sturgis sorted again through the sheets. "Apparently Moseley also made some racist remarks about a black kid from Penfield named Aman Anbessa, who Aimée had been talking to. He's one of her Penfield classmates. One woman said, 'When Aimée felt Moseley touch her, she turned and slapped him hard enough to hurt.' Seems Moseley clenched his fist in response, and it looked to the people watching like he was about to hit her back. He's a good six foot four and apparently plays football at Yale, so it sounds like he could have done some real damage. Couple of the men on the terrace moved in to stop him. But Whitby's security guy got there first and took over."

"Charles Kraft?" asked Maggie.

"Yeah. Kraft got in Moseley's face. Told the kid to leave Aimée alone. Then Edward Whitby shows up, the kid salutes, says a couple of 'yessirs,' and that was supposedly the end of it. But one person here says, 'Moseley slinked off.'"

"Is *slinked* a word?" asked Will Meserve. "Shouldn't it be *slunk*?"

"Whatever turns you on, Will," said Sturgis. "'Moseley slunk off. I thought he might come back and try to hurt Aimée.' Another one says, regarding Moseley . . ." Sturgis sorted through some sheets of paper, found what he was looking for and said, " . . . here it is. 'If looks alone could kill, both Aimée and Mr. Kraft would have dropped dead on the spot.'" Sturgis looked up. "Looks to me like Moseley's an obvious candidate."

"Yeah, except he's twenty years old. Unlikely he's got any gray hairs on his head or chest," said Maggie. "Even so, I think we ought to talk to him."

"Gray hairs could be from Knowles," said Sturgis. "He was thirty-six."

"Either way, Moseley's on the interview list," said Detective Bill Bacon. "Based on what Carl just read, I'll move him up the priority list."

"Is he one of the R.W. Moseley Moseleys?" asked McCabe.

"Yup. Son and heir. Also Edward Whitby's godson. Couple of the Penfield girls we talked to said he was Aimée's boyfriend back when she was a sophomore and he was in his last year at Penfield."

"Interesting."

"Very interesting. I interviewed a classmate of Aimée's named Kristin Chalmers," said Connie Davenport. "She was on the terrace when Moseley did his thing. Chalmers said back in junior year Aimée told her that she broke up with Moseley because 'he doesn't know what *no* means.' Chalmers asked Aimée if she was saying Moseley had tried to rape her. Aimée's answer? 'I don't think *tried* is the right word.'"

Maggie felt a small shiver of excitement. Gray hair or not, Moseley was a possible rapist who not only had a motive but was also physically far more capable of killing both Aimée and Byron Knowles than either Julia or her mother was. As Edward Whitby's godson, chances were also good that he was familiar with the details of the 1904 murder. Maybe he thought carving the *A* on someone who looked so much like the original Aimée would be a fun way to sign his work.

"Moseley ever been in trouble before?" asked McCabe.

"Not with us," said Fortier. "I'm sure of that."

"Brian, check him out with ViCAP and CODIS. Also call the New Haven PD and the Yale campus cops. See if he's been in any kind of trouble down there. Either way, find him and bring him in for a chat sooner rather than later. Be sweet about the invitation. I'd rather we didn't have Moseley Senior lawyering him up before we can talk to him. Anybody have his cell number?"

"Should be on the list Whitby's assistant sent over," said Cleary. "Yup. Here he is. 207-555-7483."

Cleary called Moseley's number three times. Each time it went to voice mail. Finally, he said the hell with it and called down to Starbucks and asked him to start a GPS search for the phone and see if they could find out where it was. Cleary also asked Starbucks to see if he could isolate a shot of Moseley and, if so, what his expression might be.

"Also ask him to isolate any shots he can find of either Julia or Deirdre McClure Whitby," said Maggie. "I want to see their reactions to our girl's grand entrance."

"A lot of people said they remembered talking with Aimée," Fortier was saying. "A few, mostly kids and teachers from Penfield, remembered talking to Byron Knowles. 'Mr. Knowles,' as they called him. Nobody mentioned seeing anything other than Moseley's bad behavior on the terrace that seemed in any way suspicious."

"Here's one that I conducted," said Bill Bacon. "With Margaux Amory? Y'know, the movie star? It was kind of interesting talking to her. She told me Aimée had enough of what she called 'star quality' to make it big in Hollywood. I asked her what she meant by that. She said if I didn't know, she couldn't explain it. Pretty full of herself, actually."

"Anybody say anything about talking with Julia?" asked Maggie.

Before anyone could answer, Sally Caldwell, the department's senior crime analyst, walked in the room. "Somebody just used Aimée Whitby's debit card. Withdrew four hundred bucks from an ATM in the mini-mart over on Washington Ave.," she announced. "Video from the machine is on its way over now."

TEN MINUTES LATER, Starbucks called to say he had the video and they could come down to take a look. Maggie, McCabe, Bill Fortier and Brian Cleary headed down to the second floor, where they found Starbucks hunched in front of one of his four flat-panel monitors, his eyes focusing on the image on the screen.

"What have we got?" asked McCabe.

"We have a full two minutes of footage, reasonable quality, of the person withdrawing the money. A lot of good full-face shots. She looks like a homeless lady."

The three of them leaned in as Starbucks went back to the beginning of the tape and started going through it frame by frame.

McCabe shook his head. "I don't think she's our killer."

"I know she's not," said Maggie. "Her name is Lucy. I don't know her last name, but she pushes her cart around my end of the hill every Tuesday night to grab the cans and bottles out of the recycling bins before Wednesday trash pickup. I say hello when I run into her. Occasionally give her a couple of bucks in addition to the bottles."

"She lives on the street?"

"Yeah. I've tried a couple of times to get her to go over to Florence House. Even told her I'd drive her there." Florence House was a shelter on Valley Street that provided both emergency and permanent housing for chronically homeless women. "She always says she will, but, as far as I know, she never has except when a blizzard's coming."

"Okay, assuming she's not the killer," said McCabe, "how did Lucy get her hands on Aimée Whitby's debit card? And when she did, did she get a look at whoever the real killer was."

"This time of year she sleeps rough. Woods off the Loring seem like as good a place as any. Which means she may have seen the whole thing. Which also means she's probably the homeless woman Scott said he saw scurrying away from the site."

"I'll have somebody take a printout over to the hospital and show it to Scott," said Fortier. "See if he can ID her."

"The other question," said McCabe, "is if she saw the bad guy, did he see her? If he did, she could be in trouble. Starbucks, would you please play the whole tape one more time from beginning to end?"

The detectives watched closely as the woman named Lucy stepped up to the ATM machine. She looked around nervously. Then reached out and inserted the debit card into the slot and pulled it out. She looked around again before entering the PIN number.

"Okay," said Fortier. "We obviously have to find her. I'll put out a high-priority ATL. Have dispatch get shots of her out to every unit in the city. Also send it to SoPo and Westbrook as well. Anywhere she could get to by bus." ATL stood for Attempt to Locate. Soon every cop in the greater Portland area would be on the lookout for Lucy McCorkle.

Chapter 47

From the journal of Edward Whitby Jr.
Entry dated July 22, 1924

That night I confronted Aimée. I entered her bedroom after the house had gone to sleep. I locked the door and put the key in my pocket.

She looked up from the magazine she was reading. "What is it, Edward?"

"What were you doing in Boston yesterday?"

"I told you. Shopping with Delphine."

"Oh really? Shopping? And what did you and Delphine buy?"

Startled by the anger in my voice she said uncertainly. "We bought nothing. We didn't see anything we liked."

"You saw nothing you liked? Nothing at all? Not even Mark Garrison?"

"No. No. Of course not."

"Not even any of Garrison's drawings? This one, perhaps?" I held up the unfinished drawing Garrison had been working on when Whelan had entered the room. "I think he captured your body rather well. Of course he captures it far better when he's fucking you, doesn't he? Then he gets to enjoy *all* you have to offer."

"He . . . I . . . we never." I'd never seen Aimée so shaken or so tongue-tied. "No," she finally managed to say. "That's not true."

"Liar!" I slapped her hard across the face. She fell back, shocked. "You lying bitch!" I hissed. Then I slapped her again. She leapt from the bed, bleeding from her lip, and tried to run for the door. I grabbed her by her hair and pulled her down before she had gone halfway. She fell hard to the floor. She tried to slither away from me, pleading, swearing she had never done anything with Garrison. I turned her on her back, pulled up her nightgown and threw myself on top of her. "Liar!" I cried.

I pinned her flat, pulled her legs apart and thrust myself inside. "Is this how Garrison does it to you?" I pushed my face an inch from hers. "Is it? Answer me, you lying, unfaithful bitch."

She stopped struggling and waited until I had finished before answering.

"No," she said in a quiet voice, tears rolling from reddened eyes, blood dripping from her mouth, lying flat on the floor where I had raped her. "He's far gentler than you. Far gentler than you've been for many years. And a much better lover than you've known how to be since we were young and newly married."

I flinched at her words. I sat down on the bed and began to weep. "Why?" I asked. "Haven't I always given you everything you wanted? Everything you asked?"

She rose from the floor, went to her armoire and began to dress. "You have," she said. "Everything except the willingness to remain the man I met and fell in love with in Paris. The man I married."

Finally she took the bedroom key from my pocket and walked out of the house. I don't know where she went that night. Perhaps to a hotel. Perhaps somewhere else. I only know that she didn't return until late the following morning.

I didn't ask where she'd been. I only begged her to forgive me for my actions the previous night. I broke down and wept. Told her through my tears that I had never loved another woman as I loved her. And that I was sure that somewhere in her heart she still loved me. As I wept I fell to my knees and buried my head in her lap as a wounded child would. She stroked my head gently and told me that all she wanted in life was for me to go back to being the man I was when we had met but that she didn't think that possible. I told her I could. I swore that I would. Begged her to forgive me and swore that I would turn the reins of the company over to Charles and that she and I and the children would go to Paris and live our lives the way she wanted if only she would come back and be my wife again.

She asked how she could trust me after what I had done. I swore over and over it would never happen again and that when we moved to Paris our relationship would truly return to what it once was.

Finally she said that if I would make that sacrifice, if I

would truly give up Portland and Whitby &Sons, she would tell Garrison she could never see him again. In turn, I had to swear I'd never repeat the violence that I had visited upon her the night before. When I asked her if we could make love, she said no. Not yet. The memory of last night was still too fresh in her mind. It would take her some time before she could trust me again. Still, I was certain that if I kept my part of the bargain, I would soon have my wife back and that as soon as I could wind up my affairs at the company, we'd be once again living the life in Paris that I'd dreamt of as a youth.

The next day my younger brother Charles and I left for New York on the noon train to wind up negotiations with the board of the Poseiden America Lines for the construction of a new transatlantic passenger steamer. I had been working hard for two years with our best designers and engineers on the project, and I felt certain the ship we were proposing would not only set a new standard for comfort and luxury but also surpass all others in the speed of the transatlantic crossing.

I debated telling Charles of my and Aimée's plans on the train but decided it might be better to tell him after our meeting with Poseidon. Upon arrival, we checked in and spent a quiet night at the Waldorf Hotel on Fifth Avenue.

At our meeting the next morning, the Poseiden board announced that they were accepting our proposal. Emerging from their offices, I asked Charles to join me in celebrating our success with a luncheon at the Union League Club. Once we were seated in the grand dining room, I ordered a bottle of my favorite champagne. I waited until the wine steward had poured us each a full measure, then raised my glass to Charles.

"I would like to propose a toast," I said, "not just to our success this morning with Poseiden but also to you, Charles, and to the continued success of Whitby & Sons under your leadership as the new president of the company."

His jaw literally dropped. "What on earth are you talking about?"

"Today," I said, "I am the happiest of men. Aimée and I have agreed that I should leave the company in your very capable hands. We will be moving back to Paris. Once settled, I will once again try to become the artist I always believed I could be."

Charles did his best to dissuade me. "Edward, you know as well as I do I'm a financial man, not a boat builder," he said. "The company may make money with me at the helm, but it is you who has the genius and vision for designing innovative ships. Without you, I fear Whitby & Sons will ulti-mately wither and perhaps die."

Deep down, I feared Charles might be right. Nonethe-less I tried to convince him otherwise. Following lunch I took a hansom cab down to Tiffany's on Union Square, where I purchased a pair of diamond and sapphire ear-rings for Aimée, which I chose because the dark blue of the sapphires very nearly matched the blue of her eyes. Leav-ing Charles behind to wrap up final details with Poseidon, I caught the overnight Pullman sleeper to Portland, where I planned to surprise her with the earrings as a symbol of our renewed commitment to each other.

Chapter 48

As far as Maggie was concerned, Munjoy Hill was getting too damned crowded for its own good. There was only one very tight parking spot on Vesper Street, and it was a good hundred yards from her house. Maggie mentally measured the space and figured her TrailBlazer could just about make it. She pulled alongside the car in front and, relying on her right-side wing mirror, she turned the wheel all the way to the right and then left and squeezed into the space in a single try. She got out of the car and looked. Damned good parking job if she did say so herself. Less than a foot from the curb and barely two inches of clearance from the cars both front and rear.

She grabbed her bag, locked the car and started walking toward the small frame house where she lived.

That's when she heard the scream.

A broken, guttural scream, barely human, it seemed filled with the emptiness of despair. Maggie stopped for a second, her hand going automatically to her Glock. Her eyes slid from one side of the street to the other, checking every house, every porch, every landing. For the next few seconds she heard nothing but a gentle breeze rustling the leaves in the trees. And then a second scream. This time she was sure the sound had come from the right. Possibly from the porch of her own house. She pulled out her gun and broke into a run. A second later, she heard the muffled sound of a shot fired by a silenced automatic. Maggie sprinted toward the sound.

From fifty yards away, she saw a smallish man, no bigger than five-six or five-seven, dragging a body down from the porch. Lucy McCorkle's head thumped on each of the three steps. Then the man pulled her toward the back of a white TrailBlazer she'd seen double parked in front of her house. Maggie crouched and pointed her gun in a two-handed stance. She shouted, "Police! Freeze!"

The man swiveled toward her. Light from the streetlamp above his head struck the bottom half of his face. He had a square jaw covered with two days' growth of gray stubble jutting out from under a blue Red Sox cap. The man dumped Lucy, looked toward Maggie and aimed.

Maggie leapt to her right, simultaneously dropping to the ground behind a hundred-year-old maple. A large-caliber slug tore off the bark inches above her head. A splinter struck her forehead, and she felt a dripping of blood. Steadying her Glock on the ground in front of her, she returned fire. Three shots in quick succession.

Maggie saw a spray of blood. The man staggered. Fell to one knee.

"Drop the gun! Freeze," she shouted. "Police."

The man's only response was a flurry of covering shots as he hoisted himself up and, using the hood of the car for support, staggered around to the front.

Maggie jumped to her feet. Fired two shots back. Both missed.

Using the car for balance, the man fired back. Three shots as Maggie sprinted zigzag toward the SUV. All three missed their target.

Taking cover behind another tree, Maggie pulled out her phone. Punched in 911. Was instantly connected to PPD dispatch Kelly Haddon.

"Vesper Street! My block," Maggie shouted breathlessly into the phone. "Shooter firing at me. Dead or wounded victim down."

She stuffed the phone in her pocket knowing Kelly would have every available unit there in minutes. Maybe even seconds if there was one nearby.

Maggie's next round struck the right rear window of the SUV, spidering the glass. The man opened the driver's door and leapt in. Slammed the door. Maggie fired again, aiming this time for the right rear tire. Missed.

The car's engine roared to life. Maggie dropped to one knee and, taking careful aim, fired at the left rear tire of the vehicle. The round went high through the plastic bumper. She fired again as the vehicle squealed out. Swore at herself as she missed again.

Maggie ran toward the bundle on the sidewalk as the car pulled out. One of Lucy McCorkle's eyes was open. The other was gone. Torn away by a bullet passing through her eye socket.

The SUV roared toward the corner. White Maine plates. Black numbers and letters. Too far away to make them out, but the letters looked like *K* and *N*.

The first black-and-white pulled up just as the white SUV swerved wildly left onto the Eastern Prom.

Maggie pulled Diane Rizzo from her cruiser, jumped in and took off after the killer, lights flashing, siren blaring.

Sliding around the corner, she could see the killer's red taillights in the distance. It had to be him. She wasn't gaining on him. But she wasn't falling farther behind either.

Maggie radioed dispatch that the suspect was fleeing in a white TrailBlazer with Maine plates. Last letters probably *KN*. "He's on the Eastern Prom heading toward Washington Ave. and maybe 295 north. Victim on Vesper Street appears to be dead."

Kelly responded by alerting all units to follow Maggie. "Stay on the line for updates."

The killer swung down and around onto Interstate 295, barely missing a car that was pulling over into the right lane. Maggie followed. She saw no other flashing lights from either Portland or state police cruisers in her rearview mirror. For now, at least, she was on her own.

The killer was pushing the TrailBlazer for all it was worth, but it was no match for the powerful Ford Interceptor's big 365-horsepower, 3.5-liter engine. She was steadily gaining on him. Probably realizing he couldn't outrun her, the bad guy swerved right onto Exit 10, and then right onto Buckham Road in Falmouth. He then took another right onto Route 9 and finally a quick left onto a small residential cul-de-sac called Jackson Way. Maggie wondered if the guy knew he was trapping himself. On the other hand, with no backup behind her, maybe he thought he was trapping her.

At the end of the cul-de-sac, the guy skidded to a stop and climbed out of his car, ignoring his wounded left leg. He was now holding what looked like an AR-15. Maggie, suddenly outgunned, turned the Interceptor so the passenger door with its reinforced ballistic side panels was facing the bad guy. She flopped down onto the seat as he fired a few bursts on full automatic, destroying both front tires and windshield. Maggie told Kelly to send Portland PD's heavily armed Special Reaction Team.

Another half a dozen rounds slammed into the side of the car. Shit. If the cavalry didn't get here soon, she was dead meat. Maggie dug into her bag and pulled out the spare magazine she always kept there. Then she slithered out the driver's side door, taking her phone with her. She put her gun over the hood and fired off a couple of blind rounds to keep the guy pinned down. Not sure how many rounds she had left, she fired once more, then stopped to change magazines.

Lights were going on in several houses around the cul-de-sac. She hoped none of the civilians would be stupid enough to come running outside to see what the ruckus was all about.

Maggie peeked over the hood to check on the guy and stared in disbelief.

He was leaning on the hood of his car and pointing a long tube in her direction. She knew exactly what it was.

Abandoning the cover of the car, she leapt into a small drainage ditch on the side of the road. Landing hard, she looked up just in time to see a cloud of gas emerge from the back end of the tube.

The last thought that entered Maggie Savage's mind before a huge blast turned her cruiser into a fiery coffin was, Who the hell did this guy work for? Al Qaeda? She didn't have time to figure out a logical answer before her world went black.

Chapter 49

MAGGIE HAD NO idea where she was or why. She could hear an odd buzzing inside her ears and seemed to be surrounded by an obnoxious mixture of burning oil and rubber. The pounding inside her head was as bad as any headache she could ever remember having. Worst of all, her eyes seemed glued together.

She felt someone pick up her hand and begin stroking it. She didn't know who was doing the stroking, but since it felt really good, maybe it didn't matter. She just hoped whoever it was would keep on doing what they were doing.

After another minute or two, Maggie made a greater effort to open her eyes. When she finally managed it, she saw a pair of McCabes sitting in identical chairs next to her bed. Not exactly two whole McCabes. More like one McCabe overlapping with another, giving her the impression that he now had three eyes, one and a half noses and a really long mouth.

"How do you feel?" one of the McCabes asked. Or maybe it was both of them.

It seemed like a stupid question, so she didn't bother answering.

"Do you know where you are?"

She looked around. "Hospital?"

"Do you know who I am?"

"Of course I know who you are. I'm just not sure why there happen to be two of you."

Both McCabes must have thought that was funny, because both their extra long mouths chuckled when she said it. Maggie didn't chuckle back. Having more than one McCabe didn't seem funny at all. Nor was a throbbing that felt like a mule had kicked her in the head any laughing matter.

As she kept looking at him, the two McCabes slowly melded into one.

"What time is it?" she asked.

"Eight thirty in the morning."

"Saturday morning?"

"Yup. Saturday."

"What time's the graduation?"

"Starts at ten."

"Can somebody give me something for the pain?"

McCabe went out into the hall. A minute later he came back with a nurse, who asked her a few questions, then gave her a Percocet.

"Now that you're awake, maybe you can give me your version of what happened."

Amazingly, she remembered it all in detail. The shoot-out in front of her house. Lucy McCorkle lying dead, half on and half off her porch steps. She recounted it all, right down to the point where the sonofabitch picked up the RPG and she dove into a ditch to avoid the explosion. "Poor old Lucy," Maggie sighed. "Never even got to spend the four hundred bucks she pulled from the ATM.

Had to be her biggest payday in years. Please don't tell me the bad guy got away."

"Yup. He got away, all right."

"Shit."

"Guess he thought you'd been killed by the explosion, or maybe he just heard the sirens coming. Either way, he raced out of that cul-de-sac like a bat out of hell and disappeared without checking to see whether or not you were dead. Couldn't have been more than a minute or so before the cavalry arrived. A couple of units reported hearing the explosion, so they may even have passed him going the other way."

"How's the car I was driving?"

"What car would that be?"

"That bad, huh?"

"A burned-out wreck. You jumped just in time to avoid being turned into a crispy critter. According to the doc, you suffered what he called a blast-related concussion. Pretty common in war zones. Not so much in Maine. They gave you a CAT scan, which didn't show any brain damage, so the neurologist thinks you'll be fine."

"Thinks?"

"Just covering his ass. Concussions are tricky."

Maggie didn't like thinking about that. At least the Percocet was taking effect and the pain in her head was fading out. "So when can I get out of here?"

"Pretty much whenever you want."

"Right now sounds like a good time to me," Maggie snorted. She kicked McCabe out of the room and changed back into her clothes.

Ten minutes later, she had checked out and was following McCabe out to the Bird. "Where to?" he asked.

"Home to shower and change. These clothes are filthy."

They headed toward Vesper Street. "I want to get that bastard," Maggie muttered, staring out the window at the empty Saturday-morning streets.

"No more than me. At least we now know for sure that it was a third man and not Byron Knowles."

"I shot him, you know."

"No. I didn't know. Where and how bad?"

"His calf, I think. If it missed the bone, it probably went straight through and out the other side. Jacoby should be able to find both the bullet and blood spatters in the road by the front of my house. Could give us the DNA we need to nail the guy."

McCabe called Bill Jacoby and told him there might be blood from two people at the Vesper Street crime scene.

"Lucy McCorkle's on the porch steps. The killer's by the curb. Get somebody over there and make sure you've got both. Then put the highest priority on getting the reads."

Ending the call, McCabe said to Maggie, "Okay, now all we need to do is find a match."

"We will if the guy is ex-military, which I think he is. If he served in Iraq, which he might have, they'll have his DNA on record. Harlan told me they recorded DNA for everybody they sent over there."

"Really? Why?"

"To identify the dead when there wasn't enough left of them to tell who they were any other way."

"Is it the RPG that makes you think he's ex-military?"

"There's that. But did I tell you I spoke with Kraft last night?"

"Yeah."

"While we were talking . . ."

"And you were flirting?"

"Yeah, and I was flirting, I asked him how he got his job with Whitby. Turns out he was recommended by the founder of Orion. It also turns out the founder of Orion is a man named Dennis McClure, who just happens to have done a substantial amount of work for Whitby Engineering & Development."

"And who just happens to have a sister named Deirdre?"

"You got it. Mrs. Deirdre McClure Whitby, the woman too upset by the killing, too *emotionally fragile* to even talk to us on the island yesterday. Her big brother runs a company crawling with contractors, both current and former employees, all of whom are certified experts in killing people. 'Gee, Dennis,' Maggie vamped, 'your little sister needs a little help.'"

"Those guys are probably certified experts in taking out vehicles with rocket-propelled grenades as well," said McCabe. "And Mrs. Whitby also has access to all the money she needs to pay the bill."

"That's what I'm thinking."

"Weird, isn't it? The idea of Edward Whitby's wife using Edward Whitby's money to kill Edward Whitby's daughter."

"Makes perfect sense though. Deirdre takes Aimée out of the picture and, bingo, just like that Julia moves up in the rankings to become Edward Whitby's new dearest, favorite little girl."

McCabe thought about that for a minute. "I wonder if there was more to it than Deirdre and Julia being jealous of Aimée."

"Like what?"

"Like money. With Aimée gone, Julia now stands to inherit twice as much of the Whitby fortune than she did two days ago. And Deirdre probably does better as well."

"I don't know. Whitby's only in his forties. Isn't he a little young for his wife to be thinking inheritance?"

"He would be. Unless Lady Macbeth and the RPG man are planning, I don't know, let's say an unfortunate helicopter accident that would tragically make her a widow. I think maybe I better have a chat with both Mr. and Mrs. Whitby."

"Not until after Casey's graduation, you don't. It starts in less than an hour."

Chapter 50

McCabe was late. Graduation was scheduled for ten o'clock, and it was well after nine when he got back to the apartment and nearly ran into Casey going the other way. She was wearing a white dress and carrying her blue robe over her arm. Her mortarboard was sitting at a silly angle on top of her head.

"There you are," she said. "I wasn't sure you were going to make it."

McCabe smiled at his daughter. Dressed up and made up as she was, it staggered him how much she looked like Sandy the day he'd first met her in a casting session at NYU Film School. Same features. Same long, dark hair. Same gorgeous blue eyes. Sandy then was the same age Casey was now. McCabe remembered falling instantly in love the minute she'd walked through the door.

"Is this where they're auditioning actresses for the student film?" she'd asked, "the one being directed by somebody named McCabe?"

McCabe forced his mind back to the present. "Sorry I'm late," he told Casey. "I'll just run up and take a shower, shave and change. You take the car. I'll grab a cab and see you at Merrill."

"You take it. I've got a ride."

"Good," he said and headed into the building.

"There's something I better tell you."

"Later," he called out and darted up the stairs.

"It's important," she called out. But he was already gone.

THE PORTLAND HIGH School graduation ceremonies were taking place in Merrill Auditorium, an elegant, white-and-gold, nineteen-hundred-seat concert hall that had been built into the side of the new city hall in 1911 and totally renovated in 1997. McCabe circled the block three times looking for a parking space, finally said the hell with it and pulled into a lot on Pearl Street, where a guy was waving a flag and collecting five bucks for parking. McCabe hated giving it to him, since the police garage was only a couple of blocks away and was free, but he had less than five minutes to get to his seat before the kids started marching in. He rushed to the entrance and threaded his way through the two hundred or so graduating seniors who filled the entry hall. Spotted Casey and waved. She waved back.

The seats at the front were reserved for the graduates, and the rest of the orchestra section was packed. McCabe stood there, scanning the place for even a single vacant seat. That's when he spotted Kyra waving to him on the far aisle about midway up. His heart skipped a beat.

He went up and slipped into the seat she'd been saving for him.

"What are you doing here?"

"I figured somebody ought to be here for Casey. You know, in loco parentis?"

"What's that supposed to mean? In loco parentis?" McCabe's whisper was louder than he intended. Several people turned and looked at him. "I'm parentis and I'm here."

"I saw the news about the Whitby murder yesterday, and knowing you like I do . . . well, at the last minute, I hopped the red-eye to Boston, rented a car and drove up here to play surrogate mother in case Casey needed one. I hope you're glad to see me."

"Of course I'm glad to see you, but if you were thinking there was any way I was going to miss my daughter's graduation, I'm afraid you were wrong. Does Casey know you're here?"

"Yes. I drove straight to the apartment. Since you were out hunting your killer, I told her I'd drive her to the ceremony."

"Nevertheless saving me a seat?"

"Hope springs eternal."

"You should have called me from the airport." He hesitated for a moment, then leaned in and kissed her on the lips. "Anyway, I'm sorry. I'm really glad to see you."

"Me too."

"How long are you here for?"

Just as Kyra whispered, "I'm not sure," music filled the hall and the two hundred plus members of Portland High School's graduating class of 2012 marched in and filled the front six rows of seats. Principal Roseanne Hatcher climbed up on the stage and welcomed parents, family members and friends of the graduates. "Before we proceed to awards," she said, "I'd like to introduce the top ten graduates of the class of 2012 and ask them each to please rise."

Casey was number five. "Cassandra McCabe," said Principal Hatcher, "is the daughter of Sergeant Michael McCabe of the Portland Police Department and Cassandra Ingram of New York City. Casey, as we call her, is a member of the class executive board and participated in the Anatomy of Leadership program. She was on the women's swimming, tennis and soccer teams and was a member of the drama club, art club and Shakespeare club. She also earned membership in the National Honor Society and was the recipient of the Brown University Book Award. Casey plans to attend Brown in the fall."

Casey stood and acknowledged the applause before returning to her seat.

The ceremony continued for another hour and a half before the graduates filed out. Kyra and McCabe caught up with Casey on Congress Street. They all spent twenty minutes chatting with Casey's friends and their parents.

"Shall we all go somewhere for brunch?" asked McCabe.

Casey scrunched her face up and said in an apologetic voice, "Sorry, Dad, I can't go."

"Why not?"

"A bunch of kids are going out to Higgins Beach for a barbecue. Since I wasn't sure you were going to be here, I promised I'd go."

"What made you think I wasn't going to be here?"

"Well . . . you know? What with the murder and all, I thought you'd be too busy. I'd cancel, but I'm in charge of hamburgers and hot dogs."

Kyra put a hand on her shoulder. "That's all right. You go with your friends. Your father and I have some catching up to do anyway."

McCabe gave Kyra a *maybe you ought to butt out* look, but he managed to hold his tongue.

FIFTEEN MINUTES LATER, the two of them were sitting in the back booth at Tallulah's.

Max came around to take their orders. "Hey, back again," she said.

"I told you I hang here a lot. This is Kyra. Kyra, Max."

"You feeling okay?" asked Max, sounding more than a little concerned.

McCabe smiled, nodded and thanked her for asking. Kyra ordered a mushroom omelet and coffee, McCabe a burger and a beer.

"Why did she want to know if you were feeling all right?"

McCabe shrugged. "No clue. Just takes an interest in my well-being, I guess. Why didn't you tell me you were coming?"

"I wasn't sure how you'd react. Then when I got to the apartment, you weren't there."

"I was at the hospital."

Kyra waited for the explanation.

"Maggie nearly got blown up last night."

"Oh, my God. What happened?"

"She found the bad guy and was chasing him. A real old-fashioned car chase, like in *The French Connection*. Unfortunately, it turned out he was more heavily armed than she thought. A whole lot more. Since her car was faster than his, he lured her into a small side road and fired a rocket-propelled grenade. Totally destroyed the car she was in."

"Is she okay?"

"Yeah, thank God," McCabe sighed. "She just managed to jump out of the way. She seems fine, and the doctor says he thinks she'll be fine. Still, she suffered a blast concussion, and you never can be sure of the long-term effects when the brain gets bounced around like that."

"Did you catch the killer?"

McCabe shook his head. "Not yet. But we will."

Max brought his beer and Kyra's coffee. Said the food would be out in a second.

McCabe reached across the table and took her hand. "How long are you staying?"

"I don't know. A few days at least. I want to see my parents while I'm here. They just opened up the house in Tenants Harbor and . . ."

"Stay a little longer," said McCabe. "Come stay at the apartment."

Kyra shook her head. "I'm sorry, but I don't think so."

"Please. We have a lot to talk about."

"Nothing we haven't talked about a dozen times before."

"I think we should give it one more try."

"Don't do this, McCabe. You're going to make me cry. And I'd feel really silly bawling like a baby in the back booth at Lou's."

"Just promise you won't go back to the coast till we've had a little time together."

"How can we have time together when you're in the middle of a murder? That's always been the problem, hasn't it?"

"I'll make time."

"What's wrong with this weekend?"

McCabe sighed. "Like you said, I'm in the middle of a murder."

Chapter 51

AT A FEW minutes after four on Saturday afternoon, McCabe watched Edward Whitby emerge from the Cathedral Church of St. Luke on State Street. Unlike their first meeting on the island, Whitby was now clean-shaven and dressed in a jacket and tie. The man next to him wore an ecclesiastical collar.

He had told McCabe that he would be spending much of the afternoon at the church, completing arrangements for Aimée's funeral. McCabe wondered what say, if any, Tracy had in the plans. Probably none. She didn't believe in religion of any kind, and Whitby liked running things.

McCabe got out of the car and approached the two men.

"Sergeant McCabe," said Whitby, "this is Bishop Stephen Crocker, who will be officiating at the service for Aimée."

McCabe extended his hand. The priest shook it.

"The sergeant is running the investigation into Aimée's murder."

"A horrible thing," said Crocker, "for someone so young who had so much to live for."

"When will the service be?"

"We're planning for Tuesday at eleven o'clock here at the cathedral."

McCabe made a mental note to attend if the case was still open. "Will there be a burial?"

"Aimée's body will be cremated and her ashes buried in the Bishop's Garden, in the cloister outside the chapel," said Whitby.

"Well," said Crocker, "I'm sure you gentlemen have much to talk about. It was a pleasure meeting you, Sergeant." He excused himself and went back inside the church.

"You wanted to talk privately," said Whitby. "Why don't you walk with me back to the house? It's not far."

McCabe agreed. He needed the exercise anyway. The two men walked up State Street, turned left, and continued on Pine. Most of the people they passed were locals out doing weekend chores and enjoying the fine weather.

"I take it Aimée's mother is comfortable with having her ashes buried there."

"Yes. We discussed it. We're both comfortable with cremation. Tracy suggested scattering her ashes to the wind. I preferred St. Luke's. Whitbys have worshiped here since shortly after the Civil War. Tracy said fine, one place was as good as any other."

"Sounds like Tracy."

"I understand you once had a brief fling with Aimée's mother."

"Did Tracy tell you that?"

"No. I had Kraft do a little background research on you."

"Investigating the investigator?"

"Yes. I wanted to make sure you and Savage are as good at what you do as your reputations suggest. According to Charles, you are. Both very good and very thorough."

"Glad to hear Charles feels that way. Yes, I did have a relationship with Tracy when I first came to Portland. Aimée was a child at the time, and I actually met her. None of that will affect how I approach the case. It was a long time ago."

"For both of us," said Whitby. "But I'm still very fond of Tracy. I've always liked strong-willed women, and she is definitely that."

"Would you describe your current wife that way?"

"Yes. Absolutely. Now, what did you want to talk about?"

"I want to do a little background research on you."

"Such as?"

"Tracy told me that when you and she were married, you asked her to sign a prenup specifying how much money she would get in the event of a divorce. She said she signed it. She also said it wasn't very much."

"I'm not sure what that's got to do with anything."

"Maybe nothing. But I'd appreciate it if you could humor me with the details."

"All right. Yes, there was a prenup. It specified that Tracy would receive exactly one hundred thousand dollars if we divorced. It also said I would take care of all the costs of child support and education. Which I have."

"One hundred thousand dollars isn't much for someone like you."

"No. But that's what she agreed to, and that's what she got."

"Did you have the same terms in your agreement with Deirdre?"

"Identical."

"What about your will?"

"What about it?"

"Who gets your money if you die?"

"I've made substantial bequests to the Portland Museum of

Art, Penfield Academy and Princeton. Smaller amounts to various other charities. However, the bulk of the estate would be split equally between Aimée and Julia and any other children we might have had. Guess now she's gone I'll have to amend it."

"How about your wife? What does she get?"

"She gets five million dollars."

"Was Deirdre familiar with the details of your great-grandmother's death?"

"Yes, she's read the newspaper accounts."

"Was she bothered by it?"

"Not especially."

"What did Deirdre feel about the portrait of Aimée you paid more than two million for?"

"She thinks it's beautiful."

"Did she tell you that?"

"No. But I'm sure she does."

"You're sure she does?"

"Well, I don't actually remember her describing it that way or really any other way. Listen, McCabe, I'm trying to be cooperative, but what in hell are you getting at?"

By this time McCabe and Whitby had reached the Western Prom.

"Why don't we sit over there on that bench and finish our conversation?" said McCabe. The two men crossed the circular road and sat down.

"Were Aimée and Deirdre particularly close?"

"I asked you before what you were getting at. What exactly are you insinuating?"

"Please, Mr. Whitby, just bear with me. Were Aimée and Deirdre particularly close?"

"I don't know. I think they were when the girls were little. She'd sometimes take them both on outings. She tried to be a good stepmother to Aimée when she was staying with us."

"Did you love Aimée more than you loved Julia?"

"How dare you?"

"Did you? Love her more, I mean? At the graduation party you apparently referred to Aimée as 'my dearest, favorite girl.'"

"I didn't say that."

"You did. I've got it right here on video."

McCabe pressed Play and handed Whitby the phone.

Whitby looked at the clip in silence. Handed the phone back.

"Sure sounds to me like you loved Aimée more."

Whitby said nothing.

"What about Julia?" asked McCabe. "What was she? Your second-dearest favorite girl? I wonder what she felt like, standing in that room surrounded by two hundred people and hearing that?"

"I am very sorry about that, but it was merely a slip of the tongue. I love my daughters equally."

McCabe waited for Whitby to say more. He didn't. He just seemed to be staring at the view of Mt. Washington outlined hazily in the distance. After a minute or so, McCabe continued. "You said the other day on the island that Deirdre didn't want to talk to us because she was so upset about the murder. You described her as emotionally fragile. Yet ten minutes ago you said you've always been attracted to strong-willed women. Would you describe Deirdre as both emotionally fragile and strong-willed?"

"An oxymoron I suppose, but in Deirdre's case, it applies."

"Deirdre's brother, Dennis McClure, is the founder and CEO of The Orion Group. According to his bio on Google, Dennis is a former officer in the Navy Seals. He started the company when he left the navy back in the late eighties to provide physical security to both government and corporate personnel required to work in dangerous places."

"That's right. I met Dennis in the early nineties when Whitby was hired by the navy to design and build marine bunkering facilities in Djibouti. We hired Orion to provide security for our engineering and construction people. They did an excellent job under difficult circumstances. We've worked with them a number of times since. In fact, it was Dennis who introduced me to Deirdre when she was looking for a job. I hired her. Then I fell in love with her, and the rest is history."

"A history that starts with the nearly simultaneous birth of two daughters by two different women?"

"Not my proudest moment, but yes."

"Over the years, hundreds, maybe thousands, of former military special operations people work or have worked with Orion. All of whom are trained experts in the fine art of killing other human beings."

"McCabe, are you suggesting someone from Orion came out to our island to kill my daughter and Byron Knowles?"

"I'm wondering about it."

"And why do you think an Orion professional might have done that? Certainly not for personal reasons."

"No. I'm sure not. What I'm wondering is if somebody familiar with Orion, somebody who perhaps knew its people, might have hired a current or possibly a former company operative to do the job."

"Somebody such as who?"

"Somebody such as Deirdre."

"That's the most ridiculous accusation I've ever heard."

"Is it? Well, let me ask you this. What if your emotionally frag-ile yet strong-willed wife believed, in spite of your denials, that you loved Tracy's daughter more than you loved her own? And what if this emotionally fragile yet strong-willed woman feared that you . . . who Tracy described to me as a serial adulterer . . . might one day hand her a check for one hundred thousand dollars and kick her out the door of that white pillared mansion over there and invite someone younger and perhaps more desirable in? And what if this emotionally fragile yet strong-willed woman feared that once you had done that, you might then set about *amending* your will, perhaps to write her and her less-loved daughter out of it, or at least to reduce that daughter's share of the pie?

"And a pretty impressive pie it is. According to *Forbes Maga-zine,* you were tied last year with two other lucky souls for the hundred and forty-third spot on their list of the four hundred richest Americans. They listed your net worth at roughly $4.3 bil-lion dollars.

"Given that number, and given the fears that your emotionally fragile yet strong-willed wife might have had, and given the fact that she once worked for Orion and thus was almost certainly fa-miliar with a number of current and former Orion operatives, is it still the most ridiculous suggestion you ever heard? If you believe it is, I suggest you ask Charles Kraft if he happens to agree with your assessment. I'd also suggest that you might want to watch where you walk and perhaps avoid riding around in helicopters for the time being."

Whitby stared at McCabe but said nothing.

"Detective Savage and I have tried a number of times to arrange to interview your wife. So far she's stonewalled us. I'm not suggesting that all the what-ifs I just outlined are necessarily true. But given the possibility, we do need to ask Deirdre some difficult questions. The help I need from you is to convince her to talk to us without lawyering up."

Chapter 52

From the journal of Edward Whitby Jr.
Entry dated July 30, 1924

I arrived at the house at a little after nine the following morning, hoping to surprise Aimée with my return a day early from New York. To my great disappointment, she was not there. The housekeeper told me she'd sailed out to the island the day before to paint and had spent the night there. Anxious to see her and eager to present her with the earrings that I hoped would serve as a symbol of our reaffirmed commitment, I decided to go out myself and surprise her. I asked Mrs. Simms to prepare a picnic lunch for the two of us. Cold pheasant, beluga caviar, a fresh baguette and two cold bottles of Perrier-Jouët. When the lunch was ready, I took the basket and drove down to the company dock.

Once on board my boat, I put the champagne in a net

bag, which I tied to the stern. The frigid Maine water would serve to keep the bottles suitably cold on my way over. Then I hoisted sails and went out to the island. As the wind caught my sails, I felt like a young suitor, alive with joy. As lighthearted as I had been on that first day at the Académie Julien when Aimée had invited me to go to the Café Lézard with her group.

I tied up at the family dock, where I found the *Aimée Marie*. Since she wasn't in her boat, I suspected I would find her at the studio.

I hurried up the path, imagining the pleasure we would have consecrating our renewed marriage vows in the island house she loved so much. When I got to the studio, I peered in the window. I instantly closed my eyes, unable to believe the scene before me. When I opened them again, what I saw utterly horrified me.

Chapter 53

McCABE WAS STILL waiting for Edward Whitby to agree to convince his wife to be interviewed without benefit of counsel. Instead Whitby stood. "Let me get something I think you should read," he said. "I'll be right back."

McCabe watched him walk across the Western Prom to the big house with the white columns and go inside. Less than five minutes later, Whitby returned. He handed McCabe a leather-bound notebook. The leather was old and cracked. McCabe flipped it open. The pages inside were handwritten in pen on the kind of lined paper one uses in school.

"What is it?" asked McCabe.

"A journal written by my great-grandfather during the summer of 1924, the last months of his life before he died of cancer. In it he describes the real story of the deaths of both Garrison and Aimée on the island that day."

"The real story?"

"Yes. Things didn't happen quite the way we discussed earlier. Garrison did not kill the first Aimée."

"So it was Edward?"

"Just read what he had to say."

"Who knows about this journal?" asked McCabe. "Who's read it?"

"Nobody ever has. Just my grandfather, my great-aunts Charlotte and Annabelle, my father and myself."

"Not Deirdre or your daughters? Not anyone else?"

"No. I keep it in my private safe, as did my father and grandfather before him. Deirdre and the girls don't have the combination. I don't think they even know of the journal's existence. I haven't looked at it myself in several years."

"And your father and your grandfather also kept it secret?"

"They did. As did Charlotte and Annabelle. A secret handed down within the immediate family."

"Why keep it such a secret?"

"My great-grandfather wanted it that way. He wanted us, his and Aimée's children and grandchildren, to know the real truth of what happened on the island that day. But no one else. Each of us in turn acceded to his wishes. The journal was written twenty years after the event, and its author, my great-grandfather, was dying as he wrote it."

McCabe flipped the pages. "Why are you breaking with that tradition and allowing me to read it now?"

"Because Aimée's death has convinced me that burying the truth all these years may have left a curse on this family that can only be expunged by ripping away the curtains and letting in the light."

"Do you believe in curses?"

"I never have. But after the events of the last three days, Aimée's death and your accusations about Deirdre, I'm beginning to think they may indeed exist."

McCabe wasn't sure how much more he would learn, but he took the old journal. He handed Whitby a business card. "This is my cell phone. Call me if anything occurs to you. Anything that seems important. Anything you want to discuss privately."

Whitby slipped the card into his jacket pocket, crossed the Prom and entered his house. McCabe watched him go, walking slowly, eyes focused on the ground, the walk of a troubled man.

Chapter 54

From the journal of Edward Whitby Jr.
Entry dated July 30, 1924

I will never forget the frightful image I saw as I peered silently through the studio window on that summer morning so long ago. On the far wall, the naked body of Mark Garrison, his eyes bulging, his mouth agape, hung by a leather belt from a stout hook attached to the wall on the far side. Directly in front of me, equally naked, her back to the window, Aimée stood gazing at herself in a mirror. In her hand she held the Tanto, the ancient, short-bladed Samurai dagger my grandfather brought home many years earlier from a voyage to Japan.

Aimée brought the razor-sharp blade up and began carving a letter into the top of her own chest as carefully and deliberately as if she'd been creating one of her works of art. My beautiful wife was concentrating so completely on her task that she failed to notice the reflection of my stricken face in the window behind her. I stood for a moment, frozen in place by what I was witnessing. But then I stirred myself and went to the door of the studio. I threw it open to discover Aimée holding the blade in the air, pointed toward her own body. I rushed to grab it before she could act, but before I could reach her to wrest the Tanto from her hands, she'd already thrust it down in an arc. The blade entered her body a few inches above and to the right of her navel. Then she pulled it out and raised the blade, intent on stabbing herself once again. Before she could, I managed to grab her wrist and pull the dagger from her hands.

"Why?" I shouted, looking into her anguished eyes. "For God's sake, why?"

She stared at me for a second and then, without a word, ran from the house, bleeding from her wounds. Stunned, I stood there, watching her go, before I finally followed. It was my failure to move faster that made all the difference. When I did at last give chase, she was well ahead of me, running far faster than I would have imagined possible, wounded as she was. She was headed directly toward the cliff. I ran as fast as I could, calling her name, and managed to close the distance between us. But then, a split second before I could reach out and grab her, she stopped and turned. She was standing at the edge of the cliff.

"Don't come another step," she warned me.

I stood frozen, afraid any movement on my part, any movement at all, would force her over the edge.

"Aimée, please," I said. "Come away from there."

"It was you, Edward!" she hissed. "It was you who killed Mark! And I helped you."

"Please come away from there and tell me what happened." I spoke in the calmest voice I could muster, my words as soothing and gentle as I could make them.

"You *know* what happened." She spat the words at my face. "I played your fool, Edward. I did exactly what you wanted. Exactly what you *forced* me to do if I ever wanted to see my children again. I told the man I loved as I have never loved another that I could never be with him again. My words broke his heart. He told me that he wouldn't, that he couldn't go on living without me. I told him that was how it would have to be. He pleaded with me to allow him to make love to me one last time. I said yes. Afterwards I slept. Hours later, when I awoke, I saw it."

"Saw what?" I asked.

"His body. His body hanging dead from that hook. As I'd slept, he'd taken his own life. And it was my fault. I spoke the words, the words you put in my mouth, that killed him."

I reached out to take hold of her arm, to bring her back from the precipice. I will never know whether it was the small movement of my arm or simply her own determination to join her lover in death that pushed her over the edge.

I did my best to grab her, but my best was not, as it never had been for Aimée, nearly good enough. I watched her body fall and land hard on the rocks below.

Certain she was dead and equally certain her death was my fault, I fell to my knees and wept for a long time. Perhaps hours.

Finally I rose and walked in a kind of daze back to the studio. I stood in the room, gazing at Garrison's lifeless body hanging from the hook, silently cursing him for ever having lived. For ever having met my beloved Aimée. And for seducing her and taking her from me.

Finally, I picked up the Tanto from the floor where I had dropped it. The blade was still red with Aimée's blood. I held it in my hands, strongly tempted to join my beloved wife in death. But the thought of Charlotte, Teddy and Annabelle growing up as orphans, believing neither of their parents loved them enough to forgo death on their behalf, stayed my hand.

I picked up the handwritten note I saw sitting on Aimée's painting table. She must have read it as soon as she woke from her slumber to find Garrison's lifeless body.

My Darling Aimée,

I am so sorry for what I am about to do. I understand your reasons for wanting to break off our relationship and return to your husband. But understanding your reasons doesn't mean I can live with them. I can only hope that we will see each other again either in heaven or in hell. Whichever God intends for us.

I read the note a dozen times and then wrote another, mimicking Garrison's hand as best I could in which he admitted killing her in rage and then himself in remorse. I left the second note for the police, tore up the first and stuffed the pieces in my pocket.

Before leaving the island, I walked back one last time to the cliff to gaze down at my beloved Aimée. As I looked, I saw some fishermen lifting her body into their boat. Presumably they were taking her back to the mainland. I went to my own boat and sailed home. There was nothing left for me to do here.

Chapter 55

DEIRDRE WAS SEATED comfortably in an oversized chair when Edward Whitby entered the room. She was dressed in a knee-length skirt, and she had her shoes off and her legs tucked up under her. She was sipping Scotch from a large cut-crystal glass and reading a copy of *Vanity Fair*. She glanced up when he came in, then turned back to her magazine without acknowledging his presence.

Edward walked to the drinks cupboard, tossed a handful of ice cubes into an identical glass and poured a Scotch for himself. He took the chair opposite his wife.

"What took you so long?" Deirdre's voice emerged from behind the photograph of whichever beautiful actress *Vanity Fair* was featuring on that month's cover.

"Will you put that damned magazine down?"

"Are we angry?" she asked, looking over the top with raised eyebrows.

"Just put it down. Please."

Deirdre closed the magazine and laid it on her lap, one finger tucked between the pages, holding her place, as if she planned to go back to reading any second. "I was in the middle of a very interesting article."

"Please. We need to talk."

She tossed the magazine onto the table at the side of the chair with an audible sigh. "So talk."

"Tracy and I have finalized funeral arrangements with Bishop Crocker." Whitby told her about the plans for the service at St. Luke's and for burying Aimée's ashes in the Bishop's Garden.

"Is that it? Is that what you wanted to talk about?"

Whitby's eyes turned away from his wife. He took a sip from his Scotch and stared down at the pattern in the antique Persian rug. The rug he had grown up with. He was struggling to find the right words to ask the question that had to be asked.

"Deirdre, how did you feel when you learned about Aimée's death?"

"Devastated, of course. We all were devastated."

"But what was your first reaction? Your immediate reaction?"

"Edward, what on earth are you getting at?"

"Have you ever heard how in wartime, a soldier's first reaction when the soldier next to him is shot and killed is often a fleeting sense of relief that it was the other guy and not him? Even if they were close friends."

"Are you asking me if I felt relieved that it was Aimée who was murdered and not Julia?"

"Yes."

She seemed to weigh her response before answering. "I suppose I did. A little. I think the reason for that is obvious. Julia is my own child. Aimée isn't . . . wasn't."

"Would you say you loved Julia more?"

"I wouldn't want to put it that way. I loved both of them."

"But did you?"

Deirdre's eyes turned to the large window that overlooked the ancient garden and the rose bushes growing profusely just beyond. A hundred blooms, large, luscious and bloodred. It had been a long time since Edward had brought her roses. Or made love to her, for that matter. She wondered briefly who he was making love to these days. Some ambitious young thing at the company? Or perhaps several ambitious young things.

"I suppose I did. Julia is my child. Sprung, as they say, from my loins. Aimée wasn't. But you don't have the same excuse. They were both your children, and I know that you loved Aimée more. You always have. Ever since they were little girls."

"I didn't. I swear to you I didn't."

"Don't lie to me, Edward. Just take another look at that painting you're so enthralled with."

"It's a painting of my great-grandmother."

"No. It's a painting of your daughter, and you know it. Aimée always had that Whitby look. Julia is a McClure through and through."

"I have always loved both my daughters equally," Whitby said, knowing even as he said it that it was a lie.

"Once again bullshit. Complete, utter and total bullshit. I know it and you know it. I could see it in your eyes at the party when your 'dearest, favorite' daughter came prancing down the stairs eager to steal the show. Julia could see it in your eyes as well. And so could every other person in the room. Julia has always adored you, and it hurt her very deeply to see that."

Whitby looked down and stared at his shoes. "I'm so sorry. I never meant for that to happen."

"I have a strong suspicion that you paid two and a half million dollars for that painting, far more than it's worth, not because it's a painting of your great-grandmother and not because it's a famous painting by a well-known artist. I think you had to have it because it's a portrait of Aimée. Not the first Aimée. Your Aimée."

"That's ridiculous. If I wanted a painting of my 'favorite' daughter, as you put it, I could have commissioned one far more cheaply."

"Yes. But then you would have had to commission paintings of both your daughters. Or one painting of the two of them. And no way would you have wanted the other daughter, the not quite so beautiful one, to share wall space with the girl, the woman who is—and let's be honest about it—the one true love of your life."

Deirdre finished her whiskey, went to the drinks cupboard, added a handful of ice cubes to her glass, and poured four more ounces of Johnnie Walker Black over them. Edward finished his own drink, got up and did the same.

"In fact, Edward," she said as he put the bottle back in its place, "I've often wondered, at least since she started growing breasts, if your love for that child . . . let me see, how can I put it delicately? Ever strayed beyond the bounds of propriety."

"How dare you?" Whitby roared. "How dare you even hint at such a thing?"

"It's true, isn't it, Edward?" said Deirdre, hissing out the words like an angry cat. "Not only did you love your little Aimée more than you loved me or Julia or anyone, you've been proving your love by fucking her all these years, haven't you?"

Edward Whitby's face reddened with rage. He drew back and slapped his wife across the face with all the strength he could muster. The blow was hard enough to knock her to the floor in front of the fireplace. The glass she was holding fell upon the stone hearth and broke into a thousand pieces.

"You're blind, aren't you, Edward?" she said, spitting the words up at him, "totally blind to the fact that your 'dearest, favorite' daughter . . . the one you loved so much, was not only a slut who fucked every man she could get her hands on but also a total bitch."

Whitby stood over his wife, his fists clenched, his face scarlet. "You killed her, didn't you?" he roared. "You called your fucking brother and paid some fucking *contractor* to kill my daughter, didn't you?"

"No, of course I didn't," Deirdre screamed. "I don't do things like that."

"Don't lie to me, you fucking bitch. You killed her!"

"You know something? I didn't kill her, but I'm glad somebody did! That dirty little slut deserved to die."

Because Deirdre McClure Whitby turned away from her husband at that instant and covered her face with her hands, she never saw Edward pick up the poker from the fireplace and swing it with all his might against the side of her head, striking her just above her right ear. She did, however, feel a brief explosion of pain as the pointed hook at the end of the poker entered her brain.

Edward Whitby stared down at his dead wife, the rage drained out of him by this singular act of violence, barely believing what he had done.

He slid to the floor and sat next to where she lay, his hand on her shoulder, blood leaking from her head and staining his trousers. He sat for a full ten minutes. The curse, he thought. The stain. It had come again. Finally he rose, took a business card from his breast pocket and punched in the number on his cell.

"This is McCabe," said a voice on the other end.

"You'd best come and get me, Sergeant. I'm afraid I just killed my wife."

Chapter 56

McCabe and Kyra had been sitting in the living room of the apartment on the Eastern Prom for the last half hour, rehashing ground they'd been over a dozen times before. He asking, or perhaps pleading was the better word, for her to come home from San Francisco. She asking him to join her out there.

"You haven't found someone else?" he asked.

"I told you I haven't been looking. It'll take me a while before I get to a point where I want to start a new relationship. What about you?"

"No. I still love you."

"What about Maggie? I could always tell there was something there by the way you looked at her, spoke of her."

"That's something that might have been but never has. At least not so far."

The insistent ringing of the phone in his pocket cut the conversation short. He resisted the temptation just to let it go to voice mail when he checked caller ID.

"This is McCabe," he said.

"You'd best come and get me, Sergeant. I'm afraid I just killed my wife."

"Where are you?"

"At the house."

"Stay right where you are," McCabe said. "Don't go any-where."

"Who was it?" asked Kyra. "What is it?"

"Another murder. Edward Whitby just killed his wife. And I have the awful feeling it might be, at least partly, my fault."

McCabe dialed 911. Andrea Simon, the PPD day shift dispatcher, came on the line.

"Get a MEDCU unit and a couple of cruisers over to the Whitby mansion on the Western Prom. ASAP. Lights and siren all the way. Get an evidence team over there as well."

McCabe next called Maggie. "Whitby just killed Deirdre."

"You've got to be kidding."

"Not kidding. He's at his house. Where are you?"

"109."

"Okay. Meet you there in five."

He ended the call. Got his jacket and weapon. "Gotta go," he told Kyra.

"I understand. I won't be here when you get back."

McCabe paused, thought about it and nodded. "I'm sorry about that."

THE TWO DETECTIVES reached the Western Prom within seconds of each other. Two cruisers and an ambulance were already there. A young cop McCabe didn't recognize was stringing yellow crime scene tape across the front of the house. Some passersby had gathered on the Prom to watch. Sergeant Pete Kenney came out to greet them. Probably his last crisis call, McCabe thought. His last homicide.

"It's pretty much a mess in there," said Kenney. "The body is in the living room to the right of the front door. She's lying by the fireplace. Had her head bashed in with a fire iron. The hook on the end went through her temple. EMTs say she died instantly. Murder weapon's lying next to her."

"Where's Whitby?" asked Maggie.

"Sitting on a chair looking at the vic. We've got him cuffed. But he's totally docile. Hasn't said a word except 'I killed her,' which he's said two or three times."

"You read him his rights?"

"No. Thought I'd let you guys do the honors."

"Anybody else in the house?"

"A woman. Name's Brenda Boatwright. Says she's the Whitbys' housekeeper. She said she heard a lot of screaming but was afraid to go into the room. Says the Whitbys fought a lot and she knew enough not to interfere. She didn't find out what happened in there until things quieted down. She's pretty much in shock herself."

The PPD evidence van pulled up. Bill Jacoby and two techs climbed out. Maggie filled them in and told them to go into the living room and start doing their thing.

Maggie and McCabe entered the house. McCabe escorted Whitby out of the living room, sat him down on a bench, then sat next to him. He turned on a small digital recording device and placed it between them. Neither man looked at the other.

"I told you we were cursed," said Whitby. "In spite of our wealth, or perhaps because of it."

"This is Detective Sergeant Michael McCabe. Today is Saturday, June 16, 2012. I'm at the home of Edward Whitby at number 22 Western Promenade, Portland, Maine. Please state your name."

"Edward Whitby."

"Edward Whitby," McCabe said, "I'm arresting you for the murder of your wife, Deirdre McClure Whitby. You have the right to remain silent. Anything you say can and will be used against you in a court of law." He went through the rest of the Miranda script, asking the required questions at the end. "Do you understand each of these rights I have explained to you?"

"Yes."

"Having these rights in mind, do you wish to talk to us now?"

"Yes."

"Mr. Whitby, would you please tell me in your own words what occurred in the living room of your home at number 22 Western Prom at approximately five fifteen this afternoon?"

Whitby began not at five fifteen but with his conversation with McCabe earlier that afternoon. He ended with his picking up the poker and killing his wife in an uncontrollable rage.

Whitby turned and looked at McCabe for the first time. "She is dead, isn't she?"

"Yes, she's dead. Prior to hitting your wife with the poker, did you ask her if she was involved in the murder this past Friday of your daughter, Veronica Aimée Whitby?"

"Yes."

McCabe took a deep breath and asked the question he knew he had to ask even though it might mean the end of his career. "And why did you do that?"

"Because of you," Whitby said. "You planted the seed in my mind when we spoke earlier. When I gave you the journal."

"How did your wife respond to your question?"

"She denied having any involvement in Aimée's death."

"Do you think she was telling the truth?"

"I don't know. She seemed to be. But then Deirdre was always an accomplished liar."

"So can you tell me what exactly made you so angry that you picked up the poker and struck her?"

"She accused me of loving Aimée."

"Of course you loved her. I love my daughter. That's part of being a father."

"I don't mean that kind of love." Whitby swallowed hard. "She accused me of sexually abusing my daughter."

McCabe frowned. "Was there any truth to what she said?"

Edward Whitby didn't answer.

"Was there any truth to what she said?"

"None whatsoever. But . . ."

"But what?" McCabe asked again.

"She was right when she accused me of loving Aimée more. More than Julia. More than Deirdre. I did love her more. She was so beautiful. Not just physically but in every way," Whitby said in little more than a whisper.

McCabe waited for more, but Whitby just sat, slumped on the bench, no longer an arrogant master of the universe but someone emotionally and, it seemed to McCabe, even physically diminished.

"Mr. Whitby," McCabe finally said, "you've admitted to killing your wife. Did you also kill Byron Knowles and your daughter Veronica Aimée Whitby at approximately 2:00 a.m. Friday morning?"

Whitby turned and looked at McCabe as if he had understood nothing "Of course not. How could I kill Aimée? She was the one person I've always loved more than anyone else in the world. The one person to whom I could refuse nothing. I don't think someone like you could possibly understand how deeply a father's love for his child can run."

Whitby was wrong. McCabe understood perfectly.

"What could possibly lead me to harm someone I loved so much?"

"The same thing that might have led your great-grandfather to kill the person he loved more than anyone else in the world. And to kill *her* lover. Rage driven by jealousy."

"But he didn't kill her. Haven't you read the journal?"

"Not all of it. Not yet."

"It doesn't matter. The answer to your question is still no. I didn't kill my daughter. Nor would I. No matter what her faults, and they were many, I would have killed myself before hurting her in any way."

McCabe turned off the recorder and went over to Sergeant Pete Kenney.

"I've arrested Edward Whitby on charges of murder," he said to Kenney. "He knows and understands his rights. I would appreciate it if you would please deliver him to the Cumberland County jail and make sure they put him on suicide watch. I don't want him escaping his guilt by killing himself."

Kenney gave McCabe an odd look but said nothing. He walked over to Whitby, took him by the elbow and led him out of the house.

Chapter 57

AT EXACTLY 5:00 A.M. on Monday morning, McCabe's cell phone alarm broke into the first few bars of Arthur "Guitar Boogie" Smith's "Feudin' Banjos." He fumbled around on his nightstand for a few seconds before he managed to find the phone and quiet the jangle. It took him a couple of seconds to remember exactly why he was getting up before dawn on a June morning. Simple, really. They still didn't know who killed Aimée, and the number one suspect, Deirdre McClure Whitby, being dead, was unfortunately unavailable for questioning. McCabe figured his next best source on whether or not Deirdre had hired a contract killer was Mr. Orion himself, her brother Dennis.

McCabe pulled himself out of bed and into the bathroom. He showered, shaved and briefly debated whether a white shirt or a blue-and-white striped one would work best with the CEO of a company that specialized in safeguarding the lives of State Department and Pentagon bigwigs. He decided on stripes. Added his only red power tie and then put on the one decent suit he owned, purchased with the advice and consent of Kyra two years earlier for her favorite uncle's funeral.

A cab was waiting downstairs. Fifteen minutes later it deposited him in front of the brand-new terminal building at the Portland International Jetport. He had time for two cups of coffee and a glazed donut before boarding the six forty-five US Airways flight to Reagan National. The flight was, as all flights seemed to be these days, totally booked, but at least he had an aisle seat and it took off on time. A little over two hours later, he emerged from a taxi in front of a nondescript modern office building on Crystal Drive in Arlington. No signs on the exterior indicating the names of any of the tenants. He walked through the revolving door and checked in with a blue-jacketed security guard seated behind a curved desk in the center of the lobby.

"How can I help you?"

"I have a 9:00 a.m. appointment with Dennis McClure of The Orion Group."

McCabe signed in as instructed and produced photo ID. The fact that he was a cop raised no eyebrows, and the security guy phoned upstairs.

"Please take a seat. Mr. McClure's assistant will be down in just a few minutes."

A few minutes turned into fifteen before a stunning black woman in a gray pants suit approached.

"Detective McCabe?"

"That's right."

"I'm Edwina Starling, Mr. McClure's assistant. I apologize for the delay, but he had an early meeting."

Orion occupied the building's top three floors. Ms. Starling pressed the button for the top floor.

The doors opened on a reception area paneled in rich walnut and decorated with some first-rate modern art. To McCabe the place looked more like a white shoe Wall Street law firm than a company that specialized in sending heavily armed security guards into the hottest of the world's hot spots.

Ms. Starling offered McCabe coffee. He declined and was then ushered into a large corner office with floor-to-ceiling window walls on both sides.

A trim, athletic-looking man in his early fifties rose from behind a large glass desk and extended his hand.

"Sergeant McCabe? Dennis McClure." McClure pointed him to the visitor seat in front of the desk, skipped any prelims and got right to the point. "I assume you're here to talk about my sister's death."

McCabe could detect no obvious signs of grieving in McClure's face or manner. No signs at all of being upset that his younger sister had had her head bashed in by her husband.

"Were you and Deirdre close?"

"Yes, we were close. I was the big brother she counted on and confided in. We spoke regularly by phone. Our families spent holidays together. Skiing. Sailing. Whatever. Last year we all went to Africa and climbed Kilimanjaro. I feel personally devastated by her death. Even more so because it was Edward who killed her. Now what else do you want to know?"

"You employ and have, over the years, employed a lot of people who know a lot about killing people."

"Correction. They know a lot about protecting people. That's what my company does. We protect both government and corporate personnel who are required to work in dangerous and unfriendly environments."

"Yes. That's what it said on your website."

"We also provide our clients with confidential intelligence and intelligence assessments, not available from public sources, about opportunities and potential problem situations in what people generally call 'hot spots.'"

"Yup. Saw that on your website too."

"So now you know all about us. How else can I help you?"

"Ever hear the line 'Will no one rid me of this troublesome priest?'"

"Not that I recall."

"It's what King Henry II supposedly called out when he was looking for somebody to knock off Thomas Becket, the Archbishop of Canterbury."

"And the significance of this bit of trivia is?"

"Did Deirdre ever ask you for the name of someone to rid her of her troublesome stepdaughter?"

McClure raised both eyebrows in obvious surprise. "You think Deirdre had something to do with Aimée's murder?"

"I think it's possible. I also think Edward may have killed your sister because he suspected that she did."

"If that's what you think, then both you and Edward are full of shit."

"A lot of people have told me that. On the other hand, most of them were people who had something to hide. Is there something you're trying to hide?"

"The answer is no, she didn't ask me for the names of any hit men."

"Would you tell me if she had?"

"Probably not. But on the other hand, Deirdre worked here for a couple of years before she headed north in search of Whitby's riches. I'd be surprised if she didn't have a contact or two of her own left over from the old days."

"That was more than twenty years ago."

"People stay in touch."

"Could you come up with a list of Orion employees who worked here at the same time Deirdre did?"

"My HR people could, but I don't think it will help you."

"Why not?"

"Deirdre was a rich and resourceful woman. If she wanted to find a contract killer, I think she could have managed it on her own without having to use any of her old Orion contacts. And she's smart enough to know it would be strategically better to hire someone who couldn't be linked to her time with the company or to her in any other way."

"Even smart people sometimes make mistakes, so if you don't mind, I'd appreciate the list anyway."

"Fine. I'll get it in the works today, but I still think you're barking up the wrong tree. I knew Deirdre better than anyone, and while my sister could be willful, spiteful and frankly a royal pain in the ass, she wasn't a killer. It just wasn't her style."

"Are you coming to Portland for the funerals?"

"Of course. Also to be with Julia. Naturally, she's in total shock over everything that's happened. If Edward ends up going to prison, and maybe even if he doesn't, I expect Julia will most likely be coming to live with us here in D.C. My wife flew up this morning, and I'll be joining her tonight. And now, Sergeant, I'm afraid you'll have to excuse me. I have another meeting starting in just a few minutes."

Chapter 58

By the time McCabe got back to Reagan National, Tom Shockley's face was peering down at him from every TV screen in the airport, alternating with file footage of Edward Whitby and still shots of Deirdre, Aimée and Byron Knowles. Obviously the Whitby murders had replaced the Syrian civil war as the major story *de jour*. On all three cable news networks it was all Whitby, all the time, most of it broadcast live from Portland.

After a brief search, McCabe managed to find a bar where the lone TV was tuned to a British soccer game. He went in and ordered a beer, taking refuge from the chief's pontificating for the half hour he had to wait until his flight boarded.

A couple of hours later McCabe was back in Portland, pushing his way past a crush of reporters, TV cameras and news vans to gain entrance to 109. He found Maggie seated at the head of the conference room table, surrounded by piles of interview reports.

"How'd it go with McClure?" she asked.

"Says he didn't give her any names and he doesn't think she did it."

"How surprising. Anything else?"

"Yeah. He's sending us a list of people who worked at Orion the same time Deirdre did. That was twenty years ago, so they all should be old enough to have gray whiskers and chest hairs. We've just got to find out if any of them also have a leg wound. Anything happen here?"

"Quite a bit actually. Judge Nelson turned down Whitby's bail request. Not because he thought Edward might fly the coop but because Burt convinced him that Whitby, given half a chance, was a definite suicide risk." "Burt" was Assistant Attorney General Burt Lund, who'd been assigned to prosecute the murder case against Edward Whitby. "He'll be arraigned this afternoon on one count of homicide for murdering his wife. Burt expects his lawyers will plead irresistible impulse. Also the board of directors of Whitby E&D met in emergency session this morning and appointed Robert W. Moseley interim CEO to serve until a permanent replacement can be found. And another thing, a white TrailBlazer with a number of bullet holes in it was found this morning in the parking lot at The Maine Mall. Whoever parked it there wiped it down for fingerprints and took his guns and rocket launcher with him. Car belonged to a Palmer Milliken lawyer named Murray Epstein, who we managed to contact in Santa Barbara, where he's vacationing. He says he parked it in the long-term lot at the Jetport over a week ago."

"Anything else?"

"Not much except a long list of people we know didn't do it. Julia seems to be in total shock. Can't eat. Can't sleep. Barely able to talk. Doctor is keeping her heavily tranquilized."

"Would Julia have had the money to hire someone to kill Aimée?"

"Yes and no. Both girls came into trust funds of a million bucks each on their eighteenth birthdays. However, Julia's money is still sitting in an investment account at Moseley and Co. Even if she hired a killer on a buy-now-pay-later basis, I don't think she would have been capable of pulling this off."

"Where is she now?"

"At home. Her aunt, Dennis McClure's wife, got there this morning and is staying with her."

"Dammit." McCabe slapped his hand on the table in frustration. "It's got to have been Deirdre. She had the motive. She had the money. And according to her brother, she had the contacts, with or without his help. She also knew both Byron and Aimée would be on the island Thursday night and that they'd probably be together."

"But her brother doesn't think she did it."

"That means absolutely nothing. Do we have her phone records and e-mails yet?"

"Came in this morning. The boys are going through them now. So far no calls, texts or other contacts that look even remotely suspicious. If she set this up, she either did it in person or got herself a disposable cell phone."

"How about money? If she hired your friend with the rocket launcher, she probably had to pay him an up-front deposit. Probably cash. Let's get a warrant to search her bank accounts and see if she withdrew any large amounts recently."

"Somebody with Whitby money could easily have an untraceable account. Cayman Islands. Belize. Wherever."

"I know. But what else can we do?"

"Beats me. I guess we just wait for the lab to get us preliminary DNA results."

Chapter 59

BETWEEN MONDAY AND Thursday no new evidence emerged in the case, and the cable news stations turned their primary attention back to the Middle East. At three thirty Thursday afternoon, the fourth-floor elevator door slid open and Joe Pines, the DNA specialist at the state lab in Augusta, walked out. Pines was a small man, no more than five foot five, who wore large round glasses that gave him an owlish look.

"What are you doing here?" asked McCabe.

"I just got preliminary reads on all the samples you guys sent up. Terri told me to drive down and brief you on this in person."

"Anything unexpected?"

"Yes."

McCabe tapped Maggie on the shoulder, and the three of them went to the conference room and shut the door.

"All right, shoot. And please, Joe, try to keep it simple. Don't go on about alleles and such."

"Okay. We analyzed all the DNA collected from Aimée Whitby's body at the autopsy. Aside from a lot of animal DNA coming from the dog, there were some additional significant findings. We analyzed DNA from human semen samples collected from her vagina. We've identified it as coming from the drowning victim Byron Knowles. No other semen. A rapist of course might have worn a condom. However, the DNA of the gray hair found on Aimée's chest and some skin cells found under her nails turned out to be a match with the DNA collected in the blood sample at the end of Maggie's driveway. In other words, the guy who shot Lucy McCorkle was also in close physical contact with Aimée Whitby."

"So Aimée managed to scratch him?"

"Yes. Deeply enough to draw blood."

"How about the samples taken from the apartment?"

"Here's where it gets interesting," said Pines.

"Go ahead."

"As expected, most of the samples Jacoby collected in the apartment matched either Byron or Aimée. There were also a few random samples that may have come from the landlord or a previous tenant. However . . ."

Here Pines stopped for dramatic effect.

"However what?"

"Several of the samples turned out not to be random. We identified them as coming from a woman who is the daughter of the man who killed Lucy McCorkle. We don't know who she is, but we do know she's his daughter."

Maggie and McCabe stared at each other.

"His daughter? Are you sure?"

"Absolutely. Every daughter gets half of her DNA from her father. The daughter in this case has half the killer's alleles. Sorry.

You didn't want me to use that word. The unidentified woman in the apartment is definitely the daughter of the killer."

"Jesus Christ." McCabe turned to Maggie. "Do y'think Deirdre would have asked her father to kill her stepdaughter?"

Maggie shrugged. "Guess it depends who her father is."

"Have you had a chance to analyze DNA from Deirdre Whitby?" McCabe asked. "The woman who was killed by her husband on Saturday."

"No," said Pines. "Nobody put a rush on that one. Wouldn't have had results this fast even if you had."

"Well, let's put a rush on it now."

"I hope this is important," said Pines. "You guys are pushing a lot of other requests further down the line."

"Joe, please. Trust me. It is important."

"Who do you suppose Deirdre's father is?" asked Maggie.

"Let's see if we can find out."

McCabe called Dennis McClure's cell phone. To his surprise, McClure answered.

"What do you want now, McCabe?"

"Did you and Deirdre have the same biological father?"

"I beg your pardon."

"Did you and Deirdre have the same biological father?"

"Yes. She was my sister. We had the same father."

"Where is he now?"

"Who?"

"Your father."

There was a long sigh on the other end. "What kind of bullshit are you chasing now, McCabe? I mean, hasn't this family suffered enough?"

"Please. It could be important."

"Our father is dead. He died three years ago in an automobile accident in Cincinnati. That's where Deirdre and I were brought up. You have any other personal requests, or can I go now?" McClure hung up anyway.

"Deirdre's father didn't do it," said McCabe. "So whose frigging father did?"

"I just thought of something," Maggie said.

Chapter 60

ON FRIDAY MORNING, exactly a week after Dean Scott's dog, Ruthie, found Aimée Whitby near death in the brambles off the Loring Trail, McCabe looked up to find Maggie peering down at him, arms folded across her chest, a grim expression on her face.

"McCabe, we screwed up big-time."

"What are you talking about?" He tossed the report he'd been reviewing onto his desk. The one that told him there were no DNA matches for the killer anywhere in either the state or federal databases. That, whoever he was, he'd never been made to submit a sample. Ditto for his daughter.

"You and me. You know, Portland's hotshot supercops? We got this whole case wrong. From beginning to end, we got it wrong. And at least one person's dead because of the stupid assumptions we made."

"All right, Mag, maybe you better stop beating us up and tell me what you're talking about."

"Come with me and I'll tell you in the car."

She turned and headed for the elevator. McCabe grabbed his jacket and followed.

"Where are we going?"

"Westbrook."

"What's in Westbrook?"

"Intex Labs."

They found an old unmarked Crown Vic in the downstairs garage. Maggie signed it out and slid into the driver's seat. McCabe got in next to her.

"All right, start talking," said McCabe as they pulled out onto Middle Street.

"You know how we assumed from the beginning that the killer's primary target was Aimée? That Knowles was basically collateral damage?"

"A reasonable assumption, given the fact that the first Aimée was killed exactly the same way. Also given that the victim was the daughter of the richest man in the state and that Knowles was a relative nobody."

"I agree. A very reasonable assumption. And a very logical trap. One which a sneaky bastard named Francis J. 'Little Frannie' Hogan, who I think I can prove is the real killer, set for us by mimicking the old murder, and which you and I, my dear Watson, bought into hook, line and sinker."

"And this Little Frannie, whoever the hell he is, you're saying he suckered us into thinking Aimée was the primary target . . ."

" . . . when it was the 'relative nobody' all the time."

"Okay, Sherlock, what exactly led you to this brilliant conclusion?"

"Actually, some variation of it occurred to me last week, but I dismissed it at the time. I went over to take a look at Aimée and

Byron's love nest on Hampshire Street, and I realized how easy it would have been for Gina to follow Byron to the place to get the goods on them. Once she did, she had an obvious motive for killing both of them."

"Jealousy."

"Jealousy. My problem was I couldn't see how Gina, eight months pregnant, and too broke, and, I assumed, too distant from the world of professional killers could afford to hire a pro. So I put it out of my mind. Until yesterday, when Joe Pines delivered his news that the DNA found in the apartment came from the daughter of the killer."

"And you figured out that Gina Knowles's maiden name just happened to be Hogan?"

"Yep. It wasn't even that hard. I just Googled Byron Knowles's wedding announcement. Turns out Byron and Gina were married here in Portland, and the *Press Herald* carried the announcement. *'Miss Gina Hogan, the youngest daughter of Mr. and Mrs. Francis J. Hogan of Boston*, Massachusetts,' blah blah blah. The next step was obviously finding out exactly who Mr. Hogan was and what he did for a living. You remember my old pal John Bell?"

"Yeah. Detective who works homicide for the Boston PD? Helped us out on the Lucas Kane case."

"Exactly. I called John and asked him if he knew anything about the father of the bride. Turns out that in his younger days, Mr. Hogan was an enforcer for the D Street Gang, one of the old Irish mobs operating in Southie. They specialized in extortion and loansharking, and Hogan was suspected of being responsible for at least ten murders over the years. Including the extermination of two leaders of a rival gang by . . . guess what? Blowing up their car with a rocket-propelled grenade."

"While they were inside?"

"Indeed."

"And this guy was never convicted?"

"Nope. Not even of stealing a newspaper. He had a reputation for being clever and for covering his tracks well. Never left any evidence or witnesses behind. At least no witnesses alive enough to testify."

"How old is Hogan?"

"According to Bell he's in his early sixties. Supposedly retired from what he used to call the insurance business about ten years ago. He moved out of Southie when the Irish gangs started falling apart and the Yuppies started moving in. Currently resides on Mussey Street in South Portland less than a mile from his loving daughter."

"His motive being to get rid of an unfaithful son-in-law?"

"I guess. Since his daughter was adamantly opposed to divorce, looks like Daddy figured the best way to end a bad marriage was by doing what he did best."

"Invoking the old *till death do us part* clause? Interesting. You think Gina was in on it?"

"I don't know. She seemed genuinely horrified when she learned of the killings. On the other hand, she also told us she had no idea who Byron was having an affair with when she obviously did, so maybe she's just a good liar."

"How'd she find out?"

"My guess is she followed Byron to the Hampshire Street apartment, waited until she saw the lovers leaving, then entered the apartment herself. She either picked the lock or, more likely, made a duplicate of a key she found on Byron's key ring. Once inside, she looked in the desk, found the old news stories and a screenplay he was writing, and read them. Maybe borrowed them and made photocopies and then gave the photocopies to Daddy or at least told him about them in detail. We're going to Intex today to ask Gina to provide us with fingerprints and a DNA sample, which will prove both that she was there and that her father was the killer. I've got a fingerprint kit and cheek swabs in my bag."

"And if she refuses?"

"Judge Washburn just signed a warrant requiring Gina to provide both. If her DNA proves she's the daughter of the guy who killed Aimée and Lucy, we've got him. I also convinced Byron's landlord to lend me a key to the apartment. I'd like to see if Gina happens to have a duplicate on her own key ring."

"Sounds like the only thing you don't have is a way to find out if Gina was complicit in the killings or whether Hogan did them on his own."

"Yeah."

They drove in silence for a while. McCabe didn't look happy.

"What's the matter?" asked Maggie.

"If you're right about Gina and Hogan and the rest of it—and I suspect you are—I feel even worse than I did before about planting the seeds in Whitby's mind that led to him killing Deirdre."

"No way you could have known where it would lead. You did what you thought was right at the time."

"But it wasn't right. I jumped in with both feet without thinking through the possibilities. In the end, all I did was provoke the murder of an innocent woman."

"Nonsense. She provoked it herself."

"Yeah maybe. Anyway, let's not talk about it anymore."

"Okay."

"I'm surprised Gina's back at work already."

"So was I, but when I called the house, her mother answered. Said being at work helps Gina not think about the murders. Also said she's already scheduled a lot of time off for maternity leave and doesn't want to miss any more."

"Does she know we're coming?"

"Yes. I called and said there were a few more odds and ends we needed to check with her. She was reluctant but finally agreed to meet us for coffee in the company cafeteria."

The Intex Corporation's headquarters building was a large, three-story low-rise covering at least an acre of land in a 1990s vintage industrial park off Route 22 in Westbrook. Maggie and McCabe parked in a visitor's spot and went through the main entrance. The interior was totally utilitarian, lacking even a hint of corporate chic.

"Hi, Detective Margaret Savage and Detective Sergeant Michael McCabe. We're here to see Gina Knowles," Maggie said to the smiling, round-faced receptionist. "She's expecting us."

The receptionist checked a directory for the right extension and called upstairs. When she hung up, she asked Maggie and McCabe to take seats in the reception area. "Mrs. Knowles will be down in a minute."

GINA KNOWLES HELD her company keycard up to a small black sensor to the left of the door to gain access to the cafeteria. It was a large room with a capacity of at least three hundred. At ten forty-five in the morning, it was mostly empty. All three of them poured themselves coffee from a large stainless steel urn and took the cups to a table in the far corner of the room. Maggie took her digital recorder from her bag and placed it on the table between them. She flicked it on and recorded the preliminaries.

"I don't have very long," said Gina. "What do you want that we didn't cover the other day?"

Maggie decided to play it low key. "No big deal. It's just some routine stuff that we forgot to take care of when we spoke to you at your house. First off, we need you to provide us with a set of fingerprints and a cheek swab."

Gina looked at Maggie suspiciously. "Why?"

"Nothing important. It's standard operating procedure in all murder cases to get prints and DNA from all persons related to the victims. We can take care of it right here if you like. Or maybe there's a small conference room if you'd like to be more private."

"Standard operating procedure?"

"That's right."

"I think you're lying. I can always tell when people are lying. Even cops."

"Fine. I won't debate the subject with you, Ms. Knowles. I simply need you to provide us with your fingerprints and a sample of your DNA."

"And if I say no?"

"I have a warrant signed by District Court Judge Paula Washburn requiring you to provide us with both. If you refuse, Sergeant McCabe and I will take you into custody on grounds of obstructing a murder investigation and get what we need at Portland police headquarters."

"Fine," said Gina, her tone more than a little petulant. "Come with me. There's a small conference room down the hall. We should have some privacy there."

They went in and closed the door. When Maggie finished taking prints and a cheek swab, Gina Knowles rose to leave. "Please sit down, Ms. Knowles. We still have a few questions we need you to answer." Maggie turned the recorder on again.

Gina sat, but she didn't look happy. "I hope this won't take very long."

"When we spoke to you at your house last Friday morning, you told us that you were certain your husband was having an affair but that you didn't know who the affair was with. You said you thought it might be with one of the other teachers in the English Department. You were lying then, weren't you?"

Gina swallowed hard. She avoided looking either Maggie or McCabe in the eye. "Yes," she finally said, "I was lying."

"May I ask why?"

"Because it occurred to me that if it ever came out that Byron was having an affair with one of his students, he'd lose his job and probably never find another one. At least not teaching. With the baby due any minute, the last thing we needed was for him to be unemployed and probably unemployable. Even after his suicide, I didn't want people thinking that an affair with one of his students had ever happened or that it was his reason for killing himself."

"Did you ever visit an apartment at 47 Hampshire Street in Portland? I would urge you not to lie about this, Ms. Knowles. The DNA swab you just provided will give us proof positive of whether or not you were ever there."

Gina sat, her eyes down, her hands folded around the bulge in her tummy.

"Yes. I was there."

"How did you get in?"

"I had a key. I made a copy of all of Byron's keys when he was out fishing with his father one Saturday last month."

"What did you do when you entered the apartment?"

"I just looked around. Especially at the art on the walls. Especially the self-portraits of the Whitby girl and I guess most especially the nude drawing of Byron. The fact that he'd allowed her to draw him that way with all his parts hanging out enraged me. I was tempted to throw it in the trash, but they obviously would have noticed."

"Then what did you do?"

"I found all the old newspaper reports of the murder in 1904. Also Byron's screenplay based on those reports. I e-mailed everything on the computer to myself. I also took all the paper stuff to FedEx Kinko's on Monument Square and copied it all. Then I returned it to the apartment."

"What did you do with the copies?"

"I gave them to my father."

"Why?"

Gina looked from one detective to the other. She said nothing.

"Did you ask your father to murder your husband and Aimée Whitby to punish them for having an illicit affair?"

"I did not ask him to murder anybody. My father is not a murderer."

Maggie wondered if Gina had any idea of what her father used to do for a living. "Did you suggest to your father that by copying the details of the 1904 murder, he would make everybody think that Byron killed Aimée in a rage and then took his own life just as Mark Garrison was supposed to have done a hundred years ago?"

"My father is not a murderer."

"Oh really?" said Maggie. "According to my sources on the Boston Police Department, your father is Francis J. 'Little Frannie' Hogan. Former member of the D Street Gang in South Boston and known to the Boston police as a mob enforcer."

"I'm not answering any more questions."

"That's your right. However, Gina Hogan Knowles, I am now placing you under arrest as an accessory to the murder of Veronica Aimée Whitby. This charge will be raised to actual murder if it turns out the killing took place with your knowledge and assent." Maggie proceeded to read Gina her Miranda rights. She also patted her down to make sure she had no weapons. "If you promise to behave, I'll allow you to walk out of here without being handcuffed, but you will have to wear cuffs in the police car that's waiting for you outside."

When Gina agreed, Maggie accompanied her to her desk, where Gina retrieved her bag and jacket. Maggie checked both for possible weapons. There were none, but she took possession of Gina's cell phone.

They left the building. Maggie put the cuffs on Gina, then deposited her in the backseat of Diane Rizzo's replacement cruiser. She told Diane to stick Gina in an interview room at 109 and not let her make any phone calls until her father was safely in custody.

Chapter 61

It took Maggie and McCabe fifteen minutes to drive to Mussey Street in South Portland. The Hogan house was a small white colonial with black shutters that looked like it had been built in the early fifties and not changed much since then. Since a two-year-old green Buick LaCrosse was pulled up on one side of the two-car driveway, and since Mrs. Hogan was at the Knowles house taking care of her granddaughter, they figured Little Frannie was likely at home. In case he was looking out the window, they drove past the house and parked at the end of the block. Far enough away so Hogan wouldn't spot them even if he was looking.

"You have a phone number for the house?" asked McCabe.

"Yup. 207-555-7843. It's a landline."

McCabe blocked out caller ID so his number would appear as Private Caller on Hogan's phone.

The phone rang four times before a croaky male voice answered, "Who's this?"

"Mr. Hogan?"

"That's right. Who're you?"

"My name is John Allen, and I'm with the Greater Portland Campaign to fight Muscular Dystrophy . . ."

There was a click on the other end. "Yup. He's home."

"No doubt accompanied by his Glock, his assault rifle and his RPG," said Maggie. "Plus God knows whatever else he has in his arsenal." She blew out a long breath. "Okay, McCabe, you're the boss. How do we play this one without getting a lot of people killed? Possibly including us."

McCabe thought about it for a minute. Then he called Detective Connie Davenport. He told her to head over to Cumberland Medical Center, where she should hang out and wait for him to call again. He next called South Portland detective Tommy Holmes.

"Hiya, McCabe, what's up?"

"We're about to take a man named Francis Hogan into custody for the murders of Byron Knowles and the Whitby girl. The guy's armed to the teeth. Including an assault rifle and an RPG. He may come peacefully, but maybe not. If he decides to start a war, we're going to need backup from a SWAT team. Since his house is in South Portland, seems to me the team ought to be yours. Is that possible?"

"Oh, yeah. I think our guys will be eager to take part in this one," Holmes said. "What's the address?"

McCabe told him.

"Let me check up the line and get back to you in five minutes," said Holmes.

He hung up, and Maggie and McCabe both put on their body armor and waited. Ten minutes later, McCabe's phone rang.

"Okay, McCabe. Everything's cool," Holmes said. "My folks are loving the idea of getting a piece of the action on this one."

McCabe instructed Holmes to have his people approach the

house quietly. No lights. No sirens. "I want you to have cruisers blocking off Mussey Street between Broadway and Third. Then I want your SWAT team to deploy quietly on foot on all four sides of Francis Hogan's house and get as close as they can without being seen. That part's important. They absolutely should not be seen. Hopefully Mr. Hogan's watching TV or taking a nap and not looking out the windows. Cool?"

"Cool so far."

"Okay. I'll fill you in on the rest of it when your people are in position."

Maggie and McCabe kept a close eye on 38 Mussey while they waited for the reinforcements to arrive. Another ten minutes passed, then Holmes approached their car and slipped into the backseat. "Okay, everybody's in place and ready to go. How do we play it?"

"I want to get this guy alive," said McCabe, "without starting World War III. He's a professional killer, and adding a couple of cops to his body count won't bother him in the least. So I'm going to try to get him out of his house without his heavy artillery."

Maggie looked doubtful. "How do you propose doing that?"

McCabe didn't answer. Just held up one finger, signaling a brief time out. Then he called Connie Davenport.

"You at the hospital?" he asked.

"I'm here. What do you need me to do?"

"Go up to the nursing station in the obstetrics unit, show them your badge and tell them you need to use one of their phones. Don't take no for an answer. Let me know when you're in place. Then you're going to call a Mr. Francis Hogan at 555-7843." McCabe waited while Connie wrote down the number. "Tell Mr. Hogan you're a nurse at Cumberland Med. Give him the real nurse's name and her extension in case he wants to call back and check. Tell him his daughter, Gina Knowles, who is eight and a half months pregnant, has been in an accident, that she might die and that you're trying to save the baby. Tell him Gina needs him to come to the hospital right away. Got it?"

"Got it."

"Good. After you've done that, you're going to call me back and let me know what he said."

McCabe hung up and turned to Holmes. "When Hogan comes out of the house and heads for his car, I'm going to block his driveway with this car. I want your guys to move fast and get between Hogan and the front door so he can't get back inside. Got it?"

"Got it."

"With any luck, he won't rush to the hospital wearing any guns. If he's unarmed, we've got him. If not, we tell him to put his hands up. If he goes for a gun, we kill him."

"What if he runs for it?"

"He's got a wounded leg. I don't think he's going to be doing any running."

"He may just hobble for it," said Maggie. "But I don't think he'll get very far."

THE SCENARIO PLAYED out exactly as McCabe described it. A very distraught Francis Hogan limped out the front door and headed for his car as soon as he got the message from the hospital. Maggie blocked the end of the driveway with the Crown Vic, and the SWAT guys moved in. Hogan instantly recognized the trap and put his hands in the air.

"Francis Hogan," said McCabe, "you're under arrest for the murders of Veronica Aimée Whitby and Lucy McCorkle."

"Who's Lucy McCorkle?" asked Hogan as Tommy Holmes pushed him spread-eagle against the Buick, frisked and cuffed him. He was unarmed.

"The old lady you blew away on the porch of my house when I was coming home," said Maggie. "I'd say that was bad timing on your part."

"Listen guys, have a heart. I've got to get to the hospital. My pregnant daughter's been in an accident. They're trying to save the baby, but she could die. I've got to see her before that happens. Can you take me there first?"

"Sorry to break it to you, Frannie," said McCabe, "but your daughter and her child are both just fine. She's being held in custody at Portland police headquarters."

It took Hogan less than a second to realize he'd been set up.

"You fucks," said Hogan. "You tricked me."

"Yeah, we did," said McCabe, with the biggest grin he'd enjoyed in what seemed like months. "Ain't life sweet?"

Chapter 62

It was the first Saturday in October, and McCabe was jogging down to the running trail that went from East End Beach and then around Back Cove. The same trail Dean Scott and Ruthie had taken the June night they'd discovered Aimée Whitby lying near death on the Loring Trail.

October was always McCabe's favorite month in Portland. The days beginning to cool but the sun still warm enough to get outside for a run wearing just a T-shirt and shorts. The trees were already well into their annual change from green to brilliant red and gold. The city itself alive with a new season of music and art and theater. Still another new hotel was opening on Fore Street, with a slick modern bar that carried a huge selection of good single malts, including The Macallan 12, which McCabe could just manage to afford, and The Macallan 18, which was truly spectacular but way above his pay grade. A new Asian fusion restaurant and a new upscale steakhouse had just opened their doors to great reviews. He hadn't tried either yet.

A small indie film company was spending the month in

town shooting exteriors for a thriller about the Russian mob's involvement in human trafficking. The director loved the small cobblestoned streets and the urban feel of the Old Port and the atmospheric grittiness of the wharfs and the waterfront. Turned out the cinematographer was a guy McCabe knew from his student days at NYU Film School, so he'd spent a fair amount of time hanging around the set. A couple of times he'd even dated one of the actresses who was playing a key supporting role as the head of the FBI team investigating the traffickers. She was good company, and he had fun talking movies with somebody who knew as much about films as he did. Still, they both knew the relationship wasn't going anywhere and that soon she'd be heading back to L.A.

Work had been fairly quiet all summer except for the fallout from the murders. On June 25, Assistant Attorney General Burt Lund recommended that charges against Gina Hogan Knowles be dropped, since there was no hard evidence that she had either conspired with her father to murder Aimée Whitby or her husband, or had any knowledge or warning that he'd planned to do so. McCabe was sure she was guilty as sin, but Lund insisted there was no way short of a confession they could prove it. And neither Hogan nor Gina would admit to a thing. Three days after Lund's decision not to prosecute, Gina gave birth to a healthy seven-pound, four-ounce baby boy. She named him George Gordon Byron Knowles in honor of her late husband, so maybe she really was innocent. She'd told Maggie, who'd driven over to South Portland to deliver a baby gift, that the boy would be called Byron.

Both McCabe and Maggie testified at the trial of Gina's father, Francis J. "Little Frannie" Hogan. He was convicted on two counts of first-degree murder for the murders of Veronica Aimée Whitby and Lucy McCorkle. The conviction was based on both the DNA evidence and Maggie Savage's eyewitness account of the McCorkle killing. Lund didn't bother filing murder charges against Hogan for killing his son-in-law. He only had circumstantial evidence for the murder of Byron, and Little Frannie was going away for the rest of his life for the other two murders anyway.

As expected, Edward Whitby's team of high-priced attorneys pleaded not guilty on account of irresistible impulse, and the trial was now going into its third month. Betting at 109 was that, in the end, Whitby would serve no time for killing his wife. Whitby's surviving daughter, Julia, was now a freshman at Princeton, where, to avoid attracting attention, she listed her last name as McClure. When not at school, Julia was living with her uncle and aunt in Washington.

McCabe's biggest problem was loneliness coupled with boredom. The Crimes Against People slate had calmed down to the usual assortment of DV and assault cases. Casey had spent most of the summer in France on a student exchange program and was now thoroughly ensconced at Brown and loving every minute of it. Kyra was still in San Francisco, and he hadn't heard from her in a while. Of course she hadn't heard from him either. Some photos on her Facebook page showed her hiking and at the beach with a guy who definitely looked like a new boyfriend and definitely didn't look like a cop. McCabe was pretty sure the Kyra chapter of his life was over.

What he really needed was either a new murder or a new girlfriend or maybe both. So far, at least, the murder wasn't happening. As for the girlfriend, he'd spent a fair amount of time checking out the Match.com and OkCupid websites. He'd gone out for drinks with three different women whose profiles he'd liked. They were all nice. All attractive. But none of them excited him enough to follow through. Apparently he hadn't excited them either.

Finally there was Maggie. They had both avoided the subject of a possible relationship since that day in June when he'd gotten so staggeringly drunk at Tallulah's. While he was now certain Kyra was gone for good, there was still the undeniable fact that Maggie worked for him and the equally undeniable fact that the department frowned on relationships between cops who worked together. McCabe ran under the highway overpass and started counterclockwise around Back Cove. For the next mile or so he argued with himself.

As he passed the Chevrus High School football field, he decided the hell with the arguments and leaned against a tree. Feeling as nervous as an adolescent, he took out his phone and punched in her number.

"Hi, McCabe. What's going on?"

He didn't answer for a minute.

"McCabe, are you there?"

"Would you like to have dinner with me tonight?"

"You mean like a date?"

"Yup. Exactly like a date."

"I'm afraid the answer is no."

"Oh."

"For one thing, I've already got a date tonight."

"Who with?"

"Not that it's any of your business, but it just happens to be with a guy named Kraft."

"As in Charles Kraft?"

"As in."

"You like him?"

"That really is none of your business."

"What about tomorrow?"

There was a pause. "Let me think about it." After a minute Maggie finally said, "We can have dinner tomorrow. But let's not call it a date. How about a working supper?"

McCabe sighed. "Okay. A working supper. Seven o'clock?"

"Seven o'clock is fine."

The whole way back to his house McCabe couldn't get the image of Maggie and Whitby E&D's head of corporate security out of his mind. He figured he'd find out whether or not there was anything to be jealous about when they got together on Sunday. And if there was, if Maggie was "taken," he supposed he'd just have to figure out how to deal with it.

Acknowledgments

I'd like to thank all those people who were helpful to me in the writing of this book. Former Detective Sergeant Tom Joyce, who once held McCabe's job on the Portland PD and who has always done his best to make sure my cops investigate crime the way cops should investigate crime. Where I stray from reality, it is my own doing and not Tom's. Former Portland detective and unofficial historian of the Portland PD, Steve Roberts, for his help in presenting an accurate picture of the way things were in 1904. Forensic pathologist Dr. Erin Presnell of the Medical College of South Carolina for graciously answering all my pestering questions about death and DNA. Dr. Bud Higgins and Dr. Robert Zeff, who both, once again, helped with medical details. Naturally, I want to thank my super agents Meg Ruley and Rebecca Scherer of the Jane Rotrosen Agency for their insights and help in getting this book right. And, of course, to my editor, Emily Krump, and my publisher, Dan Mallory, from HarperCollins Witness Impulse for their constant patience and support for this project. Finally, to my wife, Jeanne O'Toole Hayman, for putting up with my grumpiness when things weren't going right and with my lengthy solitary journeys into the imaginary world that all writers of fiction must inhabit.

I should also reiterate that *The Girl in the Glass* is most definitely a work of fiction. While my descriptions of the city of Portland are generally accurate, the Whitby family, Whitby Island, and the activities of Whitby Engineering & Development are totally figments of my imagination.

About the Author

JAMES HAYMAN, formerly creative director at one of New York's largest advertising agencies, is the author of the acclaimed McCabe and Savage series: *The Cutting, The Chill of Night, Darkness First,* and *The Girl in the Glass.*

www.jameshaymanthrillers.com
www.witnessimpulse.com

Discover great authors, exclusive offers, and more at hc.com.